I0564019

Elk of the 'Yard'
The Criminal Cases of
Inspector Elk
Volume 3

Elk of the 'Yard'
The Criminal Cases of
Inspector Elk
Volume 3

White Face

Silinski–Master Criminal

Edgar Wallace

LEONAUR

Elk of the 'Yard'
The Criminal Cases of
Inspector Elk
Volume 3
White Face
and
Silinski-Master Criminal
by Edgar Wallace

First published under the titles
White Face
and
Silinski-Master Criminal

Leonaur is an imprint of Oakpast Ltd
Copyright in this form © 2011 Oakpast Ltd

ISBN: 978-0-85706-567-4 (hardcover)
ISBN: 978-0-85706-568-1 (softcover)

http://www.leonaur.com

Publisher's Notes

TThe views expressed in this book are not necessarily
those of the publisher.

Contents

White Face

Contents

Chapter 1

Michael Quigley had a fair working knowledge of perverse humanity, having acquaintance with burglars, the better class of confidence man, professional forgers, long firm operators, swindlers, ingenious and naive, bank workers, bucket-shop keepers and pickpockets. He did not know White Face because nobody knew him, but that was a pleasure deferred. Sooner or later, the lone operator would make a mistake and come within the purview of a crime reporter.

Michael knew almost everybody at Scotland Yard and addressed chief constables by their first names. He had spent week-ends with Dumont, the hangman, and had helped him through an attack of delirium tremens. He had in his room signed photographs of *ci-devant* royalties, heavy-weight champions and leading ladies. He knew just how normal and abnormal people would behave in almost any circumstances. But personal experience failed him in the case of Janice Harman, although he had heard of such cases.

He could understand why a girl with no responsibilities (since she was an orphan) and three thousand pounds a year should want to do something useful in life and should choose to become a nurse in an East End clinic; other girls had allowed their enthusiasm for humanity to lead them into similar vocations, and Janice only differed from the majority in that she had not wearied of her philanthropy.

She was very lovely, though he could never analyse the qualities which made for loveliness. She had amazingly clear eyes and a mouth that was red and sensitive—perhaps it was the quality of her skin. He was never sure—the only thing he was certain about was that he could look at her for hours and wanted to look at her forever.

The one quality in her which made him wriggle uncomfortably was her cursed motherliness. He could never bridge the gulf which separated her from his twenty-seven years.

She was twenty-three and, as she often told him, a woman of twenty-three was at least twenty years older than a man of the same age. But twenty-three can be motherly or cruel. One night she told him something that struck all the colour out of life. It was the night they went to supper at the Howdah Club—the night of Michael's pay-day.

He knew, of course, about her romantic correspondent. Had sneered at him, raved at him, grown wearily amused about it all. The correspondence started in the most innocent fashion. One day a letter had come to Janice's flat in Bury Street, asking if she would be kind enough to place the writer in touch with his old nurse, who had fallen on evil times. This was a few months after she had begun her work in Dr. Marford's clinic and one of the newspapers had found a good story in the "rich young society woman" who had given her life to good works. The letter was written from South Africa and enclosed five pounds, which the writer begged her to hand to his old nurse if she found her, or to the funds of the clinic if she did not.

"How do you know this fellow isn't working a confidence trick on you?" demanded Michael.

"Don't be stupid," said Janice scornfully. "Because you are a wretched crime reporter you think that the world is made up of criminals."

"And I'm right," said Michael.

That the unknown stranger had arrived in England Michael did not know until ten days later. She called him up, asked him to take her to supper: she had some important things to tell him.

"You're one of the oldest friends I have, Michael," she said, speaking rather breathlessly. "And I feel that I ought to tell you."

He listened, stunned.

She might have seen how pale his face was, but she purposely did not look at him, fixing her eyes on the dancing couples on the floor.

"I want you to meet him—you may not think he is wonderful, but I've always known... from his letters, I mean... he has lived a terrible life in the wilds of Africa; I'll be terribly sorry to leave Dr. Marford... I shall have to tell him, of course..."

She was incoherent, a little hysterical.

"Let me get this right, Janice. I'll try to forget that I love you and that I was only waiting until I got my salary raised before I told you." His voice was very steady, so unemotional that there was every encouragement to look at him. Nevertheless she kept her eyes steadily averted.

"This isn't unusual—I have heard of such cases. A girl starts a correspondence with a man she has never seen. The correspondence grows more intimate, more friendly. She weaves around him a net of romance. And then she meets him and is either—disillusioned, or else falls for him. I've heard of happy marriages which started that way—I've heard of others. I can't believe it is true—but obviously it is, and I don't exactly know what to do or say."

It was at this moment that he missed something from her hand—a long oval-shaped ruby ring that she had worn since he had first known her.

Instantly she knew what he was looking for and dropped her hand out of sight.

"Where is your ring?" he asked bluntly.

She had gone very red: the question was almost unnecessary.

"I've—I don't see what it has to do with you?"

He drew a long breath.

"Nothing has to do with me—but I'm curious. An exchange of love tokens?"

He was very tactless tonight.

"It was my ring and I refuse to be cross-examined by a—by somebody who hasn't any right. You're being horrible."

"Am I?" He nodded slowly. "I suppose I am, and I know I've no right to be horrid or anything else. I won't ask you to show me what you got in exchange. A bead necklace perhaps—"

She started at this chance shot.

"How did you know? I mean, it is very valuable."

He looked long and earnestly at the girl.

"I want to vet this fellow, Janice."

She saw his face now and was in a panic—not on his behalf, but on her own.

"Vet—I don't know what you mean?"

He tried, with a smile, to minimise the offensiveness of what he had to say.

"Well, make inquiries about him. You vet a horse before you buy him—"

"I'm not buying him—he is a rich man—well, he has two farms." Her manner was cold. There was a touch of resentment in her voice. "Vet him! You'll find he is a criminal, of course; if you can't find this, your fertile imagination will invent something. Perhaps he is White Face! He is one of your specialities, isn't he?"

He groaned miserably. Yet here was an opportunity to escape from a maddening topic.

"He is not an invention; he's a fact. Ask Gasso."

Gasso, the slim *maitre d'hotel*, was near the table. Mike beckoned him.

"Ah! That White Face! Where is your so-called police? My poor friend Bussini has his restaurant ruined by the fellow."

It was to Bussini's restaurant that White Face had come in the early hours of a morning and, stepping to the side of Miss Angela Hillingcote, had relieved her of six thousand pounds worth of jewels before the dancers realised that the man in the white mask, who had appeared from nowhere, was not a guest in fancy dress. It was all over in a second or two and he was gone. A policeman at the corner of Leicester Square saw a man fly past on a motor cycle. The cycle had been seen on the Embankment going eastward. It was the third and most spectacular appearance of White Face in the West End of London.

"My patrons are nervous—who is not?" Gasso apparently shared their nervousness. "Fortunately they are refined people—" He stopped suddenly and stared at the entrance of the room. "She should not come!" he almost shrieked and darted forward to meet an unwanted guest.

This was a blonde lady who called herself Dolly de Val. It was found for her by an imaginative film agent, who thought—and rightly—that it sounded more pretentious than Annie Gootch, which name she had borne in the days of her poverty. She was not a good actress, because she could never quite remember all that the producer told her, and more often than not she was the only girl in the front line who kicked with her right leg when she should have kicked with her left. And frequently she was not in the line at all.

But there were quite a lot of people who found her attractive, and in the course of the years she became very rich, and packed a considerable amount of her fortune into platinum settings, so that in all the fashionable night clubs of London she was known as "Diamond Dolly."

Managers of such clubs and fashionable cabaret restaurants grew a little nervous after the Hillingcote affair, and when Dolly booked a supper table they rang up Scotland Yard and Superintendent Mason, who was in control of "C" area, but had an executive post at headquarters, would delegate a couple of detectives arrayed like festive gentlemen, but looking remarkably like detectives, to the club or restaurant favoured by her dazzling display, and these were generally to be found lounging in the vestibule or drinking surreptitious glasses of beer in the manager's office.

But sometimes Dolly did not notify her intentions beforehand. And she would glitter into the club surrounded by handsome young men, and a hasty table would be wedged impossibly on the packed floor and waiters would lay the table with extraordinary enthusiasm, conveying the impression that this was a favoured position for a table.

She came this night unheralded into the Howdah Club and Gasso, who was Latin and entirely without self-control, threw up his hands to the ceiling, stiff with cupids, and said things in Italian which sounded very romantic to people who only understood English.

"No room—don't be stupid, Gasso! Of course there's room. Anywhere will do, won't it, boys?"

So they put a table near the door, and Dolly sat and ordered *consomme Julienne, chicken a la Maryland*.

"I don't like you to seet here, madam," said Gasso fearfully, "with so much beautiful jewellery. . . Miss 'Illingcote—ah, what a disaster! This fellow with the white face—"

"Oh, shut up, Gasso!" Dolly snapped. "And, after that, we'll have coupe Jacques and coffee. . . "

The Russian dancers had taken the floor and had made their exit after the third encore, when—"Bail up—you!"

Dolly, who had seen the face of her escort suddenly blanch, half turned in her chair.

The man in the doorway wore a long black coat that reached to his heels, his face was covered by a white cloth in which two eye-holes had been cut.

He carried an automatic in his gloved hand, with the other, which was bare, he reached out.

There was a "snick"—the long diamond chain about Dolly's neck parted. She stood frozen with fear and saw the glittering thing vanish into his pocket.

Men had risen from the tables, women were screaming, the band stood ludicrously grouped. "After him!" yelled a voice.

But the man in the white mask was gone and the cowering footmen, who had bolted on his entrance, came out from cover.

"Don't move—I'll get you out in a minute." Mike's voice was urgent, but she heard him like one in a dream. "I'll take you home; I must get through to my paper. If you faint, I'll be rough with you!"

15

"I'm not going to faint," she quavered.

He got her out before the police came, and found a cab.

"It was dreadful; who is he?"

"I don't know," he answered shortly. Then—"What's this romantic lover's name—you've never told me?"

Her nerves were on edge; she needed the stimulant of righteous anger to recover her poise and here was an excuse.

Mike Quigley listened unmoved to her tirade.

"A good looker, I'll bet; not a gaunt-faced, tow-haired brute like me," he said savagely. "O God, what a fool you are, Janice! I'm going to meet him. Where is he staying?"

"You'll not meet him." She could have wept. "And I won't tell you where he is staying. I hope I never see you again!"

She declined the hand he offered to assist her out of the cab; did not answer his "goodnight."

Mr. Quigley went raging back to Fleet Street, and all the vicious things he wrote about White Face he meant for the handsome and romantic stranger from South Africa.

Chapter 2

A slovenly description of Janice Harman would be that she was the product of her generation. She had inherited the eternal qualities of womanhood as she enjoyed a freedom of development which was unknown in the formal age when guardians were restrictive and gloomy figures looming behind the young and beautiful heiress.

Janice had attained independence almost unconsciously; had her own banking account when she was seventeen, and left behind the tangibilities of discipline when she passed from the tutelage of the venerable head mistress of her school.

A bachelor uncle was the only relative she had possessed. In a spasmodic and jolly way he was interested in his niece, made her a lavish allowance, sent her beautiful and useless presents at Christmas and on her birthday, which he invariably remembered a month after. When he was killed in a motor accident (the three chorus girls who were driving with him escaped with a shaking) she found herself a comparatively rich young woman.

He had appointed as trustee a friend whose sole claim to his confidence lay in the fact that he was the best judge of hunters in England, and was one of the few men who could drink half a dozen glasses of port blindfolded and unerringly distinguish the vintage of each.

Janice left school with an exalted code of values and certain ideals which she religiously maintained. She had in her bedroom a framed portrait of the Prince of Wales, and she took the Sacrament on Christmas mornings.

At eighteen all men were heroes or dreadful; at nineteen she recognised a middle class which were neither heroic nor unspeakable. At twenty the high lights had receded and some of the duller tones were taking shape and perspective.

Donald Bateman belonged to the old regime of idealism. In his handsome face and athletic figure she recaptured some of the enthusiasm of the class-room. He was Romance and Adventure, the living receptacle in which were stored all the desirable virtues of the perfect man. His modesty—he no more than inferred his excellent qualities—his robust personality, his good humour, his childish views about money, his *naiveté*, were all adorable. He accepted her judgments and estimates of people and events, giving to her a sense of superiority which was very delightful.

In one respect he pleased her: he did not embarrass her more than once. He never forgot that their acquaintance was of the slightest, and the word "love" had never been uttered. The second time they had met he had kissed her, and she was ridiculously uncomfortable. He must have seen this, for he did not repeat the experiment. But they talked of marriage and their home and the wonders of South Africa; she could even discuss in a prim way the problem of children's education. A breezy figure of a man, delightfully boyish.

She was taking afternoon duty at the clinic and had been worrying about him all the morning—he had been a little depressed when she had seen him last.

"Did your money come?" she asked, with a smile.

He took out his pocket-book and drew forth two crisp notes. She saw they were each for a hundred pounds.

"It arrived this morning. I drew out these in case of emergency—I hate being without money when I'm in London. Angel, if the money hadn't turned up, I should have been borrowing from you this morning, and then what would you have thought of me?"

She smiled again. Men were so silly about money. Michael, for instance. She had wanted him to have a little car, and he had been almost churlish when she offered to help him.

He sat down and lit a cigarette, blowing a cloud of smoke to the ceiling.

"Did you enjoy your dinner?"

She made a little face.

"Not very much."

"He's a reporter, isn't he? I know a reporter on the Cape Times—quite a good chap—"

"It wasn't Michael who made the dinner a failure," she intervened loyally. "It was a man who came into the club with a white mask."

"Oh!" He raised his eyebrows. "The Howdah Club—White Face? I've been reading about it in this morning's papers. I wish I'd been

18

there. What is happening to the men in this country that they allow a fellow like that to get away with it? If I'd been within reach of him one of us would have been on the floor. The trouble with you people in England is that you're scared of firearms. I know from my own experience..."

He told a story of a prospector's camp in Rhodesia; it was a story which did not place him in an unfavourable light.

He sat facing the window, and during the narrative she had time to scrutinise him—not critically, but with indiscriminate approval. He was older than she had thought; forty, perhaps. There were little lines round his eyes, and harder ones near his mouth. That he had led a difficult and a dangerous life, she knew. One cannot starve and thirst in the desert of the Kalahari, or lie alone racked with fever on the banks of the Tuli River, or find oneself unarmed and deserted by carriers in the lion country west of Massikassi, and present an unlined and boyish face to the world. He still bore beneath his chin the long scar which a leopard's claw had left.

"Living in Africa nowadays is like living in Bond Street," he sighed. "All the old mystery has departed. I don't believe there's a lion left between Salisbury and Bulawayo. In the old days you used to find them lying in the middle of the road..."

She could listen to him for hours, but, as she explained, there was work to do.

"I'll come down and bring you home—where is it?" he asked.

She explained the exact location of Tidal Basin. "Dr. Marford— what sort of a man is he?"

"He's a darling," said Janice enthusiastically.

"We'll have him out at the Cape." He echoed her enthusiasm. "It's very easy. There's an extraordinary amount of work to be done, especially with the coloured children. If I can buy that farm next to mine, we might turn the farm building into a sort of convalescent home. It's one of those big, rambling Dutch houses and, as I've rather a nice house of my own, I shouldn't have use for the other."

She laughed at this.

"You're suffering from land hunger, Donald," she said. "I shall have to write and get particulars of this desirable property!"

He frowned. "Have you any friends at the Cape?" he asked.

She shook her head. "I know a boy there—he was a Rhodes scholar—but I haven't written to him since he left England."

"H'm!" He was rather serious now. "When strangers come into

the property market they soak 'em! Let me give you a word of advice: never try to buy land in South Africa through an agent—half of 'em are robbers, the other half an incompetent lot. One thing is certain, that the property at Paarl—that is where my farm is—will double itself in value in a couple of years. They are running a new railway through—it passes at the end of my land—and that will make an immense difference. If I had a lot of money to invest I should put every cent of it in land."

He explained, however, that the Cape Dutch, who were the largest landowners in the country, were a suspicious folk who never did business with an Englishman, except to the latter's disadvantage.

He took out the two hundred pound notes and looked at them again, rustling them affectionately.

"Why don't you put it back in the bank?" she asked.

"Because I like the feel of it," he said gaily. "These English notes are so clean-looking."

He returned the case to his pocket, and suddenly caught her by both arms. She saw a light in his eyes which she had never seen before. She was breathless and a little frightened.

"How long are we going to wait?" he asked in a low voice. "I can get a special licence; we can be married and on the Continent in two days."

She disengaged herself; discovered, to her amazement, that she was trembling, and that the prospect of an immediate marriage filled her with a sense of consternation.

"That is impossible," she said breathlessly. "I've ever such a lot of work to do, and I've got to finish up my work at the clinic. And, Donald, you said you didn't want to be married for months."

He smiled down at her.

"I can wait months or years," he said lightly, "but I can't wait for my lunch. Come along!"

She had only half an hour to give to him, but he promised to meet her and take her to dinner that night. The prospect did not arouse in her any sense of pleasurable anticipation. She told herself she loved him. He was everything that she would have him be. But immediate marriage? She shook her head.

"What are you shaking your head about?" he asked.

They were at Pussini's, and, as it was before one o'clock, the restaurant was empty save for themselves.

"I was just thinking," she said.

20

"About my farm?" He was looking at her searchingly. "No? About me?"

And then suddenly she asked: "What is your bank, Donald?"

He was completely surprised at the question.

"My bank? Well, the Standard Bank—not exactly the Standard Bank, but a bank that is affiliated with it. Why do you ask?"

She had a good and benevolent reason for putting the question, but this she was not prepared to reveal.

"I will tell you later," she said, and when she saw that she had worried him she was on the point of making her revelation. "It's really nothing, Donald."

He drove down with her to Tidal Basin, but refused the offer of her car to take him back, his excuse being that he felt nervous of the London traffic. She was secretly glad that there was some feature of London life of which he stood in awe.

Mr. Donald Bateman came back to town in a taxi and spent the afternoon in the City office of a tourist agency, examining Continental routes. He would like to have stayed in London; but then, he would like to have stayed in so many places from which expediency had dragged him. There was Inez. She had grown into quite a beautiful woman. He had seen her, though she was not aware of the fact. It was curious how women developed. He remembered her—rather sharp-featured, a gawk of a girl who had bored him utterly. In what way would Janice grow? For the moment she was very delectable, though she had qualities which exasperated him. Perfect women, he decided, were difficult to find.

When he had caught her by the shoulders that morning and looked down into her eyes, he had expected some other reaction than that fit of shivering. She had shown her alarm too clearly for him to carry the matter any further. It must be marriage, of course. But marriage was rather dangerous in a country like this. That reporter friend of hers? He hated reporters; they were a prying, unscrupulous lot. And crime reporters were the worst.

He began to feel uncomfortable, and turned relief to a contemplation of the physical perfection of Inez. From Inez his mind strayed to other women. What had become of Lorna, for example? Tommy had found her, probably, and forgiven everything. Tommy was always a weak-willed sap. But Inez!...

He and Janice dined together that night, and most resolutely he chose the Howdah Club. Already the outrage had had effect upon the attendance: the dining-room was half empty, and Gasso stalked up and down, a picture of gloom.

"This has ruined me, young miss," he said brokenly. "You were here last night with the newspaper gentleman. People will not come unless they have no jewels. And I particularly desire jewelled people here, but not jewelled as Miss Dolly!"

"I hope he comes tonight," said Donald with a quiet smile.

"You 'ope so, eh?" asked the agitated Gasso. "You desire me to be thrown into the street with only my shirt on my back? That is good for business!"

Janice was laughing, but she succeeded in pacifying the outraged *maitre d'hotel*.

"It certainly is empty, but I don't suppose we shall see our white-faced gentleman." said Donald. "It's rather like old times. I remember when I was in Australia there was a gang which held up a bank—they wore white masks, too. They got away with some money, by Jove! Ever heard of the Furses? They were brothers—the cleverest hold-up men in Australia."

"Perhaps this is one of them," she said thoughtlessly.

"Eh?"

She could have sworn he was frightened at that moment. Something she saw in his eyes. It was absurd, of course, for Donald Bateman was afraid of nothing.

"I shouldn't think so," he said.

Half-way through dinner, when they were discussing some amiable nothing, he dropped his knife and fork on the plate. Again she saw that frightened look intensified. He was staring at somebody, and she followed the direction of his eyes.

A man had come in. He must have been nearly sixty, was slim, dandified, rather fussy. He had a small party with him, and they were surrounded by waiters. Curiously enough, she knew him: curious, because she had made his acquaintance in a slum.

"Who—who is that?" His voice was strained. "That man there, with the girls? Do you—do you know him?"

"That is Dr. Rudd," she said.

"Rudd!"

"He's the police surgeon of our division—I've often seen him. In fact, he once came to the clinic. Quite an unpleasant man—he had nothing at all nice to say about our work."

"Dr. Rudd!"

The colour was coming back to his face. He had gone pale! She was astounded.

"Do you know him?" she asked in surprise.

He smiled with difficulty.

"No; he reminds me of somebody—an old friend of mine in—er—Rhodesia."

She noticed that when on their way out he passed the doctor's group Donald was patting his face with a handkerchief as though he were healing a scratch.

"Are you hurt?" she asked.

"A little neuralgia." He laughed cheerily. "That is the penalty one pays for sleeping out night after night in the rain."

He told her a story of a rainfall in Northern Rhodesia that had lasted four weeks on end.

"And all that time," he said, "I had not so much as a tent."

She left him at the door of the flat in Bury Street, and he was frankly disappointed, for he had expected to be asked up to her apartment. There was consolation on the way back to the hotel, certain anticipations of an interview he had arranged for the morrow. It was not with Janice.

Chapter 3

In his rare moments of leisure Dr. Marford was wont to stand in his surgery, behind the red calico curtains which were stretched across the big window level with the bridge of his thin, aristocratic nose, and muse, a little sourly, upon Tidal Basin, its people and its future.

He had material for speculation on those summer evenings, when the light of the brazen day still persisted in the western skies, and when every dive and tenement spilt the things that were so decently hidden in the cold days and nights of winter. On such nights the sweltering heat forced into the open the strangest beings, creatures which even the oldest inhabitants could not remember having seen before and the most hardened could hardly wish to see again.

The red calico curtain was strung across the window of the large room which was his surgery. It had been a boot store and a confectioner's parlour. Loucilensky, of infamous memory, had housed his "club" in it and found the side door which led to the little yard a convenient exit for his squalid patrons.

It was a derelict property when Dr. Marford came to found his practice here. All Tidal Basin knew that the doctor was so poor that he had painted, distempered and scrubbed the place from top to bottom with his own hands. He had probably sewn his own curtains, had certainly collected from the Caledonian Market, where you may furnish a house for a few pounds, such domestic equipment as was necessary for his well-being. Tidal Basin, which favoured those cinemas which featured pictures of high life, had despised him for his poverty. A consumptive plumber had fixed the huge sink, which was an unsightly feature of one corner of the surgery, and had received, in return, free treatment and medicine until he went the dingy way of all consumptive plumbers.

Tidal Basin had known and still knew Dr. Marford as the "penny doctor." They knew him better as the "baby doctor," for, after he had been in Tidal Basin a year, by some miracle he succeeded in founding a free clinic, where he gave ray treatment to children. He must have had influential friends, for on top of his other activities he founded a small convalescent home at the seaside.

His work was his obsession, and not a penny of the money which came to him went to his own advantage. The drab surgery remained as shabby as it had always been—a very dreary place compared with the spick and span little palace of white enamel and glass where the children of Tidal Basin were made acquainted with artificial sunlight and the beneficent quality of strange rays.

He saw Janice Harman pass the window and went to open the door to her. It was not true that this preoccupied man was hardly aware of her loveliness. He used to sit at his desk and think about her for hours on end. What strange dreams came to disorder the tidiness of his methodical mind was known only to Dr. Marford; and now, when she told him awkwardly, a little disjointedly, of her future plans, he showed no evidence of the sudden desolation and despair that crushed him.

"The oddest people fall in love with Janice," said her best friend.

"Oh!" he said, and bit his thin lip thoughtfully. "That is very unfortunate—for the clinic. What does Mr. Quigley say to all this?"

Hitherto he had felt an unreasonable antipathy to the young reporter, who had been a too frequent visitor to the clinic, and had written too much and too enthusiastically about Dr. Marford's ventures to please a man who shrank instinctively from publicity.

"Mr. Quigley has no right to raise any objections whatever." There was a note of defiance in her voice. "He is a very good friend—or was."

There was an embarrassing pause.

"But isn't any longer," said Dr. Marford gently.

He experienced an inexplicable sense of kinship with Michael Quigley.

Her native loyalty made her modify her attitude.

"I like Michael—he is extraordinarily nice, but very domineering. He was awfully good to me the other night, and I was a beast to him. I was in the Howdah Club when that dreadful man came."

He turned an inquiring face to her.

"Which dreadful man?"

"The robber—White Face."

He nodded.

"Yes, I know. I read the newspapers. I was talking to Sergeant Elk about him. There is a theory that he lives in this neighbourhood, a theory for which I am afraid your young friend is responsible. Are you wise?"

He asked the question suddenly.

"About—my marriage? Is any girl wise, Dr. Marford? Suppose I'd met this man every day of my life for years, should I know him—I mean, as one knows one's husband? Men always put on their best appearance for women, and unless one lives in the same house with them it is impossible to be absolutely sure."

Marford nodded, fondling his bony chin.

There was a long silence, which he broke.

"I shall be sorry to lose you; you have been a most enthusiastic helper."

Now she came to a delicate stage of the interview—delicate because she knew how sensitive he was on the point.

"I'd like to give the Institute a little present," she said jerkily. "A thousand pounds—"

He raised his hand; his expression was genuinely pained.

"No, no, no; I couldn't hear of it. You asked me once before if I would. No, I am satisfied that I have not paid you for the help you have given us. That is your splendid contribution to the clinic."

She knew he would be adamant on this point and had already decided that if he refused her gift it should take the form of an anonymous donation on her wedding day. Michael, in one of his more cynical moods, had once accused her of being theatrical, and the charge was so ridiculous that she had laughed. Yet there is a touch of theatricality in every sentimentalist, and Janice Harman was not without that weakness.

Unexpectedly the doctor put out his thin hand and took hers.

"I hope you will be happy," he said, and this was at once a benediction and a dismissal.

She crossed the road at Endley Street. At the corner stood a tall, good-looking man, with greying hair at his temples. To her surprise he was talking to a woman, talking confidentially it seemed. Presently the woman walked away and he came, smiling, to meet the girl.

"What a ghastly place, darling! I am so happy you're leaving it."

"Who was that woman you were speaking to?" she asked curiously.

He laughed—she loved that laugh of his.

"Woman? Oh, yes." He looked round and nodded towards a slim figure walking ahead of them on the opposite side of the road. "It was rather odd—she thought I was her brother, and when she saw she'd made a mistake she was a little embarrassed. Rather a pretty girl."

Her car was in a near-by garage—in the early days she had driven up to the clinic, which was at the far end of Endley Street, but the doctor had advised her against the practice—advice well justified, for in a week everything that was movable in the car had been stolen by the parents of the children she cared for.

She seated herself at the wheel, a radiant figure of youth, he thought, more beautiful than even he in his wildest imaginings had dreamed. The car came down the slope of the road; she saw the shabby figure of the doctor watching them, and waved her hand to him.

"Who was that?" he asked carelessly.

"That was Dr. Marford."

"Your boss, eh? I'd like to have had a look at him. He's a big noise around here."

She laughed at this.

"There isn't a tinier murmur in Tidal Basin," she said. "But he's marvellous! I sometimes think he starves himself to keep his clinic going."

She rhapsodised all the way through the City. In Cranbourn Street they were held up by a traffic block. By this time he had gained command of the conversation and the excellences of Dr. Marford were relegated to a second place. He was talking of South Africa and his two farms, one in the wilds of Rhodesia, the other amidst the beauties of Paarl. He liked talking of the Paarl property.

"It's going to be terribly slow for you, though there is some sort of social life at the Cape. I'm pretty well known—"

"There's somebody who knows you," she laughed.

He turned his head quickly, but could distinguish amongst the hurrying throng on the sidewalk no familiar face.

"Where?" he asked.

"There—that dark man." She looked back. "He is standing by the hosiers."

He looked round and frowned.

"Oh, yes, I know him—not very well, though; I got the better of him in a business deal, and he hasn't forgiven me." He uttered an exclamation. "Darling, I can't take you to the theatre tonight: I've just remembered. Will you forgive me?"

She was too happy, too completely under the fascination of this exalted adventure, to resent the missed engagement. This good-looking stranger who had come from the blue, whose name she could hardly use without an unaccountable sense of shyness, was Romance—the fulfilment of vague and delightful dreams. He was still outside the realms of reality.

She had known him for ten days; it seemed that it was a lifetime. Once or twice during the journey she was on the point of telling him of the surprise she had for him. He was a great home-lover; his self-confessed sin was that he coveted his neighbour's land. There was a farm adjoining his at Paarl that had come into the market, could be had for a mere £8,000. He waxed enthusiastic on the advantage of having this additional property—vine-yards and orange groves, new pastures for his cattle.

He returned to the subject as the car was crossing Piccadilly Circus.

"You've made me ambitious, you angel," he said. "I'm a poor farmer and can't lay my hands on a fortune, so the farm will have to go."

Again she was nearly telling him. She had a friend in Cape Town, a young lawyer, a Rhodes scholar, whom she had met at Oxford. That very morning she had wired to him, asking him to buy the property.

He parted from her at the door of her flat in Bury Street, and her chauffeur, who was waiting, drove him to his modest hotel. At parting: "I hate the thought of losing that farm—if I could cable four thousand pounds tomorrow morning I could clinch the bargain."

She smiled demurely and went up to her room to daydream of green slopes and high, sun-baked mountains where the little baboons chatter all day and night.

At ten o'clock that night, when she was undressing for bed, came a cablegram which left her white and shaking. It was in one sense remarkable that the first person she thought of to help her in her necessity was Michael Quigley; but when she reached for the telephone with a trembling hand it was to learn that Michael had left the office on a hurry call. She looked at the clock; it was by then half-past ten. She changed her mind about going to bed and began to dress quickly.

Chapter 4

After Janice had left, Dr. Marford walked slowly to that corner of the surgery where his drugs were stocked and began to dispense the medicines he had prescribed in the course of the day. This was generally his afternoon task, but he had spent most of the day at the clinic.

He wearied of the task very soon and vent to his desk. There was a heap of papers to go through—the accounts from the clinic showed a heavy deficit. The place ate money: there was always new apparatus to buy, new equipment to furnish. The daily report from the convalescent home in Eastbourne, which maintained the progress of a dozen small hooligans of Tidal Basin, was as cheerless; but it brought no sense of depression to Dr. Marford. He grudged nothing to these ventures of his—neither time nor exertion.

He was expecting a remittance almost any day. There was a man in Antwerp who sent him money regularly, and another in Birmingham—he pushed the papers aside, looked at his watch and went out by the side door into the yard.

It was a fairly large yard. At one end was the big shed in which old Gregory Wick's kept his taxicab, paying a small weekly rent.

Old Gregory Wicks had been a famous driver even in the days of the festive hansom. And always he had housed his horses and his resplendent cab in Tidal Basin, where he was born and where he hoped to end his days. In his advanced middle age came the taxicab. Gregory refused to regard motor vehicles as new-fangled crazes that would soon go out of fashion. He was one of the first to sit at a driving wheel at a motor school and solve the mysteries of clutches and gears. He found his lameness no obstacle in obtaining a cab-driver's licence—he limped from a thirty-year-old injury to his ankle.

Always he was a night bird; even in the horse cab he went clopclopping along Piccadilly in the early hours of the morning, picking up swells from the clubs and driving them unimaginable distances to their country houses. And when the taxi came he continued his nocturnal wanderings. A silent, taciturn man, who never stood on a rank or invited the confidence of his brother drivers, he was known locally and abroad for his rigid honesty. It was he who restored to a certain Austrian baron a million *kroners* in hard paper cash, left in the cab by the Herr Baron in a moment of temporary aberration caused by a quarrel with a lady friend. Old Gregory had returned thousands of pounds' worth of goods left by absent-minded riders. In the police books he was marked "Reliable; honest; very excellent record."

You could see him and his cab on certain nights prowling along Regent Street, his long, white hair hanging over the collar of his coat, his fierce white moustache bristling from his pink, emaciated face, choosing his fares with a nice discrimination. He had no respect for any man save one. In his more than seventy-year-old arms he packed a punch that was disconcerting to the punchee.

The doctor unfastened a door and passed through into Gallows Court. That narrow and unsavoury passage was alive with children— bare-legged, unwashed and happy. Nobody offered the doctor a friendly greeting. The frowsy men and women lounging in the doorways or at the upstairs windows favoured him with incurious glances. He was part of the bricks and mortar and mud of the place, one with the brick wall which separated his yard from this human sty. He belonged there, had a right in Gallows Court, and, that being so, might pass without notice or comment.

The last house in the court was No. 9; smaller than the others; the windows were clean, and even the lower one, which was heavily shuttered, had a strip of chintz curtain. He knocked at the door—three short quick raps, a pause and a fourth. This signal had been agreed as between himself and old man Wicks; for Gregory had been annoyed by runaway knocks and by the appearance on his doorstep of unwelcome visitors. He knew the regular hour at which the milkman called and the baker, and could cope with them. Whosoever else knocked at the door during the daytime received no answer. Marford heard the shuffle of feet on uncarpeted stairs and the door was opened.

"Come in, Doctor." Gregory's voice was loud and hearty. He had been a shouter all his life, and age had not diminished the volume of his tone. "Don't make a row; I expect the lodger's asleep," he said as he closed the door with a slam.

"He must be a very good sleeper if you don't wake him, you noisy old man!" said Marford, with his quiet smile.

Gregory guffawed all the way up the stairs, opened the door of his room and the doctor passed in. "How are you?"

"Fit as a flea, except this other little trouble, and I'm not going to mention that. I'm doing fine. Doctor. Sit down. Where's a chair? Here we are! What I owe to you, Doctor! If the people in Tidal Basin knew what you've done for me—"

"Yes, yes," said Marford good-humouredly. "Now let me have a look at you."

He turned the old man's face to the light and made a careful examination.

"You're no better and no worse. If anything you're a little better, I should think. I'll test your heart."

"My heart!" said the other scornfully. "I've got the heart of a lion! There was an Irish family moved in here and the woman wanted to borrow a saucepan, and when I told her just what I thought of people who borrow saucepans, along came her husband—a new fellow, full of brag and bluster! I gave him one smack in the jaw and that was his finish!"

"You shouldn't do it, Gregory. It was a stupid thing to do. I heard about it from one of my other patients."

The old man was chuckling gleefully.

"I needn't have done it at all," he said. "Any of the boys round here would have put him out if I'd said the word. I dare say the lodger would, but of course I wouldn't have wakened him up."

"Is he here today?"

Gregory shook his head. "The Lord knows! I never hear him come in or go out, except sometimes. I've never known a quieter fellow. Reformed, eh, Doctor? I'll bet you I know who reformed him! You'd never dream"—he lowered his voice —"that he was a man who'd spent half his life in stir—"

"You're giving him a chance," said Marford.

He was going, when the old man called him back. "Doctor, I want to tell you something. I made my will today—not exactly a will, but I wrote down what I wanted doing with my money."

"Have you got a lot, Gregory?" asked the other good-humouredly.

"More than you think." There was a significance in the old man's voice. "A lot more! It's not money that makes me do what I'm doing—it's pride—swank!"

To most men who had known him for years, Gregory Wicks was a taciturn and uncommunicative man. Marford was one of the few who knew him. He often thought that this loquacity which Gregory displayed at home was his natural reaction to the hours of silence on the box. Night after night for nearly half a century this old cabman had placed himself under a vow of silence. Once he explained why, and the reason was so inadequate that Marford, who was not easily amused, laughed in spite of himself. Gregory had in a talkative moment allowed a client—he always called his fares "clients"—to wish a counterfeit half-crown upon him. It was a lesson never to be forgotten.

The doctor often came in to chat with the old man, to hear stories of dead and forgotten celebrities whose names were famous in the eighties and the late seventies. As he was leaving, Gregory referred again to his lodger.

"It was a good idea putting up that shutter to keep out the noise, though personally there's nothing that would stop me sleeping. I sometimes wish he'd be a bit more lively—"

"And come up and have a little chat with you at times?" suggested Marford.

Gregory almost shuddered.

"Not that! I don't want to chat with anybody, especially strangers. I chat with you because you've been God's-brother-Bill to me, to use a vulgar expression. I don't say I'd have starved, because I shouldn't have done. But I'd have lost something that I'd rather die than lose."

He came down to the door and stood looking out after the doctor, even when Marford was out of sight. The noisy children did not gibe at him, and none of these frowsy ones hurled their inevitable and unprintable jests in his direction. A wandering policeman they would have covered with derision. Only the doctor and Gregory Wicks escaped their grimy humour; the latter because of that ready fist of his, the doctor—well, you never know when the doctor will be called in, and if he's got a grudge against you who knows what he'll slip into your medicine? Or suppose he had to use the knife, eh? Nice so-and-so fool you'd look, lying under chloroform with your inn'ards at his mercy! Fear was a governing factor of life in Gallows Court.

Chapter 5

That he had no other friends was good and sufficient reason why Mr. Elk should drop in at odd minutes to discuss with Dr. Marford the criminal tendencies and depravities of that section of the British Empire which lies between the northern end of Victoria Dock Road and the smelly drabness of Silvertown.

Elk called on the evening Janice Harman took her farewell, and found Dr. Marford's melancholy eyes fixed upon the dreary pageant of Endley Street. They were working overtime in the shipyard, which was almost opposite his surgery, and the din of mechanical riveters would go on during the night. Dr. Marford was so accustomed to this noise that it was hardly noticeable. The sound of drunken songsters, the pandemonium which accompanied amateur pugilism, the shrill din of children playing in the streets—hereabouts they played till midnight—the rumbling of heavy lorries on the way to the Eastern Trading Company's yard which went on day and night never disturbed his sleep.

"If I was sure this was hell"—Mr. Elk nodded his own gloomy face towards the thoroughfare—"I'd get religion. Not that I don't say my prayers every night—I do. I pray for the Divisional Inspector, the Area Inspector, the Big Five and the Chief Commissioner; I pray for the Examining Board and all other members of the criminal classes."

The ghost of a smile illuminated the thin face of Dr. Marford. He was a man of thirty-five who looked older. Spare of build, his greying hair was thin on the top. He wore absurd little side-whiskers half-way down his cheek, and gold-rimmed spectacles, one lens of which was usually cracked.

For a long time they stood in silence behind the calico curtains, attracting no attention from the passers-by, for there was no light in the surgery.

"My idea of hell," said Elk again.

Dr. Marford laughed softly.

"With its own particular devil, by all accounts," he said.

Detective-Sergeant Elk permitted himself to guffaw.

"That bunk! Listen, these people believe anything. Funny thing, they don't read, so they couldn't have got the idea out of books. It's one of the—what do you call the word—um—damn it! I've got it on the end of my tongue. . . "

"Legends?"

"That's it—it's like the Russians passing through England with the snow on their boots. Everybody's met the man who saw 'em, but you never meet him. Every time there's a murder nobody can explain, you see it in the newspaper bills: 'The Devil of Tidal Basin,' an' even after you've pinched the murderer an' all the earth knows that he never heard of Tidal Basin, or thinks it's a patent wash-bowl, they still hang on to the idea. These newspapers! Next summer you'll have joy-wagons full of American trippers comin' here. Limehouse has had it, why shouldn't we?"

A bright young newspaper man had invented the Devil of the Basin. It was the general opinion in Tidal Basin that he wasn't any too bright either.

"There is a devil—hundreds of 'em! The waterside crowd wouldn't think twice of putting me out. They tried one night—Dan Salligan. The flowers I sent to the man when he was in hospital is nobody's business."

Dr. Marford moved uncomfortably.

"I'm afraid I helped that legend to grow. The reporter saw me and very—er—indiscreetly, I told him of the patient who used to come to me—he hasn't been for months, by the way—always came at midnight with his face covered with a mask. It wasn't good to see the face, I mean. Explosion in a steel works."

Elk was interested.

"Where does he live?"

The doctor shook his head.

"I don't know. The reporter tried to find out but couldn't. He always paid me in gold—a pound a visit, which is forty times more than I get from my regulars."

Mr. Elk was not impressed. His eyes were fixed upon the squalling larrikins in the roadway.

"Weeds!" he said, and the doctor laughed softly.

34

"Those ugly little boys are probably great political leaders of the future, or literary geniuses. Tidal Basin may be stiff with mute, inglorious Miltons," he said.

Sergeant Elk of the Criminal Investigation Department made a noise that expressed his contempt.

"Nine-tenths of that crowd will pass through the hands of me and my successors," he said drearily, "and all your electric rays won't stop um! And such of them as don't finish in Dartmoor will end their days in the workhouse. Why they call it a workhouse, God knows. I've never known anybody to work in a workhouse except the staff. You know Mrs. Weston?" he asked suddenly. "A pretty woman. She's got the only respectable apartment in the Basin. All Ritzy—I went up there when some kids broke her windows. She's not much good."

"If she's not much good," said Marford, and again that ghost of a smile came and went, "if she's not much good, I probably know her. If she's the kind of woman who doesn't pay her doctor's bills, I certainly know her. Why do you ask?"

Elk took a cigar from his pocket and bit off the end. It was obviously a good cigar. He had hoarded it so long that it had irregular fringes of leaf. He lit it with great deliberation and puffed enjoyably.

"She was saying that she knew you," he said, fully two minutes after the question had been asked. "Naturally I said a good word for you."

"Say a few good words for the clinic," said the doctor.

"I'm always doing it," said Sergeant Elk complacently. "You're wasting your time and other people's money, but I do it. That's a pretty nurse you've got—Miss Harman. Quigley the reporter's all gooey about her."

"Yes," said Dr. Marford quietly.

He rose and pulled down the blind, went to a cupboard, took out a whisky bottle, a siphon and two glasses, and looked inquiringly at the detective.

"I'm off duty," said Elk, "if a detective is ever off duty."

He pulled up a chair to the writing table. The doctor was already in his worn leather chair. "Ever read detective stories?" asked Elk.

Dr. Marford shook his head.

At that moment the telephone rang. He took up the instrument, listened for a while, asked a few questions, and put down the receiver.

"That's why I don't read detective or any other kind of stories," he said. "The population of Tidal Basin increases at a terrific rate, but not so rapidly as some people expect."

He jotted a note down on a little pad.

"That's a come-at-once call, but I don't suppose they will require my attention till three o'clock tomorrow morning. Why detective stories?"

Sergeant Elk sipped at his whisky. He was not a man to be rushed into explanation.

"Because," he said eventually, "I'd like some of these clever Mikes to take my patrol for a couple of months. I saw an American crook play up in the West End the other night. It was all about who-did-it. First of all they introduced you to about twenty characters, told you where they were born and who their fathers were, and what money they wanted and who they were in love with—you couldn't help knowing that the fellow who did the murder was the red-nosed waiter. But that's not police work, Dr. Marford. We're not introduced to the characters in the story; we don't know one. All we've got in a murder case is the dead man. What he is, who his relations are, where he came from, what was his private business—we've got to work all that out. We make inquiries here, there and everywhere, digging into slums, asking questions of people who've got something to hide."

"Something to hide?" repeated the doctor.

Elk nodded.

"Everybody's got something to hide. Suppose you were a married man—"

"Which I am not," interrupted Marford.

"We've got to suppose that," insisted Elk. "Your wife is abroad. You take a girl into the country. . . "

The doctor made faint noises of protest.

"We're supposin' all this," conceded Elk. "Such things have happened. And in the morning you look out of your window an' see a feller cut another feller's throat. You are a doctor and cannot afford to get your name into the papers. Are you going to the police and tell them what you saw? And are you going to stand up in court and tell them what you were doing out of town and the name of the lady you were with, and take the chance of it getting into all the papers? Or are you going to say nothing? Of course you are! That happens every day. In a murder case everybody has got something to hide, and that's why it's harder to get the truth about murder than any other kind of crime. Murder is a spot-light. You've got to take the stand and face a defending counsel who's out to prove that you're the sort of fellow that no decent jurywoman could ask to meet her young daughter."

The detective sucked at his cigar for a long time in silence. Then he asked:

"Bit of a mystery, this woman Lorna Weston?"

The doctor's tired eyes surveyed him thoughtfully.

"I suppose so. They're all mysteries to me. I can't remember their names. God, what names they've got! Like the patterns of a dull wallpaper—one running into the other. Jackson, Johnson, Thompson, Beckett, Dockett, Duckett, Roon, Doon, Boon. . . eh? And some without any names at all. I attended a young woman for three months—she was just 'the young woman upstairs,' or 'Miss What's-her-name.' Her landlady didn't know it. She was a waitress working nobody knew where. If she had died I couldn't have certified her. I called her Miss Smith—had to put some sort of name on the books. What does Mrs. Weston do for a living?"

Mr. Elk made a little grimace.

"Well, you know, she's. . . well, she goes West every night all dolled up."

The doctor nodded.

"There are lots of 'em—a whole colony. Why do they live in this hell shoot? I suppose it's cheap. And their earnings are not what they were. One girl told me—but you can't believe 'em."

He sighed heavily and sighed again.

"You can't believe anybody."

Elk got up, drained his glass and reached for his hat.

"She wanted to know if you were an easy man to get on with. I got an idea she's a dope-getter. I don't know why, but I've just got that idea. There was a doctor in Silvertown who made a fortune out of it: he spent over a thousand on his defence when I got him to the Old Bailey. . . "

The doctor went out with him, and they arrived at the street door at an opportune moment.

The earlier sound of the battle had come to them in a confused hubbub of sound as they passed through the disinfected passage. As Marford opened the door he saw two men fighting, surrounded by a crowd. It was a fair fight, both men being well matched in point of physique and equally drunk. But they were too close to the granite kerb of the sidewalk. One of the combatants went down suddenly, and the grey, dusty kerbstone went red.

37

"Here—you!"

Elk made a grab at the victor and swung him round. The policemen came running and plunged through the crowd.

"Take this man."

Elk handed over his dazed prisoner and shouldered his way through the tightly packed knot of people that surrounded the man on the kerb.

"Get him inside the doctor's shop. Lift him. . . "

They carried the limp thing into the surgery and Dr. Marford made a brief examination whilst Mr. Elk bustled the bearers into the street.

"Well?" he asked when he came back. "Hospital case, isn't it?"

Marford was fixing an enormous pad of gauze and cottonwool to the head of the white-faced man.

"Yes. Do you mind ringing the ambulance? Two shillings' worth of surgical dressings and I don't get a cent for it. You can't sue their relations—they need the money for a swell funeral. Everybody has to go into black, and that costs money."

Elk screwed up his lips painfully.

"Is he booked?" he asked, looking at the figure with the awed curiosity which the living have for the dead.

"I should think so: compound fracture of the *occiput*. Get him to the London and they may do something. It costs me ten shillings a week just for surgical dressings. I'll tell you something, and you can arrest me. If I get 'em alone, I go through their pockets and take the cost of the dressing. But usually they've got some howling women with 'em who won't leave 'em. *When pain and anguish wring the brow*, eh?"

The ambulance came noisily and the patient was taken away.

It was an incident not worth remembering—except for two shillings' worth of dressing that would never be liquidated.

The doctor closed the door upon Mr. Elk, and went back to his books and his thoughts. Two inconvenient new lives were coming to Tidal Basin. The district nurses would call him in good time. Inconvenient. . . the children of an unemployable labourer and a father who was resting in one of His Majesty's prisons.

As to this Lorna Weston. . .

He knew her, of course. She often passed the surgery on her way to the provisions store next door, and once or twice she had come in to see him. A pretty woman, though her mouth was a trifle hard and straight. He never confessed to Elk that he knew anybody. Elk was a detective and respected no confidences.

There was a phone call from Elk. The fighter had died on admission to hospital. The doctor was not surprised. An inquest, of course.

"We shall want you as a witness," said Elk's voice. "He's a dock labourer from Poplar—a man named Stephens."

"How thrilling!" said the doctor, hung up the receiver and went back to his book—the intrigues of Louis's court, the scheming Polignacs and the profitable machinations of Madame de Lamballe.

He heard the shrill call of the door-bell, looked plaintively round, finally rose and went to the door. The night had come down blackly; the pavement outside was glistening: you do not hear the rain falling in the East End.

"Are you Dr. Marford?"

The woman who stood in the doorway exhaled the faint fragrance of some peculiarly delicate perfume. Her voice, thin for the moment with anxiety, had the quality of culture. She was a stranger; he had never heard that voice before.

"Yes. Will you come in?"

The surgery had no other light than the reading-lamp on the desk. He felt that she would have had it this way.

She wore a leather motoring coat and a little tight-fitting hat. She unfastened the coat hurriedly as though she were hot or had some difficulty in breathing. Under the coat she wore a neat blue costume. From some vague clue, he thought she was American. A lady undoubtedly, having no association with Tidal Basin, unless she was a passenger on the Moroccan boat which sailed with the tide from Shrimp Wharf.

"Is he—is he dead?" she asked jerkily, and in her dark eyes he read an unconquerable fear.

"Is who dead?"

He was puzzled; searched his mind rapidly for patients in extremis and could find none but old Sully, the marine store dealer, who had been dying for eighteen months.

"The man—he was brought here. . . after the fight. A policeman told me.. they were fighting in the street and he was brought here."

She stood, her hands clasped, her thin body bent forward towards him, breathless.

"A man?. . . Oh, yes; he's dead, I'm afraid."

Dr. Marford was for the moment bewildered. How could she be interested in the fate of one Stephens, dock labourer, of Poplar?

"Oh, my God!"

She whispered the words, dropped for a second. Dr. Marford's arm went round her and assisted her to a chair.

"Oh, my God!" she said again and began to cry.

He looked at her helplessly, not knowing for whom he could frame a defence—for the dead or the living.

"It was a fair fight as far as one could see," he said awkwardly. "The man fell. . . hit his head on the sharp edge of the kerb. . . "

"I begged him not to go near him," she said a little wildly. "I begged him! When he telephoned to say he was on his track and had traced him here. . . I came by cab. . . I implored him to come back."

All this and more came incoherently. Dr. Marford had to guess what she said. Some of the words were drowned in sobs. He went to his medicine shelf and took down a bottle labelled "Ap. Am. Arm.," poured a little into a medicine glass and added water.

"You drink this and tell me all about it," he said authoritatively.

She told him more than she would have told her confessor. Sorrow, remorse, the crushing tragedy of fear removed all inhibitions. The doctor listened, looking down at her, twiddling the stem of the medicine glass in his fingers.

Presently he spoke.

"This man Stephens was a dock labourer—a heavy fellow, six feet tall at least. A fair-haired man. The other man was a young fellow of twenty something. I only saw him for a second when he was in the hands of the police. He had a light, almost a white, moustache—"

She stared up at him.

"Fair. . . a young man. . . "

Dr. Marford held the glass out to her.

"Drink this; you're hysterical. I hate telling you so."

But she pushed the glass aside.

"Stephens—are you sure? Two, well, two ordinary men?. . . "

"Two labourers—both drunk. It's not unusual in this neighbourhood. We have an average of two fights a night. On Saturday nights—six. It's a dull place and they have to do something."

The colour was coming back to her face. She hesitated, reached for the glass, swallowed its contents and made a wry face.

"*Sal volatile*. . . beastly!"

She wiped her lips with a handkerchief she took from her bag and rose unsteadily to her feet.

"I'm sorry, Doctor. I've been a nuisance. I suppose if I offered to pay you for your time you'd be offended."

"I charge ten cents for a consultation," he said gravely, and she smiled.

"How accommodating you are! You think I am American? I am, of course, though I've lived in England since—oh, for a long time. Thank you, Doctor. Have I talked a lot of nonsense, and, if I have, will you forget it?"

Dr. Marford's thin face was in the shadow: he was standing between her and the lamp.

"I won't promise that; but I will not repeat it," he said.

She did not give him her name: he was wholly incurious. When he offered to walk with her until she found a cab, she declined his escort. He stood in the drizzling rain and watched her out of sight.

Police-Constable Hartford came from the direction she had taken and stopped to speak.

"They say that Stephens is dead. Well, if they will drink, they must expect trouble. I've never regretted taking the pledge myself—I'll be Chief Templar in our lodge this summer if Gawd spares me. I sent a young lady; she was makin' inquiries about Stephens. I didn't know he was gone or I'd have told her."

"Thank you, for not telling her," said Marford.

He was shy of P.C. Hartford, who was notoriously loquacious and charged with strange long words.

He locked the door and went back to his book, but the corruptions and permutations of Madame de Lamballe interested him no more.

Pulling up the surgery blind, he looked out into the deserted street. There was some sort of movement in progress under the shadow of the wall which encircles the premises of the Eastern Trading Company.

He saw a man and a woman talking. There was light enough from the street standard to reveal this much. The man was in evening dress, which was curious. The white splash of his shirt front was plainly visible. Even waiters do not wear their uniform in Tidal Basin.

Dr. Marford went out and opened the street door as the man and the woman walked in opposite directions. Then he saw the third of the trio. He was moving towards the man in evening dress, following him quickly. The doctor saw the first man stop and turn. There was an exchange of words and a scuffle. The man in dress clothes went down like a log, the second bent over him and went on quickly and disappeared under the railway arch which crosses Endley Street, opposite the Eastern Company's main gateway.

Dr. Marford watched, fascinated, was on the point of crossing to see what had happened to the inanimate heap on the pavement, when the man got up and lit a cigarette.

The clock struck ten.

Chapter 6

Louis Landor looked down at the hateful thing he had struck to the earth. He lay very still and the hate in Landor's heart was replaced by a sudden horror. He glanced across the road. Immediately opposite was a doctor's surgery—a red light burned dimly from a bracket-lamp before the house to advertise the profession of its occupant. He saw the door was open and somebody was standing there. Should he go for help? The idea came and went. His own safety was in question. He hurried along in the shadow of the high wall and had reached the railway arch, when right ahead of him appeared the shadowy figure of a policeman, and the policeman was coming his way. He looked round for some way of escape. There were two great gates on his right and in one a small wicket door. In his panic he pushed the door and it yielded. By some miracle it had been left unfastened. In a second he was inside, felt for the bolt and pushed it home. The policeman passed without being conscious of his presence.

P.C. Hartford was at that moment composing a little speech which he intended to deliver at the next lodge meeting, where matters of very considerable interest were to be discussed. His thoughts being so centred, it was not unlikely that he should miss seeing the fugitive.

A certain Harry Lamborn, who was by trade a general larcenist, and who at that moment was standing in the shelter of a deeply-recessed door on the opposite side of the road, had less excuse, except that his eye was on the approaching copper and that he had little interest in ordinary civilians. That night he had certain plans connected with No. 7 warehouse of the Eastern Trading Company, and he was waiting for P.C. Hartford to reach the end of his beat and return before he put them into operation.

He watched the constable's leisurely stride, drew back still farther into the recess which afforded him freedom from observation and protection from the falling rain, and transferred a collapsible jemmy from one pocket to another for greater comfort.

Hartford could not help seeing the man in evening dress. He stood squarely in the middle of the side-walk, wiping the mud from his black overcoat. Instantly Hartford descended from the dais of Vice-Templar and became a human police constable.

"Had a fall, sir?" he asked cheerfully.

The man turned a good-looking face to the officer and smiled. Yet he was not wholly amused, for his hands were trembling violently and the whiteness of his lips was in odd contrast to his sunburnt face. And when he spoke he was so breathless that the words came in gasps. Rain had been falling; there was a brown, muddy patch on his overcoat. He looked backward, the way he had come, and seemed relieved when he saw nobody.

"Have I had a fall?" he repeated. "Well, I think I have."

He looked past the constable. "Did you see the man?"

Police-Constable Hartford looked back along the deserted stretch of pavement.

"Which man?" he asked, and the other seemed surprised.

"He went your way; he must have passed you."

Hartford shook his head.

"No, sir, nobody's passed me."

The white-lipped man was sceptical.

"Did he do anything?" asked Hartford.

"Did he do anything?" The stranger had a trick of repeating questions and tinging them with contempt. "He punched me in the jaw, if that's anything. I played possum." His face twisted in a smile. "Scared him—I hope."

He gave a certain emphasis to the last words. Police-Constable Hartford surveyed him with greater interest.

"Would you like to charge the man?" he asked.

The other was fixing his white silk neck-cloth and shook his head.

"Do you think you could find him if I charged him?" he asked sarcastically. "No; let him go."

"A stranger to you, sir?"

P.C. Hartford had not handled a case for a month and was loath to let his fingers slide off the smooth edge of this.

"No; I know him."

"There's a bad crowd about here," began Hartford. "A drunken, dissipated——"

"I know him, I tell you." The stranger was impatient.

He dived his hand into an inside pocket, took out a silver case and opened it. P.C. Hartford stood by while the man lit his cigarette, and noticed that the hand which held the patent lighter was shaking.

"Here's a drink for you."

Hartford bridled, and waved aside the proffered coin.

"I neither touch, taste nor 'andle," he said virtuously, and stood ready to pass on his majestic way.

The stranger unbuttoned his coat and felt in his waistcoat pocket.

"Lost anything?"

"Nothing," said the other with satisfaction.

He blew a cloud of smoke, nodded, and they separated.

The man in evening dress came slowly to where a granite-paved roadway bisected the path before the gates of the Eastern Trading Company. The thief in the covered doorway saw him take his cigarette from his mouth, drop it on the pavement and put his foot upon it. And then, suddenly and without warning, he saw the white-faced man stagger; his knees gave from under him and he went down with a crash to the sidewalk.

Lamborn was an opportunist—saw here a gift from heaven in the shape of a drunken swell; looked left and right, and crossed the road with stealthy footsteps. He did not see Hartford moving towards him in the shadow of the wall. Lamborn flicked open the coat of the stricken man, dived in his hand and found a note-case. His fingers hooked to a watchguard; he pulled both out with a simultaneous jerk and then saw the running policeman. To be arrested on suspicion is one thing; to be found in possession of stolen property is another. Lamborn's hand jerked up to the high wall which surrounded the company's yard, and he turned to fly. Half a dozen paces he took, and then the hand of the law fell on him, and the familiar "Here, you!" came hatefully to his ears. He struggled impotently. Mr. Lamborn had never learned the first lesson of criminality, which is to go quietly.

Hartford thrust him against the wall, and then saw somebody crossing the road, and remembered the man lying under the lamp-post as he recognised the figure.

"Doctor—that gentleman's hurt. Will you have a look at him?"

Dr. Marford had seen the stranger fall and stooped gingerly by his side.

"Keep quiet, will yer?" said Hartford indignantly to his struggling prisoner.

His whistle sounded shrilly in the night. There were moments when even Lamborn grew intelligent.

"All right, it's a cop." he said sullenly, and ceased to struggle.

It was at that moment that the policeman heard an exclamation from the stooping, peering doctor.

"Constable—this man is dead—stabbed!"

He held up his hands for the policeman's inspection. In the light of the standard Hartford saw they were red with blood.

Elk, who was at the end of the street keeping a spieling house under observation, heard the whistle and came flying towards the sound. Every kennel in Tidal Basin heard it and was drawn. Men and women forfeited their night's rest rather than lose the thrill of experience; when they heard it was no less than murder they purred gratefully that their enterprise was rewarded. They came trickling out like rats from their burrows. There was a crowd almost before the uniformed police arrived to control it.

When Elk came back from 'phoning the divisional surgeon the doctor was washing his hands in a bucket of water that the policeman had brought for him.

"Mason's at the station; he's coming along."

"Here, Elk, what's the idea of holding me?"

Lamborn's voice was pained and hurt. He stood, a wretchedly garbed figure of uncouth manhood, between two towering policemen, but his spirit was beyond suppression.

"I've done nothing, have I? This rozzer pinched me—"

"Shut up," said Elk, not unkindly. "Mr. Mason will be along in a minute."

Lamborn groaned.

"Him!" he almost howled. "Sympathetic Mason, what a night for a party!"

Chief Detective Inspector Mason was visiting his area that night, and was in the police station when the call was put through. He came in the long, powerful police tender with a host of detectives, and a testy and elderly police surgeon. Dr. Rudd was a police surgeon because it offered him the maximum interest for the minimum of labour. He was a bachelor, with an assured income from investments, but he liked the authority which his position gave him; liked to see policemen touching their helmets to him as he passed them on the street; was impressed by the support he received from magistrates when he declared as having been drunk influential people who brought their own doctors from Harley Street to prove that they suffered from nothing more vicious than shell-shock.

He knew Dr. Marford slightly, and favoured him with a cold nod; resented his being in the case at all, for the penny doctor was one of the poor relations of the profession, not the kind of man one would call into a consultation, supposing Dr. Rudd called in anybody.

He made a careful examination of the still figure.

"Dead, of course," he said.

He gave the impression that, had he arrived a little earlier, the tragedy might have been averted.

"There is a knife wound," began Marford, "which penetrated—"

"Yes, yes," said Dr. Rudd impatiently. "Of course. Naturally."

He looked at Mr. Mason.

"Dead," he said. "I will make an examination. Obviously a knife wound. Death was probably instantaneous."

He looked at Marford.

"Were you here when it happened?"

"Soon after," said Marford; "a minute after—probably less than that."

"Ah, then," said Dr. Rudd, his hands in his pockets, his legs apart, "you'll be able to tell us something—"

Mason intervened. He was a bald man, with a humorous eye and a deep, unctuous voice.

"Yes, yes, we'll see all about that, Doctor."

He showed no resentment at this attempt to usurp his function; was almost jovial in the face of an impertinence which was not an unusual experience when Dr. Rudd was in a case.

"We'll see all about that. Doctor—"

"Marford."

"Doctor Marford, you were here when the murder was committed or soon after: you'll be able to tell us something, I'm sure. But now naturally you're a little upset."

Marford smiled and shook his head. "There's nothing I can tell you, Mr. Mason, except that I saw the man fall."

"I'm detaining this man, sir." It was Hartford, stiffly saluting, more important than a Chief Commissioner on his first case.

Mason bent down over the body and let the powerful rays of his hand-lamp pry into ugly places.

"Where is the knife?" he asked. "We want to look after that."

"There is no knife," said Elk, with gloomy satisfaction.

"Excuse me, sir." P.C. Hartford, unrebuffed, stood regimentally stiff: accuser, prosecutor and expositor all in one. "I've got a man here detained in custody."

Mason became aware of his humble subordinate, took him in from the rose on the crest of his helmet to the toes of his large, polished boots.

"He should be at the police station," he said gently.

It was Elk who explained.

"I kept the man here, sir, till you arrived."

Mr. Mason put his little finger in his ear and twiddled it impatiently.

"All right," he said. "It's a pleasure to know that everything is being done in strict accordance with the rules of procedure. You seem to have a nice bunch of highly intelligent police officers in your division, Inspector."

He addressed Divisional Inspector Bray, who accompanied him; but Bray had no sense of humour, and was entirely oblivious of sarcasm.

"They're a pretty useful lot," he said complacently.

Mr. Mason looked at the body at his feet, and thence to the man held between the two policemen, and back to the body again.

"No knife. . . You might search the body, will you, Elk? Help him, will you, Shale? Thank you."

He peered round at the crowd, and there were a few who, desiring at the moment to escape his scrutiny, melted quietly into the darkness.

At any rate he had seemed oblivious of the presence of Dr. Marford, who was silent in an atmosphere charged with hostility to penny doctors. Suddenly Elk lugged something from beneath the body.

"Here you are, sir."

It was a knife sheath, and at the moment was not pleasant to handle. Mr. Mason found an old envelope in his pocket and took it carefully.

"Is the knife there?"

"No."

Bray had joined the search party and was emphatic on the point. They had moved the body slightly.

"No knife." Mason looked up at the high wall. "It might have been thrown over there," he mused.

"Excuse me, sir." Constable Hartford froze to attention.

"Wait," said Mason. "Now tell me, Doctor, what did you see?"

He addressed Marford, who, brought suddenly into the ambit of publicity, stammered and was ill at ease.

"I came out of my surgery"—he pointed awkwardly—"that place with the red light. I—er—heard two men fighting—I thought I heard a little altercation before then—and I went in and got my hat and mackintosh—"

"So you'd have a better view of the fight, eh, Doctor?" Mason smiled blandly.

Marford could return the smile now.

"Not exactly," he said. "Fights are not a novelty in this particular neighbourhood. I was going out to see a case—a maternity case. When I came out I heard the commotion. The policeman was arresting a man when I came over—"

"Wait," said Mason sharply. "You saw two men fighting—could you distinguish them?"

"Not plainly," Marford shook his head, "although they were opposite my surgery."

"Very handy for them," said Mason. "Was one of them this man?"

Marford could not swear. He was rather inclined to think it was. He was certain one of them was in evening dress.

"You don't know him?"

Marford shook his head again.

"I should think he's a stranger in this neighbourhood; I've never seen him here before. When I saw him lying on the ground I thought that it was a resumption of the fight I had witnessed."

Mr. Mason whistled softly, fixing his eyes just under the doctor's chin. Marford thought his collar was awry and put up his hand, but that was a practice of Mr. Mason, who was sometimes called "Sympathetic Mason."

"Hartford." He beckoned the constable forward. "What did you see?"

P.C. Hartford saluted.

"Sir," said the constable punctiliously, "I had seen the deceased—"

A look of weariness passed across the face of Mr. Mason. He was not sympathetic with loquacious constables.

"Yes, yes, my boy, but you're not in court now, you know. You needn't call him 'the deceased.' I don't mind what you call him. You saw him before he fell?"

P.C. Hartford saluted again.

"Yes, sir, I saw him. He stopped me when I was passing and asked me if I'd met a man he'd had an argument with. I said 'No.'"

"Did he describe the man?"

"No, sir," said Hartford.

"He said nothing else?"

Hartford thought for a long time, and then repeated, as best he could remember, all that the white-faced man had said.

"You didn't meet his assailant—I mean, you weren't dreaming about the beer you were going to have for supper?"

P.C. Hartford was prepared with an indignant repudiation, but swallowed it.

"No, sir. A few minutes later, when I came back this way, I saw him lying under the lamp, and I saw another man walking away and I stopped him. Then I saw the doctor coming across. By this time I'd arrested Lamborn, who tried to run away."

"Oh, no!" said Mason, pained.

Mr. Lamborn grew voluble. He was running for a doctor, he protested.

"The man was on the ground before you touched him: is that what you're suggesting?" asked Mason.

The prisoner not only suggested but swore to this fact. He had a witness, a woman who carried a can in her hand. She might have preferred to remain anonymous, but that natural sense of justice which is the possession of poor and innocent people overcame her modesty. She was haled forward into the clear circle. She was a respectable woman. She had seen the man fall, had been a witness of Lamborn going across to him. If she had any private views as to the motive for his attentions she wisely restrained them.

Mason looked at her thoughtfully.

"What is in that can?" he asked.

There was a lid to the can. All her inclinations were against satisfying his curiosity, but she had a respect for the law and told the truth.

"Beer."

Mason seemed oblivious of the dead man behind him, of the thief in custody, and of the very existence of secret murderers who stalked their prey on the highway.

"Beer—that's funny." A clock chimed half-past ten. "Why are you carrying beer about the street at half-past ten, Mrs.—"

Her name was Albert. She had no explanation for the beer, except, she explained tremulously, that she was taking it home. There was

50

a sympathetic murmur in the crowd. An anonymous revolutionary said "Leave the woman alone!" There are always voices that offer the same advice to policemen in all parts of the world in similar circumstances.

P.C. Hartford was desperate. He had something to say—something vital, a solution which would sweep aside all the cobwebs of mystery which surrounded the pitiful heap lying under the electric light standard and yielding very little to the busy men who were searching it.

"I wanted to say, sir, that I saw this man throwing something over the wall."

Mason looked at the wall, as though he expected it to give confirmation of this statement.

"Lamborn, you mean?" He glanced keenly at the thief and jerked his head significantly. "Take him away," he said; "I'll see him at the station."

Mr. Lamborn went between two policemen, hurling back sanguinary defiance. There is something of a terrier in the habitual crook: he stands up to punishment most gallantly.

"I'll see you at the station, too, ma'am," said Mason.

Mrs. Albert nearly dropped her can in her agitation. She was a married woman with four children, and had never entered a police station in her life.

"It's never too late to learn," said Mason sympathetically.

Another ambulance came, one of the baser kind, hand-pushed, and then a police car, with photographers, cheerful finger-print experts and men of the Identification Bureau. Wilful murder lost its romance and passed into its business stage.

"Just plain murder," said Mason to his subordinates as he moved towards his car. "One or two queer features about it, though."

And then through the crowd came a woman. He thought she was a girl, but in the cruel light of the arc lamp saw that she had left girlhood a long way behind her. She was white-faced, wide-eyed, a ghost of a woman; her trembling lips parted, for the moment inarticulate. She stared from one to the other. Dr. Marford, from the shadows, watched her curiously; knew her for Lorna Weston, a lady of uncertain profession.

"Is it—he?"

Her voice, starting as a croak, ended in a wail.

"Who are you?" Mason stood squarely before her.

"I'm—I live around here." She spoke spasmodically; every sentence seemed an effort. "He came to see me tonight, and I warned him. . . of the danger. You see, I—I know my husband. He's a devil! I somehow know it."

"Your husband killed this man, eh?"

She tried to push past him, but he held her back with some difficulty, for fear had given this frail body the strength of a man.

"Steady, steady, my girl. It may not be your friend at all. What's his name?"

"Donald—" She checked herself. "May I see him?. . . I'll tell you."

But Mr. Mason must proceed methodically, in the way of his kind, consolidating the foundations of fact.

"This is what you say, that this man came to visit you tonight, and you warned him against your husband. Now, is your husband living in this area?"

She looked at him blankly. He realised that her mind was not upon his questions and repeated it.

"Yes," she said. There was a certain defiance in her voice.

"Where does your husband live? What's his name?"

She was moving from side to side, and stooped once to look under his arm at the still thing on the ground,

"Let me see him," she pleaded. "I shan't faint. . . it may not be he. I'm sure it's not he. Let me see him!" Her voice was a whine now.

Mr. Mason nodded to Elk, and Elk took her by the arm and led her to where the man lay, half in and half out of the circle of light. She looked down, speechless; opened her lips but could say nothing. And then:

"Donald. . . he did it! The swine! The murderer!"

She stopped speaking. Elk felt her sagging away from him and caught her round the waist. The Tidal Basin crowd watched the drama. It was well worth the loss of a night's sleep.

Mason looked round, caught Marford's eye and beckoned him forward.

"Do you mind taking this woman to the station? I think it's only a faint."

Dr. Marford protested wearily. He and a policeman carried the woman to a closed police car and they drove off. Outside a chemist's shop at the end of Basin Street, Marford stopped the car and sent the constable to ring the night bell; but the restorative he secured did not bring the woman back to consciousness. She was still silent when he got her to the station.

Mr. Mason, waiting for the return of the car, delivered himself of certain observations.

"There's murder plain and murder coloured," he said to the patient Inspector Bray. "This is murder plain. No music, no fireworks, no lady's *boudoir*, nothing sexy. A man stabbed to death under three pairs of eyes and nobody saw the murderer. No knife, no motive, no clue, no name of the dear departed."

"The woman," began Bray, "talked about a devil—"

"Let's keep religion out of it," said Mason wearily. "Who was the man that threw the knife, and how did he get it back again? That's the mystery that's beating me."

Chapter 7

Quigley, crime man of the *Post-Courier* and arch-inventor of devils, telephoned through to his newspaper:

"The devil of Tidal Basin is again abroad. This slinking and sinister shadow passed unseen through deserted Endley Street and left a dead man sprawling upon the sidewalk, stabbed to the heart. Whence he came, whither he went, none knows. Under the eyes of three independent witnesses, including Mrs. Albert, the wife of the night watchman at the Eastern Trading Company, Dr. Warley" (names were Quigley's weak point), "a highly respected medical practitioner, and Police-Constable Hartford, an innocent pedestrian was seen to stagger and fall. When the horrified spectators reached his side they were dumbfounded to see that he was stabbed. The identity of the murdered man has not yet been established. Who was this stranger in evening dress, wandering in the purlieus of Tidal Basin? What ruthless hand destroyed him, and in what mysterious manner did the unseen murderer make his escape? These are the questions which Central Detective Mason has to solve. Mason, one of the Big Five, was fortunately in the neighbourhood, and immediately took charge of the case. A man has been detained, but is he the devil of Tidal Basin?"

"Cut out all that devil stuff," said the night editor as he handed the copy to a sub. "It's been overworked."

Elk came to the police station and into the inspector's room, where Mason was sitting, ten minutes after his chief arrived. He laid two articles on the table before the great man.

"That night watchman takes a lot of waking. By the way, he's the husband of Mrs. Albert—"

"The woman with the beer?"

Elk nodded.

"I found these in the yard—obviously Lamborn threw them over when he saw the policeman."

He enumerated his finds.

"Notebook and watch; glass broken, watch stopped at ten p.m. Swiss made, and has the name of a Melbourne jeweller on the face."

Mason examined the watch.

"Careful," warned Elk. "There's a smudgy thumb-print on the back."

Mason shifted his chair a little, and invited Elk by a gesture to draw another up to his side.

"What else?" he asked.

Elk took from an inside pocket a quantity of loose paper money and put it on the table. The pocket-case, which also contained a memorandum book, he opened, and extracted two new bank-notes, each for a hundred pounds. On their backs was the stamp of the Maida Vale branch of the Midland Bank; it was a round rubber stamp, and in the centre was a date line.

"Issued yesterday."

"If he'd got an account there—" began Elk.

Mason shook his head.

"He hadn't. You don't draw hundred-pound notes out of your own account and carry them about with you. You draw them out because you want to send them away. You couldn't change a hundred-pound note in London without running the risk of being arrested. No, these notes were drawn from somebody else's account and given to him. Which means that he hasn't a banking account of his own or they'd have been paid in. Therefore he's not in trade, or he'd have a banking account."

Elk sniffed.

"Sounds like the well-known Shylock Holmes to me," he said.

He was a contemporary of Mason's who had missed promotion, and his sarcasms were licensed. "What else?" asked Mason.

"Visiting-cards—any number of them." Elk took them out and laid them on the table. Mason examined them carefully. There were addresses in Birmingham and Leicester and London, but a large proportion of them were the visiting cards of people who had a permanent address in South Africa.

"All the same colour," he said. "They've all been collected within a couple of months. That means he's been a sea voyage lately—it's extraordinary how people give away their cards to perfect strangers when they're taking an ocean trip."

He looked at the backs of one or two of them; there were pencilled notes. One said: "£10,000 a year"; another: "Made a lot of money in Namaqualand Diamonds; staying Ritz, London."

Mason smiled.

"I'll give you two guesses as to what his trade is." He picked up a third card; this time the inscription on the back was in ink: "Cheque stopped; Adam & Sills."

"I'll give you one guess now. He's a crook and a card-sharp. Adam & Sills are the lawyers who do the barking for these kind of birds. That places him. Now we'll find his name. Get on to the Yard, tell 'em to call every hotel, big and small, in the West End, and find if a man has arrived there from abroad. Say that his first name is Donald. You'll find out where he came from——"

"Cape Town," said Elk.

Mason nodded. "I expected that. How do you know?"

"His boots are new; they've got a tag to them, 'Cleghorn, Adderley Street.'"

"Then make it South Africa," said Mason. Elk was half-way across the room when Mason shouted him back.

"Ask the bureau to give you the name, private address and telephone number of the manager of the Maida Vale branch of the Midland Bank. Wait a minute, don't rush me—tell the bureau to get on to the manager and find if he remembers on whose account two notes for a hundred pounds"—he scribbled down the numbers on a slip of paper and handed them to Elk—"were issued, and, if possible, to whom they were issued. I've got an idea we shan't discover that."

When Elk returned, Mr. Mason was sitting, chin in hand, his heavy, round face more than ordinarily blank. "I'll see Lamborn," he said.

Mr. Lamborn was brought from the detention-room, voluble and truculent.

"If there's a law in this country——" he began.

"There isn't," said Mr. Mason genially. "You've broken 'em all. Sit down, Harry."

Mr. Lamborn looked at him suspiciously. "You goin' to be sympathetic?" he asked. The glamour of legend surrounded Mr. Mason. He was indeed a sympathetic man, and under the genial influence of his understanding and sympathetic heart many wrongdoers had, with misguided confidence, told him much more than they ever intended to tell, a fact which they had bitterly regretted when they stood before a jury and heard their frankness exploited with disastrous effect.

Mason beamed.

"I can't be wicked with you fellows—naturally I can't." His voice was at its most unctuous. "Life's a bit difficult for all of us, and I know just how hard it is for some of you birds to get an honest living."

"I dessay," said Lamborn icily.

"You never do any harm, Harry"—Mr. Mason laid his hand upon the other's knee and patted it softly—"by telling the police all you know. It isn't much, because, if you knew enough to come in out of the rain, you wouldn't be thieving for a living. But this is a case of murder."

"Nobody says I did it," said Lamborn quickly.

"Nobody says so at the moment," agreed Mr. Mason pleasantly; "but you never can tell what stories get around. You know Tidal Basin, Harry—they'd swear your life away for a slice of pineapple. Now let's be perfectly open and above-board."

He leaned back in his chair and surveyed the other with fatherly benevolence.

"The constable saw you go over to this man and put your hand in his pocket, take out a pocket-book and possibly a watch. When you were detected you threw them over the wall, where they have since been found by Detective-Sergeant Elk. Isn't that so, Elk?"

"I know nothing about 'em," said Lamborn loudly, and Mr. Mason shook his head with a sad smile.

"You saw this fellow fall and you thought he was soused. You went over and you dipped him for his clock and pack."

"I don't understand what you're talking about," said Mr. Lamborn rapidly. "I've never heard such expressions in me life."

"Let me put it in plain English," said Mason gently. "You put your hand in his pocket and took out his pocket-case and his watch."

"That," said Lamborn emphatically, "is a damn dirty lie'."

Mr. Mason sighed, and looked at Elk despairingly.

"What can you do with 'em?" he asked.

"I don't want none of your sympathy," said the ungracious Lamborn. "There's too many people in stir through listening to your smarming. I see the gentleman fall and I went over to render him assistance."

"Medical assistance, I'm sure," murmured Mason, "you being an M.D. of Dartmoor and having learnt first aid at Wormwood Scrubs. Now come across, Harry. You can save me a lot of trouble by telling the truth."

"I—" began Lamborn

"Wait a moment." The reservoir of Mr. Mason's urbanity was running low and his voice was a little sharper. "If you'll tell me the truth I'll undertake not to charge you. I shall hold you as a Crown witness—"

"Look here, Mr. Mason," said Lamborn hotly, "what sort of a can do you think I am? I've been treated disgraceful since I've been at this station. They stripped me naked and took all me clothes away. They haven't even a sense of decency! Give me these old duds to put on. And why did they take me clothes away? To frame up evidence by puttin' stuff in me pocket—I know the police!"

Mason sighed, and when he spoke it was very deliberately and offensively.

"If you had a little more brains you'd be half-witted," he said. "That's not an original remark, but it applies. There are men twice as sane as you living in padded cells. You poor, ignorant gutter scum, don't you understand that your clothes were taken away to see if there was any blood on them, and that your dirty hands were examined for the same reason? And don't you realise that a man of my rank wouldn't trouble even to spit at you if he hadn't a very good reason? I don't want you for murder—get that into your sawdust. I don't even want you for robbery. I want you to tell me the truth: did you, or did you not, dip this man when he was lying on the ground? And if you tell me the truth I'll otter no against you. Let me tell you this." He leaned forward and tapped the other's knee with a heavy knuckle. "You won't be able to understand it, but I'm doing my duty when I tell you. The whole of this case may swing upon whether you make a voluntary statement that you took this man's pocket-case out of his pocket—the watch doesn't matter—whilst he was lying on the ground, or that you did not."

"I didn't," said Lamborn loudly. "I defy you to prove it!"

The chief inspector groaned.

"Take him away before I forget myself," he said simply.

Elk gripped the arm of his prisoner and marched him to the desk.

"You fool," he said *en route*, "why didn't you speak?"

Lamborn snorted.

"Why didn't I speak?" he demanded scornfully. "Blimey, look what I'm getting for saying nothin'!"

A minute later he was charged before an apathetic station-sergeant, and went noisily to the cells.

Elk came back to his chief with information that had come through whilst the charge was in progress.

"The two notes were issued on the account of Mr. Louis Landor, of Teign Court, Maida Vale. Landor is either an American or has lived in America. He's an engineer, a fairly rich man, and drew out another three thousand pounds this morning—he's going abroad."

"*Bon voyage* to him," said Mason, in a cynical humour. "Going abroad, is he?"

He gazed at the knife-sheath lying on a sheet of paper before him, and pointed with his little finger to ornate initials engraved on a small gold plate.

"L.L.—they may stand for Leonard Lowe: on the other hand, they may stand for Louis Landor.'

"Who's Leonard Lowe?" asked Elk, momentarily dense.

"There is no such person," said the superintendent patiently. "Listen, Elk—living in Tidal Basin hasn't sharpened your wits, has it? I'll be moving you to the West End soon—'C' Division. You'll shine amongst that batch of suckers."

He got up from the table and walked heavily through the charge-room to the little apartment which the police matron used as a duty-room, lay Lorna Weston; her face was pale, her lips colourless.

"She might be dead," said Mason.

Dr. Marford sighed, took out his cheap American watch and looked at it.

"So might be quite a large number of my patients," he said listlessly. "I don't know whether you're interested in the phenomena of life and death, Mr. Mason—my own interest is strictly professional—but at this moment there is a lady waiting for me—"

"Yes, yes," interrupted Mason good-humouredly. "We forget nothing. I've arranged for your district nurse to phone you through to the station. We'll have to do something with this woman."

He looked dubiously down at the still figure on the bed, moved slightly the blanket that covered her and felt her hand.

"She's a dope?" he asked.

Dr. Marford nodded.

"I found a hypodermic in her bag," he said.

"Rudd thinks she should be taken a hospital or infirmary."

Marford assented reluctantly. Here was the inevitable key witness, and he was loath to leave her out of his sight.

Rudd came bustling in importantly.

"I've fixed a bed at the infirmary." he said. "Of course they told me they had no accommodation, but as soon as I mentioned my name—" He smiled jovially at Marford. "Now if it had been you dear fellow—"

"I shouldn't have asked. I should simply have taken the case there and they'd have had to find a bed for her." said Marford.

Dr. Rudd was a little ruffled.

"Yes, yes; but that is hardly the way, is it? I mean, there are certain professional—um—courtesies to be observed. The resident surgeon is a friend of mine, as it happens—Grennett; he was with me at Guy's."

He dropped Marford as being unworthy of his confidence, and addressed the superintendent.

"I'm getting the ambulance down right away."

"Have you seen the man again?" asked Mason.

"The man?" Dr. Rudd frowned. "Oh, you mean the dead man? Yes. Your Mr. Elk was there, searching him. I made one or two observations which I think may be useful to you, Superintendent. For instance, there's a bruise on the left cheek."

Mason nodded.

"Yes, he was fighting. Dr. Marford saw that."

Rudd was called away at that moment, and bustled out with an apology. The very apology was offensive to Mr. Mason, for it inferred that investigations were momentarily suspended until the police surgeon returned.

The woman on the bed showed no sign of life. The doctor, at Mason's request, exhibited two tiny punctures on the left arm.

"Recently made," he explained, "but there's no evidence that she's an addict. I can find no other punctures, for example, and the mere fact that the shot has had such an extraordinarily deadening effect upon her rather suggests that she's a novice."

He lifted the arm and dropped it; it fell lifelessly.

"When will she recover consciousness?"

Marford shook his head.

"I don't know. At present she's not in a state where I could recommend giving restoratives, but I'll leave that to the infirmary people. The resident surgeon is a personal friend of Dr. Rudd's and is therefore in all probability a man of genius."

The eyes of the two men met. Mr. Mason did not attempt to disguise his own amusement.

"Fine," he said. And then: "Have you ever been in a murder case before?"

The doctor's lips twitched with the hint of a smile.

"Manslaughter—this evening," he said. "No, I have not been called in professionally. Not one doctor in eight thousand ever attends a murder case in the whole course of his practice—not if he's wise," he added.

Mason became suddenly interested in this shabby figure with the pained eyes and the thin, starved face.

"You find living not particularly pleasant in this neighbourhood, Doctor? Couldn't you work your clinic somewhere more salubrious?"

Marford shrugged.

"It's all one to me," he said. "My own wants are very few and they are satisfied. The clinic must be where it is wanted. For myself, I do not crave for the society of intellectual men, because intellectual men bore me."

"And you've no theory about this murder?"

Mason's good-humoured eyes were smiling again.

The doctor did not answer immediately; he bit his lip and looked thoughtfully past the superintendent.

"Yes," he said quietly. "To my mind, this case is obviously a case of revenge. He was not murdered for profit, he was deliberately assassinated to right some wrong probably committed years before. And it was not in the larger sense premeditated: the murder was committed on the spur of the moment as opportunity offered."

Mason stared at him.

"Why do you say that?"

"Because I think it." Marford was smiling. "Unless you believe that this man was definitely lured to this spot with the object of killing him, and that a most elaborate scheme was formed for enticing him into this neighbourhood, you must believe that it was unpremeditated."

Superintendent Mason, fists on hips, legs wide apart, peered at Marford.

"You're not one of these amateur detectives I've been reading about, Doctor?" he challenged. "The sort of man who's going to make the police look foolish in chapter thirty-nine and take all the credit for the discovery?" Then unexpectedly he clapped his hand on Marford's bony shoulder. "You talk sense, anyway, and every doctor doesn't talk that. I could name you one, but you'd probably report me to the British Medical Association. You're quite right—your theory is my theory."

And then, suddenly: "Do you exclude the possibility that Lamborn may have knifed him?"

"Entirely," said the other emphatically, and Mason nodded.

"I might tell you"—he dropped his voice confidentially—"that that is the ground plan of Dr. Rudd's theory."

"He has another," said Marford. "I wonder he hasn't told you."

Chapter 8

Mason looked down at the woman again. She had not moved, so far as the eye could see had not even breathed, since she came in.

"She's got it locked up there." He touched the white forehead lightly. "No, it's an ordinary police case, Doctor. Everything looks mysterious until somebody squeals, and then the case is so easy that even a poor old gentleman from Scotland Yard could work it out."

He frowned at the woman.

"All right, shoot her into hospital," he said brusquely, and returned to his room.

It was Inspector Bray's room really; a cupboard of a place, with a table and chair, a last year's almanac on the wall, two volumes of the Police Code, a telephone list a foot long—and three reprints of popular fiction. They were decently hidden from view by the Police Code, and Mr. Mason took one down to the table and opened it.

A taste for thrilling fiction is not phenomenal in a detective officer. With this particular story Mr. Mason was well acquainted, and he turned the leaves casually and disparagingly. Here was a murder the like of which never came the way of the average police officer. There were beautiful ladies involved, ladies who had their own Rolls-Royces and lived in exotic apartments; gentlemen who dressed for dinner every night—even the detectives did that. Here murder had a colour and a fragrance; it was set in scenes of beauty, in half-timbered country houses, with lawns that sloped down to a quiet river; in Park Lane mansions, where nothing less than a footman in resplendent uniform could find the dead body of his master lying by the side of a broken Sevres vase. High politics came into the story; ministers of state were suspected; powerful cars sped seaward to where the steam cutter was waiting to carry its murderous owner to his floating den of vice.

Mr. Mason shook his head, scratched his cheek and closed the book, and returned to his own murder, to the drabness of Tidal Basin, with its innumerable side streets and greasy pavements, jerry-built houses all of a plan, where three families lived in a space inadequate for a Park Lane bath-room. Silent Tidal Basin, with its swing bridges over the narrow entrance to docks, and its cold electric standards revealing ugliness even on the darkest night. People were living and dying here; one death more or less surely made no difference. But because a man who was a card-sharp, probably a blackguard, had met his just end, there were lights burning in all sorts of odd rooms at Scotland Yard, men searching records, a printing press working at feverish speed, police cyclists flying to the ends of the area carrying the wet sheets which described the dead man, and in ten thousand streets and squares policemen were reading, by the light of their electric lamps, the description of a man unknown, killed by one known even less.

The machinery was working; the wheels and pistons whirled and thundered—purposeless, it would seem, save to entertain the tall men on their lonely beats with first-hand news of tragedy.

Mason got up and walked out to the entrance of the station. A dim blue light painted his bronzed cheek a sickly hue. The street was deserted. Rain was falling steadily; every window of every house that faced the station was black and menacing.

Why he shivered he did not know. He was too serious a police officer to be influenced by atmosphere. And yet the unfriendliness of this area, all its possibilities of evil, penetrated his armour of indifference.

A queer, boozy lot of people. . . A thought struck him, and he slapped the palm of his hand. There were three C.I.D. men in the charge-room; he called them and gave them instructions.

"Take a couple of guns," he said. "You may need them."

After he had seen them depart, he sent an urgent phone message to Scotland Yard. Then he went across to where Dr. Marford was standing, talking to the station clerk.

"What about this man with the white mask? You know everything that happens in this pitch. Is it a yarn, or is there any foundation for it? There used to be a man up west—had some sort of accident that upset his features—he used to wear that kind of thing."

The doctor nodded slowly.

"I think that is the man I have met," he said.

"You've met him?" asked Mason in surprise.

"Yes. Why he wore the mask I have never been able to understand, because there was really very little wrong with his face, except a large red scar. He wasn't exactly good to look at—but you can say that of a lot of people who don't wear masks. I've seen thousands looking worse."

Mason scowled and pursed his lips.

"I remember the West End man. I see that some of the newspapers are recalling the fact that he was seen years ago. If I remember rightly, he lived in a top flat in Jermyn Street. He had permission from the Commissioner to go out with this thing on his face. I haven't seen him for years, but I remember him well. What was his name—West something—not Weston?"

The doctor shrugged.

"I never knew his name. He came to me about three years ago and asked for ray treatment. He was stupidly sensitive and only came after he had fixed the interview up by telephone. He's been several times since, round about midnight, and he invariably pays me a pound."

Mason thought for a while, then went to the telephone and called a central police station off Regent Street. The sergeant in charge remembered the man at once, but was not sure of his name.

"He hasn't been seen round the West End for years," he said. "The Yard has been arguing about him—wondering if he was White Face."

"Was his name Weston?" suggested Mason, but the sergeant was without information.

Mason came back to the doctor.

"Does this man live in the neighbourhood?"

But here Dr. Marford could tell him nothing. The first time he had met his queer patient he had undoubtedly lived in the region of Piccadilly; thereafter he had only appeared at irregular intervals.

"Do you think he's our devil?" asked Mason bluntly, and the lean man chuckled.

"Devil! It's queer how normal people attribute devilry to any man or woman who is afflicted—the hunchback and the misshapen, the cross-eyed and the lame. You're almost medieval, Mr. Mason."

He could say very little that might assist the police, except that he no longer received warning when the man with the mask made his appearance. Invariably he came through the little yard that ran by the side of the surgery into the passage which Dr. Marford's patients used when they queued up for their medicine.

"I never have the side door locked—I mean the door that goes into the yard." Marford explained that he was a very heavy sleeper, and it was not unusual for his clients to come right into the house to wake him, and the first intimation of their needs was a knock on his bedroom door.

"I've nothing to lose except a few instruments and a few bottles of poison; and to do these fellows justice, I've never had a thing stolen from me since I've been in the neighbourhood. I treat these people like friends, and so long as they're reasonably wholesome I don't mind their wandering about the house."

Mr. Mason made a little grimace.

"How can you live here? You're a gentleman, you have education. How can you meet them every day, listen to their miseries, see their dirt—ugh!"

Dr. Marford sighed and looked at his watch.

"If that child's normal he's born," he said, and at that moment the sergeant called him across to the telephone at the desk.

The child had been normal and had made his appearance into the world without the doctor's assistance. The male parent, a careful man, was already disputing the right of the doctor to any fee. Dr. Marford had had previous experience of a similar character, and knew that for the fact that the baby arrived before the doctor came the mother would claim and receive the fullest credit.

"Half fee, as usual," he told the district nurse and hung up the receiver.

"I used to charge half fees, but double visiting fees if I was called in afterwards. That didn't work, because the mother was usually dead before they risked the expense of calling me in. The economy of these people is excessive."

The ambulance was ready. He and Rudd saw the woman placed in charge of a uniformed nurse, and Sergeant Elk appointed a detective officer to accompany the patient to the infirmary.

Elk was silent, and his eyes were preternaturally bright when he lounged into the inspector's room.

"This is a case which ought to get me promotion," he said, a shameless thing to say in the presence of a man who expected most of the kudos. "Here I've been working for years, and this is the first real mystery I've struck. More like a book than a police case. Quigley's nosing round the neighbourhood—I shouldn't be surprised if he didn't turn in a new devil. It's a good story for him."

Mr. Mason indicated a chair.

"Sit down, my poor fellow," he said with spurious sympathy. "What are the features of this murder which have separated it from an ordinary case of knifing?"

Elk's long arm went out, and he pointed in a direction which Mr. Mason, not wholly acquainted with the geography of the station, decided was the matron's room.

"She's it!" said Elk. His voice shook. "What happened tonight, Mr. Mason? An unknown man has a fight with another unknown man, who bolts. The first fellow walks along and meets a police officer and tells him all about it. He's alive and well; obviously he's not stabbed; yet within a few seconds after the officer moves on, this fellow drops in his track like a man shot. A cheap crook comes over and dips him, and is seen by Hartford, who tackles the man. They then discover that the fellow on the ground is stabbed. Nobody saw the blow struck. Yet there he is dead—knifed, and the knife's well away and can't be found."

Mason leaned back in his chair and closed his eyes.

"End of the first reel; the second reel will follow immediately," he murmured, but Elk was undisturbed. That bright light in his eye was now a steely glitter. He was agitated as he had never been seen before in all the years of his service.

"Out of nowhere comes Mrs. Weston. She'd warned this man he was going to be killed. She wants to be sure that it is him."

"He," murmured Mason gently.

"Never mind about grammar." Elk was frankly insubordinate in his vehemence. "She takes a look at the man on the ground and drops."

He laid his hand almost violently upon the superintendent's arm and shook it.

"I was watching her. I knew the woman, though I didn't recognise her at first. She drops—and what do we find? She's a needler—a dope. Does that mean anything to you, sir?"

"I'm glad you said 'sir,'" said Mason. "I was wondering how I'd bring you back to a sense of discipline. Yes, it means a lot to me. Now I'm going to ask you a question: does the can of beer which Mrs. Albert was carrying mean anything to you, and does that can of beer associate itself in your active and intelligent mind with the disappearance of Mr. Louis Landor—if that's the name of the man who fought with the dead one?"

Elk was frankly bewildered.

"You're trying to pull my leg."

"Heaven forbid!" said the patient Mason. "Bring in Mrs. Albert. She's waited long enough to get three kinds of panic—I want her to have the kind where she'll tell the truth."

Mrs. Albert came, a rather pale woman, sensible of her disgraceful surroundings, conscious, too, of her responsibility for four children, only three of which, Mason learned, were yet born. She still clutched in her hand the tell-tale can of beer. The liquid was now flat and uninviting and some of it had spilt in her agitation, so that she brought with her to the inspector's room a faint aroma of synthetic hops. She was quivering, more or less speechless. Mason gave her no opportunity for recovering her self-possession or her volubility.

"Sorry I've had to keep you so long, Mrs. Albert," he said. "Your husband's the night watchman at the Eastern Trading Company, isn't he?"

She nodded mutely.

"The Eastern Trading Company do not allow their night watchman to have beer?"

Mrs. Albert found her voice.

"No, sir," she piped. "The last night watchman got the sack for drinking when he was on duty."

"Exactly," said Mason, at his most brusque. "But your husband likes a drop of beer, and it's fairly easy to pass the beer through the wicket gate, isn't it?"

She could only blink at him pathetically.

"And he's in the habit of leaving the wicket gate undone every night about eleven o'clock, and you're in the habit of putting that can inside the gate?"

Her pathos grew. She could only suspect a base informer, and was undecided as to which of her five neighbours had filled that despicable role.

She was not unpretty, Mason noticed in his critical way, despite the three children—or four, if her worst fears were realised.

The superintendent turned to his subordinate.

"There's the connection," he said, "and that is where Mr. Louis Landor went—through the wicket gate. Oh, you needn't bother: I've sent some men to search the yard. But if I am any judge, Mr. Landor has gone. I've already circulated his description."

Mrs. Albert, the wife of the night watchman, drooped guiltily in her chair, her agonised dark eyes fixed on Mr. Mason. Here was tragedy for her, more poignant than the death of unknown men struck down by unseen forces; the tragedy of a husband dismissed from the only job he had held in five years, of the resumption of that daily struggle for life, of aimless wanderings for employment on his part—she could always go out as a hired help for a few shillings a day.

"He'll get the sack," she managed to breathe.

Mason looked at her and shook his head.

"I'm not reporting to the Eastern Trading Company, though you might have helped a little bit if you hadn't hidden up the truth when I asked you about the beer. I blame myself for not realising that you had something to hide, and what it was. It might have made a big difference."

"You're not reporting it, mister?" she asked tremulously, and was on the verge of tears. "I've had a very hard time. That poor woman could tell you how hard it was: she used to live with me till she came into money."

"Which poor woman is this?" asked Mason quickly.

"Mrs. Weston."

She had lost some of her fear in the face of his interest.

"She lodged with you?"

Elk had left the room. Mason motioned her to the chair which the sergeant had vacated and which was nearer to him.

"Come along and let's hear all about it," he said genially.

A bald man, with a round, amused face and a ready smile, removed all her natural suspicions.

"Oh, yes, sir, she used to lodge with me, till she got this money."

"Where did she get the money from?"

"Gawd knows," said Mrs. Albert piously. "I never ask questions. She paid me all that she owed me, that's all I know. I've been wondering, sir"—she leaned forward confidentially—"was it her husband or her young man who was killed?"

"Her young man was killed," said Mason without hesitation. "You knew them?"

She shook her head.

"You knew the husband, at any rate?"

"I've seen photographs of him in her room. They were taken in Australia—her and the two. When I say I've seen them," she corrected herself, "I was just going to take a look at 'em when she come in the room and snatched the frame out of my hand—which was funny, because it had always been on the mantelshelf before, but I never took any notice of it till she said one day it was her husband and a great friend. It was on the following day I took up the picture to have a look."

"And she snatched it out of your hand? How long ago was this?"

She thought.

"Two years last July."

Mason nodded.

"And soon after that she came into money, almost immediately after?"

Mrs. Albert was not surprised at his perspicuity. She had the impression that she had given him that information.

"Yes, sir, she left me the next day, or two days after. I haven't spoken to her since. She lives in the grand part of Tidal Basin now. I always say that when people are well off——"

"I'm perfectly sure I can guess what you always say." He was not unkind but he was very firm. "Now, what sort of a frame would this be in—leather?"

Yes, she thought rather that it was leather—or wood, covered with leather.

"I know she put it in her box because I saw her do it—a little black box she used to keep under her bed."

He questioned her and cross-checked her answers, eliminating in the process all possibility that her narrative might be embroidered by imagination. Into the lives of the poor comes no other romance than that of their own creation.

He grew suddenly vague; she could not understand the questions he put to her. They seemed to have no foundation in reason. And then suddenly he touched a high note of romance. Had she ever seen a man with a piece of white cloth on his face? She shuddered pleasurably.

"The Devil... I've heard of him, but never seen him, thank God! It was him that done it—everybody was saying so in the crowd."

"Have you ever seen him?"

She shook her head vigorously.

"No, an' I don't want to in my state. But I know people who have .. in the middle of the night."

"When they've been dreaming," suggested Mason, but she would not have this.

The Devil was a possession of Tidal Basin; not willingly would she surrender the legend. When he showed into the charge-room a woman made tearfully grateful by the knowledge that she could go to her home and her three children. Marford was waiting to say good night. Dr. Rudd had already left.

"If you want me tonight, I shall be at my surgery. I hope I may be allowed to sleep."

Mason had three things he wished to do at the same time—three errands on which he could trust nobody but himself. He decided to perform his first task single-handed and call back for Elk to assist him with the second.

Chapter 9

Michael Quigley was coming up the steps of the police station as Mason appeared in the doorway.

"Carrion," said Mason pleasantly, "the body has been removed."

"Who is it, Mason?"

Mr. Mason shook his head.

"There was once," he said jovially, "a medical student who was asked how many teeth Adam was born with, and he replied, very properly, 'God knows.'"

"Unknown, eh? A swell, they tell me?"

"He's well dressed," said Mason in his noncommittal way. "Go along and have a look at him. You know all the toughs in the West End."

Michael shook his head.

"That can wait. What is this murder—a little joke of White Face?"

"Why White Face?" demanded Mason. "Listen, Quigley, you've got a bug in your brain. White Face doesn't belong to Tidal Basin any more than your devil."

"He's been seen here," insisted the reporter, and Mason sighed.

"A man who wore a lump of lint over his face has been seen here. Dr. Marford, in a weak-minded moment, told you. You'd see the same in the neighbourhood of any hospital."

Michael Quigley was unusually silent.

"Oh. . . where are you going?"

No other reporter dared ask such a question, but Mason knew this young man rather well.

"You'll get me hung, Michael, but I'll let you come along with me. I'm going to see a green door and have a little independent search. Your encouragement and help will be welcome. How is Miss Harman?"

Mike almost showed his teeth.

"You can collect gossip, even if you can't collect murderers!" he snarled. "Miss Harman is a very good friend of mine who is going to marry somebody else."

"I congratulate her," said Mason as they stepped out towards Endley Street. "It must be a terribly unromantic life being married to a reporter."

"There is no question of my being married to anybody," said Michael savagely, "and you're getting under my skin, Mason."

"Fine," said Mason. "Someday I'll go shooting elephants."

They trudged side by side, cold anger in the heart of one and an idea that was growing into shape in the mind of Mr. Mason. He whistled softly as he walked under the high wall of the Eastern Trading Company.

"Do you mind," asked Michael with sour politeness, "choosing some other tune than the Wedding March?"

"Was I whistling that?" asked the other in surprise. "Ever noticed how like a funeral march it is? Change the time and you're there."

It was a beast of a night; a wind had risen, with the cold of the Eastern *steppes*.

"Policemen and reporters," said Mason, "get their living out of other people's misfortunes. Has that ever struck you? Here they are!"

The "they" were three men walking abreast towards them. They slackened their pace when Mason came into view and halted to receive them.

"We've found nothing and nobody," said the senior. "We searched the yard, but there wasn't a sign of a man, though there were plenty of places where he could have hidden."

"And the wicket gate?"

"That was ajar," replied the detective. "Albert, the night watchman, swore that it hadn't been opened. It's against the rules to open the wicket gate unless there's a fire."

"Maybe there was a fire," suggested Mason. "It's a good night for a fire. All right, you can come along with me."

They had only a few yards to go before they came to the place where the pavement, the private yard road and the railway arch formed a triangle.

"This is where the body was found." suggested Michael, and Mason indicated the spot.

He was still whistling when he walked to the green-painted wicket door and pushed. It was locked now. If he'd only thought of trying that door—but if there had been a man behind it he would have had the sense to have shot in the bolts. He must have been hiding in there when Elk was searching the yard for the pocket case and watch. But if Mrs. Albert had talked—

He confided his woes to Michael, a safe and sure recipient, for Michael Quigley knew just what not to print.

"You get that sort of thing in all these cases," said Michael philosophically. "And you expect it, anyway. Nobody tells the truth, because there's some twiddling little thing to hide that may bring discredit upon them. Personally, I can't understand their mentality."

His eyes roved over the pavement.

"You searched the gutter, I suppose? There's a distinct slope to this sidewalk."

Mason looked inquiringly at one of the detectives, but nobody could tell him anything except that the traps where storm water runs had been emptied and the mud at the bottom carefully searched, without anything of value being found.

Michael straddled the gutter, and, pulling up his sleeve, ran his fingers through the slowly moving water, groping. . .

"First shot!" he cried exultantly. "What's this?"

Mason took it in his hand. It looked like a button or a tiny brown electric light bulb. One of the detectives put his light upon the find as it lay in Mason's hand.

"It looks to me like a capsule," said Michael, turning it over curiously.

It was indeed a tiny capsule of thin glass, containing something the colour of which was indistinguishable.

"I seem to know the shape, too. Now where the devil have I seen those before?"

"It can go to the police analyst, anyway," said Mason, and put it carefully in his pocket. "Mike, you're lucky: try again."

Michael's wet hand went through the water, but he could find nothing. And then he saw what hundreds of pairs of eyes, focused on that strip of pavement, had not seen. It lay poised upon the sharp edge of the kerb, as if it had been carefully placed there, though it must have rolled and fallen into its position through no other agent than the force of gravity. The long stone hung over the kerb: the platinum circle was so dulled with rain that it was indistinguishable from the granite on which it rested.

He picked it up, his heart thumping painfully.

"What is this?"

Mason took it from his unwilling hand.

"A ring! To think those poor, blind bats—a ruby ring! I suppose the ruby's an imitation, but it looks ruby."

Michael Quigley said nothing. The men were swaying blurs of shadow; he found a difficulty in breathing. Something in his attitude must have attracted Mason's attention, for he looked at him sharply.

"What's the matter with you? God Almighty, you look like a dead man! It was stooping down that did it—the blood rushing to your head, eh?"

Michael knew Mason well enough to realise that Superintendent Mason was advancing an excuse for the benefit of the other detectives, and this was confirmed when he sent them left and right groping vainly through the gutters for some new clue. Then it was, he took Michael's arm.

"Son," he said kindly, "You've seen that ring before, haven't you?"

Michael shook his head.

"What's the use of telling me a lie?" Mason's voice was reproachful and hurt.

"I don't remember seeing it before," said Michael harshly. It did not sound like his voice speaking.

"Hiding up?" said Mason gently. "What's the use? Somebody's bound to come along and blow it all. You were saying only a minute ago how silly it was to keep things from the police—twiddling little things that don't count. And you couldn't understand their mentality. Are you understanding their mentality any better?"

"I've never seen that ring before."

It required a mighty effort on his part for Michael to make this statement. Mr. Mason was by nature a sceptic and not easily convinced.

"You've seen it before and you know whom it belongs to. Listen, Michael! I'm not going to be sympathetic with you and I'm not going to try any of the monkey tricks that I use with half-witted criminals. You'll save yourself a lot of trouble and somebody else more, if you take me into your confidence. It doesn't mean that the person who owns that ring is going to be pinched, or that they're booked for pads of publicity—you know me too well for that. Hiding up, as you say, is one of the curses of the business."

Michael had recovered himself by now.

"You'll be pinching me for the murder in a minute," he said lightly. "No, I don't know that stone at all. I was a little dizzy from trying to do stunts in the gutter with my head between my legs. Try it yourself and see what effect it has on you."

Mason looked at him for a long time, then at the ring.

"A lady's ring, I should say." He tried it on his little finger. "And a little finger ring. It doesn't go any farther than the top of mine. That will mean publicity," he said carelessly. "I don't want to say anything against you newspaper men, Michael, but you certainly spread yourselves on a mysterious clue like this, and I shouldn't be surprised to find a portrait of the young lady—"

He stopped suddenly.

"Not Miss Harman?"

"No," said Michael loudly.

"Liar," retorted Mr. Mason. "It's Miss Harman's ring! And you knew it the moment you saw it!"

He looked at the jewel for a while, then put it into his pocket.

"This man who was murdered was a South African?" asked Mike. Mason nodded.

"Had he come recently from South Africa?"

"We don't know, but we guess within the last week or two."

"What is his name?"

"We don't even know that, except that it's Donald."

His jaw dropped; his large protruding eyes opened to their widest extent.

"Whom is Miss Harman going to marry?" he asked.

"An Irishman named Feeney," said Michael mendaciously. "No, as a matter of fact, Mason, she's marrying me. But I've had a little tiff with her. Can I see the body?"

"Let's go together and make an evening of it," said Mason, and linked arms with him.

Their gruesome errand lasted only a few minutes and left Michael more puzzled than ever. Puzzled and terribly distressed. There was no question at all that the man who had dropped that ring, whether it was the dead man or the murderer, was the romantic lover. He must find out the truth at all costs.

He left Mason at the police station and ran out, almost knocking down a girl who was hesitating at the foot of the station steps.

"Michael. . . Michael!" she gasped, and clutched him by the arm.

76

"They told me you were here. I had to see you. . . Oh, Michael, I've been a fool and I do want help terribly badly!"

He looked at her with momentary suspicion.

"How long have you been here, Janice?" he asked.

"I've just arrived. There's my car." She pointed to its dim lights. The shoulders of her skin coat were wet with rain. "Could we go anywhere? I want to speak to you. There's been a murder, hasn't there?"

He nodded.

"How dreadful! But I'm glad I knew where I could find you. There always seem to be murders here," she shuddered. "And I've been murdered, too, Michael. All my vanity, all my pride—if it's true. And I feel that you are the only person that can bring them to life again. Where can we go?"

He hesitated. He had supplied the needs of the last edition; there was nothing more for him to write tonight, though his work was by no means done. He went back to the car. She was in so pitiable a condition that he took the wheel from her hand and drove her to Bury Street. He had never been in her flat before, so that he was a stranger to the maid who opened the door.

Janice led the way to the pretty little drawing-room and closed the door.

"Take your coat off," he commanded before she started speaking. "Your shoes and your stockings are all wet—go and change them."

She went meekly, and returned in a few minutes with a dressing-gown wrapped round her, and cowered down in a low armchair before an electric radiator.

"Here's the cablegram I had."

She handed him a folded paper without looking up.

"Wait! Before you read it I want to tell you. He said he had a farm in Paarl and he was very anxious to buy an adjoining property. . . and I was buying it for him and cabled out to Van Zyl, that awfully nice boy I spoke to you about, and told him to buy it. That is his answer."

He opened the telegram. It was a long message.

"The property you mention is not at Paarl but in Constantia adjoining the convict prison. It is not and never has been for sale. Donald Bateman, whom you mention as proprietor, is unknown as landowner either here or in Rhodesia. My friend Public Prosecutor is afraid man you mention is Donald Bateman, who served nine months imprisonment at Constantia for land frauds; tall, rather good-looking man, long scar under his chin, grey eyes. He left by *Balmoral Castle* five weeks ago *en route* England. His frauds take shape of persuading people advance money buy property and decamping with deposit. Please forgive if this little melodramatic. Always anxious to serve. Carl."

He folded the telegram and looked at her oddly.

And then he said in a strange voice:

"The scar under the chin. It's curious, that's the first thing I noticed."

She turned and looked up at him, startled.

"You haven't seen him? You told me you hadn't. When did you see him?"

Michael licked his dry lips. Donald Bateman! So that was his name! He walked across to her and laid his hand gently on her shoulder.

"My dear, how perfectly rotten for you!" he said huskily. "Isn't it?"

"Do you think that is true? That he is—what Carl says he is?"

"Yes," he said. "You gave him the ring, didn't you?"

She made an impatient little gesture.

"That was nothing; it had no value except a sentimental one— which made it rather appropriate," she added bitterly.

There was something he had to ask, something so difficult that he could hardly frame the words.

"There are no complications, are there?"

She looked up at him wonderingly.

"Complications? What do you mean, Michael?"

She saw that he avoided her gaze.

"Well, I mean, you aren't married already secretly married, you know? It can be done three days."

She shook her head.

"Why should I? Of course not."

He fetched a long sigh of relief.

"Thank the Lord for that!" he said. "Are you fond of him? Not too fond, are you, Janice?"

"No. I've been a mad schoolgirl, haven't I? I've been realising it all the evening, that I didn't—love him. I wonder if you'll believe it. . . I haven't even kissed him—ugh!"

He patted her shoulder gently.

"Naturally my pride is hurt, but I haven't crashed so utterly as I should if I—well, if this thing had gone on before I found it out. You'll never laugh at me, will you, Michael?"

She put up her hand and laid it on that which rested on her shoulder.

"No, I shan't laugh at you."

She sat gazing into the glowing electric fire, and then:

"Why did you ask about the ring?"

He made the plunge.

"Because I've been lying about it to Mason—Superintendent Mason of Scotland Yard."

She was up on her feet instantly, her eyes wide with alarm.

"Scotland Yard! Have they got the ring? Have they arrested him? Michael, what is it?" She gripped his arm. "You're hiding something—what is it?"

"I've been hiding something—yes. I've been hiding from Mason the fact that the ring was yours. It was in Endley Street. I picked it up myself, near the place where the body of a murdered man was found."

"A murdered man was found in Endley Street." She repeated the words slowly. "That was the case you were on. . . Who was it? Not Donald Bateman?"

He nodded.

"O God, how awful!"

He thought she was going to faint, but when he reached out to catch her she pushed him back.

"He was stabbed by some person unknown," said Michael. "I-I've seen him. That's how I knew about the scar."

She was very still and white but she showed no other signs of distress.

"What was he doing there?" she asked. "He didn't know the neighbourhood; he told me today he'd never been there before in his life. Nobody knows who did it?"

He shook his head.

"Nobody. When I saw the ring I recognised it at once. Like a fool I gave myself away, and Mason, who's as sharp as a packet of needles, knew I was lying when I told him I had never seen it before. He may advertise the ring tomorrow unless I tell him."

"Then tell him," she said instantly. "Dead! It's unbelievable!"

She sat down in the chair again, her face in her hands. He thought she was on the verge of a breakdown, but when she raised her face to him her eyes were tearless.

"You had better go back, my dear. I shan't do anything stupid—but I'm afraid I shan't sleep. Will you come early in the morning and let me know what has been discovered? I intended going to see Dr. Marford tomorrow to ask him to let me come back to the clinic, but I don't think I can for a day or two."

"I don't want to leave you like this," he said, but she smiled faintly.

"You're talking as if I were a mid-Victorian heroine," she said. "No, my dear, you go. I'd like to be alone for a little while."

And then, to his great embarrassment, she raised his hand and kissed it.

"I'm being motherly," she said.

If there were no tears in her eyes, pain was there. He thought it wise of him to leave at once, and he went back to Tidal Basin to find the streets alive with police, for two important things had happened; two new phases of the drama had been enacted in his absence.

Chapter 10

A framed photograph is not a difficult object to find, and black boxes in which ladies keep their treasures deposited beneath their beds are far from becoming rarities. Mason would have liked to have Elk with him, but the sergeant had gone on to join Bray. A watch was being kept on the block in which Louis Landor's apartments were situated. Bray had telephoned through that neither Mr. nor Mrs. Landor was yet at home. Evidently something was wrong here, for the servant, who had returned and was awaiting admission, told Bray that she had been sent out earlier in the day, that there had been some sort of trouble between a couple that were hitherto happily married. She had been told she need not return until late. Bray had found her waiting disconsolately outside the flat, and had persuaded her to spend the night with a sister who lived in the neighbourhood.

"One thing she told me," said Bray over the wire; "the flat is packed with South African curios. If this girl's story is true, there are two knives similar to the one with which the murder was committed—they hang on a belt in the hall. She described the sheath exactly, and said they both had the initials of Landor, and that he got them as prizes in South America, where he lived for some years."

"Hang on," were Mason's instructions. "Elk's gone up to join you. Report to me here or at Scotland Yard. I am making a search on my own."

He had on his desk the contents of Mrs. Weston's bag, including the worn hypodermic case that Dr. Marford had produced. The case puzzled him, because it was old and the little syringe had evidently been used many times. And yet Marford had given it as his opinion that the woman was not an addict and that it was only the second time that the needle had been used.

There were a few letters, a bill or two from a West End milliner.

Evidently Lorna Weston, in spite of the poverty-stricken neighbourhood in which she lived, spared no expense in the adornment of her person. He found two five-pound notes, half a dozen Treasury bills, a little silver and a bunch of keys, and it was with these keys that, in company with Sergeant Shale, he made his way to the mystery woman's apartments.

What Mrs. Albert had described as "the grand part of Tidal Basin," consisted of two or three streets of well-built villas. There were several shops here, and it was over one of these, a large grocery store, that Mrs. Weston had her apartments, which were approached by a side door and a short passage. From this ran a flight of rather steep steps to a landing above.

The place was fitted with electric light and had, he saw, a telephone of its own. He climbed the stairs and was staggered to find that the landing had been painted and decorated in the West End style. Parchment-covered walls, white metal wall-brackets and soft-shaded lamps gave the approach to the apartment the appearance of luxury.

The front room was the parlour, and was tastefully furnished, and this was the case with the other rooms, including an expensively fitted kitchenette.

Mr. Mason was essentially a man of the world. He knew that this style of living was consistent with the earnings of no profession, reputable or otherwise. Either Mrs. Weston had a private income of her own or else—

He remembered that the woman at the police station had spoken of her coming into a lot of money. That might be an explanation. But why did she choose this ghastly neighbourhood in which to live?

There was a small writing-table in the drawing-room, but a search of this—the drawers were unlocked—revealed nothing that was in any way satisfactory to the searcher. It was in the bedroom that he and his assistant decided to make their most careful scrutiny. This was the room next to the drawing-room and the last to be visited. As soon as he switched on the lights, Mason realised that something unusual had happened. The drawers of the dressing-table had been pulled out, the plate-glass door of the wardrobe stood wide open. On the floor was a medley of garments and wearing apparel, and amidst them Mason saw the corner of a black box. He went quickly to this. It had been locked, but somebody had broken open the lid. Scattered about the floor were oddments and papers. There was no framed photograph. What he did see was a small cardboard cylinder. He picked it up and squinted through it; it was empty.

The cylinder interested him, because he knew it was the kind in which marriage certificates were kept; and however unhappy a marriage might be, that little slip of paper is one with which no woman parts willingly.

"Get the men in and we'll dust the place for fingerprints," he said.

He had hardly spoken the words before he saw lying on the bed a pair of white cotton gloves. The intruder had taken no risks. He examined them carefully, but they told him nothing except that they were white cotton gloves which had been carefully washed, probably by their user.

When had the burglar come, and how had he secured admission? The door below had not been forced; only the black box, which, he guessed, had been in the bottom drawer of the bureau when it was found, for nothing in this drawer had been disturbed, and there was a space which such a box might have occupied.

Of clues by which he could judge the time, there was none.

"There's somebody knocking on the door down below," said Shale. "Shall I see who it is?"

"No, wait; I'll go."

Mason went quickly down the stairs and opened the door. A woman was standing there with a shawl over her head to protect her from the rain. She looked dubiously at Mason standing in the light, and edged farther back. It struck him that she was ready to run.

"Is everything all right?" she asked nervously.

"Everything is all wrong," said Mason. And then, recognising her timidity and guessing the reason: "Don't worry—I'm a police officer."

He saw she was relieved.

"I'm the caretaker of the house opposite; the lady is away in the country; and I was wondering whether I ought to go to the police or not."

"Then you saw somebody go into this flat tonight?" asked Mason quickly.

"I saw them come out," she said. "I wouldn't even have taken notice of that if it hadn't been for the white thing—"

"What white thing? You mean, it was somebody with a white mask?" Mason snapped the question at her.

"I won't swear to who it was, but I will swear that he had white on his face. I saw it as plain as can be in the light of the street lamp. I've had toothache all night and I've been sitting in our front parlour—"

He cut short her narrative.

"When did you see this somebody come out?" he asked.

It was less than a quarter of an hour ago. She had also seen him and Shale enter and, believing that they were police officers, she had ventured to come over and knock at the door. He questioned her closely as to how the burglar had been dressed, and the description was a familiar one: the long coat that reached to the heels, the black felt hat and the white mask. He learned one characteristic which had never before been noticed: the man limped painfully. She was very sure of this. He came in no car and went away walking, and had disappeared round the corner of the block, in the direction opposite to that which the two detectives had followed on their way to the flat.

Shale came down and took a shorthand note of her statement, and then the two men returned to the flat and made an even more careful scrutiny in the hope that White Face might have left something else behind than his gloves.

"I don't even know that these won't tell us something."

Mason put the gloves carefully into a paper bag and slipped them into his pocket.

"Then it's true, White Face is an institution here."

"They all think so," said Shale. "The little thieves round here glorify him!"

Mason returned to the station, a very much baffled man. He had two pieces of evidence, and these he had locked away in the station safe. He took out the ring and the capsule and brought them into the inspector's room. The garrulous Rudd would be able to tell him something about this. He opened the door and called to the station sergeant.

"I suppose Dr. Rudd will be in bed by now?"

"No, sir; he rang me up a quarter of an hour ago. He said he was coming round to offer rather a startling theory. Those were his words—rather a startling theory.'"

Mason groaned.

"It'll be startling all right! Get him on the 'phone and ask him if he'll step round. Don't mention the theory. I want him to identify a medicine."

He examined the ring through a magnifying-glass, but there was nothing that could tell him a twentieth of what Michael Quigley could have told.

"That Quigley knows something," grumbled Mason. "I nearly had it out of him, too."

"What could he know, sir?" asked Shale.

"He knows who owns that ring," nodded Mason. The station sergeant opened the door and looked in. "Dr. Rudd went out five minutes ago on his way, sir," he said, "and there's a message for you from the Yard."

It was from the Information Bureau. The mysterious Donald had been located.

"His name is Donald Bateman," said the reporting detective. "He arrived from South Africa three weeks ago and is staying at the Little Norfolk Hotel, Norfolk Street, The description tallies with the description you sent us, Mr. Mason."

"He's not in the hotel now by any chance?"

"No, sir, he went out this evening, wearing a dinner jacket, and said he wouldn't be back till midnight. He hasn't been seen since. He has a scar under his chin—that corresponds with your description, too—and he's about the same height as the murdered man."

"Pass his name to the Identification Bureau," said Mason, "see if we have any record of him and—don't go away, my lad—post a man in the hotel. If Mr. Donald Bateman doesn't return by seven o'clock tomorrow morning have his trunks removed to Cannon Row Police Station and held until I come and search them,"

He hung up the receiver.

"Donald Bateman, eh? That's something to go on, Mr. Bray hasn't rung up?"

"No, sir."

Mason strolled back to the inspector's room and resumed his examination of the ring and the capsule.

"Yes, Michael knows all about the ring or I'm a Dutchman. The young devil nearly fainted when he found it."

"Where could the ring and the capsule have come from?" asked Shale.

"Where else could they have come from than out of Donald Bateman's pocket? You've heard all the witnesses examined: they agree that when Bateman fell he put his hand in his waistcoat pocket and tried to get something out. He probably got both these things in his hand; they rolled down the sidewalk into the gutter, and they wouldn't have been found then but for Michael. I'll say that of the kid, he's got good instincts."

He looked at his watch.

"How far does the doctor live from here?"

"Not four minutes' walk," said Shale, who had been sent to fetch the divisional surgeon when the murder was reported.

"Then he ought to be here by now. Ring him again."

But Dr. Rudd's housekeeper insisted that he had left ten minutes before.

"Go out and see if you can find him."

Mason was suddenly serious. He mistrusted the doctor's theories; he mistrusted more his garrulity. A man who talks all the time and whose topics are limited in number must inevitably say something which the police would rather he did not say. He hoped he had not met a friend on the way.

In a little under ten minutes Shale came back. He had been as far as the doctor's house but had seen no sign of Rudd. It was a comparatively short and straightforward walk.

"He may be with Dr. Marford. Ring him."

But Marford could offer no explanation, except that he had been in his surgery and that Rudd had passed, tapping on the big surgery window to say good night.

"And frightened me out of my skin," complained Dr. Marford. "I hadn't the slightest idea who it was until I went up and looked behind the blinds."

The distance from the doctor's surgery to the police station was less than two hundred yards, but there was another way, through Gallows Alley, an unwholesome short cut, by which the distance could be cut off some fifty yards. As nobody ever went into Gallows Alley, except those lost souls who dragged out their dreary existence there, it was presumable that Rudd had taken the longest route.

The lower end of Gallows Alley ran out through a tunnel-shaped opening flush with and a few yards north of Dr. Marford's side door. In the days when drunken sailormen from the docks and wharves were as common as lamp-posts, Gallows Alley was a place of picturesque infamy. It was no longer picturesque.

A Chinaman had a tiny lodging-house there in which he housed an incredible number of his fellow countrymen. Four or five Italian families lived in another house, and other families less easy to describe dwelt in the others. It was said that the police went down Gallows Alley in pairs. That is not true. They never went at all, and only with the greatest circumspection when *bona fide* cries of "Murder!" called for their attention.

Dr. Marford was one of the few people who went down that lane day or night voluntarily and suffered no harm. Did he wish, he could tell hair-raising stories of what he had seen and heard in that malodorous thoroughfare, but he was from choice a poor raconteur.

"I shouldn't think Rudd would go down there," he said in answer to the superintendent's inquiry. "At any rate, if you have any doubt I'll go myself."

Half an hour passed, and at a quarter to two Mason gathered all his reserves and sent them on a search. A telephone call brought swift police launches to the water front, to the distress of the local gang that was illicitly breaking cargo when the boats arrived. But there was no sign of Rudd or message from him. Momentarily he had vanished from the face of the earth.

This was the situation as Michael Quigley found it when he arrived on the scene. He sought an interview with the superintendent and told him frankly, as Janice had directed him to tell, the story of the ring. Mr. Mason listened wearily.

"Hiding up!" he wailed. "What good did it do? Why couldn't you tell me right away—not that it would have made any difference, except that I should have known the name earlier. Yes, that's his name, Donald Bateman. We're getting warmer—hallo, Doctor!"

It was Marford, who had come for news of his colleague.

"None. He's probably discovered that the murderer was an Irishman and he's gone off by the night boat to Ireland to get local colour. Sit down, Doctor, and have some coffee."

He pushed a steaming cup towards Marford, who took it and sipped painfully.

"Where he's gone I don't know, and don't care." Mason yawned. "I'm a weary man, and I did hope this murder was coming out nicely. If Mr. Louis Landor would only come home like a good lad, we ought to have all the threads in our hands by the morning. But if Mr. Louis Landor has taken his passport and his three thousand pounds in a private aeroplane to the Continent, then this is going to be one of those well-known unravelled mysteries of London that reporters write about when they're too old for ordinary work."

The doctor finished his coffee and went soon after. His second case was due.

Mason walked with him to the door.

"Any more theories?"

"Yes, I've got, not a theory, but an absolute conviction now." said Marford quietly. "But for the trifling detail that I'm not in a position to supply the evidence, I think I could tell you the murderer."

Mason nodded.

"I wonder if you are thinking of the same person, Doctor?"

Marford smiled.

"For his sake, I hope not."

"Which means that you're not going to give us the benefit of your logic and deductions?"

"I'm a doctor, not a detective," said the other.

Mason came back to the charge-room fire and warmed his hands.

"No message from Bray or Elk?"

He glanced at the clock; it was a quarter-past two. He began to have his doubts whether Mr. Louis Landor would ever return to his flat.

Accompanied by the reporter, he strolled out in the direction of Gallows Alley. The rain had ceased, but the wind still blew fitfully.

"And if you're writing about this place," he said, "don't fall into an error common to all cub reporters that Gallows Alley stands on the site of Execution Dock. It doesn't. It was named after a man called Gallers, who owns a lot of property about here, and if, instead of putting up his silly clinics, the doctor would get his rich pals to buy this area and clear away the slums, he'd be doing the world a service— and the police."

The entry of Gallows Alley looked dark and formidable. Within a few yards were the gates of the doctor's yard. It was a small court-yard, at one end of which was a shed, which he hired out to the famous Gregory Wicks, a veteran owner of a taxicab. It was in another way a most useful assembling place for the doctor, who dispensed his own medicines. Almost any evening could be seen a queue of poorly-dressed men and women lined up, waiting their turn to enter the narrow passage that flanked the surgery and receive through a small hatch from the doctor's hands the medicine he had ordered and dispensed.

It's more like the waiting-room of a hospital than a private surgery," explained Michael. Mason grunted.

"Why keep 'em alive?" he asked in despair. A wall divided Gallows Alley from the doctor's yard, the houses in that by-pass being built on one side of the court only.

Mason looked up and down, and again felt that unaccountable

sensation of menace.

The road was a black canyon, and the starry arc lamps emphasised the desolation. A street of tombs; black, ugly, shoddy tombs, nailed and glued and cheaply cemented together. The dingy window-glass hardly returned the reflection of the lights; no chimney smoked, no window glowed humanly. Up Gallows Alley, where the door panels had been used for firewood, men and women slept in the open, huddled up in the deep recesses of doorways, slept through the rain and the soughing wind, old sacks drawn over their knees and shoulders.

As Mason and his companion picked a way over the slippery cobbles, a voice in the darkness chanted—the voice of a woman husky with sleep:

"I spy a copper with a shinin' collar. If he touches me I'll holler—P'lice!"

He never ceased to wonder how they could see in the dark.

"They're rats," said Mike, answering his unspoken thought.

A chuckle of sly laughter came to them.

"They never sleep," said Mason in despair. "It was the same in my time. Day and night you could go through Gallows Alley and there would be somebody watching you."

He wheeled suddenly and called a name. From an entry slunk a figure, which might have been man or woman.

"Thought it was you," said Mason.

(Who it was, or who he thought it was, Michael never learnt.)

"How are things?"

"Bad, Mr. Mason, very bad." It was the whining voice of an old man.

"Have you seen Dr. Rudd tonight?"

Again came that eerie peal of laughter from invisible depths.

"He's the coppers' man, ain't he—Rudd? No, Mr. Mason, 'we ain't seen him. Nobody comes down 'ere. Afraid of wakin' people up, they are!"

The chuckles came now like the rustle of a wind.

Mason stopped before No. 9. A man was sitting on the step, his back to the door, a bibulous man who slept noisily. An old hearth-rug was drawn over his knees and on top some belated wag of Gallows Alley had balanced an empty tomato can.

"If it doesn't fall and wake him, old man Wicks will give him a shock if he finds him there!" said Mason.

"Uncanny, isn't it?" he said when they had emerged from the

court. "They talk about Chinamen in the East End of London. Lord! they're the only decent people they've got in Gallows Alley, and old Gregory."

"I wonder what they do for a living?"

"I should hate to know," said Mason.

They came back by the way they had entered.

"I'm giving Bray another hour, and then I'm going up to the Yard."

"I'll drive you, if you like. There's nothing more to be got here."

The shadowy figure they had seen emerged from the opening, holding an old overcoat about his throat.

"White Face has been around tonight, they say, Mr. Mason."

"Do they, indeed?" said Mason politely.

"You don't treat us right, Mr. Mason. You come down 'ere an' expect us to 'nose' for you, and everybody in the court knows we're 'nosing.' If you treated us right and did the proper thing, you'd hear something. What's the matter with old Gregory, hey? That's something you don't know—and nobody else knows. What's the matter with Gregory?"

And with this cryptic remark he vanished.

"He's mad—genuinely mad. No, I don't know his name, but he's mad in a sane way. What in hell does he mean about Gregory?"

Mike could not answer. He knew old Gregory—everybody in London knew the man who housed his cab in Dr. Marford's yard and lived alone in the one decent house in Gallows Court.

"I'd give a lot to know what that crazy man knew about him— what he was driving at."

Mason was disturbed, irritable. A detective officer has an instinct for sincerity—it is two-thirds of his mental equipment, and the demented denizen of the court was not rambling. To speak ill, or hint suspicion, against Gregory Wicks was a kind of treason.

"Rum lot of devils," he said, and shrugged off his uneasiness.

Chapter 11

The telephone bell had been ringing at frequent intervals in the Landors' flat; the waiting detectives could hear it in the street: there must have been a half-open window somewhere through which the sound could come.

"It's Mason getting rattled, I should think," said Elk fretfully. "Why I came here I don't know. Madness! I get like that sometimes—just go dippy and do silly things."

"You came here," said Inspector Bray heavily, "because you were told to come by your superior officer."

Elk groaned.

"The trouble with you, Billy, is that you've no sense of unimportance," he said helplessly.

"That doesn't sound very respectful," said Mr. Bray severely.

He wanted to be very severe indeed, but you never knew with Elk. At any moment he might force you into bringing him before the Chief Constable, and invariably when he was brought before the Chief Constable he demonstrated that he and the Chief Constable were the only people in the world who took a sensible view of the circumstances. "How many men have you posted?" he asked. "I don't want to give either of these two people a chance of slipping us."

"I've posted none," said Sergeant Elk, almost brightly. "My superior officer has posted three, and takes all the responsibility. I ventured to suggest a different posting, but I was told to mind my own so-and-so business."

"I said nothing of the sort," said Bray hotly.

"You meant it," was Elk's retort.

Bray looked anxiously up and down. He was not terribly happy, working under Mason. Very few detective officers were. And he was out of his own division, which was all wrong. Moreover, Mason was very unforgiving when his subordinates fell into error, and this was a murder case, where no excuses would be accepted. On the whole, it was better to conciliate his sergeant, who was notoriously a favourite of the superintendent.

He stared up and down the road uncomfortably.

"If I've been a little short-tempered with you, Elk, I'm sorry," he said almost affectionately. "I'm so distracted with this business. Where did you say I ought to post a man?"

"In the back courtyard," said Elk promptly. "There's a reachable fire escape up which any healthy man or woman could climb, or vice versa."

Elk was on the point of withdrawing a perfectly useless patrol at the far end of the street, when a taxicab turned the corner, stopped before the main door of the apartment and a woman got out. They were watching from the corner of a front garden on the opposite side of the road.

"That looks like the lady, eh? What do you think, Elk?"

"That's madam," said Elk. "And I've seen her before somewhere."

She had paid the taxi and it drove slowly away. The watchers still waited.

As Inez Landor put the key in the front door they saw her turn her head and look anxiously round. She could see nobody. Her imagination had pictured the road packed with police officers. She hurried up to the first floor, unlocked her own door and went into the flat.

There was a small hand-lamp on the table, working from a dry battery, and it was this she switched on. There were four letters in the letter-box. She did not even trouble to take them out, but, taking the lamp in her hand, she went softly to the bedroom door, which opened from the hall, and looked in. Her heart sank when she saw that her husband had not returned. What should she do? What could she do? With a deep sigh, she took off her leather coat and hat and went into the bedroom, leaving the door open.

There had been a murder in the East End; she had seen the late edition bills and heard somebody speaking about it at supper—not that she ate supper, but usually, when she and her husband were both out, she arranged to meet Louis at Elford's. He had not appeared. She had waited till the restaurant closed, and had then gone on to a fashionable all-night coffee-house, where they went when he was very late. He was not there either. The time of waiting seemed an eternity. In despair she had gone home, not daring to buy the midnight sheets which were being sold on the street for fear. . .

She shivered. She wondered whether that nice doctor would say anything; the man with the gentle voice, who had been so sympathetic and who had given her *sal volatile*. How stupid she had been to mistake a fight between two labourers! Perhaps that was what the newspapers called murder.

She had told him so much—things she would not have told to her mother if she were living. There was hardly a step she had taken that day which she did not now bitterly regret. It was worse than folly—sheer madness, to go in search of Louis. Suppose something had happened—a fight; she dared not imagine worse. She had broadcast his motives through London.

Inez Landor drew on her dressing-gown and walked up and down the dark room, striving to settle her mind to calmness. She had had four deliriously happy years, years of dream-building. That flimsy fabric had been shivered to nothingness.

She thought she heard a sound, a step in the hall, and, opening the door, she listened. There it was again, a faint creak. There was a loose board near the hall door. She had always intended having that board replaced.

"Is that you, Louis?" she whispered.

There was no answer. She could hear the solemn ticking of the hall clock, and the far-away whirr of a motorcar passing the end of the road.

"Louis—is that you?" she raised her voice.

She must have been mistaken, then, for no answer came. She left the door ajar, and, going to the window, pulled aside the curtains carefully and looked out. A futile act, for this window looked upon the well at the back of the building.

And then she heard a faint knock. The silence in the flat was so deep that it re-echoed through the hall. She tiptoed into the hall and listened. The knock was repeated, and she crept to the door.

"Who is there?" she asked in a low voice.

"Louis."

Her heart was beating furiously. She turned the handle and admitted him, closing the door behind him.

"Put on the light, darling."

His voice was strained and old-sounding. It was the voice of a man who had been running and had not recovered his breath.

"Sitting in the dark? Turn on the lights."

"Wait!"

There was a window in the tiny lobby which could be seen from the street. She pulled down the blind and drew the thick curtains across and closed her own door before she switched the light in the hall. Save for the blue bruise under one eye, his face was colourless. Inez Landor stared at her husband with growing terror.

"What has happened?"

He shook his head. It was at once a gesture of impatience and weariness.

"Nothing very much. I have had a ghastly time. Inez, will you get me a glass of water?"

"Shall I get you some wine?"

He shook his head.

"No, darling, water."

She was gone for a few minutes; when she returned he was looking at the knife and belt that hung on the wall. It was one of many souvenirs he had collected in his travels—a broad leather belt with big brass bosses, from which hung a knife in a gaily ornamented sheath. Before this day it had meant no more than the saddle, the lasso, the spears and the strange Aztec relics that covered the wall.

"We've got to get rid of that somehow," he said.

"The knife?"

"Yes, this."

He tapped the empty frog where a second knife had been.

She did not ask him why; but what hope there was left in her heart, flickered and died. For a little while neither spoke. There were questions she wanted to ask him which her tongue refused to frame. She could only make the most trite and commonplace remarks.

"I thought I heard you in the flat a few minutes ago," she said. "You haven't been in before?"

"No."

"Why did you knock?" she asked, suddenly remembering.

He licked his lips.

"I lost my key. I don't know where—somewhere."

He drank the remainder of the water and put the glass on the top of a little desk which stood against the wall.

"I could have sworn I heard the door close a few minutes ago," she said. "I came out and called you. I heard somebody walking in the hall."

He smiled and his arm went round her shoulders. "Your nerve is going. Have you been waiting here in the dark?"

She shook her head. Should she tell him? It was not the moment for half-confidences.

"No, I have been out looking for you."

She caught his arm.

"Louis, you didn't fight? You didn't—do anything?"

Louis Landor did not answer immediately.

"I don't know," he said. "Let us go into the sitting-room."

But she pushed him back into the chair where he was sitting.

"No, no, stay here. None of these lights shows from the street."

He looked at her sharply.

"What do you mean—none of these lights shows from the street? Is anybody outside watching?"

"I'm not sure," she said. "I think so. Before I left the restaurant I telephoned here in the hope that you had returned. I thought the maid was here, and didn't realise that she couldn't get in. I knew she'd gone to her sister's and I called her up. Louis"—her lips quivered—"the police have been here."

And when he did not speak she knew—

"Has anything happened?"

Louis Landor ran his fingers through his long black hair.

"I don't know—yes—I do know, but I'm not sure how far I was involved. When I went out after him I lost sight of him, but I had an idea I should find him somewhere in the West End, and I was right."

"You spoke to him?"

He shook his head.

"No, he was in a car with a girl—a pretty girl; some poor little fool who has fallen for him. She's a nurse who works for Marford."

He saw her mouth open wide in amazement.

"For Marford—not Dr. Marford?"

"How the devil did you know that?" he asked, astonished. "Yes, he's got a clinic in the East End, I'm going to see her tomorrow and tell her the truth about Mr. Donald Bateman. I followed them in a cab to Bury Street and then back to his hotel. I wanted the chance of seeing him alone without making any kind of scandal, but he never gave me the chance. Naturally I did not want to send my name up to his room, so I waited till he came out. There wasn't the ghost of a chance of seeing him: he went to a little restaurant which was crowded with people, but I knew that if I was patient I should pick him up and settle our little matter definitely. He lingered over his dinner and I have an

95

idea that he was waiting for somebody. She came eventually—rather a pretty woman. She wasn't in evening dress and her voice was rather common. When he went out of the restaurant I followed, keeping at a distance. I think he'd recognised me this afternoon. Naturally, she complicated matters: I had to wait till he dropped her. After dinner they drove away from the restaurant. I was in the gallery upstairs and could see everything that was happening. I took a taxi and followed them—they drove to a very poor neighbourhood—Tidal Basin, they call it, I think. There she went into a flat with him—it was over a shop. It was then that I telephoned to you. Darling, you didn't follow me?"

She nodded dejectedly.

"I had an uncomfortable feeling you might. You were mad!"

"I know. Go on," she said. "What happened then?"

He asked for another glass of water and she brought it for him.

"He came out alone, and I followed him to a street which has a long wall on one side. I was just going up to him when I saw the woman run across the road. She spoke to him for a little time and then they parted. It was my opportunity. There was nobody in sight and I came up to him—"

"He had the knife?" she interrupted, and he smiled wryly.

"I gave him no chance to use it." She had seen the bruise on his face but had not the courage to ask him how he came by it. It seemed so unimportant in view of the other terrific possibility.

"—Yes, I hit him. He went down like a log. I got scared. I saw somebody standing in the doorway—a doctor's place—it must have been Marford. I ran. And then I saw a policeman walking towards me. At the place where I stopped there was a big gate which had a wicket door. By some miracle it was unlocked. I got through and bolted the door. I was in a narrow yard which surrounded the warehouse. The police came and searched it but I hid behind some packing cases."

"The police?" she gasped. "Searched it. Is Donald——?"

He nodded.

"Not dead?" she wailed.

He nodded again.

"The police have been here?"

"Yes. They've been questioning the maid. I don't know what she has told them."

He got up and walked to the little desk and felt in his pocket.

"I've lost my keys."

She took a little leather case from her bag and handed it to him. He

96

opened one of the drawers and took out a thick packet of papers.

"I suppose very few people keep three thousand pounds in the entrance hall of their flat!" His voice was now almost normal. "Whatever happens, we'll get out of the country tomorrow. If anything goes wrong with me, you take the money and get away."

She clutched at his sleeve frantically.

"What can happen to you, Louis? You didn't kill him—the knife!"

He disengaged her hand almost roughly.

"I don't know whether I killed him. Now listen," he said. "You've got to be terribly sensible about this. Even if this blackguard told everything, they can't hurt you. But I don't want you to suffer the ignominy of an inquiry—the police court and that filth."

Her senses were unnaturally keen. She heard a sound.

"There's somebody coming up the stairs," she whispered. "Go into the bedroom—go quickly!"

He hesitated, but she pushed him towards the room and ran rather than walked to the door and listened. She could hear soft, whispering voices. Switching on the table lamp, she found a book and opened it with trembling hands. There was a little sewing table in the spare room and she brought this out and had placed it near when the first thunderous knock sounded. She took one glimpse at herself in the hall mirror, used her pocket puff swiftly and opened the door.

Two men were standing there: two tall, grim-looking figures of fate.

"Who is it?" she asked.

It was an agonised effort to control her voice, but she succeeded.

"My name is Bray—Detective-Inspector Bray, Criminal Investigation Department," he said formally. "This is Detective-Sergeant Elk."

"Good evening, Mrs. Landor."

It was characteristic of Elk that he took complete charge of the proceedings from that moment. He had the affability of a man supremely confident of himself. "Come in," she said.

"All right, Mrs. Landor, I'll shut the door," said Elk. They walked into the hall. She noticed that neither of the men removed his hat.

She made one effort to appear unconcerned, tried to infuse a little gaiety into her voice.

"I should have known you were detectives. I've seen so many in cinemas and I know detectives never take their hats off," she smiled.

Mr. Bray would have taken this as a reproach. Elk was apparently amused, but supplied an explanation.

"A detective who takes his hat off, Mrs. Landor," he said, "is a detective with one hand! In other words, the other hand is occupied when he may want to use two."

"I hope you won't even want to use one," she said. "Will you sit down? Is it about Joan?"

It was cruelly unfair to make this implied libel on an honest and decent servant, but she could not afford to be nice.

"Don't make a noise, will you?" she added. "My husband is asleep."

"He got asleep very quickly, Mrs. Landor," said Bray. "He only came in a few minutes ago."

She forced a smile.

"A few minutes ago! How absurd! He's been in bed since ten."

"Excuse me, Mrs. Landor, did another man come into this flat?"

She shook her head.

"Do you ever have burglars coming up the fire escape?" he asked, eyeing her quickly. She laughed at this.

"I don't even know which way burglars come, but I never use the fire escape myself! I hope I never shall!"

Elk paid tribute to the sally with a smile.

"We'd like to see your husband," he said after a moment's consideration. "Which is his room? Is that it?" He pointed to a door near the hall.

She had seated herself at the table where the open book was lying, her hands folded on her lap that they might not testify to her agitation. She rose now.

"No—that is the maid's room. My room is here, but I can't have him disturbed. He's not very well," she said. "He's had a fall."

"Too bad," said Elk. "Which is his room?"

She did not answer but walked across to the bedroom door and knocked.

"Louis, there are some people who want to see you."

He came in immediately. He was without coat and collar, but it needed no experienced observer to realise that he had been interrupted rather in the process of taking off his clothes than of dressing.

"Were you getting up, darling?" she asked quickly.

Elk shook his head reprovingly.

"I'd rather you didn't suggest anything to him, Mrs. Landor. You may suggest the wrong things. That is a friendly tip."

Louis looked from one to the other. He had heard Inez say "detectives" under her breath, but he did not need that explanation. Inspector Bray made one effort to control the inquiry.

"I've reason to believe that you know a man who was staying at the Little Norfolk Hotel in Norfolk Street, Strand, and calling himself Donald Bateman."

"No," said Inez quickly.

"I'm asking your husband," said Bray sharply. "Well, Mr. Landor?"

Louis shrugged.

"I have no personal acquaintance with anybody named Donald Bateman."

It was here that Elk resumed charge of the examination and his superior assented.

"We don't want to know whether you're personally acquainted with him, Mr. Landor. That's entirely beside the question. Have you ever heard of, or have you in any way been associated with, a man called Donald Bateman, who arrived from South Africa in the last few weeks? Before you answer, I wish to tell you that Inspector Bray and I are investigating the circumstances under which this man met his death in Endley Street, Tidal Basin, at ten o'clock last night."

"He's dead?" said Louis. "How did he die?"

"By a knife wound," said Bray.

He saw the woman sway on her feet.

"I know nothing about it," said Louis Landor. "I have never used a knife against any man."

Elk's eyes were roving the curios on the wall. He took a step closer, and lifting the belt from the nail, laid it on the table.

"What is this supposed to be?" He tapped the knife.

"It's a knife I brought back from South America," said Louis immediately. "I had a ranch there."

"Is it yours?"

Louis nodded.

"There were two in this belt," he said. "Where is the other?"

"We lost it." Inez spoke quickly. "Louis lost it. We haven't had it for quite a long time—we've never had it in this house."

Elk ran his finger along the belt.

"There's dust here. There ought to be dust inside this empty frog," he said. "If the story is true and there has been no knife here for a long time, the inside would be thick with dust. On the other hand, if your story isn't true, there was a knife here today—"

He rubbed the inside of the leather and showed his finger practically speckless.

"I dusted it myself this morning," said Inez, and Elk smiled at her admiringly.

"Mrs. Landor!" he said in reproach.

"Well, I've got to tell the truth," she said desperately. "You want the truth, don't you?"

She was on the verge of hysteria, near to the breaking-point which would leave her morally and physically shattered.

"You're not entitled to draw inferences without my offering some explanation. God Almighty! Haven't I suffered enough through that man!"

"Which man?" asked Bray sharply.

She was silent.

"Which man, Mrs. Landor?"

Louis Landor at any rate had recovered his self-possession.

"My wife isn't quite herself tonight," he said. "I have been out rather late and she got rather worried about me."

"Now what's the use of making a mystery of something that's perfectly clear?" asked Elk.

He was almost sad as he contemplated the futility of unnecessary evasion.

"Your wife knew Donald Bateman?"

Louis did not answer.

"I'm going to be perfectly frank with you. I told you we were inquiring into the murder of this man. That is our duty as police officers. We're not asking you or your wife or anybody else who is the murderer of Donald Bateman. Understand that right, Mr. Landor. The only person we want is the murderer of this man! The people we don't want are those who didn't murder him, even though they know something of him. If either or both of you are responsible, my chief and the whole damned crowd of us at Scotland Yard will work night and day to bring you to the Old Bailey! That's treating you square. If you're not guilty, we'll do all we can to clear you. The only thing you can give us for the moment is the truth."

"We've told the truth," said Inez breathlessly.

"No, you haven't." Elk shook his head. "I didn't quite expect you would. The truth in every case like this is hidden under a heap of rubbishy lies. What are you hiding up, Mrs. Landor? It all comes down to that. You're hiding something and your husband's hiding something, that maybe doesn't matter ten loud hoots."

"I'm hiding nothing," she said.

"You knew Donald Bateman?"

"I don't remember him," she said quickly.

"You knew Donald Bateman." Elk was infinitely patient, and when she shook her head he put his hand slowly into his inside pocket. "Well, I don't want to give you an unpleasant experience, Mrs. Landor, but I've a photograph of this man—a flashlight picture taken after his death."

She reeled back, her hands out-thrust. "I won't look at it! I won't! It's beastly... you're not allowed to show me things like that... I won't see it!"

Louis's arm was round her, his cheek was against hers. He said something to her in an undertone, something which momentarily calmed her. Then he stretched out his hand to the detective.

"Perhaps I could identify this man," he said. "I know most of my wife's friends."

Elk took from his pocket an envelope, and from this drew a positive that was still damp. It was not a pretty picture, but the hand which held the photograph did not tremble.

"Yes, my wife knew this man ten years ago, when she was a girl of seventeen," said Louis.

"When did you last see him?" asked Bray.

Louis Landor thought.

"A few years ago."

"He only arrived in England last week," said Bray coldly.

"He may have come to England every year, for all you know," said Louis with a faint smile. "No, I saw his photograph."

"What did he call himself in those days, Mrs. Landor?"

She was more composed now, her voice under control.

"I knew him as Donald. He was just—an acquaintance."

She heard Elk's murmured expostulation.

"Surely, Mrs. Landor, you're not telling us the gospel truth, are you?" he asked. "Just now you told us you'd 'suffered enough from this man.' You can't suffer very deeply through any man whose name you couldn't remember except as Donald."

She did not answer.

"Can you, Mrs. Landor? You're not going to tell us? He was a very close friend, wasn't he?"

She drew a long breath.

"I suppose he was. It's not a thing I want to talk about—"

"Inez! I'm not going to allow these people to think—"

Elk interrupted him.

"Never mind what we think, Mr. Landor. Nothing's going to shock us—not me, at any rate. You knew this man before you met your husband, I suppose, or was it after?"

"It was before," she replied.

"Was he anything—to you?"

Elk found difficulty in putting the matter delicately. He saw the man's face go red and white.

"You're being damned offensive, aren't you?" Louis was glowering at him.

Elk shook his head wearily.

"That's just what I'm not being. A man has been murdered tonight, Landor—and I'm anxious to put the murderer under lock and key, and it's only possible to put him under lock and key by asking all sorts of innocent people offensive questions. And when you come to think of it, there's nothing quite so offensive as stabbing a man to the heart and leaving him stiff on the paving-stones of Tidal Basin. It's a lousy place to die. Personally, I should be very much offended if it happened to me, and I'd regard any questions similar to those I am asking as being in the nature of a bouquet—in comparison. Did you know Donald Bateman was in town?" He addressed Inez.

"No," she answered.

Bray interjected impatiently.

"Do you mean to tell us you didn't know that he was in London three or four days ago?"

"No!" Her tone was defiant.

"Mrs. Landor," said Elk, "you've been very unhappy this last day or two; your servant told us all about it. Servants will talk, and they love a little domestic tragedy."

"I've not been well," she said.

"Is it because you've seen Donald Bateman, the man from whom you suffered?"

"No," she replied.

"Nor you?" asked Bray.

"No," answered Louis.

"Tonight, for instance?" suggested Elk. "You haven't seen Donald Bateman or the man so described?"

"No," said Louis.

"Have you been in the neighbourhood of Tidal Basin tonight?" asked Elk. "Before you answer that, I must caution you to be very careful how you reply."

"No."

Elk took a slip of paper from his pocket,

"I'm going to ask you a question, Landor, which I'd like you to consider before you answer. In the pocket of the man known as Donald Bateman were found two one-hundred-pound notes, indicator number 3310 11878 and 3310 11879. They were new notes, recently issued from the Maida Vale Branch of the Midland Bank. Can you tell me anything about these banknotes?"

He was silent.

"Can you, Mrs. Landor?"

"I don't know anything about the numbers of banknotes——" she began desperately.

"That's not what we're asking," said Bray sternly. "Have you given or sent to any person during the past week two bank-notes each for a hundred pounds?"

"They come from my account," said Louis quietly. "I suppose I'd better tell the truth. We did know Donald Bateman was back in London. He wrote to us and said he was in great distress, and asked me for the loan of two hundred pounds."

"I see," nodded Bray. "You sent them to his address in Norfolk Street by letter post?"

Louis nodded.

"Did he acknowledge receipt of the money?"

"No," said Louis.

"He didn't even call to thank you?"

"No," said Inez.

She spoke a little too quickly.

"You're not going to tell us the truth, either of you." Elk's voice was rather sad. "Not the truth about this man or this money or your visit to Tidal Basin. You've a bruise on your face—been fighting?"

"No, I hit it against a cupboard door."

"Your wife said you fell down," said Elk drearily, "but it doesn't matter. Why do you keep these knives here?" He picked up the belt and dangled it in his hand.

"Why does he keep these saddles on the wall?" asked Inez impatiently. "Be reasonable, please. They are prizes he got at a rodeo in the Argentine."

"For what?" asked Bray.

"It was a knife-throwing competition——" began Louis, and stopped.

"Hiding up!" groaned Elk. "Get your coat on, Landor!"

Inez Landor darted to him and caught him frantically by the arm. "You're not going to take him away?"

"I'm taking you both away," said Elk cheerfully, "but only to Scotland Yard. You'll have to see Mr. Mason, but you needn't worry. He's a very sympathetic man—even more sympathetic than Mr. Bray."

There was a touch of malignity in this thrust which Bray did not observe.

She did not go into the bedroom with her husband; her own coat was lying on the back of a chair. She had quite forgotten that fact— saw now the absurdity of the reading-lamp, the sewing and the book whilst this raincoat of hers testified mutely to her wanderings.

Louis came back in a very short space of time and helped her into the leather jacket.

"It's all right, we've got a police-car downstairs; you needn't bother about a taxi," said Bray, in answer to his inquiry.

He was a little huffy, being conscious that whatever result had been achieved brought him little personal *kudos*.

"I shan't want you to come with me, Elk," he said shortly. "You can help shove these people into the car and then you can come back and search the flat. Would you like to see the warrant?" he asked.

Louis shook his head.

"There's nothing in the flat that I object to your seeing," he said, and pointed to the little *escritoire*. "There's about three thousand pounds in that drawer, and railway tickets. I was leaving the country tomorrow with my wife. Give Mr.——"

"Elk's my name."

"Give Mr. Elk the keys, Inez."

Without a word she handed the case to Elk.

As they walked through the door of the flat Bray put out his hand and switched off the light. He was a domesticated man with a taste for economy, and he acted instinctively.

"Save your light, Mrs. Landor," he apologised for his action.

The door closed and the sound of their movement grew fainter to the listening man who stood behind the locked door of the maid's room. He came out noiselessly, a dark figure, a black felt hat pulled down over his eyes, his face hidden behind a white mask.

Quickly he went to the desk, took something out of his pocket; there was the sound of breaking wood and the drawer slid out. A small pocket torch revealed what he sought, and he thrust money, passport and tickets into his pocket. He had hardly done so before he heard the detective returning, and moved swiftly towards the door. He was standing in its shadow when it opened. Elk's back was towards him when he heard a slight sound, and turned quickly. Not quickly enough. For the fraction of a second he glimpsed the white-faced thing, and then something struck him and he went down like a log.

White Face stooped, dragged the inanimate figure a little way from the door so that it would open, and a second later had slipped out of the flat, leaving the door ajar.

He ran up one flight of stairs, passed through an open window and went swiftly down a narrow iron stairway which brought him to the courtyard. There was no guard here, as he knew.

Ten minutes later one of the detectives waiting outside the house went upstairs to proffer his assistance to Elk. He heard a groan and, pushing the door open, found the sergeant in his least amiable mood.

Chapter 12

Superintendent Mason boasted that he could sleep anywhere at any time. He certainly needed a considerable amount of rousing when the police car reached Scotland Yard.

As for Michael Quigley, he had never felt less sleepy in his life, and the coffee which was brought to the superintendent's room was as a stimulant quite unnecessary. It brought Mr. Mason to irritable life.

His complaint was that, at whatever hour of the day or night he arrived at Scotland Yard, he was certain to find some official document waiting for his attention. There were half a dozen minutes warningly inscribed and heavily sealed.

"They can wait till the morning." He examined the two or three telephone messages that were on his desk, but they told him nothing new. There was no news from Bray. It was a quarter of an hour later that Elk and his superior had their interview with the Landors.

Michael looked at his watch. It was too late to go to bed. He wanted to see Janice early in the morning.

"You can call back and I'll tell you anything that's going," said Mason. "About that ring, Michael: I'm afraid we shall have to have a little talk with the young lady. I'll make it as pleasant as possible. Maybe you can arrange for us to meet—I don't want to bring her down to the Yard, because that would rattle her."

Michael was grateful for this concession. Ever since he had told Mason the truth about the ring, a dull little shadow of worry had rested in his mind.

"You're a pretty nice man for a policeman, Mason."

"I'm a pretty nice man for any kind of job," said the superintendent.

Michael strolled out on to the Embankment and up through Northumberland Avenue. He had reached Trafalgar Square and was standing at the corner of the Strand, wondering whether it would be sensible to go home and snatch a few hours' sleep, or whether to call at his club, which was open till four o'clock, when a taxicab went rapidly past him in the direction of the Admiralty gate. Midnight taxicabs either crawl or fly, and this one was moving quickly—not so swift, however, that he did not glimpse a familiar figure sitting on the box, a pipe clenched between his teeth. If he had been moving more slowly Michael would have hailed old Gregory Wicks.

"Did you want a cab, Mr. Quigley?" It was a a policeman by his side; Michael was fairly well known to this division. "No, thank you."

"I thought you were trying to stop that driver. They take liberties, those fellows."

Michael laughed.

"That was an old friend of mine. I suppose you know him—old Gregory Wicks?"

"Gregory, eh?" The policeman was a middle-aged man who knew his West End extremely well. "The old fellow's getting about again. I hadn't seen him for months till I saw him the other night sleeping on his box at the corner of Orange Street. He lost a good fare that night. I wanted him to take Mr. Gasso down to Scotland Yard to make a statement—I was in that case," he added a little proudly.

Chance policemen encountered in the middle of the night can be very talkative, and Michael was in no mood for conversation. But the mention of Gasso arrested his attention.

"You were in what case?"

"The Howdah case. You know, the night they held up Mrs. What's-her-name—Duval or something, and pinched her diamond chain. Naturally my name hasn't been mentioned because the case has never been into court, but I was on point duty near the Howdah Club when the robbery occurred. If anybody had screamed, or I'd heard 'em scream, I'd have been on the spot in a second. It only shows you what chances you miss because people won't behave sensibly."

Michael gathered that behaving sensibly was synonymous with screaming violently.

"Old Gregory was about here that night, was he?"

"He had his cab about fifty yards from the club. He never joins a rank, and, knowing him, we aren't very strict. If he can find a nice quiet corner to have his snooze we never disturb him."

Old Gregory! Then in a flash Michael remembered the mysterious words of the nondescript of Gallows Court: "What was the matter with Gregory?"

Here was a new angle to many problems. He made a quick decision. Calling a more leisurely taxi, he drove off to Tidal Basin. Gallows Court had something to tell, and since Gallows Court never slept it might be more instructive in the middle of the night than in the broad and hateful light of day.

Shale arrived at Scotland Yard simultaneously with the telephoned news that Bray was on his way accompanied by the two people he had been sent to seek. Mr. Mason leaned back in his chair and rubbed his hands. He was relieved. To find suspects quietly was more desirable than telling all the world they were wanted; for a suspect, having gained much undesirable publicity, very often proves to be perfectly innocent. Questions are asked in Parliament, and there have been cases where payment has had to be made as compensation for the wounded feelings of someone called urgently to police investigations.

Parliament had been playing too interfering a part in the police force lately. A new Commissioner had come and was taking credit for all the reforms his subordinates had forced upon his predecessor. The Home Office had issued new instructions which, if they were faithfully carried out, would prevent the police from asking vital questions. Every step that the crank and the busybody could devise to interfere with the administration of justice had assumed official shape.

Superintendent Mason knew the regulations by heart. One had to know them to evade them. Like every other high official of Scotland Yard, he lived at the mercy of stupid policemen and the perjury of some eminent man's light o' love. But the risk did not sit heavily upon him.

Wender, of the Identification Bureau, was ready to see him, and he sent Shale to bring that long-suffering man, with his data.

Wender was a small, stout gentleman with a tiny white moustache, and the huge horn-rimmed spectacles he wore did not add any measure of wisdom to his face, but rather emphasised its placidity. He arrived with a bundle of documents under his arm and a short briar pipe between his teeth. He was wearing a smoking-jacket, for he had been at a theatre when he was called to make a examination of the few clues which had been acquired in the case.

"Come in, Charlie," said Mason. "It's good to see somebody looking cheerful at this hour of the morning."

"I'm always cheerful because I'm always right," said Wender, pulling up a chair and sitting down.

"Why the fancy dress?" asked Shale, who was Wender's brother-in-law, and could therefore be flippant with his superior.

"Theatre," said his relative briefly.

He was indeed an equable and happy man at all hours of the day and night. Nothing disturbed him. He was, too, something more than an authority upon fingerprints. The range of his information was astounding.

"Before we start discussing whorls, islands and circles," said Mason, as he took from his pocket the capsule and laid it on the blotting-pad, "what is this?"

Wender took it up and turned it over between his fingers.

"I don't know—*butyl ammonal*, I should think. I've seen it done up in capsules like that. Where did you find it?"

Mason told him.

"I'm not sure, of course," said Wender, "not having a nose that can smell through a glass case, but it's that colour. Now, what else did you want to know?"

"Is there any record of the Landors?" asked Mason.

Mr. Wender shook his head.

"None whatever. That doesn't mean we haven't got a record under another name. It's a curious circumstance"—he smiled brightly—"that criminals occasionally give themselves names that they weren't born with. I took this particular job on myself," he explained, "because my night man is about as useful as a performing flea." He laid the documents on the table. "There you are."

"Have you got the finger-prints of the dead man?"

The identification man sorted them out

"Yes. Who took them?"

"I did," admitted Shale.

"They were of no use to me—the first lot, I mean. I had to send down and get another lot. You young officers are still rather hazy as to how to take a print."

Mason examined the cards with their black smudges. They meant nothing to him.

"Is he known?"

"Is he known!" scoffed Wender. He sorted out another document. "Donald Arthur Bateman, alias Donald Arthur, alias Donald Mackintosh. He's got more aliases than a film star."

Mason frowned heavily.

"Donald Arthur Bateman? I know that name. Why, I had him at

the London Sessions for housebreaking."

"Fraud," corrected the other. "Twelve months hard labour, 1919."

Mason nodded.

"That's right—fraud. He swindled Sir Somebody Something out of three thousand pounds—a land deal. That was his speciality. And then he was up again at the Old Bailey—"

"Acquitted," said Wender. "The prosecutor had something to hide up and was too ill to give evidence. There's a conviction here at the Exeter Assizes—eighteen months, the Teignmouth blackmail case. You won't remember that: it was in the hands of the locals; they didn't call in the Yard."

"Then he went abroad."

"And died there! Semi-officially!"

Mason read the note.

"Reported dead in Perth, Western Australia, in 1923. Doubtful. Believed to have gone to South Africa."

"He's dead enough now," he added.

He brooded over the card.

"Blackmail, fraud, fraud, blackmail. . . he was versatile. Married, of course. . . dozens of times, I should think. Went to Australia; concerned with the brothers Walter and Thomas Furse in holding up the Woomarra branch of the South Australian Bank. Offered King's evidence. . . accepted; no prosecution. Walter Furse eight years penal servitude, Thomas Furse three years. Walter an habitual criminal; Thomas, who had only arrived in Victoria from England a month before his conviction, released after two years."

He read it aloud.

"That's our Tommy," said Shale. "You remember the woman said, 'Tommy did it'?"

But Mason was reading the "confidential." It was written in minute type and he had recourse to his reading glass.

"'During their imprisonment,'" he read, "'Bateman disappeared, taking with him the young wife of Thomas.'" He looked up. "That's Lorna. 'Walter Furse died in prison in 1935.' Tommy's the murderer, Lorna's his wife, Bateman's the murdered man. It's as clear as daylight. There's the motive!"

"What do we know about Tommy? Have you any Australian records?"

Mr. Wender had laid three paper-covered books on the table. He selected one of these.

"In this office we have everything that opens and shuts," he boasted. "Here you are: 'Strictly confidential. Record of persons convicted of felony in the State of Victoria, 1922. Published by authority'—"

"Never mind about the authority," said Mason patiently.

The identification man turned over the leaves rapidly, murmuring the names that appeared at the head of each column.

"'Farrow, Felton, Ferguson, Furse'—here you are: 'Walter Furse, see volume 6, page 13.'"

He pushed the book to Mason. This collection was more interesting than most Government Blue Books, for the record of every man was in the form of a short and readable biography.

'Thomas Furse. This man was educated in England by his brother; was probably unaware of his brother's illegal occupation when he came to the Colony. Furse was certainly an assumed name (see W. Furse, Vol. 8, p. 7), and there is a possibility that he was educated under his own name by his brother and with his brother's money, though he adopted the name of Furse when he came to the Colony. He married Lorna Weston—'

Mason stopped reading to look up.

'He married Lorna Weston, whom he met on the voyage out to Australia. She disappeared after his conviction. Thomas released. . . '

He read on in silence, and presently closed the book. "The identity of these people is now positively established," he said. "The motive is here for anyone who can read. Thomas goes to Australia; within a month or two he is caught for this hold-up and gets two years. Donald Arthur Bateman turns King's evidence and disappears with Lorna. Thomas comes back to England and in some way meets Donald last night. Now the only question is: is Thomas Furse another name for Louis Landor? That's what we've got to find out. If it is, then we have the case in a nutshell."

There were one or two other documents, and he turned them over.

"What's this?" he asked. It was a large photograph of a thumb-print.

"That was on the back of the watch," said Wender. "Harry Lamborn, as plain as a visiting-card. Five convictions—"

"I know all about him," interrupted Mason.

"A fine print," said Wender ecstatically.

"You ought to have it framed, Charlie," said Mason in his more complimentary mood. "I shan't want you anymore."

111

"Then I'll toddle home to bed." Mr. Wender stretched himself and yawned. "If I haven't brought somebody to the gallows my evening has been wasted."

"You'll get the usual medal and star," said Mason.

"I know," said the other sardonically; "and when I put my expense account in—a cab from the Lyceum to Scotland Yard—they'll tell me I ought to have taken a 'bus!"

He had left when Bray came importantly into the room.

"I've got those people."

"Eh?" Mason looked up. He was reading again the account of Thomas Furse. No age was given, which was rather annoying, but he could put a beam cable inquiry through to Melbourne and find an answer waiting for him when he came back to the office.

"You've got those people, have you? Did you search the flat?"

"I left Elk to do that."

Mason nodded.

"What are they hiding up?"

"That's what I don't quite know. I should have found out, but unfortunately Elk is a little difficult. I don't want to complain, Chief, but I'm placed in an awkward position when a subordinate takes a case out of my hands and starts investigating and cross-questioning, taking no more notice of me than if I were the paper on the wall!"

"He does it with me," Mason smiled broadly. "Why shouldn't he do it with you? As a matter of fact, you oughtn't to complain. These darned regulations about questioning prisoners are so framed that it's good to have some other officer responsible for breaking them—you can always pass the kick on to him. Shoot 'em in, Bray."

He laughed quietly to himself after Bray had left. Elk was incorrigible, but Elk was invaluable. There was some odd kink in his mind which prevented his passing the educational test which would raise him to the dignity of inspector. For the fourth time Mason determined to beard the Commissioners and demand promotion for his erratic subordinate.

He rose to his feet when the door opened and Inez came in ahead of her husband. She was more composed than he had expected, not quite so white. He went across the room to shake hands with her, an unusual and unexpected greeting which momentarily took her aback.

"I'm terribly sorry to bring you out in the middle of the night, Mrs. Landor." His voice was at its most sympathetic. "If it had been any less serious case I wouldn't have bothered either you or your husband; but here we are, all of us up and doing when we want to be in bed, in the sacred name of justice, as the poet says."

He personally placed a chair for her. Shale put a chair for Mr. Landor.

"I hope we've not alarmed you—that was worrying me." His voice betrayed an almost tender solicitude. "But, as I say, in a case of this character it very often happens that decent citizens are put to inconvenience."

It was Louis Landor who answered.

"I'm not at all worried, but it is rather unpleasant for my wife."

"Naturally," agreed Mason understandingly.

He sat down and pulled his chair a little nearer to the desk, looking up at Bray.

"Now what has Mr. Landor told you?"

Bray took out a notebook. He had kept his charges at Scotland Yard for a quarter of an hour while he had jotted down with fair accuracy the gist of the statements which they had made to him.

"Mrs. Landor knew the murdered man, and Mr. Landor knew him also slightly," he read. "The two notes for a hundred pounds found in the pocket were given to the deceased by Mr. Landor, who says it was in the nature of a loan. This statement was made after Mr. Landor had said that he did not know Donald Bateman."

Mason nodded.

"Subsequently he admitted he did?"

"Yes. He also said he'd never been in Tidal Basin. Mrs. Landor said that the murdered man was a very intimate friend of hers many years ago, but she hasn't seen him since. She has been married five years, was the widow of a man named John Smith. In the flat I found a belt with a place for two knives. One of the knives I found." He put it on the table. "The other was missing."

Mason took up the knife and pulled it from its sheath, looked at the little gold plate with the initials.

"L.L.—those are your initials?"

Landor nodded.

"Where did the other knife go?"

Bray supplied the answer from his notes.

"Mrs. Landor said it was lost. Both knives were presented to her husband at a rodeo competition in Central America for his skill in knife-throwing." He closed his book with a snap. "That is all the statement they made."

Mason's face was very serious.

"You agree that that was what you said tonight to Inspector Bray?" and, when they answered in the affirmative: "Would you like to amplify or correct that statement in any way?"

"No," said Louis.

"I'd like to point out, sir," interrupted Bray, "that he has a bruise on his face. He said he knocked it against the door; Mrs. Landor said he got it as the result of a fall."

"Would you like to make a statement of any kind?" asked Mason.

Louis Landor drew a quick breath.

"No, I don't think so."

"Have you any objection if I ask you a few questions?"

Landor hesitated.

"No." The word seemed forced from him.

"Or your wife?"

Inez shook her head.

"I'll make it as easy as I can. I realise it is very trying for you. Have you ever been to Australia?"

To his surprise, Landor replied instantly.

"Yes, many years ago. I made a voyage round the world with my father. I was very young at the time."

"Did you ever meet there or at any other place a man named Donald Arthur Bateman who, I happen to know, was an ex-convict?"

He shook his head.

"You say you have never been to Tidal Basin? If I tell you that you were recognised as having been seen in the vicinity of Endley Street fighting with Bateman, would you deny it?"

It was a bluff on Mason's part, but it came off.

"I shouldn't deny it—no."

Mason beamed.

"That's sensible! There's no need to hide anything." He was his solicitous self again. "Now just forget the statement you made to Mr. Bray and we'll forget it, too," he smiled. "You're hiding something. To save you or your wife from some imaginary danger you're implicating yourself further and further in the crime of wilful murder. Now, what are you afraid of?"

Louis Landor avoided his eyes.

"You're probably hiding something that doesn't matter two hoots. What does matter"—he emphasised every sentence with a tap of his finger on the pad—"is that I have sufficient evidence to charge you with murder. You were in Tidal Basin; a knife similar to this—I have the sheath—was used in the murder of Bateman, and you have been paying, or have paid, money to the dead man which is traceable to your banking account. Now, why?"

Bray asserted himself.

"You're not going to stick to the story that you did it as an act of kindness——" he began, and then he caught Mason's eye, and saw there no encouragement to intervene.

"You were being blackmailed: isn't that the truth?"

"Yes, that's the truth." It was Inez who spoke. "That is the truth! I can tell you that."

Mr. Mason's nods were not ordinary nods: they were an inclination of head not unlike the reverent obeisance before the statue of a heathen deity.

"Exactly. The murdered man knew that you or your wife had committed some offence, whether against the law——" he paused expectantly.

"I'm not prepared to say," said Louis quickly.

"You're prepared to go in the dock on a charge of wilful murder, and your wife is prepared to let you. Is that what I understand?"

She was shaking her head, momentarily inarticulate.

"Very well, then. You were being blackmailed."

"Yes." It came faintly from Inez.

"What had you done? Had you murdered somebody? Robbed somebody?" His jaw dropped. Into his eyes came a look of intense amusement which was particularly out of place. "I know! You had committed bigamy!"

"No," said Louis.

"This man Bateman was your husband." His forefinger pointed to her. "He was alive when you married your present husband. Isn't that the truth?"

"I thought he was dead." Her voice was very low, but he heard every word. "I was sure of it. I had the newspaper cutting. He told me when I saw him that he circulated the story because he wanted the police off his track for some crime he had committed in England. I swear I didn't know."

Again Mason leaned back in his chair, and his thumbs went into the armholes of his waistcoat.

"Even Scotland Yard didn't know, Mrs. Landor. I've got it here."

He tapped the pile of documents at his elbow. "Reported dead in Australia. Good God! What a thing to worry about—bigamy! That's hardly an offence—you ought to get something out of the poor-box for that! And that's what you've been hiding up? When did you see him last?"

The eyes of the husband and wife met, and Louis nodded.

"Today," said the woman.

"You heard he was in London four days ago," interrupted Bray. "Your servant said you'd been distressed for four days."

She hesitated.

"You can answer that," said Mason, and his permission would have been a rebuff to any other man but Mr. Bray.

"He wrote—I couldn't believe he was alive."

Bateman knew they were well off; suggested she should pay him money, threatening to publish the story of her bigamy. He arrived from South Africa penniless, having met some sharper crooks on the boat, who had taken what little money he had had when he embarked. But he had excellent prospects, he told her.

"Yes," said Mason dryly, "I know her name."

He settled himself deeper in his chair and clasped his hands before him. He knew he was now coming to the really delicate part of his investigations.

"He called at your house—when?"

"Today," she said.

"Did he call yesterday—for the money?"

She shook her head.

"No, that was posted."

"Then what did he call about today? To thank you?"

She did not answer.

"Your husband was out?"

She was looking straight at the wall ahead of her; he saw her lips quivering.

"Was he—affectionate?"

Bray was nearest to her, and caught her before she slid to the floor.

"All right, get some water."

There was a water bottle on the mantelpiece. Shale poured out a glassful. Presently her eyes opened and her husband lifted her into the arm-chair which Bray pushed forward.

"You needn't ask her anything more," Landor said. "I can tell you everything."

"I think you can," said Mason. "What time did you arrive at the flat yesterday—after this man had seen your wife?"

"Immediately after. I passed him on the stairs, but didn't know who he was."

"And yet you recognised him in the photograph?"

"I've seen him since: I've admitted that, or practically admitted it, when I said I was in Tidal Basin."

"You found your wife very upset? She told you what it was all about?"

He nodded.

"And you went after him?"

"Yes," defiantly.

"With a knife similar to this?"

Inez Landor came up to her feet at this, her hand on the table.

"That's a lie! He didn't go after him with a knife," she said passionately. "Donald took the knife—he took it from me. I'll tell you the truth. I tried to kill him. I snatched the knife from the wall. I hated him! For all the years I had with him, for all that I suffered when he was out of prison, for my baby who died because of his beastliness!"

There was a silence. Mason could hear her quick breathing.

"He took the knife from you?"

"Yes. He said he'd keep it as a souvenir, and took the sheath and put it in his pocket. You know what he wanted, don't you? He wanted me to live with him again." Her voice rose. Mason had come round to the side of his desk and took her arm in his big hand and literally pushed her back into the chair.

"Gently, Mrs. Landor. Don't get rattled. You're doing fine."

He looked round to Louis.

"You followed this man to Tidal Basin and fought with him. Did you know he had the knife in his pocket?"

"I didn't know anything about it till my wife told me on the telephone. I didn't see the knife or use it."

"Why did you run away?" asked Mason.

Again Louis paused before he answered.

"I thought I'd killed him. . . my wife begged me not to touch him. He had some sort of heart disease."

Mason nodded many times.

"And carried *butyl ammonal* in his pocket?"

"Yes," said Inez eagerly, "a little thing he crushed in a handkerchief

117

and inhaled. He always carried that."

Mason began to walk slowly up and down the room, his hands in his pockets.

"You bolted, and found a door open in the gate of the Eastern Trading Company. I call it the beer door: you won't understand why, and I can't explain. And that's all you know about it?"

"As God is my judge," said Landor.

"You never threw a knife or used a knife?"

"I'll swear I never did."

"Did you hear all the commotion when we were outside the gate?"

Louis shook his head.

"No, I was trying to find a way out of the yard. I didn't come back to that gate again for an hour. I was hiding part of the time and—"

"And how did—"

Mason got so far when the door was flung violently open. Mason stared in amazement at the man who stood there. It was Elk, part of his face hidden in white bandages. He stood at the door, supporting himself by the lintel, and glared with a certain malignity at his immediate superior.

"For the love of *Allah*, what has happened?"

"Don't touch me," snarled Elk, as Bray made a motion to assist him. "I don't want anybody with a higher rank than sergeant to help me!"

He glared down at Inez.

"Did you hear anybody come into your flat before your husband returned?"

"I thought I did," she said.

"How right you were! He was there, in the maid's room, waiting for me when I came back, and coshed me. He couldn't have got in without a key."

"Where are your keys?" asked Mason, and Louis started.

"I lost them. . . I lost them in the fight. I didn't miss them until I was on my way back there, and then I found the broken end of the chain—look."

He showed it: a gold chain dangling by the side of his trousers.

Elk staggered across to where Louis was standing and tapped him heavily on the chest.

"There's a desk in your hall," he said slowly. "Did you keep anything valuable in the top drawer—money?"

Louis stared at him.

"Stop hiding up, will you?" snapped Mason. "What was in that top drawer?"

"Money, passports and tickets," said Louis Landor huskily. "I was clearing out tomorrow and taking my wife away from this man."

"How much money?" demanded Elk.

"About three thousand pounds."

Elk laughed mirthlessly.

"There's about nothing now! It's gone! The drawer was broken open and the money taken. I'll tell you something more, Mason." His outrageous familiarity passed unnoticed. "The fellow that coshed me was White Face! I'm not romancing——"

Mason interrupted him with an impatient gesture.

"Of course it was White Face. It could be nobody else but White Face. I've known that all along," he said.

Chapter 13

Michael Quigley had never been alone through Gallows Court by day or night. He stood hesitant at the entrance and experienced a qualm of uneasiness which was foreign to him. He looked up and down the street vainly for a policeman, and rather wished he had detained the taxi-driver. Yet Gallows Court differed from no other noisome thoroughfare; there were thousands of them in every great city, none more mysterious or sinister than the other. Two hundred years ago, when bravoes lurked in these dens, there might be another tale to tell; but here was the twentieth century; a highly organised police force, housing societies and sanitary inspectors prying into the darkest places without hurt to themselves. Not in the early hours of the morning, said a warning voice.

But they would be asleep now.

It was one of Mr. Mason's figures of speech that the inmates of the court never slept. But he was rather prone to exaggeration. Mike looked up at the facade of Dr. Marford's surgery. The windows of the top room were open. This was evidently his sleeping-room—he had had a faint hope that the doctor would still be about. Summoning his resolution, he walked into the dark entry. There was no sign or sound of life. Every window in the court was black.

Either the storm or some human piece of mischief had extinguished the gas-lamp at the far end of the court. Groping his way along, feeling at the wall, he presently touched the door which gave into the doctor's yard. It was fastened, and he went on a little farther. Then suddenly he stopped, with his heart in his mouth. He had heard a groan, a deep, a painful groan that ended in a long-drawn "Oh-h!"

Where had it come from? He looked around fearfully, but could see nothing. And then he heard the groan again. It seemed to come from somewhere near him. He waited, determined to locate the sound, but it was not repeated. Instead came a soft cackle of laughter which made every hair on his head stand up. And then a hoarse voice spoke.

"Go on, Mr. Reporter, nobody's going to hurt ya!"

He recognised the speaker, though he could not see him. It was the crazy man who had followed Mason and him into the street.

"Rats, ain't we? Eyes like rats," he said. "I heard ya! I hear everything!"

Michael edged towards the voice, and then saw an indistinguishable black mass huddled against the wall.

"I know where ya going!" The crazy unknown spoke in a thick whisper. "Ya going to see what's wrong with old Gregory—clever! Cleverer than Mason. Here!" An invisible hand clutched his overcoat. Michael had to use all his self-control to prevent wrenching himself free. "I'll tell you something." The whisper grew more confidential. "They ain't found Rudd—the police doctor. They're out on the river with their drags, raking up the old mud, but they ain't found him."

The unseen creature laughed until he broke into a fit of coughing.

"All the busies and all the coppers in Tidal Basin lookin' for old Rudd! Do you think he's a good doctor—I don't! I wouldn't let him doctor me. Tell 'em what I say at the station, mister—have a lark with 'em! Tell 'em he's under a barge!"

Then the detaining claws released their grip.

"Blue Face is asleep down there on old Gregory's doorstep. Blue Face—not White Face."

Again the long gurgle of laughter that ended in a paroxysm of coughing. Michael drew himself away and went on till he came to No. 9. The sleeper he had seen sat hunched up on the doorstep of Gregory Wicks, the can still balanced on his knees. His arms were folded, his head bent forward. He was snoring regularly.

Michael did not dare go back the way he had come. He went out of the lower end of the court, came round the block and found the crazy man leaning against the wall of the entry.

"Old Gregory's back—been back a quarter of an hour. An old man like him oughtn't to drive taxicabs—and I'm the only man that knows why he oughtn't! Dr. Marford knows, but he's not the feller that goes snouting on his patients."

"Snouting" meant "nosing," and "nosing" meant "informing." Dr. Marford was credited with having been the recipient of secrets which it would have terrified his more opulent brethren even to hear.

"What's wrong with old Gregory Wicks? That's what I'm asking ya?"

And then, without warning, the crazy man turned abruptly and ran noiselessly through the dark entry. He must have been either in stockinged or bare feet, for he made no sound, but moved with uncanny silence. He might have been the wraith of all that was ugly and wicked in the court.

But he had told Michael one thing he wanted to know. Gregory had returned, had been back a quarter of an hour. Michael walked slowly to the police station and interviewed the sergeant.

"No, we haven't found Dr. Rudd. The river police are searching. There's a chance he may have gone up west. He's got a flat near Langham Place and he may turn up there later. Mr. Mason is on his way here, if you want to see him."

"Why is he coming back?" asked Michael in surprise, but the station sergeant could or would give information on this point.

Michael was relieved: he wished for no better news, for he was desperately anxious to see the superintendent.

"Personally, I'm not worried about Rudd." The station sergeant could drop all ceremonious titles with a sympathetic and understanding audience. "He's a funny old chap—I don't know how old he is, but he's young compared with Methuselah. If a man's got money, he oughtn't to be messing about in this neighbourhood."

"Has he got money?"

"Whips of it," said the sergeant. "An old lady, one of his patients, died and left him a packet! If he'd been a better doctor she might have been living now," he added libellously.

He patted back a yawn.

"Yes, he's got tons of money. He owns a flat in the West End of London. Some of the Special Branch fellers from Scotland Yard tell me they often see him in the night clubs. Thank God, a man's never too old to be silly!"

Michael, who knew the area well, had never seriously considered Dr. Rudd as an individual. There are some characters who fail utterly to inspire the least interest in themselves. They are figures—men or women occupying set places, who have no existence other than the existence which is visible to their casual acquaintances. Whether they eat or drink, have home lives or private predilections, is hardly worth speculating upon. It is almost surprising to discover that they play bridge or have the gift of distinguishing between Chateau Lafitte and

Imperial Tokay. Whatever they do that is human appears as an amazing phenomenon.

He brought Dr. Rudd out of the background of his mind and tried to examine him as an entity, but he was either too tired or too bored to give this shadowy figure significance.

Mason came with Bray and Shale, and the superintendent was in his most rollicking mood. You might have thought he had risen from a long and refreshing sleep; he greeted Michael jovially.

But the news which the station sergeant gave him wiped the smile from his face.

"What?" he said. "Rudd hasn't turned up?"

He had quite forgotten Dr. Rudd, for, like Michael, he found that elusive personality difficult to place. He did not speak for a long time, but stood in front of the fire, warming his hands.

"I'm not as worried about him as I should be," he said. "He's a queer bird, and gets me on the raw quicker than any man I know, though I hope I've never shown it. I can't feel that he's anything to worry about."

"I'll tell you something to worry about, if you'll give me a few minutes," said Michael, and the superintendent looked at him sharply.

"That sounds to me like a threat. All right. Can we have your room, Bray?"

Bray looked a little sour that he was not invited to the conference. He disliked these crime reporters, and made no disguise of his antipathy. And crime reporters disliked him and maliciously spelt his name wrong if they mentioned it at all.

Behind the closed door of the inspector's room Michael revealed all his suspicions, and Mr. Mason listened, making very few comments.

"I've had that idea in my mind, too," he said. "I'm not kidding you, Mike, or trying to jump in and take credit for your brain's work. But old Gregory Wicks is as straight as a die. I've known him since I was a boy. I was born in this neighbourhood, but don't want you to tell anybody this. Gregory's got the finest record of any cabman in London—the amount of property that fellow's restored to the rightful owners runs into five figures."

"He limps, doesn't he?" asked Michael, and Mason's brows knitted.

"Yes, he limps," he said slowly. "He was thrown from the seat of a cab years ago. Of course he limps," he went on thoughtfully. "Now, why on earth did I forget that?"

"You told me that the man who was seen coming out of Mrs. Weston's flat also limped?"

Mason nodded.

"Yes; I hadn't connected the two people. But Gregory Wicks!" He laughed. "The idea's ridiculous! The old boy is seventy-six if he's a day, and he's the most rumbustiously straight man I know."

"That crazy fellow in the court asked you to find out what's wrong with him, didn't he?" asked Michael quietly.

Mason rubbed his bald head.

"There are too many crazy people giving me theories," he said pointedly. "No, I don't mean you, Michael."

"What about asking the doctor?"

"Marford? Must I tell him I've pulled him out of bed to confirm what a lunatic has said about one of his patients? And would he tell? That's the one thing you can't compel a doctor to do unless you get him into the witness stand, and even then the Medical Association raise a hullabaloo if a lawyer goes a little too far."

"Wake him up on some other excuse," suggested Michael. "After all, he may be able to help us with Rudd."

Mr. Mason thrust his hands more deeply into his pockets and rattled his loose change irritably.

"He certainly limped, if the woman witness was telling the truth. And now I come to remember it, White Face has always been a limper. That was one of the first descriptions circulated. He used to ride a motor-cycle, you remember—that rather knocks your idea on the head."

"Motor-cyclists have been seen coming from the scene of a robbery, but nobody could swear that those particular cyclists were the robbers," said Michael. "The motor-cycle theory is one that everybody has jumped to, that after he did his dirty work he made his getaway on a pop-pop! When you come to think of it, motor-bikes are the most conspicuous things in London after a certain hour. Isn't it more likely that he made his grand exit on the box of a taxicab?"

"Or," said Mason, "is it more likely that a man with a fifty-year record for honesty, a man with a bit of money put by, with no relations or friends, no vices, a man who never goes out, has never done a dishonest thing in his life, should suddenly turn crook? And listen, Michael! You've been a witness to a White Face raid and you've read about the others. What has invariably happened? He's come into the restaurant and he's said two words—what are those words?"

"'Bail up,'" said Michael.

Mason nodded vehemently.

"Exactly—'bail up'! It was an expression of the old Australian bushrangers. It's still used by the hold-up men in Australia. Gregory's never been out of London in his life, except to drive a drunken fare into the country. The only knowledge he has of the word 'bail' is that it's something to do with getting a man out of a police station after he's pinched. I'll tell you who White Face is—Tommy Furse."

"And who in hell is Tommy Furse?" asked Michael, in surprise.

"You shall have the story when it's properly cooked—at present the oven is just heating up."

He got up quickly from his chair.

"I'll call the doctor and tell him I want to come round and see him. Or Bray can do it."

He opened the door, shouted for the inspector, and when he came gave him instructions.

"Tell him I'm very worried about Dr. Rudd and I would like to consult him."

"As a matter of fact," he added, when Bray had gone, "I'm not feeling too happy about Rudd, though what Dr. Marford can tell me I don't know."

"May I come?"

"You can come, but you'd better stay outside. I can't very well introduce you into an official inquiry."

"Anyway, he doesn't like me very much," said Michael, with a recollection of Dr. Marford's former coldness.

When the superintendent reached the surgery he found Dr. Marford dressed. He had not been to bed that night, had only returned from a patient a few minutes before the 'phone message came through.

"A boy or a girl?" asked Mr. Mason blandly.

"In this event it was both," said the doctor.

He very much disliked discussing his cases, as Bray, who knew him better than Mason, was well aware.

"I'm not worried at all about Dr. Rudd. I didn't like to say so before, for fear you might think I was saying something disparaging of him. By the way, I called in at the infirmary to see that woman, but as she seemed to be sleeping the house surgeon thought I'd better not see her."

"Mrs. Weston?"

Marford nodded.

"When will she be fit to make a statement?"

"Tomorrow—this morning, I should think."

He took a whisky bottle from a cupboard and put it with a siphon on the table.

"This is all I can offer you. I keep it exclusively for my visitors. Personally, I never drink after ten o'clock in the evening."

He had no suggestions to offer with regard to Rudd.

"He'll turn up," he said confidentially, "and I prophesy that he'll turn up with a headache and be quite incapable of transacting any kind of business for a day or two."

"What on earth do you think he's done?" asked Mason, and the doctor smiled.

"I would rather not say."

"You'd rather not say things about quite a lot of people, Doctor." Mason helped himself to some whisky and splashed in soda.

"They tell me you could hang half Gallows Court and send the other half to prison for the term of their natural lives?"

"If I could, I should do it," said Marford. "Believe me, I have no sympathy with that ghastly crowd—"

"Except Gregory Wicks?" suggested Mason, and a shadow passed over the doctor's face.

"Except Gregory Wicks," he said slowly.

"Gregory Wicks," began Bray, "is one of the nicest people living in this area—"

"Yes, yes, I'm sure the doctor will agree," said Mason. "But why not Gregory Wicks?"

"For many reasons," replied Marford. "He's a good fellow—"

"What is the matter with him? You attend him, don't you?"

Dr. Marford smiled faintly.

"I attend a good many people, but I never say what is the matter with them, even to entertain eminent police officers."

"There's something the matter with him, isn't there?" insisted Mason, and Marford nodded.

"*Anno Domini!* You can't get to the age of seventy-six without running a little threadbare. There are worn spots in men of that age, certain weaknesses, peculiar mental and physical failings which no doctor can patch. It's amazing to me that he can do what he does at his age. I've never seen him really sick or sorry—he has certainly got the loudest voice in Tidal Basin; and I can testify, for I attended the victim, that he can still deliver a blow that would knock out the average pugilist. Why are you interested?"

He stepped back from Mason and surveyed him with a troubled face.

"Do you know, Mr. Mason," he said slowly, "I've got an instinctive idea that you've come here not to talk about Mr. Rudd but to talk about this old taxi-driver. There is a half-witted man who lives in the court, whose name I forget—he used to be a shoeblack—who has an obsession about Gregory. Every time I go into the court he catches my arm and asks me what is wrong with Gregory Wicks—I wonder if he's been asking you the same thing?"

Mason was momentarily embarrassed. It did not add to his self-esteem that he should have been detected acting as a lunatic's mouth-piece.

"Well, yes," he said, and laughed awkwardly. "I've heard the man—in fact, he's asked me the same question. But of course I shouldn't be stupid enough to come round in the middle of the night to pass on a crazy inquiry. I'm interested in the old boy."

The doctor was behind his desk, leaning down on his outstretched arms, looking terribly tired. Mason found himself being thankful that he had not been born in so favourable a position that his parents could afford to educate him as a doctor.

"You'll have to ask the old man in the morning. I'm very sorry; I'd like to oblige you, Mr. Mason. It isn't entirely a question of professional secrecy—I certainly wouldn't let that stand in my way with a police officer who was investigating a very serious crime—though what poor old Gregory's got to do with it I can't imagine. But I owe Gregory something more than perfunctory loyalty. He's by way of being a crony of mine, and I'm afraid you'll have to ask him yourself tomorrow."

"He has something the matter with his face, hasn't he?"

Marford hesitated.

"Yes," he said; "you could describe it that way."

And then he raised his eyes slowly to Mason.

"You will not suggest"—his lips twitched—"that the old man is your White Face?"

"I'm suggesting nothing of the sort," said Mason hastily and re-proachfully. "Of course I'm not! I'm merely curious. That crazy fellow's got on my nerves—I'll admit it. Certainly, I'll ask Gregory himself in the morning. I'd ask him tonight if it wasn't for disturbing that mackerel who's been sleeping on Gregory's doorstep ever since midnight."

"Is it a very red-nosed man?" asked Bray, interested. "If it is, he's often there. I've seen him myself. I very often go through Gallows Court alone—more or less alone. A drunken-looking man with a red nose—

"I never inspected his nose," said Mason icily. "It probably went red through sticking it into other people's investigations."

"Very likely," said Mr. Bray, and Shale could only marvel at his clouded intelligence.

"Do you believe every man who wears a lint mask is a criminal?" Marford asked quietly. "Of course you don't: you're too sensible. Any more than you believe that all Chinamen are wicked. I ask you this,"—he spoke very slowly—"because the man of whom you spoke earlier this evening is coming"—he looked at his watch—"in less than ten minutes."

"White Face?" said Mason in amazement.

"He telephoned me just before you came."

"Tell me, Dr. Marford"—Bray could not be repressed—"how is this White Face man dressed when you see him?"

Marford considered a moment.

"He usually wears a very long coat reaching almost to his heels, and a soft dark hat."

"Black?" asked Bray eagerly.

"It may be. I've never really noticed."

"Why is he coming this morning?" asked Mason.

"He said he would have come earlier in the night, but the streets were full of policemen. I'm telling you what he told me. It doesn't sound too good of any man that he's afraid of the police. But anyone super-sensitive as this fellow is, might very easily shrink from being seen."

"He telephoned you from where?"

"I'm not sure. It certainly wasn't our local exchange, because the calls we get through on the local exchange are always indicated by continuous ringing, and these signals came at intervals."

He walked to the big window, drew aside the blind and looked out.

"There's somebody out there," he said. "Is it a police officer? No, it isn't, I see. It's the reporter, isn't it?"

"Yes."

"Ask him to come in."

Mason nodded to his subordinate, and Sergeant Shale went out to admit the reporter.

"If I could stop you getting a big beat I would, Michael, but this matter isn't entirely in my hands. You'll probably have to use your well-known discretion—I think I can trust you to keep out of your paper just what I want you to keep out."

"The idea being?" asked Michael.

"White Face," said Mr. Bray, and coughed when he caught his superior's chilly eye.

"As that active and discreet officer said, it's somebody with a white face; a man who's been seen in this neighbourhood, and probably in other neighbourhoods—I think you met him at the Howdah Club. And he's due here almost at once. I don't suppose he wants to see a lot of people here"—he addressed Marford—"but you realise I'll have to ask him to give an account of himself."

The doctor, who was arranging an instrument that looked like a huge aluminium funnel, nodded his agreement.

"As a matter of fact, he's very shy, but if I am to betray anybody in the interests of justice I might as well betray him. It isn't very admirable and I can't say that I'm very proud of myself."

He brought the lamp nearer to his desk and turned the switch, and Mason saw a circle of green light appear on the floor. The shadows which the other lights cast ran through the circle redly. Marford turned off the lamp and explained that the current came, not from the main electric supply, but from an accumulator.

"I warn you," he said, "that this man may refuse to enter the surgery. It took me a long while to persuade him the last time he was here."

"Which way does he come?"

"Through the yard and up that passage to that door." He pointed to the door near the medicine cupboard. "He gives me a signal—two long rings and two short ones; that was my own arrangement on account of his incurable shyness. I shall never get him in if he sees any of you."

Mason tried the door; it was locked. The telephone bell rang at a moment when all nerves were tense. Marford sat on the desk and took up the instrument.

"Yes, he's here," he said. "It is Dr. Marford speaking. . . better, is she?

I'm glad of that. . . Certainly."

He handed the instrument to Mason.

"The woman Weston is quite conscious and wants to come to the station to see you."

Mason listened, giving monosyllabic interruptions. He put up the receiver and looked very thoughtful.

"She wants to come to the station. It was Elk—I thought I recognised the voice. I wonder if I could get him here in time," said Mason thoughtfully. "He'd be very much interested to meet White Face—he's met him once this evening."

"There may be time—" began Marford.

A bell in the room rang shrilly and long, rang again, then came two short rings. The men looked at one another.

"That is your White Face, is it?"

Mason's voice was husky. His hand dropped mechanically to his pocket, and Bray was satisfied now: the rumour that Mason always carried a gun was true.

Michael Quigley, a silent participator, felt a little shiver run down his spine as Mason made a gesture to his two subordinates.

"Behind those curtains, you two fellows. Michael, you'd better go out into the front hall. I'll get behind the desk if you don't mind."

"What do you want me to do?" asked Marford, as he took a key from his pocket.

"Let him in, that's all. I'll see that he doesn't get out again," said Mason. "You can help us by shutting and locking the door on him."

Marford nodded. He turned the key and pulled open the door slowly. Watching him from the cover of the desk, Mason saw him smile.

"Good evening," he said. "Won't you come in?" He went a little out of sight and they heard the rumble of a voice saying something which was indistinguishable. It might have been a voice that spoke behind a muffling mask.

"My dear fellow," they heard Marford say, "I have never promised you that I can be absolutely alone, but you have nothing to fear—come along."

He disappeared from view into the passage and Mason held his breath. Then suddenly the door slammed; there was the sound of a bolt being drawn, and in another second:

"Help!" It was Marford's voice. "Mason. . . Mason! For God's sake!"

Then came an unearthly scream that turned the hearers' blood cold.

Mason was on his feet instantly. He was half-way to the door when the lights of the room went out. From the passage came the faint sound of a struggle.

"Bray! Go to the front door, quick! Go with him, Shale!"

They came to the front door to find it was locked from the inside and did not yield to their frantic tugging. Mason remembered that the doctor had told him he kept that part of the premises which contained the surgery locked and double-locked, and that he invariably used the back door himself.

They stumbled back through the darkness, and as Mason picked up a chair and sent it smashing a the panel, a ray from Bray's torch glittered on the lamp.

"This works."

He fumbled for the switch and found it, and the ghostly green circle appeared on the floor. It gave them enough light to work by. Within a few moments two panels were gone. Bray, the taller, reached through, found the bolt and drew it. There was another at the bottom, and it was some minutes before the third panel was broken and enabled them to reach this.

Bray was the first in the passage. It was empty. The door at the end stood wide open. He ran out into the yard—there was nobody in sight.

"There's blood here," he said. "I can't see Marford. Can you bring the lamp out?"

Shale examined the flex: there was enough to carry the ray lamp into the corridor. It revealed nothing except patches of something red and shining on the floor and walls The doctor and his assailant had vanished.

Chapter 14

To the man in the yard outside came the sound of splintering panels. White Face had no need to crank up his machine: the taxi engine was running softly. He pulled open the two gates and took a look inside the cab. On the floor was a huddled figure.

"Doctor," said White Face pleasantly, "I'm afraid I shall have to take you for an uncomfortable journey."

He could have left him behind for the detectives to find, but it was most undesirable that this medical practitioner should tell his experience; for he had seen White Face without his mask.

The car ran swiftly into the street. As he passed he thought he could hear somebody trying to get out of the front door. He passed a policeman on the corner of the street; the man shouted out to him, "Goodnight, Gregory." White Face smiled to himself.

The hands which gripped the wheel were wet and stained with the red liquid which he had poured from a bottle on to the floor and walls of the passage. He hoped it would look like blood, would at least throw his pursuers off the track until the morning.

He hadn't too much time. Mentally he calculated how long it would take Mason to telephone a description of the cab to Scotland Yard, and just how much longer time would be wasted whilst the description was being circulated through London. He gave himself a good half-hour, providing he kept to the outskirts. So he made his way northward, and in half an hour had reached the outskirts of Epping Forest. It was certain that the Yard would telephone to the outlying stations the number of the cab, and that made it imperative that he should keep to the secondary roads and avoid those key points where the Essex police patrols could establish a barrage.

With any luck he could reach the little farm undetected. It lay between Epping and Chelmsford, not a long journey if he had dared the direct route.

He came at last to a place where an uninviting country lane ran off at right angles to the road, and turned his car down this. He had to move with the greatest caution, for he had extinguished his lamps. The road was uneven, but not quite so bad as the cart track into which he guided the taxi. Here he had to move very carefully. The only thing that concerned him was whether the noise of the car in low gear would attract the attention of an inquisitive policeman, but apparently it had not.

Without any knowledge of the time, he could make a rough guess—thought it must be four o'clock. There was no sign of dawn in the sky.

He came at last to an old barn, which was built by the side of a squat and shapeless building, and, stopping the cab without stopping the engine, he got down, opened the cab door and, lifting out the unconscious doctor, laid him on the grass. Then he backed the machine into the barn and, closing the big gate of it, went back to open the door of the house. This done, he returned to the place where he had left the doctor and half carried, half dragged him into the passage.

Except for a few ugly, dilapidated articles which the previous owner had not thought it worthwhile to move, the house was unfurnished. There was a dingy carpet running the length of the hall, and in the room to where White Face carried his burden, an old sofa to which he hoisted the doctor. He stood for some time looking at his prisoner. "It was a great mistake for you to try to set the police on me, and I hope no harm comes to you," he said.

Lately White Face had acquired the habit of talking aloud.

He finished his examination of the unconscious man, then went out to the barn, and presently came back with a small bottle of champagne and a box of biscuits: emergency rations which he kept in a box under the cab seat.

The taxi was of no more use to him. He must make his way across country to Harwich by another means. And those means were ready to his hand. He had compiled from week to week, with scrupulous care, a list of motor excursions out of London. There was one leaving in the morning from Forest Gate to Felixstowe, and he had already decided that this was the route he would take. He would not be noticed in an excursion crowd.

The doctor was a difficulty. Almost he wished he had not brought him; but he was too dangerous to leave.

White Face drank his wine out of an old cup he found in the kitchen, poured out another cup and took it back to where he had left his charge. Placing the lamp which he carried on the table, and by the side of this the cup, White Face sat on the edge of the bed and waited. Presently he saw the doctor's eyes flicker; they opened, looked wonderingly round the room and fixed themselves finally upon the man who was sitting on the bed.

"Where is this place?" he spoke huskily.

"This place is a little farm near Romford," said the other calmly. "And may I tell you what your friend Mason has already guessed—that I am White Face."

The doctor looked at him incredulously. "You?"

The man nodded.

"Weird, isn't it? But I think you guessed it yourself and were prepared to tell your friends of Scotland Yard. I am not going to chloroform you or drug you again or do any of the things which I might do. Unless I am greatly mistaken, you will go to sleep and you will sleep for a very long time; and when you wake up you will find your way to the nearest police station. If you drive a car, I must tell you there is a taxi in the barn—I invariably use a taxi. My landlord"—he laughed at the word—"was Mr. Gregory Wicks. I invariably use a taxi—Gregory Wicks's taxi. That may or may not convey something to you, but I rather fancy your mind is incapable of grasping important essentials."

The doctor was staring at him.

"Turn on your side," commanded White Face, and was obeyed instantly. "Close your eyes."

He waited a few minutes until the drugged man was asleep, and then he went out, taking the lamp with him. He made another journey to the garage, brought in a suitcase and laid out such toilet articles as he required.

Chapter 15

Mason had found the governing light switch and brought on all the lights in Marford's house. Bray, who had searched the yard, came back with his report.

"There's blood everywhere," he said. "Look at that!" He pointed to an uneven smudge near the door. "They carried him out this way."

"Is there any other way he could have been carried out?" snapped Mason.

In the courtyard the gates were wide open, and so were the doors of the empty garage. Gregory Wick's taxicab had gone. When they came out to the street they had heard the faint, dying whine of it as it sped westwards.

"They've got him in the cab," said Bray incoherently. "There must have been two or three of them."

"Why not four or five?" snarled Mason, "Or six or seven?"

"I only want to say," began the aggrieved inspector, "that one man couldn't have outed him and lifted him. I'd better call up assistance."

The police whistle was half-way to his mouth when Mason knocked it out of his hand.

"What's the matter with the telephone?" he asked fiercely. "I want to know who's awake in this neighbourhood, and I don't want any excuse for their being awake, either! Call every man you can lay your hands on. The reserves will be in by now."

When Bray had gone, the superintendent made a quick search of the yard. There was an open pit surrounded by a low fencing. He struck a match, drew his own lamp from his pocket and cast the rays down. A long way below the surface of the ground he saw the glint of water. A well. How deep was it? There was something there, too, something that looked like a sack. And then he heard a voice behind him. "Found the well?"

135

He looked round; it was Elk, a ghostly figure, with his white-bandaged head. "Did you know there was a well here?"

"Yes, the winch is above your head—handle on the wall."

Looking up, Mason saw an iron bracket. "Something down there?" asked Elk, and peered curiously. "Gregory's cab's gone, of course. I guessed something was happening and came round."

The two men went up to the empty garage and made a search. There was nothing there except a few tools, a spare tyre or two and a dozen tins of petrol. They picked up the blood trail in the garage. Mason looked at these ominous stains and shook his head.

"All my ideas have gone west," he said in despair.

"Mine have stayed strictly put, working for the good of humanity," said Elk. "White Face, wasn't it? And he's kidnapped the doctor—that fellow's got a nerve!"

They heard Michael's step and looked round. "Well, are you going to interview Gregory?" he asked. "Gregory—I presume he's with his cab."

"Let's see," said Michael.

They discovered that the door leading into Gallows Court was fastened with a spring lock and offered no difficulty. Elk examined this door carefully and grunted.

"As full of clues as a milkshop," he said.

They walked quickly down the court and came to the doorway of No. 9. The sleeper still snored; the tin remained balanced on his knee.

"Whoever put that tin there were helping the police a lot," said Mason. "It'd break their hearts to know it, but it's a fact."

He knocked heavily at the door, but there was no answer. After a little while he knocked again-still no reply.

"He must have gone out."

Michael shook his head emphatically.

"How could he go in or out with that man sitting there? He must have moved him."

The sleeper was now aroused; the tin fell noisily from his knee as he stood up, groaning, and Bray recognised him as a famous local tippler. He had been there, he said, since about—he didn't know the time; he thought it was about half an hour after the public-houses had closed. He could not remember anybody passing, cither going in or out. Mason knocked again.

Gallows Court was alive now—alive with dark shapes that had

136

melted out of the walls, silent things that just looked and gave no evidence of their humanness. Curious watchers, eager to see somebody, something happen. If they had chatted amongst themselves Michael could have borne their presence, but they were terribly silent, edging nearer and nearer.

Then suddenly the upper window of No. 9 was raised creakily.

"Who's that?"

It was old Gregory Wicks's strident voice, unmistakably so.

"I want to see you, Gregory."

"Who is it?"

"Superintendent Mason. You remember me?"

The old man cogitated.

"I don't know no Superintendent Mason. There used to be a young feller called Sergeant Mason a few years ago."

"A good few, Gregory," said Mason with a chuckle. "I'm Sergeant Mason. Come down and let us in."

"What do you want?" asked the old man cautiously.

"I want to have a talk with you."

The man above hesitated, but after a while he put down the window and Mason heard his feet descending the stairs. The door opened noisily.

"Come on up to my room," he said.

There was no light in the house save the lamp which the police brought, nor in his little sitting-room.

"Come in and sit down. Here's a chair, Sergeant—Superintendent, eh? Gosh! Time goes on!"

"Haven't you got a lamp?"

The question seemed to embarrass the old man.

"Lamp? Well, yes, I've got a lamp somewhere. You'll find it in the kitchen, mister. There are three of you, ain't there? My eyes are not as good as they used to be, but I sort of heard three lots of feet on the stairs besides mine."

It was Michael who went downstairs and found the lamp half filled with oil. He lit it, fixed the glass chimney and carried it carefully up the stairs into the room where the three men were. And then, to Mason's surprise, he said:

"I couldn't find your lamp anywhere, Mr. Wicks."

This in face of the fairly bright light he carried in his hand. The old man smiled.

"What do you call that you've brought into the room?" he said.

"Put it on the table, young man, and don't try to take liberties with me."

The look of chagrin in Michael's face brought joy to Superintendent Mason's heart.

"Now sit down, everybody. What do you want to know?"

"Have you been out tonight, Gregory?" Mason asked.

Gregory felt his scrubby chin.

"For a little while," he said cautiously. "I always pop up to the West End. Why?"

"Does anybody else drive your cab?"

"I've let it out before now," said Gregory. "I'm not so young as I was, and an owner-driver has got to live, and he can only live if he works his machine all the time."

"Who takes your car out?"

The old man did not answer, and Mason repeated the question.

"Well. . . my lodger takes it out."

"The man who lives downstairs?"

"That's right, Sergeant—I mean, Superintendent! Bless me life, fancy you being a superintendent! I remember you getting your first stripe."

Mason patted him gently on the knee.

"Of course you do. And I remember summonsing you for using abusive language and the magistrate dismissing the charge."

Gregory gurgled with laughter at the recollection.

"I was always a hard one to get the better of," he said smugly.

"Where is your lodger now?"

Again the hesitation.

"Out, I suppose. He usually goes out at night. Rather a nice young feller. Very quiet. He's about thirty-five, and he's had a lot of trouble: that's all I know about him." Then, in sudden alarm: "He's not been in trouble again?"

"Oh, that's the kind of trouble, is it?" said Mason. "Gregory, where is your badge?"

Now, a cabman's badge is an almost sacred thing. It is to the driver what marriage lines are to a woman. The effect of the question on the old man was extraordinary. He fidgeted in his chair and rubbed his chin.

"I've put it away somewhere," he said lamely.

"Gregory, where is your badge? If you've been out tonight, you must have been wearing it," said Mason. "As a matter of fact, you haven't been out tonight; you haven't been out any night for months; you know that, old pal."

Again he pressed the old man's knee affectionately, and this time his sympathy was genuine.

"You know why you haven't been out. The doctor knows."

"He hasn't told?" said Gregory quickly.

"No, I've told myself. You knew there was a lamp came in the room because you could smell it, but you couldn't see it, Gregory—only dimly. Isn't that true?"

The old man shrank back.

"I've been a licensed cabman for fifty-five years, Mr. Mason," he pleaded.

"I know. I hope you'll be a licensed cabman all the days of your life. Only you mustn't drive cabs, Gregory—when you're blind!"

He saw the old man wince, and cursed himself for his brutality.

"I'm not exactly blind, but I can't see very well."

The blustering Gregory Wicks had suddenly become an oddly pathetic figure.

"My eyes are not what they were, Mr. Mason, but I never like to admit it. I've had my licence and badge all these years, and naturally I didn't want to part with it; so when this young lodger of mine, who's been in trouble and couldn't get a licence, said he'd like to take out the cab, I—well—I lent him my badge. That's an offence, I know, but I'm willing to take my medicine."

"Then you've never seen your lodger?"

"No, I haven't seen him; I've heard him. He comes in sometimes; I hear him moving about; and he pays me regularly."

"How do you know he's thirty-five, and a nice young man who's going to be married?"

"I heard he was—a friend of mine told me."

They left him bemoaning the loss of the thing which was more precious to him than any other possession—the stamped licence that had been issued every one of the fifty-five years of his active life, and which might never be issued again. Mason went downstairs and tried the door of the lower room. The lock was not difficult to pick—did not, if they had known, require picking at all, for the key of the upstairs room fitted both doors. In five minutes it swung open and Mason went in, followed by Bray, who carried the oil lamp.

There was a bed in one corner, but evidently it had not been slept in for a long time: the blankets were folded, the pillow was without cover. The floor had a large square of carpet in the centre, and that, with a table, a chair, and a square mirror over the fireplace, seemed all that the room contained, until Elk began to test the mirror, and found that it hid a roughly hewn hole in the wall, large enough to take a heavy steel box.

"This will tell us something," said Mason.

The lid opened squeakily, and he stared down into the interior at what it contained.

It was a short, stout knife, the blade stained and smeared red. Carefully he picked it out and as carefully laid it on the bare table.

"Here is the knife that killed Donald Bateman," he said.

Chapter 16

Only one man in the court had ever seen Gregory's lodger, or would admit they had seen him. At the very hint of an inquiry the crowd that filled the court melted back into the walls again; only the crazy, nameless man remained.

"Didn't I tell you? Didn't I tell you?" he almost screamed when he caught sight of Mason. "You and the reporter fellow—what's wrong with Gregory, eh? I knew!" He tapped his nose. "I'll bet the doctor knew, but he wouldn't squeak. Here!" He detained Mason. "Is it true that they got the doctor?. . . Somebody'll be murdered if they touch him! Everybody in Gallows Court will go and find the man and bring him in here and put him down into a cellar, and put clay in his mouth and tear little bits off him till he dies!"

The awful face grinned up at the superintendent.

"In which case," said Mason, "I shall come and do a bit of pinching myself, and somebody else will die. No, I don't know who has taken the doctor."

"I heard him—shouting, screaming something awful. And then the cab went out," whispered the man. "If we'd known it was the doctor we'd have been after 'em."

"What is this lodger like?"

The man shook his head.

"A tall feller—that's all I know. Seen him once or twice go in and out, generally at night; but I've never seen him any closer than that. He didn't sleep there—old Gregory thought he did, but he didn't."

This was so near to the conclusion that Mason formed that he was inclined to listen to other opinions with respect, but Shoey—as they called him—said no more.

There was one good quality about Inspector Bray: he was an excellent telephonist. Before Mason left the surgery, Scotland Yard knew all about a taxicab No. 93458—its colour, its appearance generally and the direction it had taken. And Scotland Yard knew all about the missing Dr. Marford and the chauffeur who lived with old Gregory Wicks.

That busy printing press at the Yard worked furiously to carry the news to the outermost beat, and the early workers straggling into the City saw police cyclists disregarding all speed rules.

Lorna Weston sat in the infirmary hall waiting for the ambulance which was to take her to the police station. A pallid, shaken woman, her eyes weary and heavy, she barely noticed or heard the laborious platitudes of Police Constable Hartford, who sat by her side—all the more laborious because he had decided that her condition was due to excessive indulgence in alcohol, and had set himself the task of opening her eyes to the evil that men (and women) put in their mouths to steal away their brains.

One of the policemen who came with the ambulance gave a fragmentary and generally inaccurate resume of what had happened to Dr. Marford. P.C. Hartford clicked his lips unhappily.

"It only shows, Mrs. Weston, what drink will do to a man," he said. "They were probably all drinking together up at the doctor's surgery, and naturally something happened. It's never too late to turn. Take me: five years ago there wasn't a man who loved a glass of beer more than myself. I used to call myself a moderate drinker, but was I? No man who drinks can be a moderate drinker. Then one day I was induced to take the pledge, and look at me today!"

She did not look at him. She hardly heard him. If she had looked, she would have realised that if there had been any improvement in P.C. Hartford's appearance, he must have looked very dreadful in his moderately drinking days. But she heard nothing except a buzz of voices that had been going on all night—whispering, buzzing voices that came from another planet; and there was a little pain in her left arm which irritated her; and through all her confusion of mind and dread, formless reality which could not be reduced to any dimensions or advanced into clear perspective.

When she spoke it was mechanically to repeat:

"I want to see the Chief of Police. I must see the Chief of Police."

She repeated this monotonously. Part of the mechanism of her reason was working; some tremendous motive power impelled a demand of which she was not conscious. She had little flashes of complete understanding; knew she was sitting on a hard form in a long and dimly-lit corridor, with bare, discoloured walls. In the next second she was sitting in an arm-chair in a small room, which was so light that it hurt her eyes; and a different lot of people were around her.

"Why did the infirmary people let her go?" asked Mason, in despair.

"I want to see the Chief of Police," she said. "I want to make a statement."

"So you've told me a dozen times, my dear," said Mason, patting her hand. "Now wake up. You know where you are—I'm Superintendent Mason."

She looked at him searchingly and shook her head.

"Where's the matron?" asked Mason. "Oh, here you are, Miss Leverett. Let her lie down; give her some coffee. Where's that damned—oh, there you are, Bray! Is there any report?"

"None, sir," said the inspector. And then, painfully: "I don't think I can stand much more, sir. I shall have to go to sleep. After all, I'm only human."

"You're not human at all"—Mason was distinctly offensive—"you're a policeman. You haven't been awake twenty-four hours, and you'll certainly be awake another twenty-four; the first forty-eight hours are the worst."

"My own belief is," said Bray, "that this fellow drove the cab straight into the Thames——"

"Yes, yes, I'm sure he did," said Mason soothingly, "or into the British Museum, possibly. You might put an inquiry through."

Inspector Bray considered this.

"I shouldn't think they'd go to the British Museum, sir——" he began.

Mason pointed to the door. He felt that another ten minutes of Inspector Bray would reduce him to a state of imbecility.

He returned to the inspector's room, now littered with a medley of articles which had been removed from the "lodger's" home. There were one or two very important documents which he had found in a tin case, which had been half filled with platinum settings. Searching the box he found tweezers, awls and instruments of the jeweller's art by the dozen. White Face had himself removed the stones from their settings—the wonder is that he had not disposed of the platinum. He must have felt himself perfectly safe under the aegis of old Gregory, whose very honesty was the lodger's best credential.

A diligent search had been made for evidence of firearms, and as

143

a matter of precaution, to the circulation of the description of the wanted man had been added the warning: "May carry a pistol." But there was no proof that he carried anything of the sort. Neither cartridge nor cartridge box was found and, except for the knife, no arms whatsoever.

In the bottom of the cupboard they had unearthed a cardboard box bearing a Lyons label, which was filled with bundles of white cotton gloves, and in another part of the room half a dozen squares of twill into which eyeholes had been roughly cut. To the edge of each was fastened a strip of whalebone and a piece of elastic; the whalebone kept the mask rigid, and the elastic obviously fitted over the ears. Except for the eye-holes they might have been parts of the hangman's ghastly equipment.

White Face was well found in all matters pertaining to dress. There were two new long black coats, obviously of foreign make, three pairs of rubber galoshes, only one pair of which had been used and, most curious of all, a dummy automatic pistol. It was the kind that is used in theatres, was made of wood, and was a lifelike representation of the real article. Until he had picked it up in his hand and had felt its lightness, Mason had been absolutely certain that it was the real thing.

In his own mind he was convinced that White Face had no other weapon and that this was the gun he carried on his unlawful occasions, the weapon which had cowed crowded restaurants and night clubs, and had reduced porters and waiters to trembling jelly.

Elk was half dozing in the room when Mason entered. "Do you know what I think, sir?"

"You thinking, too?" growled Mason. "All right, I'll buy it."

"There's one man who is going to get White Face acquitted. You can look at it any way you like, but it comes back to the same thing. You couldn't work a conviction against him—if Lamborn sticks to his story."

"Oh!" Mason's face fell. "Lamborn—that's the pickpocket. H'm!"

He pondered on the matter for a long time.

"You're quite right, Elk," he said at last. "In the face of what that dirty little thief has said it would be very difficult to get a verdict. When I say 'we couldn't,' we mightn't. It's a shade of odds how the jury would take it."

"The jury," said Mr. Elk oracularly, "is a body or institution which gives everybody the benefit of the doubt except the police. Juries don't think; they deliberate; juries——"

"Don't let us get clever," said Mason. He went out through the charge-room (where he borrowed a key), down a passage lined on one side with yellow cell doors, and stopped before No. 9, pulled back the grating and looked in. Mr. Lamborn was lying uneasily on a plank bed, two blankets drawn up over his shoulders. He was awake, and at the movement of the grating lifted his head.

"Hallo, Lamborn! Sleeping well?"

The thief blinked at him, swung his legs clear of the plank and sat up.

"If there's a law in this country, Mason, you're going to get fired out of the force for this what I might call outrage!"

"Invincible soul," said Mason admiringly. He put the key in the lock and turned it. "Come out and have some coffee with me?"

"Poisoned?" asked Lamborn suspiciously. "A little strychnine— nothing serious," said Mason. He conducted his prisoner along the corridor, handed over the key of the cell to an amused jailer and ushered Lamborn into the little room. At the sight of Elk's bandaged head the prisoner brightened visibly.

"Hallo! Had a coshing?" he asked. "Prayers are answered sometimes! I hope you're not seriously injured, Mr. Elk?"

"He means," interpreted Elk, "that he hopes I'm fatally injured. Sit down, you poor, cheap, butter-fingered whizzer."

"I shouldn't like to see you killed—flowers ain't cheap just now."

Lamborn sat, still smirking, and when the inevitable coffee was brought, half filled a cup with sugar. "Got the murderer?" he asked pleasantly.

"We've got you, Harry," said Mr. Mason in the same tone, and Lamborn snorted.

"You couldn't prove anything against me, except by the well-known perjury methods of the London police. I dare say you'll put half a dozen of your tame noses in the box and swear me life away, but Gawd's in his heaven!"

"Where did you learn that bit?" asked Mason curiously.

Lamborn shrugged his shoulders theatrically.

"When I'm in stir I only read poetry," he explained. "The book lasts longer because you can't understand it."

He sipped noisily at his coffee, put down the cup with a clatter and leaned towards Mason.

"You haven't got a chance of convicting me. I've been thinking it out in the cell."

Mason smiled pityingly.

"The moment you start thinking, Harry, you're lost," he said. "It's like putting a cow on a tight-rope. You're not built for it. I don't want to convict you."

His tone changed: he was so earnest that he carried conviction even to the sceptical hearer.

"All I wanted then, and all I want now, is that you should tell the truth. Have you ever known me to take all this trouble to get a little whizzer a couple of months' hard labour? Use your sense, Lamborn! Does a Superintendent of Scotland Yard, one of the Big Five, come down here to Tidal Basin and waste his night trying to get a conviction against a poor little hook like you? It would be like calling on the Navy to kill an earwig!"

Mr. Lamborn was impressed. The logic was irresistible. He rubbed his chin uneasily.

"Well, it does seem funny," he said.

"Funny? It's ludicrous! There must have been some reason why I wanted you to tell me this, and some reason why I should promise to withdraw the charge against you. You're wide, Lamborn—as wide as any lad in this district. Use your common sense and tell me why I should take all this trouble if I hadn't something behind it."

Lamborn avoided his eyes. "It does seem funny," he said again.

"Then laugh!" growled Elk.

The man was not listening; he was frowning down at the table, obviously making up his mind. He made his decision at last.

"All right, guv'nor, it's a bet!"

He put out his hand and Mason gripped it, and that grip was a pledge, an oath and a covenant.

"I dipped him—yes. I saw him drop and I thought he was soused. I went over and I was knocked out to find he was a swell."

"He was lying on his side, his face away from the lamp, wasn't he?" asked Mason.

The man nodded.

"Just tell me what you did—one moment."

He raised his voice and called for Bray.

"Lie down there, Bray." He pointed to the floor. "I want to reconstruct Lamborn's petty larceny."

Mr. Bray looked with some meaning at Elk.

"Elk can't lie down because of his head," said Mason irritably.

Bray went down on his knees and stretched himself, and Lamborn stood over him.

"I flicked open his coat—so. I put my hand in his inside pocket—"

"Left side or right side?" asked Mason.

"The left side. Then I hooked his clock—his watch, I mean—with my little finger—like this."

His hands moved swiftly. There happened to be a pocket-case in Mr. Bray's inside pocket. It also happened to contain the photograph of a very pretty girl, which fell on the floor. Bray retrieved it quickly and made a wrathful protest.

"And he's married!" was Elk's shocked murmur.

Bray went very red.

"All right, you can get up."

Taking a sheet of paper out of a drawer, Mason began writing quickly. When he had finished he handed the sheet to Lamborn, who read it over and eventually affixed his sprawling signature to the statement.

"Why did you want to know, guv'nor?" he asked. "What's my robbery got to do with the murder?"

Mason smiled.

"You'll read all about it in one of the evening papers—I'll try to arrange that your photograph's published."

Elk laughed hollowly.

"What's the matter with his finger-prints?"

"But why do you want me to tell, Mr. Mason?"

Mason did not explain.

"Release this man, Bray. Mark the charge 'withdrawn.' You'll have to attend the police court tomorrow morning, but you needn't go into the dock."

"It's the only part of it he knows," said Elk *sotto voce*.

Lamborn shook hands forgivingly with the chief and with Elk.

"One thing, Harry," said Mason, and the released prisoner paused at the door. "You'll be given back all your possessions except the jemmy we found in your pocket. I didn't tell you, but I was putting a felony charge against you in the morning—'Loitering with intent.' Congratulations!"

Lamborn made a hurried exit from the police station. Until morning came he lay in his bed, puzzling to find a solution of the strange philosophy of Superintendent Mason, and could discover no answer that was consistent with his knowledge of English police methods.

Chapter 17

Lamborn had hardly left before the superintendent came into the charge-room hurriedly and the police reporter heard his name called.

"Michael, this young lady of yours—what was she at the clinic?"

"I believe she acted as Marford's secretary," said Michael, surprised. And then, anxiously: "You're not going to see her tonight, are you?"

Mason was undecided.

"Yes, I think I will. Somebody ought to be told about the doctor—I mean, somebody that matters. Besides, she may give us some very valuable help."

"What help could she give you?" asked Michael suspiciously.

Mason rolled his head impatiently.

"If you imagine I'm waking her up in the middle of the night on any old excuse for the sake of seeing her in her negligee, you're nattering me. I'm out to find all the threads that lead to and from everybody who has played a part in this crime," he said. "I want to know who were Marford's friends, who were his enemies, and I can think of nobody else who can tell me. She can, because she worked with him, and Elk's got an idea that he was sweet on her."

"Rubbish!" said Michael scornfully. "I don't suppose he ever looked at her twice."

"Once is enough for most men," said Mason. "Are you going to take me up and introduce me?"

When they were huddled up under heavy rugs, for a cold wind made an open car a death trap, Michael gave expression to his fears.

"It's going to be a terrible shock to Janice—Miss Harman."

"Call her Janice: it sounds more friendly. Yes, I suppose it is. Marford is a fellow who got a lot of affection and sympathy without asking for it."

"His body hasn't been found?"

Mason shook his head.

"And it won't be, in spite of the blood. If he'd been dead, White Face would have left him, wouldn't he?"

It was the first encouraging statement Mason had made.

Bury Street was lifeless when the car drew up before the flat, and it was a quarter of an hour before they could arouse the porter. Mason identified himself, and the two men climbed up to the first floor.

The maid was a heavy sleeper; it was Janice who heard the bell and, getting into her dressing-gown, opened the door to them. The first person she saw was Mason, whom she did not recognise.

"Don't be worried, Miss Harman. I have a friend of yours with me."

And then she saw Michael and her alarm was stilled. She took them into the drawing-room, went off to wake her maid (there was something old-ladyish about Janice, Michael decided), and came back to the drawing-room to learn the reason for this visitation.

"I'm afraid I've got rather bad news for you. Miss Harman," said Mason.

Invariably he adapted his tone to the subject of his speech, and he was so melancholy that she thought he could have come only on one subject, the murder of Donald Bateman.

"I know. Mr. Quigley has told me," she said. "You want to ask me about the ring? I gave it——"

He shook his head.

"No. Dr. Marford has disappeared."

She stared at him.

"You mean—he is not hurt?"

"I hope not," said Mason. "I sincerely hope not."

It was remarkable to Michael that this man, whom he had regarded as a stout, unimaginative and fairly commonplace officer of police, could tell the story with such little offence, and suppress so much without losing any of the main facts. She listened: the news was less shocking than that of Bateman's death, but it left her with a deeper heartache, for Marford was one of the ideals which experience and disillusionment had left undisturbed.

"The trouble is, we know nothing about the doctor or any of his friends, and we don't know where to start our inquiries. You were his secretary——"

"No, not his secretary," she corrected. "I kept the accounts of the

149

clinic, and sometimes of the convalescent home, and I was helping him to get Annerford ready—he has been trying for a year to open a tuberculosis institute for the children of Tidal Basin."

"Where is Annerford?" asked Mason, and she told him and described the work which the doctor had set himself to do.

He had planned greatly, it seemed; had, in one of the drawers of his desk, blue prints of a princely building. His appeal to the wealthy public was already typewritten, and he had discussed with her many of the details.

"Now, Miss Harman," said Mason, "you know the people of the clinic. Is there anybody there who had a grudge against the doctor, or did he have any great friend there—man or woman?"

She shook her head.

"There was an elderly nurse and one or two occasional helpers. The staff at Eastbourne consisted of a matron and a nurse. He was trying to raise money to enlarge these homes," she said; "it was always a source of distress to the doctor that the places were understaffed, but they cost an awful lot of money."

"There was nobody at any of these places—the clinic, the home at Eastbourne or at Annerford—who was in the doctor's confidence?"

She smiled at this.

"Not at Annerford. No, I know of nobody. He had no friends." Her lip quivered. "You don't think. . . any harm has come to him?"

Mason did not reply.

"Did Bateman have any friends?" he asked.

She considered the question.

"Yes, there was a man who came over with him from South Africa, but he never mentioned his name. The only other person he seemed to know was Dr. Rudd."

Mason opened his eyes wide. "Dr. Rudd?" he said. "Are you sure?"

She nodded. She told him the story of the dinner and Bateman's perturbation when he had seen the doctor, resplendent in evening dress.

"That certainly beats me. Where could he have met Rudd?" said Mason. "All gay and beautiful, was he—the doctor, I mean? Yes, I knew he knocked about a little bit in the West End, but I didn't realise—h'm!"

He looked down at the carpet for a long time, deep in thought.

"Yes," he said suddenly. "Of course. I understand now. Naturally he didn't want to meet Rudd."

He looked at Michael quizzically.

"Are you going to stay to breakfast?" he asked, and Michael returned an indignant denial.

"You'd better go down to Tidal Basin and wait for me. I'm only calling at Scotland Yard to check up a few dates; I'll be with you in an hour. I'm sending a police car back—you can use that."

★★★★★★

White Face waited patiently for daylight. He had changed his clothes, and the suit he wore now would attract no attention when he lined up at Forest Gate for his *char-a-banc* ticket to the coast. Once or twice he went in to see his unwilling companion, and on each occasion found the doctor sleeping peacefully.

From his pocket he took an evening paper which he had not had time to read before. There was quite a lot about White Face, of course. He was a star turn in those days. Great authors, who catered exclusively for the intelligentsia, stepped down from their high pedestals to speculate upon what one called "this amusing malefactor." The Howdah affair was still topical. There was a revival of the "Devil of Tidal Basin"; some gross plagiarist had attempted to revitalise the myth, but it needed Michael Quigley's skilful touch to make it live.

He dropped the paper on to the table, walked out into the open and stood listening. From far away he could hear the sound of distant motor-cars, and whilst he stood there, he saw a white magnesium rocket, probably a Verey light, flame in the air and die. So the police had put on the barrage! He knew that signal. A suspected car had been seen, and the white flare was the order to the nearest police control to stop and search it. Ingenious people, the London police, in their quiet untheatrical way. Very difficult, very dangerous to fool with. And yet they were not men of education—just common policemen who had raised themselves out of the rut, established their own little hierarchy, and attained by some extraordinary method a complete efficiency.

He did not despise them nor did he fear them. The odds against his escaping were twenty to one—there was enough of the gambler in him to fancy his chance.

No man who was wanted, and whose photograph was procurable, had ever escaped from England. Perhaps some did, but the police never admitted the exceptions.

As he came back along the passage he heard a faint voice call from the open door of the darkened room.

"Can I have some water, please?"

He carried a glass in to the doctor, who drank it and thanked him.

"You're in considerable danger, my friend. I hope you realise that?" said the voice from the sofa weakly.

"My dear Doctor, I have been in danger for quite a long time—go to sleep, and don't worry about me."

He waited till he heard the doctor's regular breathing, and then came out, closing the door softly behind him.

Danger! It had no significance for White Face. He feared nothing, literally and figuratively feared nothing. He did not regret one act of his life; regretted least of all that which had sent Donald Bateman into nothingness. Perhaps Walter would not have approved, but then Walter was weak—a daring man, but weak. White Face approved his own deed, which approval was more important than self-glorification.

Poor old Gregory! As for the doctor, he would put water and some kind of refreshment ready to his hand. In the morning he would be well enough to drive the taxi to the nearest police station.

Only one regret he had, and that he did not allow his mind to rest upon. But to give up life was an easy matter if necessity arose; with life one surrendered all aspirations.

He had finished his shaving, using cream instead of soap and water, when he heard a footstep in the passage. The doctor, then, was awake; that was unfortunate. He took one step towards the door when it opened. Mason stood there; an untidy Mason with his hat on the back of his head and his overcoat unfastened.

"I took the liberty of coming through a back window; most of them are open," he said. "I want you, of course."

"Naturally," said White Face. There was no tremor in his voice. "You'll find the doctor in the next room. I don't think there's very much the matter with him."

He held out his hands, but Mason shook his head.

"Handcuffs are old-fashioned. Have you got a gun?"

White Face shook his head.

"Then we'll step along," said Mason politely, and guided him by the arm into the darkness outside.

Stopping to despatch his men to look after the doctor, he led his prisoner to where the police car was waiting.

"You weren't seen, but you were heard," he explained.

White Face laughed.

"A taxicab in low gear is a menace to the security of the criminal classes," he said lightly.

Chapter 18

There was a complete dearth of news when Michael Quigley reached the station. Negative reports are never sent to minor stations, and the absence of anything positive was sufficient to indicate that the search for the missing taxicab had so far been fruitless.

To kill time he wandered up and down the streets, revisited the scene of the murder, would have gone again to Gallows Court for news, if Gallows Court had not come out to meet him.

Michael was turning over the mud in the gutter with the toe of his boot when he saw the odd figure of the crazy man crossing the road. This strange apparition had one curious (and welcome) characteristic. He avoided the light, and no sooner had he come within the range of the arc lamp, than he halted and half turned away from its searching beams.

"Come over here, reporter! I've got something to tell you."

"You can tell me your name to start with."

The oddity chuckled. "I ain't got a name. My parents forgot to give me one." (This astounding statement, Michael discovered was true.) "People call me anything they like—Shoey, some of 'em, because I used to black shoes."

"What have you got to tell me?" asked Michael.

"He took the doctor away."

He said this in a hoarse whisper.

"Who—White Face?"

Shoey nodded violently.

"I've got all the rights of it now. He took him in his cab—he was layin' there on the floor and nobody knew."

He doubled up with silent laughter and slapped his knees in an agony of enjoyment.

"That makes me laugh! Mason don't know! All these clever busies from Scotland Yard, and they don't know that!"

"What are the 'rights of it'?" asked Michael.

Sometimes, Mason had said, this strange creature was nearer to the truth than a saner man.

"Elk knows."

The man without a name stuck a grimy forefinger into Michael's ribs to point his remark.

"That fellow's wider than Broad Street. Elk! I'll bet you he knowed all the time! But he likes to keep things to hisself until he's got 'em all cleared up. I've heard Bray say that—Bray's got no more brains than a rabbit," he added.

Somebody was walking along the sidewalk towards them.

"That's him!" whispered the ragged object and melted across the street.

Bray was at such a distance that it seemed impossible for anybody to recognise that it was he. It appeared that he was walking off a grievance.

"As soon as this affair is over I'm going to put things straight," he said aggressively. "Mason really shouldn't do it! You understand, Quigley, that an officer of my rank has his position to uphold; and how can I uphold it if important inquiries are placed in the hands of subordinates? Insubordinates, I call 'em!"

"What's Elk been doing now?"

There was no need to ask who was the offender.

"Mason is a good fellow," Bray went on, "one of the best men in the force and one of the cutest. It you ever get a chance of dropping a hint that I said that, I'd be obliged, Quigley. You needn't make a point of repeating the conversation, but just mention it accidentally—he takes a lot of notice of what you say. But he's altogether wrong about Elk. Evil," he went on poetically, "is wrought by want of thought as well as want of heart—"

"Shakespeare?" murmured Michael.

"I dare say," said Bray, who had no idea that American citizens wrote poetry. "Mason does these things thoughtlessly. I told him I was willing to cross-examine this woman as soon as she came round and was in a fit state to talk. But no, Elk must do it! Elk knows her, apparently. But I ask you, Quigley, is it necessary to know a person before you question 'em? Was I properly introduced to Lamborn—there's another scandal; he's out on bail!"

To shorten the length of the grievance, Michael suggested that they should walk back together to the station. They arrived at an interesting time for Inspector Bray, because Lorna Weston had decided to talk.

She had refused to go into the inspector's office, and was seated in the charge-room, the bandaged Elk towering over her. Michael could see that it was not his but Bray's presence which brought that demoniacal frown to the sergeant's face when they appeared.

"All right, let's have all the press in, Bray," he said savagely. "Won't you come into the private office, Mrs. Weston?"

"No, I won't." The pale-faced woman was determined on the point. "I'll say what I want to say here."

"All right," said Elk grimly. And to Shale, who was the stenographer of the party: "Get your book. You're known as Lorna Weston," he began, "and you're the wife of——?"

She had parted her lips to speak when Mason came in briskly; behind him came two detectives and between them walked their prisoner.

Lorna Weston came up to her feet, her eyes fixed upon the smiling man who stood between the two guards—unconcerned, perfectly at his ease, not by so much as the droop of an eye betraying consciousness of his deadly peril.

"There he is! There he is!" she shrieked, pointing at him. "The murderer! You killed him! You said you would if you ever met him, and you did it!"

Mason watched the prisoner curiously, but he made no response.

"It wasn't for me you hated him. It wasn't because he took me away from you—it was because of your brother who died in prison."

The man nodded.

"It was because of that," he said simply. "If he could be brought to life and I were free, I'd kill him again."

"Do you hear him?" she shrieked. "My husband—Tommy Furse!"

"Call me by my real name," said the other. "Thomas Marford! It is a pretty good name, though it has been borne by some pretty bad people."

He turned smilingly to Mason.

"You won't want this lady, I think? I can tell you all you wish to know, and I will clear up any point which may seem to you to be obscure."

Michael Quigley stood petrified, unable to speak or move. Marford! This self-possessed man...White Face...hold-up man, murderer. ..He must be dreaming. But no, here was the reality.

Marford, as unemotional as the crowd of detectives who stood around him, was twiddling his watch-chain, looking half amused, half pityingly at the shivering woman who called herself his wife.

He was evidently considering something else than his own position.

"I hope Dr. Rudd will feel no ill-effects from his unhappy experience," he said. "As I told you earlier in the morning, I don't think he will suffer anything worse than a headache, which he can easily remedy. He has been in my garage all the night. You see," he was almost apologetic, "Rudd had a theory, which was to me a very dangerous theory on the lips of a rather loquacious and not terribly clever man. His view, which he was developing most uncomfortably, was that there was only one person who could possibly have killed Bateman—and that was myself! He thought it was a huge joke, but it wasn't a joke to me; and when he called in at my surgery on the way to the station to put his ideas before you, I realised at once that I was in considerable danger. I realised more than this," he added calmly, "that my life's work was done, that my clinic and my convalescent home and my new rest-house at Annerford—how did you find your way to Annerford Farm, by the way? But perhaps you wouldn't like to tell me—were things of the past, and that I must save myself at all costs."

He looked round and caught Elk's eye and shook his head sadly.

"I had to do it, Elk. I'm terribly sorry. You're the last man in the world I would have hurt."

To Mason's surprise, Elk grinned amiably.

"I don't know anyone I'd rather take a coshing from," he said handsomely.

"You were a dangerous man, too," smiled Marford, "but I couldn't give you a whisky and soda with a little shot of drug in it, as I gave to Dr. Rudd. Just enough to put him under for a few minutes. What I did then was to dope him and put him in the garage. I was afraid he had betrayed me later, when I heard him groaning. You probably heard him groaning, too; I think you mentioned the fact to me?"

He addressed the reporter, and Michael remembered the noise he had heard as he had moved through Gallows Court in the dead of the night.

"There is one other matter I'm concerned about—how is old Gregory? I'm afraid he's taken it rather badly."

He talked fluently enough, but with a little slur in his voice. It was the first time Mason had noticed that he had an impediment of speech which caused him to lisp a little. "I'm rather anxious you should take my statement now."

Mason nodded.

"I must caution you, Dr. Marford—I suppose you are a doctor, Marford?"

Marford inclined his head.

"Yes, I am qualified: lay anything to my door but the charge of being a quack! You can confirm this by a visit to my surgery, where you will find the certificates."

"I have to warn you," Mason went on conventionally, "that what you now say may be taken down and used at your trial."

"That I understand," said Marford.

He looked at his wife; she had approached more closely to him; her dark eyes were blazing with hate; the straight, white mouth was bloodless.

"You'll hang for this, Tommy!" she breathed. "Oh, God, I'm glad—you'll hang for it!"

"Why not?" he asked coolly, and, turning on his heels, followed Mason into the inspector's office.

"A nice woman," was his only comment on his wife's outburst. "Her loyalty to her unfortunate friend is almost touching—but then, loyalty invariably is. I cannot let myself think about poor Gregory Wicks."

He was sincere: Mason had no doubt of it. There was no cynicism in his tone. Whatever else he might be, Thomas Marford was not a hypocrite.

Mason offered him a glass of water, which he refused.

He sat down by the side of the writing-table; his only request was that somebody should open a window, for the room was unpleasantly crowded. And then he told his story. He did not refuse a cigarette, but through most of the narrative he held it and its many successors between his fingers and only occasionally raised it to his lips.

"Are you ready?" he asked, and Sergeant Shale, who had opened a new notebook, tested his fountain pen and nodded.

Chapter 19

"One always tries to find a beginning to these stories" said Dr. Marford, "and usually one chooses to enumerate the virtues and describe the splendid domestic qualities of one's father and mother. That I do not purpose doing, for many reasons.

"My brother and I were left orphans at an early age. I was at a preparatory school when Walter went out to Australia to try his luck. He was a decent fellow, the best brother any man could wish to have. The little money that came to us from the sale of my father's practice—oh, yes, he was a doctor—he put in the hands of a lawyer for my education. He hadn't been in Australia long before he found work, and half his salary used to come to the lawyer every month.

"I don't know what date his criminal career began, but when I was about fifteen I had a letter from him, asking me to address all future letters to 'Walter Furse.' He was then in Perth, Western Australia. His full name was Walter Furse Marford. Naturally, I did as I was asked, and soon after larger monthly sums came to the lawyer and were very welcome, for I had been living practically without pocket money, and my clothes were the scorn of the school.

"By this time I was at a high school, or, as they call it in England, a public school, which I shall also refrain from mentioning, because every public schoolboy has a sneaking pride in his school. One day the lawyer came to see me. He asked me whether I had heard from my brother, and I told him I had not had a letter from him for four months. He told me that he was in a similar case, but that, previous to my brother's ceasing to correspond, he had sent a thousand pounds. But all the lawyer's letters asking how he would like this money invested had been unanswered. I was a little alarmed, naturally, because I had a very deep affection for Walter, and realised, as I had grown older, just what I owed to him. I was to go to a hospital and take up the profession of my father—it was my brother's money which made this possible.

"The mystery of Walter's silence was explained when I received, in a roundabout way, a letter which had been sent to a friend of his, and which was by him transmitted to me. It was written on blue paper, and when I saw on the heading the name of an Australian convict prison I nearly fainted. But it was the truth: Walter hid nothing in the letter, though in justice to him it contained no cant of repentance. He had been arrested after holding up a bank, where he and his gang had got away with nearly twenty thousand pounds. He asked me to think as well of him as I could, and said that he was telling me because he was afraid the authorities might trace me, and I should hear from some unsympathetic person the story of his fall.

"I will tell the truth. After the first shock I was not horrified at the revelation. Walter had always been an adventurous sort, and at my age I had that touch of romanticism which exaggerates certain picturesque types of crime into deeds almost worthy of a Paladin. My reaction to the blow was that I felt an increasing love for the man who had made such sacrifices and had taken such risks in order to fit his brother for membership of a noble profession.

"I exalted him above all men, and I yet do. But for the burden which my education and living imposed upon him, he could have afforded to live honestly, and I know, though he never told me, that I and I alone was responsible for his entering into the crooked path.

"The letter which I sent to him was, I am afraid, rather disjointed, and had in it a suggestion of hero-worship, for when he was released from prison he answered me very straightly; pointed out that there was nothing admirable in what he was doing, and that he would sooner see me dead than go the way he had gone.

"I worked like the devil at the hospital, determined to justify his sacrifice, if it could be justified. From time to time he wrote me, now from Melbourne, once from Brisbane, several times from a town in New South Wales, the name of which I cannot at the moment recall. Apparently he was going straight, for there were no delays in his letters; he told me that he was thinking of buying a 'station,' that he had already acquired a house and a few hundred acres in the hope to extend these by the purchase of other land.

"It was in this letter that I first heard of Donald Bateman. He said that he had met a very clever crook and had nearly been caught by him in connection with a land deal, but that a mutual friend, who had been in prison with Walter, had made them known to one another, Bateman had apologised, and they were now chums.

"Bateman apparently made his money out of persuading innocent purchasers to put up a deposit on imaginary properties, but he did a little other crook work on the side, and was one of the best-informed men in Australia on one topic—the security and deposit of banks. He himself was not a bank robber, but he supplied the various gangs with exact information which enabled them to operate at a minimum risk. Usually he stood in for his corner—by which I mean——"

"I know what you mean," said Mason.

"As soon as my final examinations were over Walter wanted me to come out to Australia and stay with him for six months, to discuss future plans. He asked me if I would mind adopting the name of Furse. He said he could arrange to get me my passport and ticket in that name. The only awkward point about this arrangement was that my examinations finished on the Friday, I was to leave for Australia on the Saturday, and I could not know the result of the exams, except by letter. I arranged, however, with the manager of the bank which carried my account to have the certificates addressed care of the bank and for him to send them on to an address which my brother had given me. I had to invent a family reason why I was calling myself Furse in Australia, and he seemed satisfied.

"The work at the hospital grew increasingly hard. The last days of the examination came, and on the Friday I handed in my final papers with a heartfelt sense of thankfulness. The results would not be known for some weeks, but I had a pretty good idea that I had passed except in one subject. As it happened, my highest marks were for the subject in which I thought I had failed!

"The next morning, as happy as a child, I drove off to St. Pancras and Tilbury, and on the Saturday afternoon was steaming down the Channel, so excited that I hardly knew what to do with myself.

"The boat had a full complement of passengers. I was travelling second-class, because, although my brother had sent the first-class fare, I wanted to save him as much as possible, and second-class on a P. & O. steamer is extraordinarily comfortable,

"This particular ship was crowded with people, the majority of whom were bound for India and quite a number for Colombo. We dropped the Indian passengers at Port Said or Suez—I'm not sure which—and now that the dining-room was thinned out and there was space to walk about the decks, one began to take notice of one's

161

fellow passengers.

"I had seen Lorna Weston the day we left England, but I did not speak to her until we were passing through the Suez Canal, and then only to exchange a few words about the scenery.

"It was at Colombo, where we both went ashore, that I came to know her. She was very pretty and vivacious, and was, she told me, travelling to Australia to take a position as nursery governess. Looking back from my present age, I can see that, if I had had more experience of life, I should have known she was much too young for the job, and should have guessed, what I later knew, that she was going out in the hope of finding easy money.

"I told her very little about myself, except that I was a medical student, but for some reason or other she got it into her head that I was a wealthy young man or had wealthy relatives. She may have got this idea because I was travelling second from choice, or because I had a lot of money in my possession—I had a couple of hundred pounds in notes which I had managed to save from my allowance. I had an idiotic idea that it would please Walter if I handed him back this colossal sum, as it appeared to me, out of the money he had so generously sent me.

"If you know anything about ship travel you will understand that it takes no more than a few days for an ordinary friendship between a young man and a girl to develop into a raging passion. We were not five days out of Colombo when, if she had asked me to jump over the side of the ship, I should have obeyed. I adored her. I loved her, and she loved me. So we told each other. I'm not complaining about her, I'm not reproaching her, and I don't want to say one single word that's going to make life any harder for her, except that I must tell the truth to explain why she was living in Tidal Basin.

"She only loved one man in her life, and that was Bateman. I say this without bitterness or hatred. She probably loved the worst man she has ever met or is ever destined to meet. It is not necessary for me to tell you what happened during the remainder of the voyage. I had moments of exaltation, of despair, or I resolve, or terrible depression. I wondered what Walter would say when I told him that at the outset of my career, before I was in a position to earn a penny, I had engaged myself to a girl who had been a perfect stranger to me when I went on board.

"He came down to the dock to meet me, and I introduced him to Lorna, but I did not tell him of my intentions until we were back in the hotel where he was staying and where he had rented a room for me. To my surprise, he took it very well.

"'You're a bit young, Tommy, but I'm not so sure that it's a bad thing for you. If I had married I mightn't have made such a fool of myself. But don't you think you could wait for a year?'

"I told him there were imperative reasons why we should marry almost at once, and his face fell.

"'She told you that, I suppose? She may be mistaken.'

"But I couldn't argue the matter, and after a while Walter agreed.

"'I'm going through a pretty bad time,' he said. 'I've been speculating on the Stock Exchange, and I've lost quite a lot of money racing. But things will take a turn soon, and you shall have the best wedding present that money can buy.'

"How bad was his financial position I only discovered by accident. He had sold his little property and for the moment was without occupation. His prison life had naturally brought him into contact with all sorts of undesirables, but so far he had resisted their solicitations, and had steered a straight path.

"Walter was not a strong character. Viewed dispassionately, he was a weakling, because he invariably took the easiest route. But he had the heart of a good woman, and I can't help feeling that again it was to make some provision for me that he fell back into his old ways. In fact, I am sure of it. His wedding present to me was five hundred pounds, and it didn't make me a bit happy, because I had read in the papers that a country bank had been stuck up the day before and a considerable sum of money had been stolen. In fact, I taxed him with it, but he laughed it off.

"It was a few days after the wedding that I made up my mind. I left Lorna at the hotel and went in search of Walter. I found him in a restaurant which was also a bar, and that was the first time I met Donald Bateman. Bateman went out, and I took this opportunity to put forward my proposal, which was no less than that I should share a little of his risk.

"'You're mad,' he said, when it dawned upon him what I meant.

"I suppose I was. But if I were to analyse my motive from the standpoint of my experience, I should say I was no more than stupidly quixotic. He wouldn't hear of it, but I insisted.

"'You've been taking these risks for me all these years. You've suffered imprisonment. Every time you go out on one of your adventures you stand the risk of being killed. Let me take a little of it.'

"Bateman came back at that moment, and I realised he was well in Walter's confidence. I tried to put the matter hypothetically to Bateman, without betraying myself and Walter, but it was a fairly childish effort, and he saw through it at once.

"'Why not, Walter? It's better than taking in any of these roustabouts—Grayling or the Dutchman. Besides, he's a gentleman, and nobody would imagine he was a member of a gang of crooks.'

"Walter was furious, but his fury did not last long: he was, as I say, weak, though I'm not blaming him, for, if he had refused, I believe I should have gone off and stuck up a bank of my own out of sheer bravado.

"We all three went back to the hotel, and I introduced my wife to Bateman. He was a good-looking fellow in those days and terribly popular with women; the worse they were the more was the fascination he seemed to exercise. Although I was only a kid, I could see she was tremendously attracted by him, and the next day, when I went out with Walter to talk matters over with him, I came back to find that Bateman had lunched with her, and thereafter they hardly left one another. I wasn't jealous; I'd got over my first madness and realised that I'd made a ghastly mistake.

"Naturally, I didn't want any complications with Bateman, who I knew was married and had left his wife in England. As a matter of fact, he was married before he met and married the present Mrs. Landor—the lady who came to my surgery on the night I killed Bateman and told me, to my amazement—however, that can wait.

"Walter at last agreed that I should stand in and help him with the robbery of a country bank which carried a considerable amount of paper currency, especially during week-ends. The job was to be done 'two-handed,' as we say, and Bateman, of course, took no part in the actual hold-up, but was the man who spied out the land, supplied us with all particulars as to the movements and habits of the staff, and could discover, in some way I've never understood, almost to a pound how much cash reserve a branch office was holding.

"It was a little town about sixty-five miles from Melbourne, and Walter and I drove out overnight in a motorcar and stayed with a friend of his till morning. Naturally I was wild with excitement, and I was all for carrying a gun. Walter wouldn't hear of this. He never carried firearms, the only pistol he used being a dummy—that was a lesson I never forgot.

"'You're either going to murder or you're not going to murder,' said Walter. 'If you're going out to rob, a dummy pistol's as good as any. It's its persuasive power and its frightening power that are important.'

"He was a man of extraordinary principles, and held very strong views on criminals who used firearms.

"'It's the job of a bank official to defend his property, and if you kill him you're a coward,' he said. 'It's the job of a copper to arrest you, and if you shoot at him you're a blackguard.'

"But he had no especial affection for the police; no faith in them; and before we went out, he had insisted on my having all my pockets sewn up with strong packthread.

"'You only want a handkerchief, and you can carry that in your sleeve,' he said.

"I didn't see why he took this precaution, until he explained that it was not unusual, if the police caught a prisoner, to slip a gun into his pocket in order to get him a longer sentence. I don't know whether this was true. It may be one of the yarns that crooks invent and believe in.

"We carried our dummy pistols in a belt under our waistcoats. You'll find all the particulars of the raid we made upon the branch bank, in a little scrap-book in my bedroom. It was successful. At the appointed minute we entered the bank with white masks on our faces; I held up the cashier and his assistant with my dummy pistol whilst Walter passed round the counter, pulled the safe open—it was already unfastened—and took out three bundles of notes. We were out of the town before the police had wakened up from their midday sleep.

"We came back to Melbourne by a circuitous route, and I'll swear there was nobody in the town who would have recognised us or who could have identified us in any way That evening the Melbourne papers were full of the robbery, and announced that the Bank of Australasia were offering five thousand pounds for the arrest of the robbers, and this was supplemented by a statement issued on behalf of the Government, through the police, that a free pardon would be granted to any person, other than one of the perpetrators, or any accomplice, who might turn King's Evidence. Walter was worried about this notice. He knew Donald Bateman better than I.

"'If he gets the reward as well as the pardon, we're cooked,' he said, and when he put through a telephone inquiry to the newspaper office and heard that the reward was to go to anybody, accomplice or not, he went white.

"'Go and find your wife, Tommy,' he said. 'We've got to slip out of this town quick! There's a boat leaving for San Francisco this afternoon. We might both go on that. I'll see the purser and we can travel in different classes.'

"I went to the hotel, but Lorna was out; the porter told me she had gone with Mr. Bateman to the races, and I returned to Walter and told him.

"'Maybe he won't see the offer until after the races are over. That is our only chance,' he said. 'You'd better leave her a note and some money, tell her you'll let her know where she can join you.'

"Returning to the hotel, I packed a few things and wrote the note. When I walked out of the elevator into the vestibule, the first person I saw was Big Jock Riley, Chief of the Melbourne Detective Service. I only knew him because he'd been pointed out to me as a man to avoid. I'll say this about him—he's dead now, poor chap!—that he was a decent fellow. I knew what was going to happen when he came towards me and took the suit-case out of my hand and gave it to another man.

"'You'd better pay your bill, Tommy,' he said. 'It will save everybody a lot of bother.'

"He went with me to the cashier, and I paid the bill, and then he took me to a taxi and we drove to the police station. The first person I saw when I got in was Walter. They'd taken him soon after I had left, and I learnt that I had been followed to the hotel, and they had only waited until I had collected my kit before they arrested me. That was one of Riley's peculiarities, that he made all crooks pay their hotel bills before he arrested them. They said that his wife owned three hotels in Melbourne, but that is probably another invention.

"The police found most of the money—not all, for Walter had planted four thousand pounds, and had paid two thousand to Bateman, which Bateman returned when he found he was going to get the five thousand reward.

"Bateman was the informer, of course. He hadn't gone to the races: he was sitting in another room at the police office when we were brought in, and he came out to identify us. Walter said nothing; he didn't look at him. I think he must have had a premonition that this had been his last day of freedom, he was so utterly broken and dejected. But I met Bateman's eyes, and he knew that if ever he and I met, there would be a reckoning. Is that melodramatic? I'm afraid it is.

"There's very little to tell about the court proceedings. The prosecution was fair, and we were sentenced, Walter to eight years and I to three. I never saw Walter after we left the cells until I was taken to the prison hospital where he was dying. He was too far gone to recognise me. Riley was there; he'd come to see if he could get any information about the four thousand that was *cached*. He told me, while I was waiting to be taken back, that if I would tell him he would get me a year's remission of my sentence. I was so utterly miserable that I was on the point of telling him, but I thought better of it, and told him only half the truth.

"There was two thousand planted in one place and two thousand in another. I needn't tell you where, but one was a respectable bank. I told him the hardest, and I believe he went away and recovered it, because within a week I had my order of release. Riley never broke a promise.

"I hung around Melbourne for a month. I didn't have to look for Lorna: I knew she'd gone—you get news in prison—and that Bateman had gone with her. That didn't worry me at all. I was certain that Bateman and I would meet sooner or later. It's curious how Walter's warning always stayed with me. I have never owned a pistol in my life, and even in my most revengeful mood I never dreamt of buying one.

"The police left me alone when I came out. Riley may have suspected that there was more money to collect, but probably he wasn't bothering his head about that. I had had all my English letters sent to a certain address in Melbourne, and when I went to this place I found a dozen old bills, receipts, letters from hospital friends, and a long envelope.

"Sometimes when I was in prison I used to wonder what had been the result of those examinations, but after a time I ceased to take any interest in them. It seemed that whatever honest career I had had was finished. I should be struck off the Medical Register on conviction, and that was the end of my doctoring. I didn't realise that the Australian authorities knew nothing of 'Marford'—knew only Tommy Furse—and it was only when I opened the envelope and took out the stiff parchment certificate that the truth dawned on me. In England I was Dr. Marford, a duly and properly qualified medical man. I could begin practice at once. A new and wonderful *vista* was opened, for I was terribly keen on my work, and had determined to specialise in the diseases of childhood.

"I collected the two thousand, and after a reasonable interval left Australia for England, travelling third class as far as Colombo and transferring to first class from that port. It was a little too sultry in the steerage, and I could afford better accommodation. I stopped off in Egypt; I wanted to break completely all association with Australia, to snap the links of acquaintanceship formed on the ship which might extend to somebody who knew me and my record. In Cairo I presented my credentials to the British Minister, obtained a new passport in place of one which I said I'd lost, and travelled overland through Italy and Switzerland, arriving in London at the end of September.

"My intentions were to buy a small practice, and I had no sooner arrived in London than I called on an agent, who promised me very considerable help, said he had the very thing for me, but who proved to be worse than useless, submitting propositions which I could not afford to buy or country practices which I knew I could not keep. Country people are very conservative where doctors are concerned, and do not trust any medical man until he has grown a white beard or lost his eyesight."

"I decided to build up a practice of my own in London. I had fifteen hundred pounds left of my money, and by a system of strict economy I knew I could live for five years without a patient—three years if I carried out my big plan, which was to establish a sunlight clinic for babies. I have always had a natural enthusiasm for work amongst children. I love children, and if I had not been interrupted by Donald Bateman and my wife, I should within a few years have opened a great institution, which would have cost twenty thousand pounds to build and ten thousand a year to maintain. That was my ambition.

"It is common knowledge that I opened a surgery in Endley Street and started my practice as cheaply as any practice has ever been founded. From the first I was successful in obtaining patients. They were of the cheapest kind, and required nineteen shillings back for every pound they spent, but it was interesting work, and in a burst of enthusiasm I arranged to open my first clinic at the farther end of Endley Street. I reckoned that by the practice of the strictest economy I could live on the earnings from my practice, and that the money I had so carefully hoarded could keep the clinic running for two years.

"And then one day a thunderbolt fell. A woman walked into my consulting-room. At the time I was at my desk, writing a prescription for a patient who had seen me a few minutes before. I saw her sit down without looking at her; and then, as I asked, 'What can I do for you?' I looked up—into the eyes of Lorna Marford, my wife!

"I had forgotten her. That is no exaggeration. Literally she had passed out of my life and out of my memory. I had half forgotten

Donald Bateman. For a moment I did not recognise her, and then she smiled, and my heart felt like a piece of lead.

"'What do you want?' I asked.

"She was very poorly dressed and shabby-looking, and was lodging at that time with a Mrs. Albert. She was, she told me, three or four weeks behind with her rent.

"'I want money,' she said coolly.

"'Isn't there a man called Bateman?' I asked.

"She laughed at this and made a little gesture. I knew from that that she was still fond of him, and that he'd left her.

"'Bateman's gone. He and I have not seen each other for over two years,' she said.

"She told me the kind of life she had been living, how she had been forced into a slum by sheer poverty. I felt sorry for her—I find it very easy to be sorry for women. But I remembered also that she had taken her share of the blood money, and had probably helped in our betrayal. There were a lot of little happenings that I remembered afterwards in prison which gave colour to this view. And I remembered Walter, dying in a prison hospital, so friendless, so lonely, so heartbroken.

"'You'll get no money from me,' I said. 'You had your share of the reward, I suppose?'

"'I had a bit of it,' she answered coolly. 'Not so much as I deserved. The police would never have found your white masks but for me.'

"Her coolness took my breath away. I got up from the table and opened the door.

"'You can go,' I said, but she did not stir.

"'I want a hundred pounds,' she said. 'I'm sick of living in poverty.'

"I could only look at her; I was speechless.

"'Why should I give you a hundred pounds, supposing I had it?'

"'Because,' she answered slowly, 'if you don't give me a hundred pounds I shall tell somebody that you are an ex-convict. And then where will you be—doctor?'

"From that day onwards she blackmailed me. Within three months I had only half the money that I had put aside for the clinic, and I had committed myself to twice as much: ordered lamps, beds, structural alterations, and had practically placed myself under an obligation to buy the premises in five years' time.

"If I could have got her to leave the neighbourhood I might have had some respite; but though I was giving her a big sum every week, and she could have lived in comfort in the West End, she insisted, when she changed her lodgings, upon taking rooms locally, and upon these she spent a sum equivalent to my yearly income.

"Why she refused to live somewhere else I did not know. It puzzled me, until one day there flashed upon me the solution. She believed that sooner or later I should meet Donald Bateman—she wanted to be on hand to watch every movement of mine, so that she might save her lover. She may have had a premonition. That phenomenon is outside the ambit of my knowledge. I am a physiologist; mental and psychic phenomena I know nothing about.

"It seemed there was not one chance in a million that I should ever see Donald Bateman again. Suppose he came to London, what likelihood was there that he should come to such an out-of-the—way spot as Tidal Basin? And yet I had met with some odd coincidences. The very first doctor I met, when I came to the place, was Dr. Rudd—and I had heard Bateman speak of Rudd. Rudd had been prison doctor at a county jail where Bateman had served two years' hard labour! I remembered the name and the description the moment I saw him. It is quite possible that he also saw the doctor in London, but of that I know nothing. He hated Rudd, who had been the cause of his getting extra punishment for malingering whilst he was in prison, and he often described him—unflatteringly, but, I must say, faithfully.

"The demands from the clinic increased with the growth of my ambition. I was desperately hard pressed for money. On the one hand, by the legitimate expansion of my experiment, on the other by the increasing demands from Lorna.

"I don't know what gave me the idea; I rather think it was the pathetic distress of old Gregory Wicks when I told him that he could never take out his cab again except at the gravest risk to himself and to the community. He was nearly blind, and his misery at the idea of surrendering the licence he had held for fifty-five years touched me. I thought how useful a taxicab might be, and how easily one might make up as Gregory. One thought suggested another, and when the idea took definite shape I was thrilled by the prospect. Isn't there a legend of an old highwayman who robbed the rich to give to the poor? That would not have amused me; but to take toll of those wealthy people who had ignored the appeals I had hectographed and posted broadcast, and use the money to extend my clinic—that was a fantastic but a fascinating thought.

"I don't think I was ever completely happy until I began my raids. I planned everything, spent nights in the West End, observing, timing and arranging my first coup. I invented, for the benefit of Gregory Wicks, a fictitious convict who could not obtain a licence, but who was a good and careful driver. I took lodgings for him in Gregory's house, and the old man was delighted. It is not true that he never allowed another man to take out the cab. He is colossally vain of his own individuality, poor old fellow, and the idea that somebody would go out looking very much like him, ply for hire and keep alive the traditions of his taciturnity and his hardihood appealed to the simple man. Only one stipulation he made, and it was that his substitute should place himself under a solemn vow to return any lost property he found in the cab. He was inordinately proud of his record.

"The first raid was ridiculously simple. I took my taxicab to the vicinity of a restaurant where smart people go to supper, and, walking boldly into the hall, I held up the room with a dummy pistol and got away with the jewels of a large, florid woman. I have no regrets. She is probably not starving, for I left on her person considerably over ten thousand pounds' worth of diamonds.

"The underworld had given me its confidence. I knew a receiver in Antwerp and another in Birmingham, with whom I could place the stones, and the first coup gave me enough money to completely re-equip the clinic and to open my Eastbourne convalescent home.

"But I had reckoned without Lorna. She had read an account of the stick-up, and it so happened that, unknown to me, she had witnessed my return. She came the next morning and demanded her share. Subsequently I gave her nearly a thousand pounds. I should have hated her if I was not a philosopher. It was much easier for me to pretend she had no existence.

"The second and third raids were as successful as the first. I paid Lorna her share. She was now the talk of the neighbourhood, with her smart dresses. She paid visits to the West End in hired cars and was probably living more expensively than she had ever lived in her life.

"If I had any qualms about the work on which I was engaged, they were caused by my association with a girl who shall be nameless. I seldom spoke to her. She was largely a creature of dreams: her sweetness and her purity were all the more transcendent in contrast with the character of my wife.

"Of Bateman I had seen nothing. I had no idea that he was in England and that Lorna had met him by accident in the West End and had asked him to come down and see her. The first mention of him I had came one night when I was visited at my surgery by a lady who was under the impression that her husband had been engaged in a fight and had killed his assailant. She was hysterical, and in her hysteria she took me into her confidence, told me of a man who was blackmailing her, mentioned his name—Donald Bateman! When I heard it the room seemed to spin round. Bateman was in England—was in that very neighbourhood! Imagine the devil that took possession of me.

"She grew calm when I assured her that the two men who had been fighting were labourers from the docks, and she went away, leaving me in a kind of passive delirium. I was almost incapable of thinking reasonably. The old loathing for the informer had come back to me. I could see, as plainly as though he were before me, the pinched face of my dying brother. It came back vividly and seemed to reproach me, that I had let it pass from my mind. Yet all in me that was sane told me that it was impossible that I could do anything, that it was unlikely I should ever meet Bateman. Could I go wandering round the streets of London looking for this blackguard? I should know him, of course: he had a knife scar under his chin—a woman did that in Australia. It had only just healed when I arrived in Melbourne.

"I was still thinking over things after Mrs. Landor had left, when I heard voices on the other side of the street. It was raining, and that had driven the crowds away and left Endley Street empty. I saw a man in evening dress, and I saw a woman run across to him. He had been to her flat, and apparently had left something behind. I knew Bateman suffered from *angina pectoris,* and invariably carried a phial of *butyl ammonal* to be used in case of emergency. Apparently he had left this behind at Lorna's flat. I heard him thank her. And then I saw them looking across the road towards me, and knew that she had already told him who I was. He did not dream that I was as well aware of his identity!

"He sent her back; didn't move till she was out of sight; then he began to walk on slowly, and I was preparing to follow, when I saw a man come up to him—it was Landor—heard a few words, and then saw Landor lash out and Donald Bateman fall. He was always a tricky sort of fellow, and it was a favourite dodge of his in a fight to pretend he'd been knocked out. In this way he saved himself from further punishment. It succeeded with Landor, for after a while he walked quickly away, and I lost sight of him.

"I still hesitated as to what I should do. I knew P.C. Hartford was on his beat, saw the flicker of his helmet as he passed under a distant street lamp. I could do nothing now.

"And then Bateman got up, dusted himself and began to walk the way that Hartford had come. I saw the man and the constable talking together, and Hartford came on. He didn't come far; presently he turned round, and at that moment Donald Bateman dropped as if he'd been shot.

"I knew exactly what had happened: he had a heart attack. My professional instincts urged me forward, but at that moment a figure crossed the road and crouched over the fallen man—and Hartford had seen him. He went back, quickening his stride, and I followed. As I came along the pavement I saw something lying at my feet. It was a broken key-chain, attached to which was a bunch of keys. I picked it up and put it in my pocket. The man who was searching Bateman's pockets was a well-known local thief named Lamborn. He, too, saw the policeman and started to run, but before he could go far Hartford had grabbed him.

"While they were struggling, I came up. Then I saw, lying by the side of the man I hated, a sheath knife. It had evidently fallen out of his pocket. I had to make my decision quickly. There he lay—the liar, the traitor, the wronger of women, the man who had killed my brother. I don't remember taking the knife from its sheath or using it. He never moved—must have died instantly.

"The struggle between the policeman and the thief was subsiding. I slipped the red knife into my pocket. There was excuse for the blood on my hands—I was a doctor handling a murdered man. Nobody questioned me or suspected me. A policeman brought me a bucket of water to wash my hands. I didn't regret it long. I do not regret it now. I am glad I killed him—proud I killed him!

"Then came Rudd, an imbecile theorist; but even imbecile theorists sometimes and by accident hit upon solutions with diabolical accuracy. And Elk suspected. I knew he suspected me from the first. But the real danger threatened when Lorna came on to the scene. Her woman's instinct had told her something was wrong. She had heard that a man had been murdered, pushed her way through the crowd, and went whimpering over the man who had made her what she was, if indeed she was not born with more than her share of original sin.

"She didn't see me in the crowd. I knew she was going to speak, and wondered how I could stop her. Fortunately, nature intervened and she fainted. I was asked to take her to the station. It was the opportunity I could have prayed for. We got her into the car and drove a little way till we came to a chemist's shop, and I sent the policeman who accompanied me to wake up a chemist. He had hardly gone before I slipped a hypodermic syringe out of my pocket. It was one I kept loaded, and had prepared for a maternity case. The drug was working by the time the policeman came back with a restorative, which certainly would not restore her. I waited my opportunity while she was in the matron's room, and gave her a second dose—enough, as I thought, to keep her quiet for the rest of the night. It was easy to explain her condition when I put the hypodermic syringe and its case in her bag. I would have given her a third shot, and called at the infirmary for that purpose, but the house surgeon would not allow me to sec her.

"To dispose of her was one thing, to silence Rudd another. I heard he'd gone home to bed. I was amazed when he tapped at my window on his way to the station and came in with this astounding theory—astounding in him because it was true.

"'The man (he said) must have been murdered between the time the policeman arrested Lamborn and the time I said he was stabbed.' He was working on the same grounds as you, Mason. If Lamborn had told the truth at first your task would have been simplified. Obviously, Bateman could not have been stabbed when the little thief picked his pocket, or his pocket-book and Lamborn's hands would have been covered with blood. That was Rudd's theory, too. He jokingly accused me of being the murderer, and pointed out certain stains on my coat which could not have been there had I not been by the body at the moment of killing.

"Rudd had to be silenced at all costs. I invited him to drink a glass of wine with me—he preferred whisky and soda. Getting his attention fixed on my new ray lamp, I doctored his drink. Curiously enough, he detected nothing wrong, though he had very little time to detect anything, for he was on the ground in ten seconds. I served him as I had served Lorna—carried him into the garage and left him there.

"I had to get away: I knew that was imperative. But to travel needed money, tickets, passport—things I did not possess. And then, standing near the door of the inspector's room, I heard that Landor had a large sum of money in his flat. This was my only chance. I went home, got out the taxi and drove to a road at the back of Landor's house. I guessed that the place was under observation, but I was desperate. Happily, there was a fire escape and up this I went.

"I had the keys of Landor's flat—I had picked them up on the night of the fight. I had to take my chance—wasn't even sure whether the flat was on the first or the second floor. But I had luck. Landor's name was on a brass plate, and I opened the door and went in. I had hardly closed the door behind me when I was startled to hear a woman's voice asking if I was Louis. I have a memory for voices, and I recognised it instantly as the lady who had called at my surgery that night. I kept quiet, fearing that at any moment she would come out and put on the lights. But she went back into her room and I crept along, looking for a hiding-place. There was a small room which, from its furnishing, was, I guessed, a maid's room. I got into here; the key was on the inside and I turned it. Landor arrived two minutes afterwards; and then, to my embarrassment, I heard Elk and Inspector Bray. Again I was fortunate: the detectives left with the Landors and gave me a few minutes to get the money and tickets—though neither these nor the passport could have been of much use to me. They had been located for me by Landor, who had told the detectives what was in the drawer.

"I had hoped to take the money and make my getaway before Elk returned, but he came back too soon, and the life-preserver, which was the only weapon I carried, had to be employed. I can't say how sorry I was to strike down a man whom I have always regarded as a friend.

"And there was another danger, I discovered when I got back to the surgery. Rudd was returning to consciousness. I heard him groan as I went along the yard to give him a second injection, and I wondered who else had.

"There was one chance of getting away, but when I had finished my preparations and had brought the car to the back door I was rung up from the police station with the news that Mason was on his way. I knew my last minute of safety had arrived, and on the spur of the moment I invented the forthcoming visit of the man with the white mask. I planned it all out, sprinkled the passage with a bottle of beef extract, which would look like blood in artificial light, tested the switches and oiled the bolts outside the door, between the time the detectives left the station and arrived at the surgery.

"I still had to get out, but I had arranged that, too. There is on my desk a bell-push which rings in the passage, and which I use as a signal for the next patient to come in. I waited my opportunity and rang the bell, using the signal which I had said White Face invariably used. Thereafter it was easy; to hold an imaginary conversation with somebody in the hall was a simple matter. To slam suddenly and lock the door, pretend that I had been attacked, switch out the lights and get away in the cab, occupied a few minutes. I had already put Rudd there, since I dared not leave him behind.

"I made, as you know, for the farm-house I had bought, and which I intended turning into a home for tubercular children. Perhaps some philanthropist will carry on the good work.

"I don't think there is anything more that I can tell you. If there is, I shall be able to supply any deficiency."

Chapter 20

Dr. Marford stretched back in his chair, a smile on his weary face.

"Tired, Doctor?" said Mason.

He nodded.

"Very, very tired," he said.

"I never knew you had a lisp before?"

The doctor ignored the question.

"Tell me, how did you find me at Annerford? Oh, I know." He smiled. "You interviewed poor Miss Harman, and she told you that I had another institution and naturally you went there."

Mason nodded.

"You have no questions to ask me?"

Mr. Mason considered.

"I don't think there is anything I can ask you, Doctor. You won't tell me the names of the two fences who bought the diamonds you stole?"

Marford shook his head slowly, laughter in his eyes.

"That would be unprofessional, wouldn't it?" he said.

"That crazy man in the court—did he know?"

"He's a very good guesser. I sometimes think he's psychic," said Marford. "Every time I met him he used to give me just the oddest, understanding look."

"I was talking about your lisp just now, Doctor. I've never noticed it before," said Mason again.

"I haven't a lisp"—Dr. Marford stretched himself luxuriously in his chair—"and I haven't any impediment of speech. But, you see, I recognise inevitabilities, and for the last hour and a half I have had in my mouth—it is now between my teeth—a little glass phial of cyanide of potassium——"

Three detectives flung themselves upon him, but it was too late.

He shuddered slightly; a spasm of pain passed over his face, and he stiffened. There was no other movement.

Mason looked at him in admiration.

"Game, eh?" he said huskily. "By God, how game!"

He turned abruptly and walked across to the charge-room, and came, bare-headed, into the street, to breathe the sweet air of morning. The day was breaking.

Silinski-Master Criminal

Contents

CHAPTER 1

Eclipse

Men who think in millions, usually pay in instalments, but this was not the case with Silinski, who had a mind for small things, and between whiles, when mighty financial schemes were not occupying the screen, had time to work out his landlady's bill and detect the altogether fallacious addition of

3 *peseta* 25 *centimes*.
4   "   50 "
_____

As 8 *peseta* 75 *centimes*

He might, indeed, have hailed from Andalusia as did the *Senora* with her thrifty additions and her buxom red and white and black beauty, for he counted his pennies carefully and never received a *duoro* without testing it with his teeth.

He was a tall man with a stoop, and dressed invariably in black, which is the colour of Spain. Seeing him, on windy days, when bleak, icy air-streams poured down from the circling *Sierras*, and made life in Madrid insupportable, you might have marked him down as a Spaniard. His black felt hat and his velvet-lined *cappa* with its high collar would show him to be such from a distance, whilst nearer at hand, his long melancholy face, with a thin nose that drooped over a trim black moustache slightly upturned, would confirm the distant impression. He spoke Spanish fluently, and affected a blazing diamond ring—such as a well-to-do Spaniard would delight in.

Silinski was, in fact, a Pole, and had been for many years a patriot, finding the calling lucrative.

Of all the bad men of whose history I have knowledge, or whose acquaintance I have made, none more than Silinski looked the part.

He was the transpontine villain to the life, and is the only instance I can recall of such a creature. He was in appearance so clever, so cunning, so snake-like, suave, and well-mannered, that men, and not a few womwn, trusted him from sheer perversity, reasoning, no doubt, that no man who looked so utterly untrustworthy could do anything but good at bottom. Reflecting on the bad men I have known, I enter into the spirit of reasoning. Jan Muller was benevolent of face, with a kindly eye that twinkled behind gold-rimmed spectacles—yet Mulle's record is known, and for the five murders that were brought home to him, a score were undiscovered. Bawker had the face of a clown, with his loose lip and the puckered eyes of a lover of good living—Bawker was a cold-hearted murderer. Agma Cymon—I doubt if that was his real name—was a cold severe, just man, infinitely precise and methodical; a mean man who would fight over a penny, and who invariably had his clothing patched, and his shoes re-soled, yet Cymon's defalcations amounted to £127,000, and the bulk of the money went to the upkeep of an establishment over which the beautiful Madame Carron-Setter presided.

Silinski looked what he was, yet people did not shake their heads over him. Rather they received him in their homes, and some, more intimately acquainted, joked with him on his Mephistophelian ensemble.

Silinski came to Burgos, from Madrid, by an excursion train that travelled all night, yet he was the trimmest and most alert of the crowd which thronged the Callo do Vitoria, a crowd made up of peasants, tourists, and soldiers.

He made slow progress, for the crowd grew thicker in the vicinity of the Casa del Cordon, where the loyal country-folk waited patiently for a glimpse of their king.

Silinski stood for a little while looking up at the expressionless windows of the Casa, innocent of curtain, but strangely clean. He speculated on the value of life—of royal life.

"If I were to kill the King," he mused, "Europe would dissolve into one big shudder. If, being dead, I came forward offering to restore him to life for fifty million *francs* the money would be instantly forthcoming on the proof of my ability. Yet were I to go now to the King's minister saying—'It is easy for me to kill the King, but if you will give me the money you would spend on his obsequies. I will stay my hand,' I should be kicked out, arrested, and possibly confined as a lunatic."

He nodded his head slowly, and as he turned away he took a little notebook from his pocket, and inscribed—"The greatest of miracles is self restraint." Then he rolled a cigarette and walked slowly back to the Café Suiso in the Espollon.

A clean-shaven priest, with a thin, intellectual face, was stirring his coffee at one of the tables, and since this was the least occupied Silinski made for it. He raised his hat to the priest and sat down.

"I apologize for intruding myself, father," he said, "but the other tables—"

The priest smiled and raised a protesting hand.

"The table is at your disposition, my son," he said.

He was about the same age as Silinski, but he spoke with the assurance of years. Silinski noted that the priest's voice was modulated, his accent refined, his presence that of a gentleman.

"A Jesuit," thought Silinski, and regarded him with politely veiled curiosity. Jesuits had a fascination for him. They were clever, and they were good; but principally they were a mysterious force that rode triumphant over the prejudice of the world and the hatred in the church.

"If I were not an adventurer," he said aloud, and with that air of simplicity which ever proved to be his most valuable asset, "I should be a Jesuit."

The priest smiled again, looking at Silinski with calm interest.

"My son," he said, "if I were not a Jesuit priest, I should be suspicious of your well-simulated frankness."

Here would have come a deadlock to a man of lesser parts than Silinski, but he was a very adaptable man. None the less, he was surprised into a laugh which showed his white teeth.

"In Spain," he said, "no gambit to conversation is known. I might have spoken of the weather, of the crowd, of the King—I chose to voice my faults."

The priest shook his head, still smiling.

"It is of no importance," he said quietly, "you are a Pole, of course?"

Silinski stared at him blankly. These Jesuits—strange stories had been told about them. A body with a secret organization, spread over the world—it had been said that they were hand-in-hand with the police.

"I knew you were a Pole; I lived for some time in Poland. Besides, you are only Spanish to your feet," the Jesuit looked down at Silinski's boots, "they are not Spanish; they are too short and too heavy."

Silinski laughed again. After all, this was a confirmation of his views of Jesuits.

"You, my father," he accused in his turn, "are a teacher; a professor at the college in Madrid; a professor of languages," he stopped and looked up to the awning that spread above him, seeking inspiration. "A professor of Greek," he said slowly.

"Arabic," corrected the other, "but that deduction isn't clever, because the Jesuits at Madrid are all engaged in scholastic work."

"But I knew you came from Madrid," smiled Silinski.

"Because we both came by the same train," said the calm priest, "and for the same purpose."

Silinski's eyes narrowed.

"For what purpose, father?" he asked.

"To witness the eclipse," said the priest.

A few minutes later, Silinski watched the black-robed figure with the broad-rimmed hat disappearing in the crowd with a little feeling of irritation.

He had not come to Burgos to witness the eclipse of the sun, but because he knew that the phenomenon would attract to the ancient stronghold of the Cid many notabilities. Notabilities were usually rich men, and these Silinski was anxious to meet. A Spanish gentleman, who could speak fluently French, English, German, and Italian, might, if he played his cards well, secure introductions at such a time as this, which ordinarily would be out of his reach. The guarded circles of Paris and London, through which the unknown could not hope to penetrate, would be assailable here.

A stately Spanish *grandee* (which was Silinski's role) might call on my lord in Berkeley Square, and receive no happier welcome than the suspicious scrutiny of an under footman. His ability to speak English would not serve him in a city where 6,000,000 of people spoke it indifferently as well.

Silinski had come to Burgos as another man might go to a horse fair, in the hope of picking up a bargain; only, in the case of the Pole, it was a human bargain he desired, a profitable investment which he could secure for a hundred *pesetas*—for that was the exact amount of capital he at the moment controlled.

So with Silinski in Burgos, with crowds hurrying to the hill above the cathedral to witness the eclipse, and with no other actor in this strange drama upon the stage, the story of the Nine Bears begins.

Silinski scrawled a platitude in his notebook—had it been an epigram I would have recorded it—drank the remainder of his *café au lait*, signed to the waiter and paid him the exact amount due. Leaving the outraged servant speechless, he stepped into the stream and was swept up the hill to where a number of English people were gathered, with one eye upon their watches and another upon the livid shadow that lay upon the western sky.

Silinski found a place on the slope of the hill tolerably clear of sightseers, and spread a handkerchief carefully on the bare baked earth and sat down. He had invested a penny in a strip of smoked glass, and through this he peered critically at the sun. The hour of contact was at hand, and he could see the thin rim of the obstruction cover the glaring ball.

He had all the clever man's respect for the astuteness of the scientist, and as he waited he wondered by what method astronomers were able to so accurately foretell to the minute, to the second, nay to the thousandth part of a second, the time of eclipse. Perhaps—

"Say, this place will do, it's not so crowded."

Silinski looked up at the newcomers.

One was short and stout and breathed stertorously, having recently climbed the hill, the other, the speaker, was tall, well-groomed and unmistakeably an American, with his rimless glasses and his square-toed boots.

"Phew!" wheezed the fat man. "Don't know which was worse, the climb or the crowd." He tapped his inside pocket apprehensively. "Hate crowds," he grumbled, "lose things."

"Have you lost anything?" asked the other. The fat man shook his head, but felt his pocket again. Silinski saw this out of the corner of his eye—inside breast pocket on the left, he noted.

"Baggin," said the fat man suddenly, "I've a feelin' that we oughtn't to have come here."

"You make me tired," said the American wearily.

"We oughtn't to be seen together," persisted the other; "all sorts of people are here, eh? Fellers I know slightly, chaps in the city, eh? They'll smell a rat."

He was querulous and worrying, and had a trick of asking for corroboration where none was likely to be offered.

"You're a fool," said the other.

There was a long pause, and Silinski knew that the American was making dumb signals of warning. They were nodding at him, he felt sure, so he raised his hat and asked politely:

"At what hour is the eclipse?"

"No *savvy*," said the fat man, "*no hablo espagnol.*"

Silinski shrugged his shoulders, and turned again to the contemplation of the plain below.

"He doesn't speak English," said the fat man, "none of these beggars do."

The American made no reply, but after a silence of a few minutes, he said quietly and in English:

"Look at that balloon."

But Silinski was too experienced a warrior to be trapped by a simple trick like that, and continued his solid regard of the landscape; besides, he had seen the balloons parked on the outskirts of the town, and knew that intrepid scientists would make the ascent to gather data.

He took another look at the sun. The disc was half-way across its surface, and the west was grey and blue, and the little clouds that flecked the sky were iridescent. Crowds still poured up the hill, and the slope was now covered with people. He had to stand up, and in doing so he found himself side by side with the fat man.

A strange light was coming to the world; there were triple shadows on the ground, and the stout man, whose name was Meyers, shifted uneasily.

"Don't like this, Baggin," he said fretfully; "it's hateful—never did like these wonders of the sky, they make me nervous—am frightened, Baggin, eh? It's awful, it's damned awful. Look out there, out west behind you, eh? It's black, black—it's like the end of the world!"

"Cut it out!" said his unimaginative companion.

Then of a sudden the black shadow in the west leaped across the sky, and the world went grey black. Where the sun had been was a hoop of fire, a bubbling, boiling circle of golden light, and the circling horizon was a dado of bright yellow. It was as though the sun had set its zenith, and the sunset glows were shown, east, west, north, and south.

"My God! My God!" the fat man shook in his terror; "it's horrible, horrible."

He covered his face with his hands, oblivious to everything, save a gripping fear of the unknown that clawed at his heart.

He was blind and deaf to the hustling, murmuring crowd about him; only he knew he stood in the darkness at high noon, and that something was happening he could not compress within the limits of his understanding.

Three minutes the eclipse lasted, then as suddenly as it began, it ended.

A blazing, blinding wave of light flooded the world, and the stars that had studded the sky went out.

"Yes—yes, I know I'm a fool." His face was bathed in perspiration, although with the darkness had come the chill of death. "It's—it's my temperament, eh? But never again! It's an experience."

He shook his head, as his trembling legs carried him down the hillside; then he tapped his pocket mechanically and stopped dead.

"Gone! By hell!" he roared. "Fifty thousand *francs*—gone—I've been robbed, Baggin—"

"You must expect that sort of thing in a crowd." Said the philosophical American.

★★★★★★

Silinski went into the cathedral to count the money—it was very quiet in the cathedral.

189

CHAPTER 2

Silinski has a Plan

Silinski had sister who was beautiful. She enjoyed a vogue in Madrid as Foudonitya, a great dancer. She went her own way, having no reason for showing respect for her brother, or regard for his authority. This did not greatly exercise Silinski. But her way—so easy a way!—led to outrageous unconventionalities, and there were certain happenings which need not be particularized. She was solemnly excommunicated by the Archbishop of Toledo, and the evening newspapers published her photograph.

Silinski was annoyed.

"Child," he had said gravely to her, "you did wrong to come into conflict with the Church."

"It will be a good advertisement," she said.

Silinski shook his head, and said nothing.

That night Foudonitya was hissed off the stage of the Casino, and came to her brother, not weeping or storming, but philosophically alarmed.

"What am I to do?" she asked.

"Go away into the country and perform good works; be kind to the poor, hire a *duenna*, and make the acquaintance of the local correspondent of the *Heraldo de Madrid*."

"It will cost money," said the practical Catherine—this was her name.

"You can do nothing without money," said Silinski, and would have entered the saying in his notebook, but the for the fact that it sounded trite.

So Catherine went into the country, and from time to time there appeared notes of her charity in the Madrid papers. She was still in the country when the ban of excommunication was withdrawn and she did penance at Cordova.

Silinski was not greatly surprised to see her dining at the Hotel de Paris at Burgos, on the night of the eclipse, but her hosts—they could not be her guests, for Catherine was one of the frugal sort—gave him occasion for thought. He stood in the doorway watching them. He had been looking for an empty table when he saw Catherine, and after a first glance he would have turned and departed, waiting until his sister was disengaged, but the fat man saw him.

"Hi!" he bellowed, "there he is—stop him, somebody!"

Silinski required no stopping; rather he came forward with a smile, offering his hand to the beautiful girl.

"That was the fellow who was standing near me when I lost the money," fumed the fat man, and looked helplessly round for a policeman.

There was a scraping of chairs, a confusion of voices; people rose from their seats craning their necks in an endeavour to secure a better view of what was happening, in the midst of which Mr. Meyers found himself pulled to his chair.

"Keep quiet—you," hissed Baggin's voice in his ear; "you fool, you're getting exactly a million dollars' worth of the wrong kind of publicity—he knows the girl." He leaned across the table and smiled crookedly at Silinski. "Sit down, won't you? My friend thinks he knows you—introduce us, *Senora*."

The commotion died down as it had begun, occasional curious glances being thrown at the strange *quartette*.

"Your brother?" Baggin looked keenly at the bowing stranger. "Well, we've met him before, and my friend entertained rather unjust suspicions—but they were preposterous, of course."

Silinski bowed again with a grave and patient smile.

"He didn't understand English on the hill, eh?"

Meyers choked as his suspicions found fresh food. "Don't like it Baggin, don't *like* it, I tell you!" He had a trick of dropping pronouns, which gave his speech an extraordinary rapidity of utterance.

"We had the pleasure of meeting your sister in Ronda a few weeks ago," Baggin went on smoothly, and Silinski nodded. He did not ask by what means this prosperous-looking American had secured an introduction in this land of *punctilio*. On Catherine's hand blazed a ring he had not remembered seeing before. "As we are leaving Spain tomorrow, we offered her a parting feast—"

He was feeling his way with Silinski, not quite sure of his ground.

Silinski might be the outraged relative, the proud *hidalgo*, quickly and easily affronted, terrible in his vengeance. The girl needed some explaining away.

As for Silinski, did Baggin but know, the girl had explained her presence when she laid her hand on the white table-cloth and the fires of her ring leaped and fell in the gas-light.

"*Senor*," said Silinski benevolently, "I am gratified beyond measure with your courtesy. We Bohemians, we artists, ask nor offer excuse for our departures from the convention. My little one—" he patted Catherine's white hand—"makes friends quickly, but"—here he shrugged his shoulders and turned a pained face to the wheezing Mr. Meyers—"some observations have been made which reflect upon my honour."

"No offence," growled Meyers sulkily.

"Pardon," Silinski raised his hand, dignity and respect in every pose, "pardon, *Senor*, I could not fail to comprehend your accusation. I stood by your side on the hill, so absorbed, so rapt in the glories of the phenomena, that I could not bring my elated mind to the level of understanding." He resolved to remember this phrase. "I understood nothing, heard nothing, saw nothing, but the astral splendour—"

"No offence, no offence," grumbled the fat man, "didn't think before I spoke; worried, worried, worried!" He waggled his fat hand to and fro as though illustrating the process of perturbation.

"As to that," said Silinski, with a magnificent sweep of hand, "we agree to forget; but you lost money—"

"Lost money!" the fat man glared, "lost more than money, important documents, eh? *Precioco*—precious, *savvy*? Letter from feller in the city, no possible value except to owner, see?"

"Let us go on with our dinner," said Baggin roughly; "you talk too much, Louis."

"Letters have been lost, seemingly, irredeemably lost," persisted Silinski, who was not at all anxious to change the subject, "yet, by such agencies as I have at present in my mind, have been restored to their grateful and generous owners."

"Detectives, eh?" Meyers' glare was now ferocious. "Spyin', pryin', lyin' detectives? *No!* By—"

Baggin looked across at the girl in patient despair.

"I was not thinking of detectives—by the way, Burgos seems filled with these gentlemen," Silinski went on. "I was thinking of a genius who makes this country his home. His name"—Silinski's voice was emphatic as he created from his mind the wonderful investigator—"his name is Senor don Sylvester de Gracia, and he is a personal friend of mine."

"Oh! Let the thing go," interrupted Baggin impatiently. "You've lost it, and there's an end to it; the thief will be satisfied with the money and tear the letter up."

"Unless," mused Silinski, "the thief is arrested by the police, and the letter is found upon him. Then the authorities might send for Senor T. B. Smith—eh?"

Meyers' face went ashen, and his thick lips began to quiver like a child on the point of crying.

"Smith? T. B. Smith? Commissioner, Scotland Yard! Not here, eh? Damn it, he's not here!"

"I passed him in the Plaza Mayos less than an hour ago; a gentleman very easily amused."

"Smith!" Meyers' shaking hand poured out a glass of amber wine. "Bah! Mistaken!"

"I know him slightly," said Silinski modestly (it was T. B. Smith who had marked him for deportation under the Undesirable Aliens Act); "I never forget a face."

The fat man pushed back his chair, wiping his big mouth clumsily with a serviette.

"Then it's *up*," he said. "He's here for something; my name's mud in the city—"

"Be quiet!" Baggin turned with a snarl upon his companion. "Look here," he said, facing Silinski, "my friend is not quite himself—I'll take him up to my room for a minute or so; will you wait here? You might be of service to us."

Without waiting for an answer the two men left the room, Baggin with one hand clenched on the fat man's arm.

When they had gone Silinski turned to his sister.

"I hope you haven't scared them," she said in German.

"I think not," said her amiable relative, and the two exchanged confidences.

"What have they done?" she asked.

"Nothing—as yet," he said diplomatically.

"You have this letter?" she asked, but Silinski shook his head.

"If I had," he said, "I could tell you all you want to know. Unfortunately I am in the dark."

"And the money?"

"I know no more about the money than you," he replied, with charming frankness. "Who are they?"

She laughed, showing two straight, white rows of teeth, and there was genuine amusement in her big grey eyes. "You have the money, of course, and the letter—you must tell me, Gregory. I must know where I am with them; it is due to me."

"As to the money," said Silinski, without shame, "it is some fifty thousand *francs*; one might live for a year in luxury upon fifty thousand *francs*. As for the letter—why, that is an annuity forever."

He leaned over the table, and as he looked his eyes were lowered to the cloth, like a man ransacking his memory for elusive facts.

"These men are part of an epidemic—a wave of financial instability is rushing across the world—no, I will put it inimitably: There are props of rotten finances; sometimes one pole snaps and the structure trembles, sometimes two snap and the structure lurches, but does not fall, for there is strength in union, and it is more difficult to break a bundle of worm-eaten sticks than one honest stave. But suppose all the props are withdrawn at once—what happens? *Ph-tt!* And suppose the weaker props say—'The big fellow is going—it is time for us to move'?"

Catherine listened patiently.

"I would rather you spoke less like a priest, in parables," she said.

"Naturally," said Silinski, with an easy inclination of his head, as though this were the very comment he expected, "yet I must deal in parables. Amongst your accomplishments, do you speak English?"

"A little." Catherine shrugged her shoulders carelessly. "I can say 'my dear' and 'I like you very much'."

"Which hardly fulfils all commercial requirements," said Silinski thoughtfully. "I will translate to you the interesting letter, which may be condensed into one comprehensive sentence towards the end— 'When you are ready to say "jump."'"

Here Baggin appeared in the doorway, and beckoned to the polite Silinski, and that worthy made his way through the crowded room.

"Can you get that letter?" asked Baggin, without any preliminary, "or were you only joshing?"

"I can not only get the letter, but I have the letter," said the other calmly, and Baggin's lids narrowed. "Further your plans are very foolish," the Pole went on smoothly, "because you have no plans. Spain will not hold nine defaulting bucket-shop keepers—that is the idiom, is it not?—unless your retirement is organized with considerably more skill than you have up to this moment displayed."

The American said nothing.

"I have a plan, a great plan," said Silinski, and he drew himself erect in the pride of his authorship; "but you must take me into its working."

"You are a damned villain," said Baggin, "a blackmailer—"

Silinski's brows darkened.

"Villain, yes," he said; "blackmailer, no—I am a genius—that is all."

CHAPTER 3

Some Disappearances

In the month of March, 1904, a notice was posted on the doors of the London, Manhattan and Jersey Syndicate, in the Moorgate Street. It was brief, but it was to the point—

"Owing to the disappearance of Mr. George T. Baggin, the L. M. and J. Syndicate has suspended operations."

With Mr. Baggin had disappeared the sum of £247,000. An examination of the books of the firm revealed the fact that the London, Manhattan, and Jersey Syndicate was—Mr. Baggin; that its imposing title thinly disguised the operations of a bucket-shop, and the vanished bullion had been most systematically collected in gold and foreign notes.

Mr. Baggin had disappeared as though the earth had swallowed him up. He was traced to Liverpool; a ticket to New York had been purchased by a man answering to his description, and he had embarked on the *Luciana*. The liner called at Queenstown, and the night she left Mr. "Coleman" was missing. His clothing and trunks were found intact in his cabin, and a pathetic note addressed to the chief steward was pinned to his pillow. It said in the extravagant language of remorse, that overwhelmed by the horror of his position, the writer had decided to leave this world for a better, and he trusted, brighter life. It was signed "George T. Baggin." The ship was searched from stem to stern, but no trace of the unfortunate man could be discovered.

The evening newspapers flared forth with "Tragic End of a Defaulting Banker," but Scotland Yard, ever sceptical, set foot certain enquiries and learnt that a stranger had been seen in Queenstown after the ship had sailed. A stranger who left for Dublin, and who doubled back to Heysham; who came, *via* Manchester, back to London again. In London he had vanished completely. Whether or not this was the redoubtable George T. Baggin, was a matter for conjecture.

T. B. Smith, of Scotland Yard, into whose hands the case was put, had no doubt at all. He believed that Biggin was alive. Two months after the disappearance, the firm of Woolfe, Meyers, Limited, crumbled into dust—for Louis Meyers himself failed to take his place one fine morning in the lavishly furnished board-room in King William Street. Meyers was a dealer in premium Bonds. A stout man, scant of breath, loose-lipped, sparing pronouns. His ingenious method of trading may be summarised in a sentence. You paid your money and he took his choice.

"There can be no doubt at all," said the *Daily Megaphone*, in commenting on his disappearance, "that this wretched man, face to face with exposure which was inevitable, has taken the supreme and desperate step of suicide. His overcoat, in which was a letter to the coroner, was found on one of the seats of the Thames Embankment. . . ."

Yet Scotland Yard took no trouble to find the body. Instead, it sent its most experienced detectives to watch the seaports. T. B. Smith's instructions to his watchful subordinates were marked with sardonic levity.

"You will recognise the body of the late Louis Meyers," he wrote, "from the fact that it will be smoking a big cigar and carrying a portmanteau containing £150,000's worth of French and German notes; it speaks English with a slight lisp."

Most artistic of all was the passing of Lucas Damant, the Company Promoter. Damant's defalcations were the heaviest, for his opportunities were greater. He dealt in millions and stole in millions. Taking his summer holidays in Switzerland, Mr. Damant foolishly essayed the ascent of the Matterhorn without a guide. His *alpenstock* was picked up at the edge of a deep *crevasse*, and (I again quote the *Megaphone*) "yet another Alpine disaster was added to the alarming list of mountaineering tragedies." What time four expert guides were endeavouring to extricate the lost man from a bottomless pit, sixteen chartered accountants were engaged in extracting from the chaos of his documentary remains the true position of Mr. Damant's affairs, but the sixteen accountants, had they been sixteen hundred, and the space of time occupied in their investigations a thousand years, would never have been able to balance the Company Promoter's estate to the satisfaction of all concerned, for between debit and credit yawned an unfathomable chasm that close on a million pounds could not have spanned.

In the course of time a fickle public forgot the sensational disappearance of these men; in course of time their victims died or sought admission to the workhouse. There were spasmodic discussions that arose in smoke-rooms and tap-rooms, and the question as to whether they were dead or whether they had merely bolted, was hotly debated, but it may be truthfully said that they were forgotten; but not by Scotland Yard, which neither forgets nor forgives.

The Official Memory sits in a big office that overlooks the Thames Embankment. It is embodied in a man who checks, day by day, hour by hour, and minute by minute, the dark happenings of the world. He is an inconsiderable person, as personalities go, for he enters no witness-box to testify against a pallid prisoner. He grants no interviews to curious newspaper reporters, he appears in no magazine as a picturesque detector of crime, but silently, earnestly, and remorselessly, he marks certain little square cards, makes grim entries in strange ledgers, consults maps, and pores over foreign newspaper reports.

Sometimes he prepares a *dossier*, as a cheap-jack make up a prize packet, with a paper from this cabinet, a photograph from that drawer, a newspaper cutting, a docketed deposition with the sprawling signature of a dying man, a finger-print card—and all these he places in a large envelope, and addresses it in a clerkly hand to Chief Inspector So-and-So, or to the "Director of Public Prosecutions." When the case is over and a dazed man sits in a cell at Wormwood Scrubbs pondering his sentence, or, as it sometimes happens, when convict masons are at work carving initials over a grave in a prison yard, the envelope comes back to the man in the office, and he sorts the contents jealously. It is nothing to him, the sum of misery they have cast, or the colour of death that permeates them. He receives them unemotionally, distributes the contents to their cabinets, pigeon-holes, guard-books, and drawers, and proceeds to make up yet another *dossier*.

All things come to him; crime in all its aspects is veritably his stock-in-trade.

When George Baggin disappeared in 1904, his simple arrangement of indexing showed the connection between the passing of Lucas Damant six months later, and the obliteration of Meyers between these times. The Official Memory knew, too, what the public had no knowledge of—namely, that there had been half a dozen minor, but no less mysterious, flittings in the space of two years.

Their stories, briefly and pithily told, were inscribed on cards in the silent man's cabinet. Underneath was the significant word, "Incomplete." They were stories to be continued; some other hand than his might take up the tale at a future time, and subscribe *"Finis"* to their grim chapters. He was satisfied to carry the story forward as far as his information allowed him.

There never was a more fascinating office than this of the Silent Recorder's. It was terribly businesslike with its banked files, its innumerable drawers, its rows of deep cabinets, "A,B,C,D," they ran, then began all over again, "AA, BB, CC," except the big index drawer where "Aabot, Aaron, Aato, Abard, Abart," commenced the record of infamous men. There were forgers here, murderers, coiners, defaulters, great and small (Silinski's autobiography occupies a folder by itself). There are stories of great swindles, and of suspected swindles, of events apparently innocent in themselves, behind which lie unsuspected criminalities.

I show you this office, the merest glimpse of it, so that as this story progresses, and information comes mysteriously to the hand of the chief actor, you will understand that no miracle has been performed, no heaven-sent divination of purpose has come to him, but that at the back of the knowledge he employs with such assurance, is this big office at New Scotland Yard. A pleasant office overlooking the Embankment with its green trees and its sunny river and its very pleasant sights—none of which the Recorder ever sees, being short-sighted from overmuch study of criminal records.

CHAPTER 4

Introducing T. B. Smith

In the month of October the market, that unfailing barometer of public nerves, moved slowly in an upward direction.

If the "House" was jubilant, the "Street" was no less gratified, for since the "Baggin Failure" and financial cataclysm which dragged down the little investors to ruin, there had been a sad flatness in the world of shares. There are many places of public resort where the "Street" people meet—those speculators who daily, year in and out, promenade the pavement of Throgmorton Street, buying and selling on an "eighth" margin.

To them from time to time come the bareheaded clerks with news of this or that rise or fall, to receive instructions gravely imparted, and as gravely accepted, and to retire to the mysterious deeps of the "House" to execute their commissions.

The market was rising steadily, as the waters of a river rise; that was the most pleasant knowledge of all. It did not jump or leap or flare; it progressed by sixteenths, by thirty-seconds, by sixty-fourths; but all down the money columns in the financial papers of the press were tiny little plus marks which brought joy to the small investor, who is by nature a "bull."

Many people who are not directly interested in finance regarded the signs with sympathy. The slaves of the street, 'busmen, cabmen, the sellers of clamorous little financial papers, all these partook in the general cheeriness.

Slowly, slowly, climbed the market.

"Like old times," said a hurrying clerk; but the man he spoke to sniffed contemptuously, being by nature one of that sour class from which all beardom is recruited.

"Like old times!" chuckled a man standing at the Bodega bar, a little dazed with his prosperity. Somebody reminded him of the other booms that had come and undergone sudden collapse, but the man standing at the counter twiddled the stem of the glass in his hand and smiled indulgently.

"Industrials are the feature," said an evening paper, and indeed the biggest figures behind the tiny pus marks were those against the famous commercial concerns best known in the city. The breweries, the bakeries, the cotton corporations, the textile manufacturing companies enjoying quotation in the share list—all these participated in the upward rush; nay, led the van.

Into Old Broad Street on one day at the height of the boom, came a man a little above middle height, clean-shaven, his face the brick tan of one who spends much of his life in the open air. He wore a suit of blue serge, well cut but plain, a spotless grey Tirai hat, broad-rimmed, white spats over his patent shoes, and a thin cane in his hand. "A fellow in the *Kaffir* market" guessed one of the group about the corner of Change Valley, but somebody better informed turned hastily when he saw the quick striding figure approaching, and dived down a side court.

A showily-attired young man, standing on the edge of the pavement chewing a quill toothpick thoughtfully, did not see the newcomer until he was close on him, then started and changed colour. The man in the wide-brimmed hat recognised him and nodded. He checked his walk and stopped.

"Here's Moss," he said. He had a snappy, curt delivery and a disconcerting habit of addressing one in the third person. "How is Moss? Straight now? Straight as a die, I'll swear. He's given up rigging, given up Punk Prospectuses for Petty Punters. Oh, Moss! Moss!"

He shook his head with gentle melancholy, though a light twinkled in his humorous grey eyes.

"I don't know why you're so 'ard on me, Mister Smith," said the embarrassed Moss; "we've all got our faults—"

"Not me, Mr. Moss," said T. B. Smith promptly.

"I dessay even you, sir," insisted the other. "I've 'ad my flutter; and I failed. There's lots of people who've done more than I ever done, worse things, and crookeder things, who are livin' in what I might call the odour of sanctity.

"There's people in the 'Ouse," Moss wagged an admonitory finger towards 'Change, and his tone was bitter but envious, "who've robbed by the million, an' what do we see?"

T. B. Smith shook his head.

"We see," said the indignant young man, "motorcars, an' yachts, an' racehorses—because they 'aven't been found out!"

"Moral," mused T. B. Smith, "don't allow yourself—"

"I know, I know," Moss loftily waved aside the dubious morality of Mr. Assistant-Commissioner Smith. "But I *was* found out. Twelve months in the second division. Is that justice?"

"It all depends," cautiously, "what you mean by justice. I thought the sentence was rather light."

"Look here, Mr. Smith," said Mr. Moss firmly; "let's put the matter another way round. Here's Baggin's case, an' Meyers' case. Now I ask you, man to man, are these chaps dead?"

T. B. Smith was discreetly silent.

"Are they dead?" again demanded Moss, with emotion. "You know jolly well they ain't. You know as well as I do who's at the bottom of these bear raids to send the market into the mud. I know them raids!" in his excitement Mr. Moss got further and further away from the language of his adoption; "they smell o' Baggin, George T. Baggin; he's operatin' somewhere. I recognise the touch. George T. Baggin, I tell you, an' as the good book says, his right hand hath not lost its cunnin'."

"And," said T. B. Smith, blandly ignoring the startling hypothesis; "what is Mr. Moss doing now to earn the bread, butter, and *etceteras* of life?"

"Me? Oh, I'm in the East mostly," said the other moodily; "got a client or two; give a tip an' get a tip now an' again. Small money an' small profits."

He dropped his eyes under the steady and pseudo-benevolent gaze of the other.

"No companies?" said the detective softly. "No companies, Mr. Moss? No Amalgamated Peruvian Concessions, eh? No Brazilian Rubber and Exploitation Syndicate?"

The young man shifted his feet uneasily.

"Genuine concerns, them," he said doggedly; "an' besides, I'm only a shareholder."

"Not promoter. Mr. Moss is not a promoter?"

In desperation the badgered shareholder turned.

"How in 'eaven's name you get hold of things I don't know," he said in helpless annoyance. "An' all I can say—excuse me."

T. B. Smith saw his expression undergo a sudden change.

"Don't look round, sir" said the other breathlessly; "there's one o' my clients comin' along; genuine business, Mr. Smith; don't crab the deal."

In his agitation he grew a little incoherent.

T. B. Smith might have walked on discreetly, leaving Moss to transact his business in quiet and peace. Indeed, the young man's light blue eyes pleaded for this indulgence; but the gentleman from Scotland Yard was singularly obtuse this morning.

"You don't want to meet him," urged Mr. Moss. "He's not in your line, sir; he's a gentleman."

"I think you're very rude, Mr. Moss," said T. B. Smith, and waited, whilst Moss and client met.

The client may have been a gentleman; he was certainly opulent. The day being fairly mild, T. B. Smith thought the client's fur-lined coat a superfluity, but the silk hat which overtopped the client's face was most correct.

"Permit me," said Moss with all the grace he could summon at a moment's notice, "to introduce you to a friend of mine—name of Smith—in the Government."

The stranger bowed and offered a gloved hand.

"Er—" said T. B., hesitant. "I did not quite catch your name."

"Count Poltavo," said Mr. Moss defiantly; "a friend of mine an' a client."

"Delighted to make your acquaintance, Count. I have met you somewhere."

The Count bowed.

"It is ver' likely. I have been in England before."

T. B. Smith with his head on one side, so ridiculously reminiscent of an inquisitive bird, surveyed the imperturbable foreigner with interest.

"But for the integrity of Mr. Moss," he said, "I should believe that I had been introduced to quite an old friend of mine—Gregory Silinski, to wit."

The foreigner smiled, showing two regular rows of white teeth.

"You think of my cousin, of whom there is some resemblance—a bad lot." He shook his head sternly and reprovingly.

"A bad lot, indeed," agreed T. B. Smith, and offered his hand to Moss.

"Good-day to you, Mr. Moss," he said; "keep out of mischief; goodbye, Mr. Silinski." He looked at his watch. "It wants four minutes

203

to twelve; and if by five minutes to twelve tomorrow you are still in England, I shall arrest you. *Comprenez?*"

"*Parfaitement*," said Silinski, who prided himself upon his ability to accept a situation.

T. B. Smith resumed his walk. At the corner of Threadneedle Street an able-bodied hawker offered him his choice of a box of matches or a pair of bootlaces.

"Neither in mine," said T. B. Smith. "Have you got a hawker's license, my man?"

"Yes, sir."

The hawker produced from the inside pocket of his frowsy jacket a folded paper, and T. B. Smith examined it carefully. He must have read every word of it twice. After a while, he handed it back and what he said was not about hawkers, or licenses.

"I know they are here," he said as though referring to people whose names were inscribed on the paper he had been reading, "but they don't count, they are too small. Silinski, do you know him?"

"I've seen him," said the hawker; "wasn't he deported over the Griffon Street affair?"

T. B. Smith nodded.

"He's way along," he said, with a jerk of his head in the direction of Moss and client; "get one of your men to watch and report."

"Very good, sir."

T. B. Smith continued in the direction of the Mansion House. A famous banker passing in his motor brougham, waved his hand in salute; a city policeman stolidly ignored him.

Along Cheapside, with the deliberate air of a sightseer, the man in the grey felt hat strolled, turning over in his mind the problem of the boom.

For it was a problem.

If you see on one hand ice forming on a pool, and on the other a thermometer rising slowly to blood-heat, you may be satisfied in your mind that something is wrong somewhere. Nature cannot make mistakes. Thermometers are equally infallible. Look for the human agency at work on the mercury bulb, for the jet of hot air directed to the instrument. In this parable is explained the market position, and T. B. Smith, who dealt with huge, vague problems like markets and wars and national prosperity, was looking for the hot-air current.

The market rises because big people buy big quantities of shares; it falls because these same people sell, it falls because these same people sell, and T. B. Smith happened to know that nobody was buying. That is, nobody of account—Eckhardt's, Tollington's, or Bronte's Bank. You can account for the rise of a particular share by some local and favourable circumstance, but when the market as a whole moves up—?

"We can trace no transactions," wrote Mr. Louis Vell, of the firm of Vell, Vallings & Boys, Brokers, "carried out by or on behalf of the leading jobbers. The marked improvement in Industrial Stocks is due, as far as we can gather, to Continental buying—an unusual circumstance."

Who was the "philanthropist" who was making a market in stagnant stocks? Whoever it was, he or they repented long before T. B. Smith had reached the Central Criminal Court, which was his objective.

He was a witness in the Gildie Bank fraud case, and his cross-examination at the hands of one of the most relentless of counsel occupied three hours. This concluded to everybody's satisfaction, save counsel, T. B. Smith, who hated the law courts, walked out into the Old Bailey to find newsboys loudly proclaiming, "Slump on the Stock Exchange!"

"Thank heaven, that bubble's burst!" said T. B. Piously, and walked back to Scotland Yard, whistling.

He did not doubt that the artificial rise had failed, and that the market had gone back to normal.

At the corner of the Thames Embankment he bought a paper, and the first item of news he read was:

"Consols have fallen to 84."

Now, Consuls that morning had stood at 90, and T. B. Smith stopped whistling.

CHAPTER 5

The Anticipators

T. B. Smith strolled into the room of Superintendent Elk.

Elk was a detective officer chiefly remarkable for his memory. A tall, thin, sad man, who affects a low turned-down collar and the merest wisp of a black tie. If he has any other pose than his desire to be taken for a lay preacher, it is his pose of ignorance on most subjects. Elk's attitude to the world at large is comprehended in the phrase, "I am a child in these things," which accounts to a very great extent for the rapidity of his promotion in the Criminal Investigation Department.

T. B.'s face wore a frown, and he twirled a paper-knife irritably.

"Elk," he said, without any preliminary, "the market has gone to the devil."

"Again?" said Elk politely, having knowledge without interest.

"Again," said T. B. emphatically, "for the fourth time this year. I've just seen one of the Stock Exchange Committee, and he's in a terrible state of mind. Stocks and shares are nothing to me," the Commissioner went on, seeing the patient boredom on the other's face, "and I know there is a fairly well-defined law that governs the condition of the Stock Exchange. Prices go see-sawing up and down, and that is part of the day's work, but for the fourth time, and for no apparent reason, the market is broken. Consols are down to 84."

"I once had some shares in an American copper mine," reflected Elk, "and a disinterested stock-jobber advised me to hold on to them; I'm still holding, but it never occurred to me—I lost £500—that it was a matter for police investigation."

The Commissioner stopped in his walk and looked at the detective.

"There's little romance in finance," he mused, "but there *is* something behind all this; do you remember the break of January 4th?"

Elk nodded; he saw there was a police side to this slump, and grew alert and knowledgeable.

"Yankees and gilt-edged American stock came tumbling down as though their financial foundations had been dug away. What was the cause?"

Elk thought.

"Wasn't it the suicide of the President of the 11th National Bank?" he asked.

"I happened after the crash," said T. B. promptly. "Do you remember the extraordinary slump in Russian Fours in April—a slump which, like the drop in Yankees, affected every market? What was the cause?"

"The attempt on the *Czar*."

"Again you're wrong," said the other; "the slump anticipated the attempt, it did not follow it. Then we have the business of the 9th of August."

"The *Kaffir* slump?"

"Yes."

"But, surely, the reason for that may be traced," said Elk; "it followed the decision of the Cabinet to abolish coloured labour on the mines."

"It anticipated it," corrected his chief, with a twinkle in his eye, "and do you remember no other occurrence that filled the public mind about that time?"

Elk thought with knit brows.

"There was the airship disaster at the Palace. Hike Mills was put away just about then for blackmail; there was the Vermont case—and the Sud Express wreck—"

"That's it," said the Commissioner, "wrecked outside Valladolid, three killed, many injured—do you remember who was killed?"

"Yes," said Elk slowly, "a Frenchman whose name I've forgotten, Mr. Arthur Saintsbury, a King's Messenger—by George!"

The connection dawned upon him, and T. B. grinned.

"Killed whilst carrying dispatches to the King of Portugal," he said.

"Those dispatches related to the proposed withdrawal of native labour—much of which is recruited in Portuguese West Africa"; he paused a moment, and added as an afterthought, "his dispatch-box was never found."

There was silence.

"You suggest?" said Elk suddenly.

"I suggest there is an intelligent anticipator in existence who is much too intelligent to be at large." The Commissioner walked to the door.

He stood for a moment irresolutely.

"I offer you two suggestions," he said; "the first is that the method which our unknown operator is employing is not unlike the method of Mr. George Baggin who departed this life some four years ago. The second is, that if by any chance I am correct in my first surmise, we may lay this ghost for good and all."

CHAPTER 6

At Bronte's Bank

It was two days later, when Consols touched 80, that T. B. Smith gathered in Elk and marched him into the City.

The agitated Committee-man of the Stock Exchange met them in his office and led them to his private room.

"I must tell you the whole story," he said, after he had carefully shut and locked the door. "Last Wednesday, the market still rising and a genuine boom in sight, Mogseys—they're the biggest firm of brokers in the city—got a wire from their Paris agents, which was to this effect: 'Sell Consols down to 80.' They were standing then at 90, and were on the upgrade. Immediately following the wire, and before it could be confirmed, came another instruction in which they were told to sell some gilt-edged stocks—this was on a rising market, too—down to prices specified. I have seen the list, and taking the prices as they stood on Wednesday morning and the price they stand at today, the difference is enormous—something like three millions."

"Which means—?"

"Which means that the unknown bears have pocketed that amount. Well, Mogseys were paralysed at the magnitude of the order, and cabled away to their agent asking for particulars, and were equally dumbfounded to learn that they were acting on behalf of the Credit Bourbonaise, one of the biggest banks in the South of France. There was nothing else to do but to carry out the order, and on Thursday morning they had hammered stocks down ten points—stocks that have never fluctuated five points each way in mortal memory!"

The Committee-man, speaking in tones of reverence of these imperturbable securities, mopped his forehead with a tumultuous *bandana*.

"Now," he resumed, "we know all the bears throughout all the world. The biggest of 'em is dead. That was George T. Baggin, one of the most daring and unscrupulous operators we have ever had in London. We know every man or woman or corporation likely to jump on to the market with both feet and set it snagging—but there isn't a single known bear who has a hand in this. We've tried to discover his identity, but we've always come up against a blank wall—the bank. The bank can't give away its client, and even if it did, I doubt very much whether we should be any wiser, for he's pretty sure to have hidden himself too deep. We'd probably find the bank was instructed by a broker, and the broker by another bank, and we'd be as far off a solution as ever."

"Is there any cause for the present break?"

"I'm coming to that. In all previous slumps there has been a very good excuse for a panic hanging round. In the present instance no such excuse exists. There is a good feeling abroad, money is free and the Bank Rate is low, and the recent spurt in *Kaffirs* and Yankee rails has put a good heart into the market—why even Bronte's have dealt!"

He mentioned the name of the great bank which in the City of London, ranks only second to the Bank of England.

"I don't know exactly the details of their dealing, but it is pretty generally known in the City that they have increased their commitments, and when a conservative house like Bronte's take advantage of a spell of prosperity, you may be sure that peace is in the very air we breathe.

T. B. Smith was thoughtfully rolling a glass paperweight up and down a blotting-pad, and Elk was regarding the ceiling with an air of pained resignation.

Neither of the two spoke when the Committee-man finished his recital, or when he looked from one to the other, secretly disappointed that two men of whom he expected so much should be so little perturbed, indeed, so little interested, by his story. He waited a little longer for them to offer some remark, and, finding that neither had any comment to make, he asked a little impatiently—

"Well?"

T. B. roused himself from his reverie, and Elk brought his gaze to earth.

"Would you mind telling me the names of the stocks again?" asked T. B., "the stocks that are being attacked."

The member recited a list.

"Um!" said the Commissioner thoughtfully. "Industrials, breweries, manufactories—the very shares that enjoyed the boom and are now undergoing the slump!

"Will you give me a Stock Exchange Year-book?"

"Certainly."

He unlocked the door and went out, reappearing shortly with a fat brown volume.

T. B. turned the pages of the book with quick, nervous fingers, consulting the list at his side from time to time.

"Thank you," he said at length, pushing the book from him and rising.

"Have you any idea—?" the broker began, and T. B. laughed.

"you nearly said 'clue,'" he smiled; "yes, I've lots of ideas—I'm just going to work one of them out."

He bowed slightly and the two detectives left the building together.

At the corner of Threadneedle Street he bought an evening paper.

"Issued at 4:10," he said, glancing at the "fudge" space, where the result of a race had been printed, " and nothing has happened."

He hailed a passing cab and the two men got in.

"Bronte's Bank, Holborn," was the direction he gave.

"Like the immortal Mrs. Harris, there ain't no Bronte, as you know," he said. "The head of the business is Sir George Calliper. He's an austere young man of thirty-five or thereabouts. President of philosophical societies and patron of innumerable philanthropies."

"Has no vices," added Elk.

"And therefore a little inhuman," commented T. B. "Here we are."

They drew up before the severe *façade* of Bronte's, and dismissed the cab.

The bank was closed, but there was a side door—if, indeed, such an insignificant title could be applied to the magnificent portal of mahogany and brass—and a bell, which was answered by a uniformed porter.

"The bank is closed, gentlemen," he said when T. B. had stated his errand.

"My business is very urgent," said T. B. imperatively, and the man hesitated.

"I am afraid Sir George has left the building," he said, "but if you will give me your cards I will see."

T. B. Smith drew a card from his case. He also produced a tiny envelope, in which he inserted the card.

A few minutes later the messenger returned.

"Sir George will see you," he said and ushered them into an ante-room. "Just a moment, gentlemen, Sir George is engaged."

Ten minutes passed before he came again. Then he reappeared, and they followed him along a marble-tiled corridor to the *sanctum* of the great man.

It was a large room, solidly and comfortably furnished and thickly carpeted. The only ornamentation was the beautifully carved mantel, over which hung the portrait of Septimus Bronte, who, in 1743, had founded the institution which bore his name.

Sir George Calliper rose to meet them.

He was a tall young man with sandy hair and a high, bald forehead. From his square-toed boots to his black satin cravat he was commercial solidity personified. T. B. noted the black ribbon watch-guard, the heavy, dull signet-ring, the immaculately manicured nails, the dangling, black-rimmed monocle, and catalogued his observations for future reference. Elk, who saw with another eye and from a different point of view, mentally recorded a rosebud on the carpet and a handkerchief.

"Now, what can I do for you?" asked Sir George; he picked up the card from the desk and refreshed his memory.

"We're very sorry to trouble you," began T. B. conventionally, but the baronet waved the apology aside.

"I gather you have not come to see me out of office hours without cause," he said, and his tone rather suggested that it would be unpleasant even for an Assistant-Commissioner, if he had.

"No, but I've come to make myself a nuisance—I want to ask you questions," said T. B. coolly,

"So long as they are pertinent to the business in hand, I shall have every pleasure in answering," replied Sir George.

"First and foremost, is there the slightest danger of Bronte's Bank failing?" asked T. B. Smith calmly.

The audacity of the question struck the baronet dumb.

"Failing?" he repeated, "Bronte's fail—Mr. Smith, are you jesting?"

"I was never more in earnest," said T. B. "Think what you like of my impertinence, but humour me please."

The banker looked hard at the man before him, as though to detect some evidence of ill-timed humour.

"It is no more possible for Bronte's to fail, than the Bank of England," he said brusquely.

"I am not very well acquainted with the practise of banking," said T. B., "and I should be grateful if you would explain why it is impossible for a bank to fail."

If Sir George Calliper had been a little less sure of himself, he would have detected the monstrous inaccuracy of T. B.'s confession of ignorance.

"But are you really in earnest?"

"I assure you," said T. B. seriously, "that I regard this matter as being one of life and death."

"Well," said the banker, with a perplexed frown, "I will explain. The solvency of a bank, as of an individual, is merely a matter of assets and liabilities. The liabilities are the elementary debts, deposits, loans, calls, and such like, that are due from the bank to its clients and shareholders. Sometimes the liability takes the form of a guarantee for the performance of certain obligations—that is clear enough?"

T. B. nodded.

"Assets may be represented as gold, Government securities and stock convertible into gold, properties, freehold, leasehold, land; but you know, of course, the exact significance of the word assets?"

T. B. nodded again.

"Well, it is a matter of balance," said the banker; "allowing a liberal margin for the fluctuation of securities, we endeavour to and succeed in keeping a balance of assets in excess of our liabilities."

"Do you keep gold in any quantity on the premises?—what would be the result, say, of a successful burglary that cleared your vaults?"

"It would be inconvenient," said Sir George, with a dry smile, "but it would not be disastrous."

"What is your greatest outstanding liability?" demanded T. B.

The banker looked at him strangely.

"It is queer you should ask," he said slowly, "it was the subject of a discussion at my board meeting this afternoon—it is the Wady Semlik Barrage."

"The Egyptian irrigation scheme?" asked T. B. quickly.

"Yes the bank's liability was very limited until a short time ago. There was always a danger that the physical disabilities of the Soudan would bring about a *fiasco*. So we farmed our liability, if you understand the phrase. But with the completion of the dam, and the report of our engineer that it had been submitted to the severest test, we

213

curtailed the expensive insurance."

"When are the works to be handed over to the Egyptian Government?"

Sir George smiled.

"That I cannot tell you," he said, "it is a secret known only to the directors and myself."

"But until it is officially handed over, you are liable?"

"Yes, to an extent. As a matter of fact, we shall be liable for one day. For there is a clause in the agreement which binds the Government to accept the responsibilities for the work seven days after inspection by the works department, and the bulk of our insurances run on till within twenty-four hours of that date. I will tell you this much: the inspection has taken place, I cannot give you the date—and the fact that it was made earlier than we anticipated is responsible for the cancellation of the insurances."

"One more question, Sir George," said T. B. "Suppose, through any cause, the Wady Semlok Barrage broke on that day—the day upon which the bank was completely liable—what would be the effect on Bronte's?"

A shadow passed over the banker's face.

"That is a contingency I do not care to contemplate," he said curtly.

He glanced at his watch.

"I have not asked you to explain your mysterious visit," he said with a smile, "and I am afraid I must curb my curiosity, for I have an appointment in ten minutes, as far west as Portland Place. In the meantime, it may interest you to read the bank's balance-sheet."

Elk's vacant eye was on him as he opened a drawer in his desk.

He closed it again hurriedly with a little frown. He opened another drawer and produced a printed sheet. "Here it is," he said. "Would you care to see me again at ten tomorrow?"

T. B. might have told him that for the next twelve hours the banker would hardly be out of sight for an hour, but he replied—

"I shall be very pleased."

He had shaken hands with Sir George, and was on his way to the door, when Elk gave a sign which meant "cover my movements," and T. B. turned again.

"By the way," he said, pointing to the picture over the fireplace, "that is *the* Bronte, is it not?"

Sir George turned to the picture.

"Yes," said he, and then with a smile, "I wonder Mr. Bronte did not fall from his frame at some of your questions."

T. B. chuckled softly as he followed the uniformed doorkeeper along the ornate corridor.

In a cab being driven rapidly westward, Elk solemnly produced his finds.

"A little rose and a handkerchief," he said.

T. B. took the last-named article in his hand. It was a delicate piece of flimsiness, all lace and fragrance. Also it was damp.

"Here's romance," said T. B., folding it carefully and putting it in his pocket. "Somebody has been crying. And I'll bet it wasn't our friend the banker.

Chapter 7

Silinski Explains

T. B. Smith was dressing for dinner in his room at the Savoy, his mind occupied by speculations that centred round a mill dam, when there came a gentle tap at the door.

"Come in," he said, having all but completed his somewhat elaborate toilet—he was ever a little fastidious in the matter of personal adornment.

The door opened, and there came into his room a gentleman in evening dress, very beautiful to behold.

His shirt-front was soft and pleated, and there were three little diamond buttons to fasten it. His dress suit fitted him almost as well as the white gloves on his hands, and if the velvet collar of his coat was a little daring, he had the distinguished air of the educated and refined foreigner to carry off his sartorial extravagance.

"Come in, Silsinki," said T. B., without turning round. "Twenty-four hours I gave you—when do you leave?"

"May I take a chair?"

Silsinki was suave, polite, deferential, all the things that a well-bred man of the world should be.

"Sorry—chuck those things of mine from the chair by the bed."

So far from "chucking" anything anywhere, Silsinki removed the various articles of attire one by one, folded them, and placed them in a neat pile on the bed.

Then he seated himself carefully.

"Mr. Smith," he began, "it was written by the illustrious philosopher Epictetus—"

"Do not," begged T. B., in the throes of manipulating a dress tie, "do not quote any of your disreputable friends, I beg."

"Then," said Silsinki, unabashed, "let me put the matter in another way. Medical authority has it that all human-kind changes once in every seven years. New tissues replace the old, of superior or inferior quality according to age and temperament; but assuredly an entire change comes to every man."

"The last man who cited to me the born-again theory—which, by the way, is an old one in criminal circles," interrupted T. B., "is now living in retirement near Princetown because unfortunately, there was enough of the old tissue left in him to induce him to commit crimes for which, I do not doubt, the new tissue experienced the greatest shame and indignation."

"It is foolish," reflected Silinski, clasping his knee and gazing pensively at the ceiling, "To attempt to pit one's feeble wit against a philosopher and a gentleman of your calibre. Coming down to foundations—that is your idiom, I believe—is it necessary that I should leave England?"

"It is," said T. B., confronting him now.

"Because years ago I was indiscreet," pursued Silinski, "a poor waif without a friend in this vast city; hungry, alone, half mad with solitude and starvation; because in those far-off days I stole a little, is my sin to be visited on my head in the days of my affluence?"

The unsympathetic T. B. grinned.

"What a liar you are, Silinski," he said admiringly. "Friendless! Starving! Why, you beggar, you were living on the fat of Europe! Have you forgotten the reason for your deportation? A friend of yours threw a bomb—"

Silinski raised a protesting hand.

"There is no need to go father," he said with dignity, "the circumstances of my persecution had for the moment escaped my memory. I must go?"

T. B. nodded. He nodded most emphatically.

"Go you must," he transposed, and Silinski rose to his feet slowly, and sadly.

"You would favour me if you extended the period," he said. "I have many interests in this country which will require time to realise. Also my sister is here, with obligation of a character not to be overridden: she is not without some little fame."

He took from the breast pocket of his coat a highly-coloured picture postcard, and handed it to the detective.

"You might not know that La Belle Espagna, whose dancing at the Philharmonic has aroused the populace to enthusiasm, has the misfortune to have for a brother Gregory Silinski, patriot and outcast."

He struck a little attitude, and T. B. smiled again.

"I have been aware of that fact for many months," he said, and Silinski could not control the look of astonishment and uneasiness that crossed his face.

"In fact, my dear friend," said T. B., dropping easily into French. "I know everything."

He watched carelessly for some sign of alarm in the other, and was immediately gratified. The wonder was that one of Silinski's experience should have been deceived by the bluff T. B. was making.

"Because I know of these things," continued T. B. Smith, enjoying the mystery he was creating, "I desire your absence. Let us, however, extend the period of grace to three days, at the end of which time I would have you in a land where your genius is appreciated to a greater extent than in this land of England."

Silinski stood in the centre of the room, his head bent forward, his whole attitude suggestive of feline activity, and suddenly T. B. felt the airy badinage of his own tone ring hollow, and there came to him a realisation that in some indefinable way he was in deadly peril.

What secret had he surprised—what strange devilment was behind this man?

T. B. had no other regard for Silinski than as a political extremist, a mischievous egger-on of other and bolder spirits. He had never thought of Silinski as a source of danger. T. B. Smith was quick to act.

"My man," he said evenly, "for some reason I do not like your present state of mind, and if you do monkey tricks I shall take you by the scruff of your neck and drop you out of the window."

Silinski's face was extraordinarily pale, but he did not move.

"You know—what?" he said steadily. "I am anxious *monsieur*, to see where I stand. If you know what you may know, I have bungled—and if I have not, then somebody else has."

"As to my information," said T. B., "I am not prepared to extend my confidence to you. I can only warn you that you will be watched, and any attempt on your part to further certain political propaganda"—he saw a look of relief come to the other's face, and was satisfied—"will be instantly and violently suppressed."

He escorted his visitor to the lift and exchanged conventional farewells for the benefit of the liftman, and returned slowly to his room. Then he sat down to untangle the mystery.

1. Silinski, an anarchist (see Dossier R.P.D., 9423, record Department), and by his own confession.

2. Deported for inciting to murder.

3. His sister comes to London to fulfil an engagement at a first-class music-hall. ("No particular significance in this," thought T. B. "We are all liable to be cursed with unspeakable relations.")

"By the way!"

He walked across the room to where a telephone stood on the little table, and called up Elk at Scotland Yard.

"Is anything known about La Belle Espagna—the dancing girl at the Philharmonic? Yes, I know all about her brother. Eh, what's that?—people desperately in love with her? You surprise me! Who? A young lord? Elk, there is so much awe in your voice that I could not catch that last. Who is the lord? Carleby? Never heard of him. Is that all? Thanks."

He hung the receiver up.

4. Silinski reappears, imposing prosperous. He knows Moss, frankly, a thief.

Could they have business together, fearing detection in which, Silinski goes white? Hardly.

Then what was Silinski doing in London? Was he—a bear! T. B. Had not connected the man with the bear raid. But that sort of thing was not in Silinski's line.

He sat meditating till he realised that he was hungry, and taking his overcoat from a peg behind the door, struggled into it and went out.

Elk met him at ten o'clock, and together they drove back to the Yard. There was need to dismiss Silinski from his mind.

This business of the Egyptian barrage was sufficient to occupy his thoughts.

Dimly, he began to see the workings of the gigantic combination that was spreading destruction throughout the world, anticipating disaster profitably.

Who they might guess; where their headquarters were situated he could not understand. In two days telegraph and cable office had been systematically ransacked for evidence upon this point. Every code, private and official, had been employed in the deciphering of messages that had arrived in London on the day of the slump and the day preceding it. The secret police of a dozen countries were acting in concert; for now that Scotland Yard had begun its investigations, many things were remembered. The Berlin financial crisis, coincided with the discovery of stolen plans, which had all but precipitated a war with Austria. Every country had its tale to tell of unaccountable depression, and their secret forces worked in unison to discover wherefore.

CHAPTER 8

Murder

"I've got two men on to Sir George," said T. B.—they were at the Yard—"I've given them instructions not to leave him day or night. Now, the question is, how will the 'bears' discover the fatal day the barrage is to be handed over to the guileless *Fellaheen?*"

"Through the Egyptian Government?"

"That I doubt. It seems a simple proposition, but the issues are so important that you may be sure our mysterious friends will not strike until they are absolutely certain. In the meantime—"

He unlocked the safe and took out a book. This, too, was fastened by two locks. He opened it, laid it down and began writing on a sheet of paper, carefully, laboriously checking the result.

That night the gentleman who is responsible for the good order of Egypt received a telegram which ran—

Premium Fellow Collect Wady Barage Meridian Tainted in-oculate Weary Sulphur.

There was a great deal more written in the same interesting style. When the Egyptian Chief of Police unlocked his book to decode the message, he was humming a little tune that he had heard the band playing outside Shepheard's Hotel. Long before he had finished decoding the message his humming stopped.

Ten minutes later the wires were humming, and a battalion of infantry was hastily entrained from Khartoum.

Having dispatched the wire, T. B. turned to the other man, who was sitting solemnly regarding a small gossamer handkerchief and a crushed rosebud that lay on the table.

"Well," demanded T. B. Smith, leaning over the table, "what do you make of 'em?"

"They are not Sir George's," replied the cautious Elk.

"So much I gather," said T. B. "A client's?"

"A very depressed and agitated client—feel."

T. B.'s fingers touched the little handkerchief; it was still quite damp. He nodded.

"The rosebud?"

"Did you notice our austere banker's buttonhole?"

"Not particularly—but I remember no flowers."

"No," agreed Elk absently, "there were no flowers. I noticed particularly that his buttonhole was sewn and yet—"

"And yet?"

"Hidden in one of those drawers was a bunch of these roses. I saw them when he was getting your balance-sheet."

"H'm!" T. B. tapped the table impatiently.

"So you see," Elk went on, "we have an interest in this lady client of his, who comes after office hours, weeps copiously, and leaves a bunch of rosebuds as a souvenir of her visit. It may have been a client of course."

"And the roses may have been security for an overdraft," said the ironic T. B. "What do you make of the handkerchief?"

It was an exquisite little thing of the most delicate cambric. Along one hem, in letters minutely embroidered in flowing script, there ran a line of writing. T. B. took up a magnifying glass and read it.

"'*Que Dieu tu garde*'," he read, "and a little monogram—a gift of some sort, I gather. As far as I can see, the lettering is 'N. H. C.'—and what that means, heaven knows! I'm afraid that beyond intruding to an unjustifiable extent into the private affairs of our banker, we get no further. Well Jones?"

With a knock at the door an officer had entered.

"Sir George has returned to his house. We have just received a telephone message from one of our men."

"What has he been doing tonight—Sir George?"

He dined at home; went to his club, and returned; he does not go out again."

T. B. nodded.

"Watch the house and report," he said, and the man saluted and left.

T. B. turned again to the contemplation of the handkerchief.

"If I were one of those funny detectives who live in books," he said sadly, "I could weave quite an interesting theory from this." He held the handkerchief to his nose and smelt it. "The scent is '*Sympatico*,' therefore the owner must have lived in Spain, the workmanship is Parisian, therefore—" He threw the flimsy thing from him with a laugh. "This takes us no nearer to the mysterious millionaires who 'bear' the shares of worthy brewers. Let us go out into the open, Elk, and ask heaven to drop a clue at our feet."

The two men turned their steps towards Whitehall, and were halfway to Trafalgar Square when a panting constable overtook them.

"There is a message from the man watching Sir George Calliper's house, sir," he said; "he wants you to go there at once."

"What is wrong?" asked T. B. Quickly.

"A drunken man sir, so far as I could understand."

"A what?"

T. B.'s eyebrows rose, and he smiled incredulously.

"A drunken man," repeated the man, "he's made two attempts to see Sir George—"

"Hail that cab, Elk," said T. B. "We'll drive round and see this extraordinary person."

A drunken man is not usually a problem so difficult that it is necessary to requisition the services of an Assistant-Commissioner. This much T. B. pointed out to the detective who awaited him at the corner of St. James's Square.

"But this man is different," said the officer; "he's well-dressed; he has plenty of money—he gave the cab-driver a sovereign—and he talks."

"Nothing remarkable in that, dear lad," said T. B. reproachfully; "we all talk."

"But he talks business. Sir," persisted the officer; boasts that he's got Bronte's bank in his pocket."

"The devil he does!" T. B.'s eyebrows had a trick of rising. "Did he say anything else?"

"The second time he came," said the detective, "the butler pushed him down the steps, and that seemed to annoy him—he talked pretty freely then, called Sir George all the names he could lay his tongue to, and finished up by saying that he could ruin him."

T. B. nodded.

"And Sir George? He could not, of course, hear this unpleasant conversation? He would be out of earshot."

"Beg pardon, sir," said the plain clothes man, "but that's where you're mistaken. I distinctly saw Sir George through the half-opened door. He was standing behind his servant."

"It's a pity—" began T. B., when the detective pointed along the street in the direction of the Square.

"There he is, sir," he whispered, "he's coming again."

Along the pavement, a little unsteadily, a young man walked. In the brilliant light of a street lamp T. B. Saw that he was well dressed in a glaring way. The Assistant-Commissioner waited until the newcomer reached the next lamp, then walked to meet him.

A young man, expensively garbed, red of face, and flashily jewelled—at a distance T. B. classified him as one of the more offensive type of *nouveau riche*. The stranger would have passed on his way, but T. B. stepped in front of him.

"Excuse me Mr. —" He stopped with an incredulous gasp. "Mr. Moss!" he said wonderingly. "Mr. Lewis Moss, sometime of Token-house Yard, company promoter."

"Here, stash it, Mr. Smith," begged the young man. He stood unsteadily, and in his eye was defiance. "Drop all that—reformed—me. Look 'ere"—he lurched forward and caught T. B. by the lapel of his coat, and his breath was reminiscent of a distillery—"if you knew what I know, ah!"

The "Ah!" was triumph in a word.

"If you know what I know," continued Mr. Moss with relish, "but you don't. You fellers at your game think you know *toot*, as old Silinski says; but you don't." He wagged his head wisely.

T. B. waited.

"I'm goin' to see Calliper," Mr. Moss went on, with gross familiarity, "an' what I've got to say to him is worth millions—millions, I tell you. An' when Calliper says to me, 'Mr. Moss, I thank you!' and has done the right thing, I'll come to you—see?"

"I see," said T. B.; "but you mustn't annoy Sir George any more tonight."

"Look here, Smith," Mr. Moss went off at a tangent, "you want to know how I got acquainted with Silinski—well, I'll tell you. There's a feller named Hyatt that I used to do a bit of business with. Quiet young feller who got marvellous tips—made a lot o' money, he did, all because he bowled out Silenski—see?"

He stopped short, for it evidently dawned upon him that he was talking too much.

"He sent you, eh?" Mr. Moss jerked the point of a gold-mounted stick in the direction of sir George's house. "Come down off his high 'orse"—the third "h" was too much for him—"and very wisely, very wisely." He shook his head with drunken gravity. "As a man of the world," he went on, "you bein' one an' me bein' another, it only remains to fix a meeting between self an' client—your client—an' I can give him a few tips."

"That," said T. B. "is precisely my desire." He had ever the happy knack of dealing satisfactorily with drunken men. "Now let us review the position."

"First of all," said Mr. Moss firmly, "who are these people?" He indicated Elk and the detective. "If they're friends of yours, ole feller, say the word," and his gesture was generous, "friends of yours ? Right!" Once more he became the man of affairs.

"Let us get to the bottom of the matter," said T. B. "Firstly, you wish to see Sir George Calliper?"

The young man, leaning against some happily placed railings, nodded several times.

"Although," T. B. went on, shaking his head reprovingly, " you are not exactly—"

"A bottle of fizz—a couple, nothing to cloud the mind," said the young man airily. "I've never been drunk in me life."

"It seems to me that I have heard that remark before," said T. B., "but that's beside the matter; you were talking about a man called Hyatt who bowled Silinski."

The young man pulled himself erect.

"In a sense I was," he said with dignity, "in a sense I wasn't; and now I must be toddling."

T. B. saw the sudden suspicion that came to him. "What do you know about the barrage?" he asked abruptly.

The man stared back, sobered.

"Nothing," he said harshly. "I know nothing. I know you, though Mr. Bloomin' Smith, and you ain't goin' to pump me. Here I'm going."

He pushed T. B. aside. Elk would have stopped him but for a look from his chief.

"let him go," he said. "I have a feeling that—"

The young man was crossing St. James's Street, and disappeared for a moment in the gloom between the street lamps. T. B. waited a time for him to reappear, but he did not come into sight.

"That's rum," murmured Elk, "he couldn't have gone into Sir George's; his house is on the other side of the street—hello, there he is!"

A man appeared momentarily in the rays of the lamp they were watching, and walked rapidly away.

"That isn't him," said T. B., puzzled, "he's too tall; it must be somebody from one of the houses. Let us stroll along and see what has become of Mr. Moss."

The little party crossed the street. The thoroughfare was deserted now, save for the disappearing figure of the tall gentleman.

The black patch where Mr. Moss had disappeared was the entrance of the mews.

"He must have mistaken this for a thoroughfare," said T. B. "We'll probably find him asleep in a corner somewhere." He took a little electric lamp from his pocket and shot a white beam into the darkness.

"I don't see him anywhere," he said, and walked into the mews.

"There he is!" said Elk suddenly.

The man was lying flat on his back, his eyes wide open, one arm moving feebly.

"Drunk!" said T. B., and leaned over him. Then he saw the blood and the wound in the man's throat.

"Murder! By the lord!" he cried.

He was not dead, but even as the sound of Elk's running feet grew fainter, T. B. knew that this was a case beyond the power of the divisional surgeon. The man tried to speak, and the detective bent his head to listen. "Can't tell you all," the poor wreck whispered, "get Hyatt or the man on the Eiffel Tower—they know. His sister's got the book—Hyatt's sister—down in Falmouth—you'll find N. H. C. I don't know who they are, but you'll find them." He muttered a little incoherently, and T. B. strained his ears, but heard nothing. "N. H. C." he repeated under his breath, and remembered the handkerchief.

The man on the ground spoke again—"The Admiralty—they could fix it for you."

Then he died.

CHAPTER 9

Hyatt

"Get Hyatt or the man on the Eiffel Tower!"

It sounded like the raving of a dying man, and T. B. shook his head as he walked back to his chambers in the early hours of the morning.

"Hyatt—the man on the Eiffel Tower—the Wady Barrage—the mysterious bears—what connection was there one with another?"

To—Hyatt, a friend of the late Lewis Moss.
Information concerning the whereabouts of the above-mentioned Hyatt is urgently required. Immediate communication should be made to the nearest police-station.

This notice appeared under the heading, "Too late for classification" in every London newspaper the morning following the murder of Moss.

"It is possible that the name is an assumed one," said T. B., "but the Falmouth clue narrows the search."

An "all-station" message was flashed throughout the metropolis.

Arrest and detain Gregory Silinski (here followed a description), on suspicion of being concerned in the murder of Lewis Moss.

But the surprising Silinski anticipated the arrest, for hardly had the last message been dispatched when he himself entered the *portico* of Scotland Yard and requested an interview with T. B.

"Yes," he said sadly, "I knew this young man. Poor fellow."

He gave a very frank account of his dealings with Moss, offered a very full explanation of his own movements on the night of the murder, threw in not a few moral sayings of the futility of life and endeavour, and was finally dismissed by a perplexed Commissioner, who detached an officer to verify all that Silinski had said.

He did not know Hyatt, confessed Silinski, had never heard the name; yet it seemed to T. B. Smith that at the mention of the mysterious Hyatt's name Silinski's lips tightened and his eyes narrowed.

T. B. was worried, and showed it after his own fashion. He sent Elk by an early train to pursue his inquiries, and then went into the City.

An interview with the head of the banking-house of Bronte was not satisfactory.

"I am satisfied," said T. B., "that an attempt will be made to destroy the barrage on the day for which you are liable. All the features of the present market position point to this fact."

"In that case," said the banker, "the 'bears' must be clairvoyant. The day on which the barrage comes into the hands of the Egyptian Government is known to two persons only. I am one, and the other is a gentleman, the mere mention of whose name will satisfy you to his integrity."

"And none other?"

"None other," said the banker. And that was all he would say.

But at six o'clock that night T. B. received a message. It was written in pencil on the torn edges of a newspaper.

Tonight Sir George Calliper is dining with the Spanish dancing girl, La Belle Espagna.

That, and an initial, was all the note contained, but it came from the most reliable man in the Criminal Investigation Department, and T. B. whistled his astonishment.

CHAPTER 10

Sir George Dines

Sir George Calliper lived in St. James's Street. A bachelor—some regarded him as a misogynist—his establishment was nevertheless a model of order; and if you had missed the indefinable something that betrays a woman's hand in the arrangement of furniture, you recognised that the controlling spirit of the household was one possessed of a rigid sense of domesticity, that found expression in solid comfort and sober luxury.

The banker sat in his study engaged in writing a letter. He was in evening dress, and the little French clock on the mantel had just chimed seven.

He finished the note and folded it in its envelope. Then he pressed a bell. A servant entered.

"I am dining out," said Sir George shortly. "I shall be home at eleven." It was characteristic that he did not say "may be home," or "at about eleven."

"Shall I order the car, Sir George?"

"No; I'll take a cab."

A shrill whistle brought a taxi-cab to the door.

A passing commissionaire stopped to ask the cabman which was the nearest way to Berkley Square as the banker came down the two steps of the house.

"Meggioli's," he instructed the cabman, and added, "the Vine Street entrance."

The commissionaire stood back respectfully as the whining taxi jerked forward.

"Meggioli's!" murmured the commissionaire, "and by the private door! That's rum. I wonder whether Elk has started for Cornwall yet?"

He walked into St. James's Square, and a smart one-horse brougham that had been idly moving round the circle of garden in the centre, pulled up at the kerb by his side.

"Meggioli's—front entrance," said the commissionaire.

It was a uniformed man who entered the carriage; it was T. B. Smith in his well-fitting dress clothes who emerged at Meggioli's.

"I want a private room," he informed the proprietor, who came to meet him, with a bow.

"I'm ver' sorry, Mr. Smith, but I have not—"

"But you have three," said T. B. indignantly.

"I offer a thousand regrets," said the distressed restaurateur; "they are engaged. If you had only—"

"But, name of dog! Name of sacred pipe!" expostulated T. B. unscrupulously. Was it not possible to pretend that there had been a mistake; that one room had already been engaged?"

"Impossible, *m'sieur!* In No. 1 we have no less a person than the Premier of South-West Australia, who is being dined by his fellow-colonists; in No. 2 a family party of Lord Redlands; in No. 3—ah! In No. 3—"

"Ah, in No. 3!" repeated T. B. cunningly, and the proprietor dropped his voice to a whisper.

"La Belle Espagna!" he murmured. He named the great Spanish dancer with relish. "She, and her *fiancé's* friend, eh?"

"Her *fiancé's?* I didn't know—"

"It is a secret—" he looked round as if he were fearful of eavesdroppers, "but it is said that La Belle Espagna is to be married to a rich admirer."

"Name?" asked T. B. carelessly.

The proprietor shrugged his shoulders.

"I do not inquire the name of my patrons," he said, "but I understand that it is to be the young Lord Carleby."

The name told T. B. nothing.

"Well," he said easily, "I will take a table in the restaurant. I do not wish to interrupt a *tête-à-tête.*"

"Oh, it is not Carleby tonight," the proprietor hastened to assure him. "I think *mamzelle* would prefer that it was—not; it is a stranger."

T. B. sauntered into the brilliantly lighted room, having handed his hat and coat to a waiter. He found a deserted table. Luck was with him to an extraordinary extent; that Sir George should have chosen Meggioli's was the greatest good fortune of all.

At that time Count Menshikoff was paying one of his visits to England. The master of the St. Petersburg secret police was a responsibility. For his protection it was necessary that a small army of men should be detailed, and since Meggioli's was the only restaurant he favoured, at least one man of the Criminal Investigation Department was permanently employed at that establishment.

T. B. called a waiter, and the man came swiftly. He had a large white face, big unwinking black eyes, and heavy bushy eyebrows, that stamped his face as one out of the common. His name—which is unimportant—was Vellair, and foreign notabilities his speciality.

"Soup—*consommé, crème de—*"

T. B., studying his menu, asked quietly, "is it possible to see and hear what is going on in No. 3?"

"The private room?"

"Yes."

The waiter adjusted the table with a soft professional touch. "There is a small ante-room, and a ventilator, a table that might be pushed against the wall, and a chair," said the waiter, concisely. "If you remain here I will make sure."

He scribbled a mythical order on his little pad and disappeared.

He came back in five minutes with a small tureen of soup. As he emptied its contents into the plate before T. B. he said, "All right; the key is on the inside. The door is numbered 11."

T. B. picked up the wine list.

"Cover me when I leave," he said.

He had finished his soup when the waiter brought him a note. He broke open the envelope and read the contents with an expression of annoyance.

"I shall be back in a few minutes," he said rising; "reserve this table."

The waiter bowed.

CHAPTER 11

The Dancing Girl

T. B. reached the second floor. The corridor was deserted; he walked quickly to No. 11. The door yielded to his push. He closed it behind him and noiselessly locked it. He took a tiny electric lamp from his pocket and threw the light cautiously round.

He found the table and chair place ready for him, and blessed Vellair silently.

The ventilator was a small one, he had located it easily enough when he had entered the room by the gleam of light that came through it. Very carefully he mounted the table, stepped lightly on to the chair, and looked down into the next chamber.

It was an ordinary kind of private dining-room. The only light came from two shaded electric lamps on the table in the centre.

Sir George with a frown was regarding his beautiful *vis-a vis*. That she was lovely beyond ordinary loveliness T. B. knew from repute. He had expected the high colourings, the blacks and scarlets of the Andalusian; but this girl had the creamy complexion of the well-bred Spaniard, with eyes that might have been hazel or violet in the uncertain light, but which were decidedly not black. Her lips, now tightly compressed, were neither too full nor too thin, her nose straight, her hair, brushed back from her forehead in an unfamiliar style, was that exact tint between bronze and brown that your connoisseur so greatly values.

A plain *filet* of dull gold about her head, and the broad collar of pearls around her neck, were the only jewels she displayed. Her dress was black, unrelieved by any touch of colour. She was talking rapidly in Spanish, a language with which T. B. was very well conversant.

"—but Sir George," she pleaded, "it would be horrible, wicked, cruel not to see him again!"

"It would be worse if you saw him," said the other drily. "You know, my dear young lady, you would both be miserable in a month. The title would be no compensation for you; Carleby would bore you; Carleby House would drive you mad; Carleby's relatives would incite you to murder."

"You are one!" she blazed.

"Exactly; and I do not exasperate you? Think of me magnified by a hundred. Come, come, there are much better men than Carleby in the world, and you are young, you are little more than a child."

"But I love him," she sobbed.

"I suppose you do," T. B. from his hiding-place bestowed an admiring grin upon the patronage in the baronet's tone. "When did you meet him first?"

"Three weeks ago." She spoke with a catch in her voice that affected T. B. strangely.

"That girl is acting," he thought.

"Three weeks?" mused the banker. "Um—when did you discover he was a relative of mine?"

"A few days since," she said eagerly. "I was in Cornwall, visiting some friends—"

"Cornwall!" T. B. had hard work to suppress an exclamation.

"—and I learned from them that you were related. I did not know of any other relation. My friends told me it would be wicked to marry without the knowledge of his people. 'Go to Sir George Calliper and explain,' they said; 'he will help you'; instead of which—"

The banker smiled again.

"Instead of which I pointed out how impossible it was eh? And persuaded you to give up all idea of marrying Carleby. Yes, I suppose you think I am a heartless brute."

She sat with bent head.

"You will give him my message?" she asked suddenly.

He nodded.

"And the flowers?"

"And the flowers," he repeated gravely.

("That clears the banker," thought T. B.)

"I shall leave for Spain tomorrow. It was good of you to let me have this talk."

"It was good of you to come."

"Somehow," she said drearily. "I cannot help feeling that it is for the best."

Again T. B. thought he detected a note of insincerity.

"When will you see him?"

"Carleby?" he asked.

"Tomorrow?"

"Not tomorrow."

"The next day?"

T. B. was alert now; he saw in a flash the significance of this interview; saw the plot which had lured a foolish relative of Calliper's to a love affair; and now, the manoeuvring to the crucial moment of the interview which she had so cleverly planed.

"Nor the next day," smiled Sir George.

"Well, the *next* day?"

He shook his head. "That is the day of all days I am not likely to leave London."

"Why?" she asked innocently, her eyes wide open and her lips parted.

"I have some very important business to transact on that day," he said briefly.

"Oh, I forgot," she said, with a hint of awe in her voice. "You're a great banker, aren't you?" she smiled. "Oh, yes, Carleby told me—"

"I thought you didn't know about me until your Cornish friends told you?" he asked.

"Not that you were related to him," she rejoined quickly, "but he spoke of the great house of Bronte—"

("Neat," approved the hidden T. B.)

"So Thursday will be the day," she mused.

"The day you will see Carleby," she said, with a look of surprise.

"I said *not* Thursday on any account, but possibly the next day," said Sir George stiffly.

"She has the information she wants," said T. B. to himself, "and so have I," he reflected. "I will now retire."

He stepped carefully down, and reached the floor, and was feeling his way to the door, when a strange noise attracted his attention. It came, not from the next room, but from that in which he stood. He stood stock still, holding his breath, and the noise he heard was repeated.

Somebody was in the room with him. Somebody was moving stealthily along the wall at the opposite side of the apartment. T. B. waited for a moment to locate his man, then leaped noiselessly in the direction of the sound. His strong hands grasped a man's shoulder; another instant and his fingers were at the spy's throat. "Utter a word and I'll knock your head off!" he hissed. No terrible threat when uttered facetiously, but T. B.'s words were the reverse to humorous. Retaining a hold of his prisoner he waited until the noise of a door closing told him that the diners in the next room had departed, then he dragged his man to where he judged the light switch would be. His fingers found the button, turned it, and the room was flooded with light.

He released the man with a little push, and stood with his back to the door.

"Now, sir," said T. B. virtuously, "will you kindly explain what you mean by spying on me?"

The man was tall and thin. He was under thirty and decently dressed; but it was his face that held the detective's attention. It was the face of a man in mortal terror—the eyes staring, the lips tremulous, the cheeks lined and seamed like an old man's. He stood blinking in the light for a moment, and when he spoke he was incoherent and hoarse.

"You're T. B. Smith," he croaked. "I know you; I've been wanting to find you."

"Well, you've found me," said the detective grimly.

"I wasn't looking for you—now. I'm Hyatt."

He said this simply enough, and it was the detective's turn to stare.

"I'm Hyatt," the man went on, "and I've a communication to make; King's evidence; but you've got to hide me!" He came forward and laid his hand on the other's arm. "I'm not going to be done in like Moss; it's your responsibility, and you'll be blamed if anything happens to me," he almost whispered in his fear. "They've had Moss, and they'll try to have me. They've played me false because they thought I'd get to know the day the barrage was to be handed over, and spoil their market. They brought me up to London, because I'd have found out if I'd been in Cornwall—"

"Steady, steady!" T. B. checked the man. He was talking at express rate, and between terror and wrath was well nigh incomprehensible. "Now, begin at the beginning. Who are 'they'?"

"N. H. C., I told you," snarled the other impatiently. "I knew they were going to get that date from the banker. That was Catherine's scheme; she got introduced to his nephew so that she might get at the uncle. But I'm giving King's evidence. I shall get off, shan't I?"

His anxiety was pitiable.

T. B. thought quickly. Here were two ends to the mystery; which was the most important? He decided. This man would keep; the urgent business was to prevent Catherine from communicating her news to her friends.

"Take this card," he said, and scribbled a few words hastily upon a visiting-card; "that will admit you to my rooms at the Savoy. Make yourself comfortable until I return."

He gave the man a few directions, piloted him from the restaurant, saw him enter a cab, then turned his steps towards Baker Street.

CHAPTER 12

"Mary Brown"

Pentonby Mansions are within a stone's throw of Baker Street Station. T. B. jumped out of his cab some distance from the great entrance hall, and paid the driver. Just before he turned into the vestibule a man strolling toward him asked him for a match.

"Well?"

"She came straight from the restaurant and has been inside ten minutes," reported the man ostentatiously lighting his pipe.

"She hasn't sent a telegram?"

"So far as I know, no, sir."

In the vestibule a hall porter sat reading the evening paper.

"Can I telephone from here?" asked T. B.

"Yes, sir," said the man, and T. B.'s heart sank, for he had overlooked the possibility.

"I suppose you have 'phones in every room?" he asked carelessly.

But the man shook his head.

"No, sir," he said; "there is some talk of putting 'em in, but so far this 'phone in my office is the only one in the building."

T. B. smiled genially.

"And I suppose," he said, "that you're bothered day and night with calls from tenants?" He waited anxiously for the answer.

"Sometimes I am, and sometimes I go a whole day without calls. Now today, for instance, I haven't had a message since five o'clock."

T. B. murmured polite surprise and began his ascent of the stairs. So far, so good. His business was to prevent the girl communicating with her brother, whom he did not doubt now was the agent of the "bears," if not worse.

He had already formed a plan in his mind.

Turning at the first landing, he walked briskly along the corridor to the left.

"29, 32, 33," he counted, "35, 37. Here we are." The corridor was empty; he slipped his skeleton key from his pocket, deftly manipulated it.

The door opened noiselessly. He was in a dark little hallway. At the end was a door and a gleam of light shone under it. He closed the door behind him, stepped softly along the carpeted floor, and his hand was on the handle of the further door, when a sweet voice called him by name from the room.

"*Adelante! Senor Smit*," it said; and, obeying the summons, T. B. entered.

The room was well, if floridly, furnished; but T. B. had no eyes save for the graceful figure lounging in a big wicker chair, a thin cigarette between her red lips, and her hands carelessly folded on her lap.

"Come in," she repeated. "I have been expecting you."

T. B. bowed slightly.

"Gregory told me that I should probably receive a visit from you."

"First," said T. B. gently, let me relieve you of that ugly toy."

Before she could realise what was happening, two strong hands seized her wrists and lifted them. Then one hand clasped her two, and a tiny pistol that lay in her lap was in the detective's possession.

******

"Let us talk," said T. B. He laid her tiny pistol on the table, with his thumb raised the safety catch.

"You are not afraid of a toy pistol?" she scoffed.

"I am afraid of anything that carries a nickel bullet," he confessed, without shame. "I know by experience that your 'toy' throws a shot that penetrates an inch of pinewood and comes out on the other side. I cannot offer the same resistance as pinewood," he added modestly.

"I have been warned about you," she said, with a faint smile.

"So you were warned." T. B. was mildly amused and just a trifle annoyed. It piqued him to know that whilst, as he thought, he had been working in the shadow, he had been under a searchlight.

"Your excellent brother, I do not doubt," he said.

"You are—what do you call it in England?—smug," she said, "but what are you going to do with me?"

She had let fall her cloak and was again leaning lazily in the big armchair. The question was put in the most matter-of-fact tones.

"That, you shall see," said T. B. cheerfully. "I am mainly concerned now in preventing you from communicating with brother Gregory."

"It will be rather difficult?" she challenged with a smile. "I am not proscribed; my character does not admit—"

"As to your character," said T. B. magnanimously, "we will not go into question. So far as you are concerned, I shall take you into custody on a charge of obtaining property by false pretences," said T. B. calmly.

"What?"

"Your name is Mary Brown, and I shall charge you with having obtained the sum of £350 by a trick from a West Indian gentleman at Barbadoes last March."

She sprang to her feet, her eyes blazing.

"You know that is false and ridiculous," she said steadily. "What is the meaning of it?"

T. B. shrugged his shoulders.

"Would you prefer that I should charge La Belle Espagna with being an accessory to murder?" he asked, with a lift of his eye brows.

"You could not prove it!" she challenged.

"Of that I am aware," he said. "I have taken the trouble to trace your movements. When these murders were committed you were fulfilling an engagement at the 'Philharmonic,' but you knew of the murder, I'll swear—you are an agent of N. H. C."

"So it was you who found my handkerchief?"

"No; a discerning friend of mine is entitled to the discovery—are you ready, Mary Brown?"

"Wait."

She stood plucking at her dress nervously. "What good can my arrest do to you—tomorrow it will be known all over the world."

"There," said T. B., "you are mistaken"

"To arrest me is to sign your death-warrant—you must know that—the nine men will strike—"

"Ah!!"

T. B.'s eyes were dancing with excitement.

"Nine men!" he repeated slowly, "*Neuf hommes*—N.H. What does the 'C' stand for?"

"That much you will doubtless discover," she said coldly, "but they will strike surely and effectively."

The detective had regained his composure.

"I'm a bit of a striker myself," he said in English.

CHAPTER 13

Deportation

T. B. found the Chief Commissioner of Police at his club, and unfolded his plan.

The Chief looked grave.

"It might very easily lead to a worse if I don't," said T. B. brutally, "I am too young to die. At the worst it can only be a 'police blunder,' such as you read about in every evening newspaper that's published," he urged, "and I look at the other side of the picture. If this woman communicates with her principals, nothing is more certain than that Thursday will see the blowing up of the Wady Semik Barrage. These 'Nine Bears' are operating on the sure knowledge that Bronte's Bank is going to break. The stocks they are attacking are companies banking with Bronte, and it's ten chances to one they will kill Sir George Calliper in order to give an artistic finish to the failure."

The Commissioner bit his lip thoughtfully.

"And," urged T. B. Smith, "the N. H. C. will be warned, and bang goes our only chance of bagging the lot!"

The Commissioner smiled.

"Your language, T. B.!" he deplored; then, "do as you wish—but what about the real Mary Brown?"

"Oh, she can be sent on next week with apologies. We can get a new warrant if necessary."

"Where is she?"

"At Bow Street."

"No,; I mean the Spanish lady?"

T. B. grinned.

"She's locked up in your office, sir," he said cheerfully.

The Commissioner said nothing, but T. B. declined to meet his eye.

At four o'clock the next morning, a woman attendant woke La Belle Espagna from a fitful sleep, and a few minutes afterwards T. B., dressed for a journey and accompanied by a hard-faced wardress and a detective came in.

"Where are you going to take me?" she demanded; but T. B.'s reply was not very informing.

A closed carriage deposited them at Euston in time to catch the early morning train.

In the compartment reserved for her and the wardress—it was a corridor carriage, and T. B. and his man occupied the next compartment—she found a dainty breakfast waiting for her, and a supply of literature. She slept the greater part of the journey and woke at the jolting of a shunting engine being attached to the carriage.

"Where are we?" she asked.

"We're there," was the cryptic reply of the woman attendant.

She was soon to discover, for when the carriage finally came to a standstill and the door was opened, she stepped down on to a wind-swept quay. Ahead of her the great white hull of a steamer rose, and before she could realise the situation she had been hurried up the sloping gangway on to the deck.

Evidently T. B.'s night had been profitably spent, for he was expected. The purser met him.

"We got your telegrams," he said. "Is this the lady?"

T. B. nodded.

The purser led the way down the spacious companion.

"I have prepared 'C' suite," he said, and ushered the party into a beautifully appointed cabin.

She noticed that a steel grating had been newly fixed to the port-hole, but that was the only indication of her captivity.

"I have enlisted the help of the stewardess," said T. B., "and you will find all the clothing you are likely to require for the voyage. I am also instructed to hand you three hundred pounds. You will find your little library well stocked. I, myself," he stated with all the extravagance to which the Iberian tongue lends itself, "have denuded my own poor stock of Spanish and French novels in order that you might not be dull."

"I understand that I am to be deported?" she said.

"That is an excellent understanding," he replied.

"By what authority?" she demanded. "It is necessary to obtain an order from the Court."

"For the next fourteen days, and until this ship reaches Jamaica, you will be Mary Brown, who was formally extradited last Saturday on a charge of fraud," said T. B. "If you are wise, you will have no trouble, and nobody on board need have an inkling that you are a prisoner. You can enjoy the voyage, and at the end—"

"At the end?" she asked, seeing that he paused.

"At the end we shall discover our mistake," said T. B., "and you may return.

"I will summon the captain and demand to be put ashore!" she cried.

"A very natural request on the part of a prisoner," said T. B. meditatively, "but I doubt very much whether it would have any effect upon an unimaginative seaman."

He left her raging.

For the rest of the day he idled about the ship. The *Port Sybil* was due to leave at four o'clock, and when the first warning bell had sounded he went below to take his leave.

He found her much calmer.

"I would like to ask you one question," she said. "It is not like the police to provide me with money, and to reserve such a cabin as this for my use—who is behind this?"

"I wondered whether you would ask that," said T. B. "Sir George was very generous—"

"Sir George Calliper!" she gasped. "You have not dared—"

"Yes, it needed some daring," admitted T. B., "to wake an eminent banker out of his beauty sleep to relate such a story as I had to tell—but he was very nice about it."

She brooded for some moments.

"You will be sorry for this," she said. "The Nine Men will know much sooner than you imagine."

"Before they know this, they will know other things," he said. And with this cryptic utterance he left her.

He stood watching the great steamer moving slowly down the Mersey. He had left the wardress on board to make the voyage, and the other detective had remained to report.

As the vessel swung round a bend of the Mersey out of sight, he murmured flippantly:

"Next stop—Jamaica!"

★★★★★★

T. B. reached his chambers at noon that day. He stopped to ask a question of the porter.

"Yes, sir," said the worthy, "he arrived all right with your card last night. I made him comfortable for the night, got him some supper, and told my mate who is on duty at night to look after him."

T. B. nodded. Declining the lift-boy's services, he mounted the marble stairs.

He reached the door of his flat and inserted the key.

"Now for Mr. Hyatt," he thought, and opened the door.

There was a little hall-way to his chambers, in which the electric light still burned, in spite of the flood of sunlight that came from a long window at the end.

"Extravagant beggar!" muttered T. B.

The dining-room was empty, and the blinds were drawn, and here too, the electric light was full on. There was a spare bedroom to the left, and to this T. B. made his way.

He threw open the door.

"Hyatt!" he called; but there was no answer, and he entered.

Hyatt lay on the bed, fully dressed. The handle of a knife protruded from his breast, and T. B., who understood these things, knew that the man had been dead for many hours.

CHAPTER 14

When the Market Rose

Consols were up.

There was no doubt whatever about the fact, and the industrial market was a humming hive of industry.

Breweries, bakeries, and candlestick makeries—their shares bounded joyously as though a spirit, as of early spring had entered into these intimate and soulless things.

The mysterious "bears" were buying, buying, buying.

Frantically, recklessly buying.

Whatever coup had been contemplated by the Nine Men had failed, and their agents and brokers were working at fever heat to cover their losses.

It is significant that on the morning the boom started, there appeared in all the early editions of the evening newspapers one little paragraph. It appeared in the "late news" space and was condensed.

Wady Barrage was handed over to Egyptian Government early this morning in presence of Minister of Works. Overnight rumours were prevalent that attempt made to destroy section dam by dynamite and that Italian named Soccori shot dead by sentry of West Kent Regiment in act of placing explosives on works. No official confirmation.

Interesting enough, but hardly to be associated by the crowd which thronged the approaches of the House with the rising market.

All day long the excitement in the City continued, all day long bare-headed clerks ran aimlessly—to all appearances—from 'Change to pavement, from pavement to 'Change, like so many agitated ants.

Sir George Calliper, sitting alone in the magnificence of his private office, watched the "boom" thoughtfully, and wondered exactly what would have happened if "an Italian named Soccori" had succeeded in placing his explosive.

The echoes of the boom came to T. B. Smith in his little room overlooking the Thames Embankment, but brought him little satisfaction. The Nine Men had failed this time. Would they fail on the next occasion?

Who they were he could guess. From what centre they operated, he neither knew nor guessed. For T. B. they had taken on a new aspect. Hitherto they had been regarded merely as a band of dangerous and clever swindlers, Napoleonic in their method; now, they were murderers—dangerous, devilish men, without pity or remorse.

The man Moss by some accident had been associated with them—a tool perhaps, but a tool who had surprised their secret. He was not the type of man who, of his own intelligence, would have made discoveries. He mentioned Hyatt and "the man on the Eiffel Tower." That might have been the wanderings of a dying man, but Hyatt had come to light.

Hyatt, with his curiously intellectual face; here, thought T. B., was the man, if any, who had unearthed the secret of the Nine.

Likely enough he shared confidence with Moss; indeed, there was already evidence in T. B.'s hands that the two men had business dealings. And the third—"the man on the Eiffel Tower"? Here T. B. came against a wall of improbability. His report to the Chief Commissioner deserves quotation on the point.

Hyatt occupied rooms in Albany Street, (he wrote). So far as we have been able to ascertain, he paid rare visits to London. His landlady thought he came from the South of England, but could give me no reason for this supposition. He paid £2 a week for his chambers, and although, as I say, he was seldom in London, he kept these rooms on, which leads to the assumption that he was a man of some means. The only documents we found in our search were two penny memorandum books, filled with notes regarding share transactions. Hyatt seems to have speculated very heavily and very successively, and it is significant that he participated in all the big 'Nine Men' operations.

I found a bag with two hotel labels half obliterated. One of these is unquestionably the label of the Hotel de Calais in the Rue de Capucines, and the other is the representation of a white ensign. Comparing this with the hotel labels indexed on the Record Department at Scotland Yard, I am led to the belief that it was affixed at the Grand Hotel, Gibraltar. It is a fact, as you know, that amongst the possessions of Moss we discovered a handbag with a Paris label, but in these two bags there is a more important clue. There is affixed to both a 'Repository' label—that is, the label of a French cloak-room.

In the case of Moss the number of the ticket is '01795,' on Hyatt's bag there is still discernible '—796.' From this we know that not only were the two men in Paris at the same time, but that they arrived by the same train, and going together to the depository, left their bags—which were numbered consecutively.

I am now, therefore, inclined to take a more serious view of the statement made by Moss before he died. His words were, you remember—

'Get Hyatt or the man on the Eiffel Tower. His sister's got the book—Hyatt's sister down in Falmouth.'

Then he went on to say that 'the Admiralty would fix it for you.'

At the time I thought the poor chap was raving; but Hyatt is a fact, and we are now searching for his sister, and this 'book' of his. As to the reference to the Admiralty I confess I am stumped, for nobody at Whitehall has ever heard of Hyatt.

There remains the man on the Eiffel Tower. Who was he, or is he? A theory advanced by Elk is that he is a man casually met; some acquaintance made in the course of a morning's sightseeing. If this is so, the business of discovering his identity promises to be an extremely difficult one. We have communicated with Lepine in Paris, but naturally the little man wants something more tangible. More definite then the description we have been able to give him. . . .In the meantime I have had Hyatt's body removed, and so far nothing has got into the papers about that murder. We must issue a statement tonight, if the fact does not leak out before. By the way, Silinski, the man I referred to in my minute of the 10th, was under observation at the time of the murder, and the detective engaged in shadowing him informs me that it is impossible that he could have been implicated.

CHAPTER 15

In the "Journal" Office

The room was a long one, full of dazzling islands of light where shaded lamps above the isolated sub-editors' desks threw their white circles. This room, too, was smirched with black shadows; there were odd corners where light never came. It never shone upon the big bookcase over the mantelpiece, or in the corner behind the man who conned the foreign exchanges, or on the nest of pigeon holes over against the chief "sub."

When he would refer to these he must needs emerge blinking from the blinking light in which he worked and go groping in the darkness for the needed memorandum.

He was sitting at his desk now, intent upon his work.

At his elbow stood a pad, on which he wrote from time to time.

Seemingly his task was a aimless one. He wrote nothing save the neat jottings upon his pad. Bundles of manuscript came to him, blue books, cuttings from other newspapers; these he looked at rather than read, looked at them in a hard, strained fashion, put them in this basket or that, as the fancy seized him, chose another bundle, stared at it, fluttered the leaves rapidly and so continued. He had the appearance of a man solving some puzzle, piecing together intricate parts to make one comprehensive whole. When he hesitated, as he sometimes did, and seemed momentarily doubtful as to which basket a manuscript should be consigned, you felt the suggestion of mystery with which his movements were enveloped, and held your breath. When he had decided upon the basket, you hoped for the best, but wondered vaguely what would have happened if he had chosen the other.

Once he leaned back and dived into the darkness. When he came back to light his hand held a little book, carefully indexed and filled with written notes.

He glanced dubiously at a bundle of copy before him, opened the book at "E," ran his finger down the page, turned the page over, made another search, and frowned.

Elling was there: George Elling, who sold the *Journal* a story about a suicide that had never happened. He had derived a fairly comfortable and regular income from reporting mythical happenings till the *Journal* sent a special man to investigate. Then the fraud was detected and "our own correspondent" at Gravesport was "fired," and his name and the record of his infamy entered in the little book with the green covers. Edwards was there too. Edwards had written a little pamphlet attacking "The Office"—a vulgarly abusive, hysterical, foolish, and illogical little pamphlet, in which personal grievances and incoherent appeals to the sanity of the country were hopelessly interwoven. Essard was there, on the second page of the "E's" No crime stood against his name, but the chief sub. Smiled faintly as he passed the name, for Essard had once dared to contribute a paragraph with a "business end." In other words, the wretched Essard had had the temerity to write under the guise of a news-story, the most barefaced advertisement of a firm of engineers, thereby wickedly, maliciously, and feloniously attempting to deprive the directors and shareholders of the *Amalgamated Newspapers, Limited,* of their just and proper revenue.

But the sub-editor sought in vain for the name of the man under review. He closed the book and looked across the table to his assistant.

"Who is Escoltier?" he asked.

The assistant looked up.

"Escoltier? Never heard of the gentleman. What has he done?"

"Is he barred?"

"Barred—Escoltier?" This was a serious question and not to be treated with flippancy. "No, I can't remember Escoltier—rum name—being barred; in fact, I can't remember Escoltier."

The chief sub. Stared at the manuscript on the desk before him.

He shook his head; hesitated, then dropped it into basket three.

The door that opened into the tape-room was swinging constantly now, for it wanted twenty minutes to eleven. Five tickers chattered incessantly, and there was a constant procession of agency boys and telegraph messengers passing in and out the vestibule of the silent building. And the pneumatic tubes that ran from the front hall to the subs'. room hissed and exploded periodically, and little leathern carriers rattled into the wire basket at the chief sub.'s elbow.

News! News! News!

A timber fire at Rotherhithe; the sudden rise in Consols; the *Sultan* of Turkey grants amnesty to political offenders; a man kills his wife at Wolverhampton; a woman cyclist run down by a motorcar; the Bishop of Elford denounces Nonconformists—

News for tomorrow's breakfast table; intellectual stimulant for the weary people who are even now kicking off their shoes with a sleepy yawn and wondering whether there will be anything in the paper tomorrow.

News to be carried by fast expresses north, east, south, and west. The history of the world for one day, told by eye-witnesses, recorded, mailed, and written in the office at first hand.

A boy came flying through the swing door of the tape-room, carrying in his hand a slip of paper.

He laid it before the chief sub.

That restless man looked at it, then looked at the clock.

"Take it to Mr. Greene," he said shortly, and reached for the speaking-tube that connected him with the printer.

"There will be a three-column splash on page five," he said in a matter-of-fact voice.

"What's up?" His startled assistant was on his feet.

"A man found murdered in T. B. Smith's chambers," he said.

The inquest was over, the stuffy little court discharged its morbid public, jurymen gathered in little knots on the pavement permitted themselves to theorise, feeling, perhaps, that the official version of "murder against some person or persons unknown" needs amplification.

"My own opinion is," said the stout foreman, "that nobody could have done it, except somebody who could have got into his chambers unknown."

"That's my opinion, too," said another juryman.

"I should have liked to add a rider," the foreman went on, "something like this: 'We call the coroner's attention to the number of undiscovered murders nowadays, and severely censure the police,' but he wouldn't have it."

"They 'ang together," said a gloomy little man; "p'lice and coroners and doctors, they 'ang together, there's corruption somewhere. I've always said it."

"Here's a feller murdered," the foreman went on, "in a detective's room, the same detective that's in charge of the Moss murder. We're told his name's Hyatt, we're told he was sent to that room by the detective whilst he's engaged in some fanciful business in the north—is that sense?"

"Then there's the *Journal*," interrupted the man of gloom, "it comes out this mornin' with a cock an' bull story about these two murders being connected with the slump—why, there ain't any slump! The market went up the very day this chap Hyatt was discovered."

"Sensation," said the foreman, waving deprecating hands, "newspaper sensation. Any lie to sell the newspapers, that's their motto."

The conversation ended abruptly, as T. B. Smith appeared at the entrance to the court. His face was impassive, his attire, as usual, immaculate, but those who knew him best detected signs of worry.

"For heaven's sake," he said to a young man who approached him, "don't talk to me now—you beggar, your wretched rag has upset all my plans."

"But Mr. Smith," pleaded the reporter, "what we said was true, wasn't it?"

"A lie that is half the truth," quoted T. B. solemnly.

"But it is true—there is some connection between the murders and the slump, and I say, do your people know anything about the dancing girl from the Philharmonic?"

"Oh, child of sin!" T. B. shook his head reprovingly. "Oh, collector of romance."

"One last question," said the reporter. "Do you know a man named Escoltier?"

"Not," said T. B. flippantly, "from a crow—why? Is he suspected of abducting your dancing lady?"

"No," said the reporter, "he's suspected of pulling our editor's leg."

T. B. was all this time walking away from the Court, and the reporter kept step with him.

"And what is the nature of his hoax?" demanded T. B.

He was not desirous of talking about nothing—it had been a trying day for him.

"Oh, the usual thing; wants to tell us the greatest crime that ever happened—a great London crime that the police have not discovered."

"Dear me!" said T. B. politely, "wants payment in advance?"

"no, that's the curious thing about it," said the reporter. "All he wants is protection."

T. B. stopped dead and faced the young man. He dropped the air of boredom right away.

"Protection?" he said quickly, "from whom?"

"That is just what he doesn't say—in fact, he's rather vague on that point—why don't you go up and see Delawn, the editor?"

T. B. thought for a moment.

"Yes," he nodded. "That is an idea. For the moment, however, I have engaged myself to meet another gentleman who may throw a light upon any matters which are at present obscure."

CHAPTER 16

Silinski is Interviewed

There was no apparent connection between Homborgstrasse 22, Berlin, and No. 14, Rue de Cent, Paris, nor between the big barren-looking house in the Calle de Recoletos in Madrid and 375, St. John Street, W. C. Nor, for the matter of that, between the little house perched upon one of the seven hills overlooking the Tagus and the pension near Novski Prospekt in Petersburg.

One feature they had in common, and that was a stout flagstaff, upon which on festal days fluttered the flag of the respective nations.

Silinski, who was responsible, for the hiring or purchasing of all these properties, could have told you another connection less apparent, but Silinski was a notoriously silent man, and said little or nothing.

He sat in his well-furnished study in St. John street, and round him and about was evidence of his refinement and taste. Rare prints hung on the wall, the furniture was sombrely magnificent, the carpet beneath his feet soft and thick and of sober hue, the desk before him such an one as a successful man of letters might affect.

There were photographs of eminent personages, kings, statesmen, ambassadors, great *prima donnas*. Some of these were autographed "*a cher Silinski*"; some were framed in silver, and, in the case of royalties, surmounted by tiny gilt crowns.

Silinski had never met royalty in his life, though he had once robbed a grand duke at Monte Carlo, and the autographs and loving messages written upon the purchased photographs were in Silinski's own hand, though this fact was not generally known. This was Silinski's weakness; many a greater man has shared it.

There came a gentle tap at his door and a man entered.

"Well?" demanded Silinski suavely.

"The police, illustrious," said the man in Spanish, and with no particular sign of agitation.

Silinski nodded gravely.

"Admit," he said, and in a few seconds T. B. Smith walked into the room.

"And what is your pleasure, gentlemen?" demanded Silinski.

"Little enough, Silinski," said the other blandly. He looked round as though seeking a comfortable chair. In reality he was taking a rapid survey of the apartment. "I have a few questions to ask you."

Silinski bowed and motioned the Assistant-Commissioner to a seat.

"It is my misfortune," he said, leaning back in his chair and crossing his legs, "that I have incurred your enmity' none the less, it will give me the greatest pleasure to afford you such assistance as lies in my power."

T. B. smiled grimly.

"You have incurred nobody's enmity, as I understand the situation," he said. He looked again round the room. "You are very comfortably circumstanced, Silinski."

"Fortune has been kind," said the Pole suavely.

"One successful speculation," mused T. B. aloud, "might found the fortunes of such a man as you."

"I am no speculator," said the other hastily. "It is too risky—I do not approve of gambling."

"Yet you had dealings with Moss?"

"Investments, m'sieur—not speculations."

"And with Hyatt?"

"As to Hyatt—I do not know him. I have never heard of him."

"And the man," T. B. paused, "from the—er—Eiffel Tower?"

Perhaps Silinski's face grew a shade whiter, and the lines about his mouth hardened.

"These riddles you set me are beyond my understanding," he said harshly. In a moment, however, he had recovered his equanimity.

"You are much too clever for me, Mr. Smith," he said, with a smile.

"There is a fourth person who would seem to be in some way associated with your complicated financial affairs," T. B. resumed. "Do you know a Mr. Escoltier?"

Silinski sprang to his feet.

"Fourth person—M'sieur Escoltier?" he stammered. "What do you mean? I tell you, you are speaking in riddles. I do not understand you—I do not wish to understand you." His voice grew louder and louder as he spoke. His energy seemed out of all proportion to the importance of the topic, and T. B. knit his brow in perplexity.

Then he suddenly sprang to his feet.

"Stop!" he said, "Stop talking" You are bellowing because something is happening in this house that you do not wish me to hear—stop!"

But the frenzy of the Pole rose. He roared indignant, unintelligible protestations; he shouted denunciations of police espionage.

T. B., with bent head and every sense alert, stood before him. Through the flood of impassioned words he detected the sound; it was a noise strangely like the rattling of dried peas in a tin can.

Then as suddenly as he began, Silinski ceased, and the two men faced each other in silence.

"Silinski," said T. B. at last, "before God, I believe you are a wicked murderer."

"Then arrest me," challenged the man; "call in the police who have been watching this house day and night since the death of Moss. Arrest me, as you did my sister!"

T. B. had all his work to suppress the exclamation of surprise that came to his lips.

"Extradite me under a false name, as you did her," sneered Silinski; "carry me up to Liverpool in the dead of night and smuggle me on board a West Indian steamer."

"I am not as a rule a curious man," said T. B. slowly, "but I must confess that I should like to know where you secured all these valuable data."

"Pooh!"

It was the old Silinski who paced the floor and snapped his fingers—the Silinski assured, arrogant, the hint of a swagger in his walk.

"You think, you English police, that the world goes blind at your command. My friend"—he stopped and pointed a lean forefinger at the other—"I can tell you many things. The hour you left London, the hour you arrived, the number of the state-room in which you place my poor, ill-used sister; your very words to her at parting."

He stopped, biting his lips; he had said too much, and he knew it. In the enjoyment of puzzling an astute member of a profession regarded by him as made up of his natural enemies, he had allowed boastfulness to outrun discretion.

"So you know my last words to her," repeated T. B., more slowly than ever, "although she and I were alone, although a thousand miles of sea separate you at this moment. I see."

He said no more, but with a slight nod, and without any further talk, he descended the stairs that led to the big entrance-hall, and Silinski, pulling nervously at his moustache, heard the great door of the house close behind him.

CHAPTER 17

The Man from the Eiffel Tower

In the holy of holies, the inner room within the inner room wherein the editor of the London Morning Journal saw those visitors who were privileged to pass the outer portal, T. B. Smith sat, a sorely puzzled man, a scrap of disfigured paper in his hands.

He read it again and looked up at the editor.

"This might, of course, be a fake," he said.

"It doesn't read like a fake," said the other.

"Admitting your authority on the subject of fakes, Tom," said T. B.,—they were members of the same club, which fact in itself is a license for rudeness—"I am still in the dark. Why does this—what is his name?"

"Escoltier."

"Why does this man Escoltier write to a newspaper, instead of coming straight to the police?"

"Because he is a Frenchman, I should imagine," said the editor. "The French have the newspaper instinct more highly developed than the English."

T. B. looked at his watch.

"Will he come, do you think?"

"I have wired to him," said the editor.

T. B. read the paper again. It was written in execrable English, but its purport was clear.

The writer could solve the mystery of Hyatt's death, and, for the matter of that, of the Moss murder.

T. B. read it again and shook his head.

"This sort of thing is fairly common," he said; "There never was a bad murder yet, but what the Yard received solutions by the score."

A little bell tinkled on the editor's desk, and he took up the receiver of the telephone.

"Yes?" he said, and listened. Then, "Send him up."

"Is it—?"

"M. Escoltier," said the editor.

A few seconds later the door was opened, and a man was ushered into the room. Short and thickset, with a two days' growth of beard on his chin, his nationality was apparent long before he spoke in the argot of the lowly-born Parisian.

His face was haggard, his eyes heavy from lack of sleep, and the hand that strayed to his mouth shook tremulously.

"I have to tell you," he began, "about M'sieur Moss and M'sieur Hyatt." His voice was thick, and as he spoke he glanced from side to side as though fearful of observation. There was something in his actions that vividly reminded the detective of his interview with Hyatt. "You understand," the man went on incoherently, "that I had long suspected N. H. C.—it was always so unintelligible. There was no such station and—"

"You must calm yourself, *monsieur*," said T. B., speaking in French; "begin at the beginning, for as yet my friend and myself are entirely in the dark. What is N. H. C., and what does it mean?" It was some time before the man could be brought to a condition of coherence. The editor pushed him gently to the settee that ran the length of the bay window of his office.

"Wait," said the journalist, and unlocking a drawer, he produced a silver flask.

"Drink some of this," he said.

The man raised the brandy to his lips with a hand that shook violently, and drank eagerly.

"*C'est bien*," he muttered, and looked from one to the other.

"I tell you this story because I am afraid to go to the police—they are watching the police office—"

"In the first place, who are you?" demanded T. B.

"As to who I and what I am," said the stranger, nodding his head to emphasize his words, "it would be better that I should remain silent."

"I do not see the necessity," said the detective calmly. "So far as I can judge from what information I have, you are a French soldier—an engineer. You are a wireless telegraph operator, and your post of duty is on the Eiffel Tower."

The man stared at the speaker, and his jaw dropped.

"*M'sieur!*" he gasped.

"Hyatt was also a wireless operator; probably in the employ of the Marconi Company in the West of England. Between you, you surprised the secret of a mysterious agency which employs wireless installations to communicate with its agents. What benefits you yourself may have derived from your discovery I cannot say. It is certain that Hyatt, operating through Moss, made a small fortune; it is equally certain that, detecting a leakage, the 'Nine Men' have sent a clever agent to discover the cause—"

But the man from the Eiffel Tower had fainted.

"I shall rely on you to keep the matter an absolute secret until we are ready," said T. B, and the editor nodded. "I tumbled to the whole scheme when a gentleman who shall be nameless, boasted to me that he knew certain things which it was not humanly possible for him to know—until I remembered that a certain ship was fitted with wireless telegraphy. Then it came to me in a flash. The Eiffel Tower! Who lives on the Eiffel Tower? Telegraph operators. Our friend is recovering."

He looked down at the pallid man lying limply in an armchair.

"I am anxious to know what brings him to London. Fright, I suppose. It was the death of Moss that brought Hyatt, the killing of Hyatt that produced Monsieur Escoltier."

The telegraphist recovered consciousness with a shiver and a groan. For a quarter of an hour he sat with his face hidden in his hands. Another pull at the editor's flask aroused him to tell his story—a narrative which is valuable as being the first piece of definite evidence laid against the Nine Bears.

He began hesitantly, but as the story of his complicity was unfolded he warmed to his task. With the true Gaul's love for the dramatic, he declaimed with elaborate gesture and sonorous phrase the part he played.

My name is Jules Escoltier, I am a telegraphist in the corps of Engineers. On the establishment of the wireless telegraphy station on the Eiffel Tower in connection with the Casa Blanca affair, I was appointed one of the operators. Strange as it may sound, one does not frequently intercept messages, but I was surprised a year ago to find myself taking code dispatches from a station which calls itself 'N. H. C.' There is no such station known, so far as I am aware, and copies of the dispatches which I forwarded to my superiors were always returned to me as 'non-decodable.'

One day I received a message in English, which I can read. It ran—

'All those who know N. H. C. call H. A.'

Although I did not know who N. H. C. was, I had the curiosity to look up H. A. on the telegraph map, and found it was the Cornish Marconi Station. Taking advantage of the absence of my officer, I sent a wireless message, 'I desire information, L. L.' That is not the Paris 'indicator,' but I knew that I should get the reply. I had hardly sent the message when another message came in. It was from Monsieur Hyatt. I got the message distinctly—'Can you meet me in London on the 9th, Gallini's Restaurant?'

To this I replied, 'No, impossible.' After this I had a long talk with the Cornishman, and then it was that he told me that his name was Hyatt. He told me that he was able to decode the N. H. C. messages, that he had a book, and that it was possible to make huge sums of money for the information contained in them. I thought that it was very indiscreet to speak so openly, and told him so.

He asked me for my name, and I gave it, and thereafter I regularly received letters from him, and a correspondence began.

Not being *au fait* in matters affecting the Bourse, I did not know of what value the information we secured from N. H. C. could be, but Hyatt said he had a friend who was interested in such matters, and that if I 'took off' all N. H. C. messages that I got, and repeated them to him, I should share the proceeds. I was of great value to Hyatt, because I received messages that never reached him. In this way he was able to keep in touch with all the operations in which N. H. C. were engaged.

By arrangement, we met in Paris—Hyatt, his friend of the London Bourse (Monsieur Moss), and myself, and Hyatt handed to me notes for 20,000 *francs* (£800); that was the first payment I received from him. He returned to England, and things continued in very much the same way as they had done, I receiving and forwarding N. H. C. messages. I never understood any of them, but Hyatt was clever, and he discovered the code and worked it out.

About a fortnight ago I received from him 3,000 *francs* in notes, a letter that spoke of a great coup contemplated by N. H. C. 'If this materialises,' he wrote 'I hope to send you half a million *francs* by the end of next week.'

The next morning I received this message—

He fumbled in his pocket and produced a strip of paper, on which was hastily scrawled—

From N. H. C. to L. L. Meet me in London on the sixth, Charing Cross Station."

It was, as you see, in French, and as it came I scribbled it down. I would have ignored it, but that night I got a message from Hyatt saying that N. H. C. Had discovered we shared their secret and had offered to pay us £5,000 each to preserve silence, and that as they would probably alter the code I should be a fool not to accept. So I got leave of absence and bought a suit of clothing, left Paris, and arrived in London the following night. A dark young man who said his name was Silinski met me at the station, and invited me to come home with him.

He had a motorcar at the entrance of the station, and after some hesitation I accepted. We drove through the streets filled with people, for the theatres were just emptying, and after an interminable ride we reached the open country. Silinski drove the car and I was the only other occupant. I asked him where was Hyatt, and where we were going, but he refused to speak. When I pressed him, he informed me he was taking me to a rendezvous near the sea.

We had been driving for close on three hours, when we reached a lonely lane. By the lights of the car I could see a steep hill before us, and I could hear the roar of the waves somewhere ahead.

Suddenly he threw a lever over, and as the car bounded forward, he sprang to the ground with a mocking laugh.

Before I could realise what had happened, the machine was flying down the steep gradient, rocking from side to side.

I have sufficient knowledge of motorcar engineering to manipulate a car, and I at once sprang to the wheel and felt for the brake. But both foot and hand brake were useless. In some manner he had contrived to disconnect them.

It was pitch dark, and all that I could hope to do was to keep the car to the centre of the road. Instinctively I knew that I was rushing to certain death, and *messieurs*, I was! I was flying down a steep gradient to inevitable destruction, for at the bottom of the hill the road turned sharply, and confronting me, although I did not know this, was a stone sea wall.

I resolved on taking my life in my hands, and putting the car at one of the steep banks which ran on either side, I turned the steering wheel and shut my eyes. I expected instant death. Instead, the car bounded up at an angle that almost threw me from my seat. I heard the crash of wood, and flying splinters struck my neck, and the next thing I remember was a series of bumps as the car jolted over a ploughed field.

I had achieved the impossible. At the point I had chosen to leave the road was a gate leading to a field, and by an act of Providence, I had found the only way of escape.

I found myself practically at the very edge of the sea, and in my first terror I would have given every *sou* I had to escape to France. All night long I waited by the broken car, and with the dawn some peasants came and told me I was only five miles distant from Dover. I embraced the man who told me this, and would have hired a conveyance to drive me to Dover, *en route* for France. I knew that N. H. C. Could trace me, and then I was anxious to get in touch with Hyatt and Moss. Then it was that I saw in an English newspaper that Moss was dead.

He stopped and moistened his lips.

"*M'sieur!*" he went on, with a characteristic gesture, "I decided that I would come to London and find Hyatt. I took a train, but I was watched. At a little junction called Sandgate, a man sauntered past my carriage. I did not know him, he looked like an Italian. As the train left the station something smashed the window, and I heard a thud. There was no report, but I knew that I had been fired at with an airgun, for the bullet I found embedded in the woodwork of the carriage."

"Did nothing further happen?" asked T. B.

"Nothing till I reached Charing Cross; then when I stopped to ask a policeman to direct me to the Central Police Bureau I saw a man pass me in a motorcar, eying me closely. It was Silinski."

"And then?"

"Then I saw my danger. I was afraid of the police. I saw a newspaper sheet. It was a great newspaper—I wrote a letter—and sought lodgings in a little hotel near the river. There was no answer to my letter. I waited in hiding for two days before I realised that I had given no address. I wrote again. All this time I have been seeking Hyatt. I have telegraphed to Cornwall, but the reply comes that he is not there. Then in the newspaper I learn of his death. *M'sieur*, I am afraid."

He wiped the drops of sweat from his forehead with a shaky hand.

He was indeed in a pitiable condition of fright, and T. B., upon whose nerves the mysterious "bears" were already beginning to work, appreciated his fear without sharing it.

There came a knock at the outer door of the office, and the editor moved to answer it.

There was a whispered conversation at the door, the door closed again, and the editor returned with raised brows.

"T. B." he said, "that wretched market has gone again."

"Gone?"

"Gone to blazes! Spanish fours are so low that you'd get a pain in your back if you stooped to pick them up."

T. B. nodded.

"I'll use your telephone," he said, and stooped over the desk. He called for a number and after an interval—

"Yes—that you, Mainland? Go to 375 St. John Street, and take into custody Gregory Silinski on a charge of murder. Take with you fifty men and surround the place. Detain every caller, and every person you find in the house."

He hung up the receiver.

"Now, my friend," he said in French, "what shall we do with you?"

The Frenchman shrugged his shoulders listlessly.

"What does it matter?" he said, "they will have me—it is only a matter of hours."

"I take a brighter view," said T. B. cheerily; "you shall walk with us to Scotland Yard and there you shall be taken care of."

But the Frenchman shrunk back.

"Come, there is no danger," smiled T. B.

Reluctantly the engineer accompanied the detective and the editor from the building. A yellow fog lay like a damp cloth over London, and the Thames Embankment was almost deserted.

"Do you think he followed you here?" asked T. B.

"I am sure." The Frenchman looked from left to right in agony of apprehension. "He killed Hyatt and he killed Moss—of that I am certain—and now—"

A motorcar loomed suddenly through the fog, coming from the

direction of Northumberland Avenue, and overtook them. A man leaned out of the window as the car swept abreast. His face was masked but his actions were deliberate.

"Look out!" cried the editor, and clutched the Frenchman's arm.

The pistol that was levelled from the window of the car cracked twice and T. B. felt the wind of the bullets as they passed his head.

Then the car disappeared into the mist, leaving behind three men, one half-fainting with terror, one immensely pleased with the novel sensation—our editor, you may be sure—and one using language unbecoming to an Assistant-Commissioner of Police, for T. B. knew that the mask was Silinski, and that the detectives even now on their way to St. John Street would find the cage empty and the bird flown.

CHAPTER 18

The Affair of the "Castilia"

There was no apparent reason for the slump in Spanish Fours. Spanish credit never stood so high as it did at the moment of the panic. Catalonia had been appeased by the restoration of the constitution, the crops throughout Spain had been excellent, and the opening of the Porta Ciento mines, combined with the extension of the mining industry in the north, had all helped to bring about a condition of financial confidence in Spanish securities.

The "bear" attack, which was made simultaneously on every European bourse, was, in the face of these facts, madness.

The Spanish Government rose to the situation and with praiseworthy promptness, issued broadcast warnings to the investing public. Ministers seized any opportunity for speaking on the subject of national financial stability, but the "raid" went on. No stock even remotely associated with, or dependent upon, Spain's national security was left unassailed. Telegraphs, railways, mines—they suffered in common.

Then happened that remarkable tragedy that set the whole of Europe gasping. It was a happening tragic in its futility, comic in its very tragedy. Europe was dumbfounded, speechless. There are two accounts given; there is that contained in Blue Book 7541/,09, and there is that issued by the Spanish Government as a white paper. The latter, although it is little more than a reprint of a number of articles published in the *Heraldo de Madrid* and the *Correspondencia*, is as accurate and contains more detail. I have taken these accounts and summarised the story of the momentous occurrence from both.

On the morning of the 29th of January, the Spanish cruise *Castilia* was lying in Vigo Bay. She had been engaged in gun practise on the coast, and had come to Vigo for stores and to give leave to her crew.

The ship had been coaled, ammunition and stores taken on board, and the warship steamed out to sea. Her commander was Captain Alfonso Tirez, a singularly capable officer who had served with distinction in the Spanish-American War.

The movements of the ship subsequent to her departure from Vigo Bay are fairly well known.

She was seen by a fishing fleet heading south, and was sighted level with Oporto by the Portuguese gunboat *Braganza*. More than this, she exchanged signals with the *Braganza*, making "All's well."

From this point, her voyage is something of a mystery, although it is evident that she continued a straight course.

She was not sighted again until the third of February, four days after her departure from Vigo, and the particulars of her reappearance are contained in the report made by Captain Somburn, R. N., of H. M. S. *Inveterate*, a first-class cruiser.

The *Inveterate* was detached from the Atlantic Squadron, then lying at Gibraltar, by order of the Commander-in-Chief, to cruise along the Morocco coast as far south as Mogador, and she was returning when the incident to Captain Somburn, so graphically described, occurred.

The ship's (the *Inveterate's*) position at 7.45 was approximately Lat. 35 north and Long. 10 west, and we were due west of Cape Cantin when the *Castilia* was sighted, (wrote Captain Somburn).

She was making a course as to pass us on our starboard bow. Recognising her, I ordered the ensign to be flown. Nothing untoward happened, and the ship came nearer and nearer.

There had been some trouble just before I arrived at Mogador, some little fighting with a Moorish tribe, and thinking that it was on this account that the cruiser was going south, and that possibly the later news I had would be of interest to her captain, I ordered a signal to be made.

'Mogador all quiet; rising quelled.'

To my astonishment, no notice was taken of this, and not even so much as an answering pennant was hoisted.

The officer of the watch, who had been looking at the vessel through his telescope, then reported to me that the *Castilia* was cleared for action, and that her gun crews were standing by.

I thought that we were interrupting some manoeuvre such as 'man and arm ship,' and readily forgave her commander, who was so absorbed in his drill that he ignored my signal.

The next minute, however, the *Castilia* opened fire on me with her forward guns. Both shots missed, one passing our stern and the other just clearing our quarterdeck.

I signalled 'Your firing practise is endangering me,'

For, even then, I could not bring myself to a realisation that the captain of the *Castilia* was in earnest.

I was soon undeceived, however. A shell from his after four-inch gun struck and carried away a portion of the navigation bridge.

I immediately ordered general stations, and in twenty seconds I had cleared the starboard batteries for action. In this time the *Castilia* had out three shells into the *Inveterate*. The first killed an able seaman and seriously wounded the gunnery-lieutenant, the second did little or no damage, but the third destroyed No. 3 9.6 gun and killed four of its crew.

I at once opened fire on the *Castilia* with two six-inch guns. Both shots took effect, one, as I have since ascertained, below her water line, and she immediately heeled over to port.

Seeing she was helpless, and sinking rapidly, I ordered away my life-boats, at the same time signalling 'I am coming to your assistance.' No further shots were fired, and the officers and crew of the *Castilia*, together with nineteen wounded men, were taken off.

The *Castilia* sank at 8.19, the action having lasted, from the time of firing the first shot to the moment of crippling, 5 minutes, 48 seconds.

I made no immediate attempt to ascertain the cause of the extraordinary conduct of the *Castilia*, because Captain Tirez, when I received him on board, was in a dying condition. He had been struck by a fragment of shell and never regained consciousness, expiring that afternoon, but before my arrival at Gibraltar I interviewed the Spanish officer who was acting as navigating lieutenant. From him I learned the incident was inexplicable to him, as to the rest of the crew. The captain had received a wireless telegram, coded in the secret cipher of the Admiralty. This telegram had perplexed and distressed him, but the only remark he had made to his officers had been—

'The Government is sending us to our deaths—but I can do nothing else than obey.'

From this it would seem that Captain Tirez—whom I know personally to have been a very able and gallant gentleman—was acting on orders which were open to no other interpretation than as direct instructions to shell the *Inveterate*.

So much for the laconic report of the officer.

He compressed within the limits of a sheet of notepaper a tragedy, the news of which appalled the civilised world.

The battle occurred at between seven and eight in the morning. The news was in London by ten that the *Inveterate* had been sunk by a Spanish cruiser and that a fierce and sanguinary battle had preceded its sinking.

Who sent the descriptive telegram from Gibraltar will never be known, though its source was obvious.

It bore the name of a world-famous news agency, and was issued to the Press from the London office of the Agency, but the Gibraltar correspondent had no knowledge of its sending. All England was in an uproar when the official version of the incident came to hand.

Spain! Why Spain! What was the cause? What had we done, what insult had we offered? There were writers in plenty to rush into print to prove that whatever had happened it was England's fault, but even these gentlemen could offer no elucidation.

Captain Somburn's report was telegraphed to the Admiralty immediately on his arrival at Gibraltar, and issued to the Press. Side by side in the morning newspapers appeared the official disclaimer of the Spanish government.

His Majesty's Government has no knowledge of any circumstance leading up to or responsible for the recent lamentable disaster off the coast of Morocco. It has issued directly or indirectly no instructions, orders, or suggestions to Captain Tirez, and has had no communication with him other than the conventional exchange of documents, peculiar to routine.

CHAPTER 19

The Book

T. B. Smith was one of many millions, who read this statement. He was one of many thousands who believed it implicitly. He was one of twelve who understood the madness of the dead Spanish Captain.

He saw, too, villainy behind it all; the greed of gold that had sent a gallant ship to the bottom, that had brought death and mutilation in most horrible form to brave men.

Silinski had slipped through his fingers—Silinski, arch-agent of the Nine.

The house in St. John Street had been raided. In a little room on the top floor there was evidence that an instrument of some considerable size had been hastily dismantled. Broken ends of wire were hanging from the wall, and one other room on the same floor was packed with storage batteries. Pursuing their investigations, the detective ascended to the roof through a trap door. Here was the flagstaff and the arrangement for hoisting the wires. Apparently, night was usually chosen for the reception and dispatch of messages. By night, taut strands of wire would not attract attention. Only in cases of extremest urgency were they employed in daylight.

Such an occasion had been that when T. B. had interviewed Silinski. He understood now why the Pole had talked so loudly. It was to drown the peculiar sound of a wireless instrument at work.

Silinski was gone—vanished, in spite of the fact that every railway terminus in London had been watched, every ocean-going passenger scrutinised.

Now, on top of his disappearance came the *Castilia* disaster with the irresponsible public of two nations howling for a scapegoat. T. B. Smith attended a specially convened meeting of Ministers in downing Street and related all that he knew.

"Give me two days," he said "and you may publish the whole of the facts. But to show our hand now would be disastrous. The police of every city are engaged in tracking down the wireless stations. There is one in every capital, of that much we are sure. To get the whole gang, however, I must find out where they are operating from."

"Is that possible?" asked the grave Prime Minister.

"Absolutely, sir," said T. B.

In the end they agreed.

A more difficult man to persuade was the editor of the *London Morning Journal.*

"I have got the story, why not let me publish?" was a not unnatural request.

"In two days you shall have the complete story' what I am anxious to avoid is anything in the nature of to-be-continued- in-our-next! I want the whole thing rounded off and finished for good."

Reluctantly, the editor agreed.

He had two days to get the "book"; this code which the unfortunate Hyatt had deciphered to his undoing. Moss had said Hyatt's sister had it, but the country had been searched from end to end for Hyatt's sister. It had not been difficult to trace her. Elk, after half an hour's search in Falmouth had discovered her abode, but the girl was not there.

"She left for London yesterday," he was informed.

From that moment Miss Hyatt had disappeared.

A telegram had reached her on the very day of Hyatt's death. It said "Come."

There was no name, no address. The telegram had been handed in at St. Martin's-le-Grand; unearthed, it was found to be in typewritten characters, and the address at its back a fictitious one.

One other item of news Elk secured; there had been a lady on the same errand as himself. "A foreign lady," said the good folks of Falmouth. When T. B. played the spy to the banker and the Spanish dancer, he had heard her speak of a visit to Cornwall; this, then, was the visit.

He had some two days to discover Eva Hyatt—this was her name.

Silinski might have killed her; he was large in his views and generous murderous, and one life more or less would not count. T. B. paced his room, his head sunk on his breast.

Where was the girl?

The telegram said "Come." It suggested some pre-arranged plan in which the girl had acquiesced; she was to leave Falmouth and go somewhere.

Who sent the telegram? Not Silinski; this Eva Hyatt, by all showing, was one of the class that sticks for the proprieties.

Suppose she had come to London, where would Catherine Silinski have placed her? Near at hand; a thought struck T. B.

He had been satisfied with deporting the dancing girl, a fruitless precaution, as it turned out; he had made no search of her flat. Had she been arrested in the ordinary way, the search would have followed, but her arrest was a little irregular.

He took down his overcoat and struggled into it, made a selection of keys from his pocket, and went out. It was a forlorn hope, but forlorn hopes had often been the forerunners of victory with him, and there was nothing to be lost by trying. He came to the great hall of the mansion in Baker street. The hall porter recognised him and touched his cap.

"Evening, sir." Then, "I suppose you know the young lady hasn't come back yet?"

T. B. did know, but said nothing. The porter was in a talkative mood.

"She sent me a wire from Liverpool, saying that she'd been called away suddenly."

T. B. nodded. He knew this, too, for it was he who had sent the wire.

"What the other young lady couldn't understand," continued the porter, and T. B.'s heart gave a leap., "was why—"

"Why she hadn't wired her, eh?" the detective jumped in.

"Well, you see, she was so busy—"

"Of course!" The porter clucked his lips impatiently. "Of course, you saw her off, didn't you, sir?"

"I saw her off," said T. B. gravely.

"I'd forgotten that; why, you went away together, an' I never told the young lady. She's upstairs in Miss Silinski's flat at this moment. My word, she's been horribly worried—"

"I'll go up and see her. As a matter of fact, I've come here for the purpose," said T. B. quickly.

He took the lift to the second floor, and walked along the corridor. He reached No. 43 and his hand was raised to press the little electric bell of the suite when the door opened quickly and a girl stepped out. She gave a startled cry as she saw the detective, and drew back.

"I beg your pardon," said T. B. with a smile. "I'm afraid I startled you."

She was a big florid girl with a certain awkwardness of movement.

"Well-dressed but *gauche*," mentally summarised the detective. "Provincial! She'll talk."

"I *was* a little startled," she said, with a ready smile. "I thought it was the postman."

"But surely postmen do not deliver letters in this palatial dwelling," he laughed. "I thought the hall porter—"

"Oh, but this is a registered letter," she said importantly, "from America."

All the time T. B. was thinking out some method by which he might introduce the object of his visit. An idea struck him.

"Is your mother—" she looked blank, "er—aunt within?" he asked.

He saw the slow suspicion gathering on her face.

"I'm not a burglar," he smiled, "in spite of my alarming question, but I'm in rather a quandary. I've a friend—well, not exactly a friend—but I have business with Miss Silinski, and—"

"Here's the postman," she interrupted.

A quick step sounded in the passage, and the bearer of the King's mails, with a flat parcel in his hand and his eyessearcking the door numbers, stopped before them.

"Hyatt?" he asked, glancing at the address.

"Yes," said the girl; "is that my parcel?"

"Yes, miss, will you sign?"

"Hyatt?" murmured T. B., "what an extraordinary coincidence. You are not by any chance related to the unfortunate young man, the story of whose sad death has been filling the newspapers?"

She flushed and her lips trembled.

"He was my brother; did you know him?"

"I knew of him," said T. B. quietly, "but I did not know you lived in London."

"Nor do I," said the girl; "it is only by the great kindness of Senora Silinski that I am here."

There was no time for delicate finesse. He slid his card-case from his pocket.

"Will you let me come in and talk with you?" he said; then, as he saw again the evidence of her suspicion, "I am a police-officer, and what I have to ask you is of the greatest importance to you and to me."

She took the pasteboard, and, as T. B. had anticipated, fell into a flutter of agitation.

"Oh, please come in! Was it wrong to come to London? The *Senora* was so anxious that nobody should know I was here. I've been so worried about her—"

She led the way into a handsomely furnished sitting-room.

"First of all," said T. B. quietly, "you must tell me how the *Senora* found you."

"She came to Falmouth and sought me out. It was not difficult. I have a little millinery establishment there, and my name is well known. She came one morning, eight days—no—yes, it was seven days ago, and—"

"What did she want?"

"She said she had known Charles, he had some awfully swagger friends; that is what got him into trouble at the post office; it was a great blow to us because—"

"What did she want?" asked T. B., cutting short the loquacity.

"She said that Charles had something of hers—a book which she had lent him, years before. Now, the strange thing was that on the very day poor Charles was killed I had a telegram which ran: 'If anything happens, tell Escoltier book is at Antaxia, New York.' It was unsigned, and I did not connect it with Charles. You see, I hadn't heard from him for years.

"She was a great friend of Charles'—the *Senora*—and she came down especially about the book. She said Charles had got into trouble and she wanted the book to save him. Then I showed her the telegram. I was confused, but I wanted to help Charles." She gulped down a sob. "I asked her who Escoltier was."

"Yes?" asked T. B. quickly.

"She said he was a friend of hers who was interested in the book. She went away, but came back soon afterwards and told me that 'Antaxia' was the telegraphic address of a safe deposit box in New York. She was very nice and offered to pay for a cable to the deposit. So I wired: 'Please forward by registered post the book deposited by Charles Hyatt'; and I signed it 'Eva Hyatt' and gave my address. By the evening the reply came: 'Forwarded; your previous wire did not comply with our instructions.'"

"I see," said T. B.

"Well, that is more than I can," said the girl, with a smile, "because only one wire was sent. The *Senora* was surprised, too, and a little annoyed, and said: 'How foolish it was of me not to ask you your Christian name.' Well, then the *Senora* insisted upon my coming to stay with her till the book came. I came expecting I should find Charles, but—but—"

Her eyes were filled with tears.

"I read in a newspaper that he was dead. It was the first thing I saw in London, the bill of a newspaper—"

T. B. gave her time to recover her voice.

"And the *Senora?*"

"She took this furnished flat near to hers," said the girl; "she lives here—"

"Does she?" asked T. B. artlessly. He took up the registered parcel which she had put on the table.

It was fairly light.

"Now, Miss Hyatt," he said, "I want you to do something for me; and I must tell you that, although I ask it as a favour, I can enforce my wishes as a right."

"I will do anything," said the girl eagerly.

"Very well; you must let me take this book away."

"But it's not mine; it belongs to the *Senora*," she protested; "and it is to save my brother's name—"

"Miss Hyatt," said T. B. gently, "I must take this book which has so providentially come into my hands, not to save your brother's name, but to bring to justice the men who took his life."

As he spoke there came a knock at the door; and, hastily drying her eyes, the girl opened it.

A porter handed her a telegram, and she came back into the light of the room to open it.

She read it, and re-read it; then looked at T. B. with bewilderment written on her face. "What does this mean?" she said.

T. B. took the telegram from her hand; it had been re-addressed from Falmouth, and ran:

By wireless from Port Sybil. Do not part with book to anybody on any account,

Catherine Silinski.

T. B. handed the telegram back.

"It means," he said, "that our friend is just two minutes too late."

273

CHAPTER 20

At the Admiralty

Wherever men met they spoke of one thing; they had one subject of conversation; in train or in club-room; in bar or meeting-place, in barristers' robbing-room; in prisoners' waiting hall—the *Castilia* and Spain.

Small doubt but that there were demands, irresponsible demands for satisfaction, after satisfaction had been given. But tangible satisfaction was needed. Spain had dared.....insult to the might and majesty of Britain—war must be a logical outcome—and the like.

These outpourings appeared in many newspapers under the heading, "Letters to the Editor." Some newspapers would not print them because of a curious resemblance between them.

The Editor of the *London Journal* made this discovery.

The *Journal* is a newspaper controlled by a great syndicate which owns a newspaper in every one of the great centres of industry throughout Great Britain. It has a system of exchanging confidences, and as a result, it was found that a letter addressed to *The Northern Journal and Times* was identical, word for word, with a letter addressed to the London paper. With this difference, that whilst one was signed "J. B. Barver," the other bore the magnificent signature of "Orlando T. Sabout." The editor sent both letters to T. B. Smith, and T. B. grinned unpleasantly, but with some admiration for the completeness of the Nine Men's organisation.

On top of these letters, was revived a form of publicity which had long since fallen into desuetude—the pamphlet was mooked.

Three pamphlets were shot suddenly into the market. This was the second day after the sinking of the *Castilia*.

One, the more virulent, was called *A Blow at Protestantism*, and was an invitation to England to sweep Europe clear of the "Catholic

Menace."

Neither pamphlet could have been written in two days. They must have been prepared a fortnight to a month in advance of the disaster. They bore no publisher's imprint or printer's advertisement.

"This business is a little too hot to hold," said the editor in a final interview with T. B. "Tonight I must tell the whole story."

T. B. nodded.

"Tonight," said T. B., "you can tell what you like. I shall have played my stake for good or ill.

"I have been talking with Escoltier; we have got him lodged in Scotland Yard—though you needn't mention that fact in your account—and I think we know enough now to trap the Nine Men."

"Who are they and what does the 'C' stand for in 'N. H. C.'?"

"I can only guess," said T. B. cautiously. "Do you know anything about wireless telegraphy?" he demanded.

"Not much," admitted the editor.

"Well, you know enough to realise that the further you wish to communicate the more electrical energy you require?"

"That much I understand," said the journalist. "The principle is the 'rings on the pond.' You throw a stone into still water, and immediately rings grow outward. The bigger the stone, the farther reaching the rings."

"At Poldhu," continued T. B., "Hyatt was in charge of the long-distance instrument. As a matter of fact, the work he was engaged on was merely experimental, but his endeavour seemed to be centred in securing the necessary energy for communicating nine hundred miles. Of course, wireless telegraphy is practicable up to and beyond 3,000 miles, but few installations are capable of transmitting that distance."

"So 'C' is, you think, within 900 miles of Cornwall?"

T. B. nodded.

"I have a feeling that I know 'C'," he said. "I have another feeling that these wireless messages do not come from 'C' at all, but from a place adjacent. However,"—he took from his pocket a flat exercise book filled with closely-written columns of words and figures—"we shall see."

He took a cab from Fleet Street; and, arriving at the block of Government buildings which sheltered the Lords Commissioners of the Admiralty, he entered its gloomy doors.

A messenger came forward to inquire his business, but was forestalled by a keen little man with tanned face and twinkling eyes. "Sailor" was written on every line of his mahogany face. "Hullo, my noble policeman!" he greeted T. B. "Who is the victim—the First Sea Lord or the Controller of the Victualling Department?"

"To be precise, Almack," said T. B. "I have come to arrest Reform, which I gather—"

"No politics,," smiled Captain Jack Almack, R. N. "What is the game?"

"It is what our mutual friend Napoleon would call a negative problem in strategy," the Assistant-Commissioner replied. "I want to ask an ethereal friend, who exists somewhere in space, to come in and be killed."

Captain Almack led the way up a flight of stairs.

"We got a request from your Commissioner; and of course, the Lord of Admiralty are only too pleased to put the instrument at your disposal."

"They are very charming," murmured T. B.

"They instructed me to keep a watchful eye on you. We have missed things since your last visit."

"That sounds like a jovial lie," said T. B. frankly.

In the orderly instrument room they found an operator in attendance, and T. B. lost no time.

"Call N. H. C.," he said; and, whilst the instrument clicked and snapped obedient to the man's hand, T. B. opened his little exercise book and composed a message. He had finished his work long before any answer came to the call. For half an hour they waited whilst the instrument clicked monotonously. "*Dash-dot, dot-dot-dot, dash-dot-dash-dot,*"

And over and over again.

"*Dash-dot, dot-dot-dot, dash-dot-dash-dot.*"

Then suddenly the operator stopped, and there came a new sound.

They waited in tense silence.

"Answered," said the operator.

"Take this." T. B. handed him a slip of paper.

As the man sent the message out with emphatic tappings, Captain Almack took the translation that T. B. handed him.

"To N. H. C. There is trouble here. I must see you. Important. Can you meet me in Paris tomorrow?"

After this message had gone through there was a wait of five minutes. Then the answer came, and the man at the instrument wrote down unintelligible words which T. B. translated.

"Impossible. Come to M. Will meet S. E. Have you got the book?"

"Reply 'Podaba'," instructed T. B., spelling the word. "Now send this." He handed another slip of paper across the table, and passed the translation back to the man behind him.

"Is Gibraltar intercepting messaged?" it ran. Again the wait, and again the *staccato* reply.

"Unlikely, but will send round tomorrow to make sure. Goodnight."

As the instrument clicked its farewell, T. B. executed a silent wardance to the scandal of the solemn operator, and the delight of the little captain.

"T. B., you'll get me hung!" he warned. "You'll upset all kinds of delicate instruments, to say nothing of the telegraphist's sense of decency. Come away."

"Now," demanded Captain Almack, when he had led him to his snug little office; "what is the mystery?"

T. B. related as much of the story as was necessary, and the officer whistled.

"The devils!" he swore. "And so that's the explanation of the poor old *Castilia's* sinking is it?"

"The discovery I was trying to make," T. B. went on, "was the exact location of N. H. C. I asked him or them to come to Paris. As a matter of fact, I wanted to know if they were within twenty-four hours' distance of Paris. 'Impossible,' they reply. But they will come to Madrid, and offer to meet the Sud Express. So they must be in Spain and south of Madrid, otherwise there would be no impossibility about meeting me in Paris tomorrow. Where are they? Within reach of Gibraltar apparently, because they talk of sending round tomorrow. Now, that phrase 'sending round' is significant, for it proves beyond the shadow of a doubt exactly in what part of Andalusia they live."

"How?"

"When people who live within reach of the fortress talk of going to Gibraltar, as you know, they either say that they are 'going across to Gibraltar' or that they are 'going round.' By the first, they indicate the route *via* Algeciras and across the bay; by the latter, they refer to the journey by way of Cadiz and Tangier—"

"Cadiz!"

The exclamation came from his hearers.

"Cadiz," repeated T. B. He bent his head forward and rested it for a moment in his hands. When he lifted it, they saw that his face was grave.

"It's worth trying," he muttered. "And," he continued aloud, "it will be bringing down two birds with one stone."

"May I use the instrument again?" he asked.

"Certainly," said the officer readily.

T. B. rose.

"I'm going to Scotland Yard, and I shall not be away for more than ten minutes," he said; and in a few seconds he was crossing Whitehall at a run.

He passed through the entrance and made straight for the big bureau, where day in and day out the silent recorder sat with his pen, his cabinets and his everlasting *dossier*.

T. B. knew he would be there, because there was a heavy calendar at the Old Bailey, and the silent man was working far into the night—arranging, sorting, and rearranging.

The detective was back at the Admiralty within the ten minutes, and together the two made their way to the Instrument Room.

"N. H. C." responded almost at once, and T. B. sent his message.

"Tell George T. Baggin that another warrant has been issued for his arrest."

The reply came immediately.

"Thanks. Get further particulars, but do not use names."

T. B. read the reply and handed it without a word to the other.

"Please God, I'll hang the man who sent that message," he said, with unusual earnestness.

CHAPTER 21

Silinski Strikes

It was half-past nine when T. B. sent and received the last message; and an hour later he had interviewed the Commissioner.

"Get your lady away all right?" his chief greeted him.

"Well away, sir," said T. B. serenely. "Out of reach of Silinski—his agents were watching the flat—there was a burglary there the very night the book arrived."

"And the lady?"

"She is due in Jamaica in a few days."

"And now—"

T. B. told the story of the developments.

The Commissioner nodded from time to time.

"You're an ingenious young man," he said. "One of these fine days somebody will badly want your blood."

"It has often happened," T. B. granted. "There was Spedding, the forger; you remember him, sir? There was—oh, I could give you a dozen instances."

He sat over a companionable cigar and a whisky and soda, talking until the hands of the clock were near on midnight; then he rose to take his leave.

"You will leave for Spain tomorrow?" asked the Chief.

"Yes; by the first train. I can get the warrants from the Yard before I leave, and the Spanish authorities will give me all the help I need."

"And what of Silinski?" asked the Chief Commissioner.

T. B. shrugged his shoulders.

"We had a murderer there," he said. "I am satisfied that with all his alibis, he killed Moss. Whether he actually stabbed Hyatt, I am not sure. The man had such a perfect organisation in London that it is possible that one of his cut-throat friends served him in the case of that unfortunate young man. Silinski can wait. If we get the others, we shall get him."

"Goodnight, sir."

He grasped the proffered hand, and his host ushered him into the silent street.

He took two steps forward, when a man rose apparently from the ground, and two shots rang out. T. B. had drawn his revolver and fired from his hip, and his assailant staggered back cursing as a dark shadow came running from the opposite side of the road to his help.

Then T. B. swayed, his knees bent under him, and he fell back into the Commissioner's arms.

"I'm done," he said, and the third man, whose name was Silinski, hesitating a moment in the roadway, slipped his revolver back into his pocket and fled.

CHAPTER 22

The Convict from Ceutra

The streets of Cadiz were deserted; only by the Quay was there any sign of life, for here the crew of the Brazilian warship, the *Maria Braganza*, were languidly embarking stores on flat-bottomed lighters, and discussing, with a wealth of language and in no complementary terms, the energy of their commander. It was obvious, so they said in their picturesque language, that a warship was never intended to carry cargo, and if the Brazilian Government was foolish enough to purchase war stores in Spain, it should go a little farther, and charter a Spanish merchant ship to carry them.

So they cursed Captain Lombrosa for a dog and the son of a dog, and predicted for him an eternity of particular discomfort.

Captain Lombrosa, a short, swarthy man, knew nothing of his unpopularity, and probably cared less. He was sitting in the cafe of the Five Nations, near the Plaza de Mayor, picking his teeth thoughtfully and reading from time to time the cablegram from his Government which informed him that certain defalcations of his had been discovered by the Paymaster-General of the Navy, and demanding peremptorily his return to Rio de Janeiro.

To say that Captain Lombrosa was unperturbed would be to exaggerate. No man who builds his house upon sand can calmly regard the shifting foundations of his edifice. But he was not especially depressed for many reasons. The Government had merely anticipated events by a week or so.

He read the cablegram with its pencilled decodation, smiled sadly, put up his feet on a chair, and called for another bottle of *Rioja*.

There is an unlovely road through the dreary waste that leads from Cadiz to San Fernando. Beyond the city and beyond the Arsenal the road winds through the bleak salt marshes to Jerez, that Xeres de la

Fonterra which has given its name to the amber wine of Spain.

A solitary horseman cantered into San Fernando, his clothing white with brackish dust. He drew rein before the Cafe Cruz Blanca and dismounted; an untidy barefooted boy leading his horse away.

There were few people in the saloon of the case, for a chill wind was abroad, and the *cappa* is a very poor protection against the icy breezes that blow from the *Sierras*.

A man greeted the horseman as he entered—an outrageously stout man with bulging cheeks and puffy eyes. He breathed wheezily, and his fat hands moved with strange restlessness.

They hailed each other in the Andalusian dialect, and the newcomer ordered "*Cafe c'leche*."

"Well, friend?" asked the stout man, when the waiter had disappeared. "What is the news?"

He spoke in English.

"The best," replied the other, in the same language. "T. B. is finished."

"No!"

"It's a fact."

"Ramundo shot him at close range, but the devil went down fighting. They've got Ramundo."

The fat man snorted.

"Isn't that dangerous?" he asked.

"For us, no; for him, yes," said the man carelessly. "Ramundo knows nothing except that he has been living in the lap of luxury for two years in London on the wages of an unknown employer."

"What will he get?" asked the stout man nervously.

The man looked at him curiously.

"You are getting jumpy, friend Meyers," he said coolly.

"I am getting sick of this life," said Meyers. "We're making money by the million, but what is the use of it? We're exiled and damned and there is no future."

"You might as well be here as in prison," philosophised his friend. "And in prison you most certainly would be, if not worse—"

"We had no hand in the murders," interrupted Meyers pleadingly. "Now did we Baggin?"

"I know little about the English law," drawled George T. Baggin, sometime treasurer of the London and Manhattan securities Syndicate. "But such knowledge as I have enables me to say with certainty that we should be hanged—sure."

The fat man collapsed, mopping his brow.

"Ramundo killed one and Silinski the other," he mumbled. "What about Silinski?"

"He was standing by when T. B. was shot; but as soon as he saw the policeman was down and out, he skipped. He arrives tonight."

Some thought came to him which was not quite agreeable, for he frowned.

"Silinski, of course, knows," he went on meditatively. "Silinski is one with us."

"He has been a good servant," the fat man ventured.

"Had been," said the other, emphasising the first word.

"What do you mean? Was it not he who established our stations and got the right men to work 'em? Why, he has got the whole thing at his fingers' ends."

"Yes," agreed Baggin, with a wry smile. "And he has us at his fingers' ends also—where are our friends?—the other matter I have arranged without calling in Silinski?"

"They are returning tonight." The fat man shifted uncomfortably. "You were saying about this T. B. fellow—he is dead?"

"Not dead, but nearly; Silinski saw him carried into the house, and a little later an ambulance came flying to the door. He saw him carried out."

Meyers lowered his voice.

"Is Silinski—?" He did not complete his sentence.

"He's dangerous. I tell you, Meyers, we are on tender ice; there's a cracking and a creaking in the air."

Meyers licked his dry lips.

"I've been havin' dreams lately," he rumbled. "Horrid dreams about prison—"

"Haw—cut it out," said the disgusted American. "There's no time for fool dreaming. I'm going to the committee tonight; you back me up. Hullo?"

A beggar had sidled into the Cafe in the waiter's absence. He moved with the furtive shuffle of the practised mendicant.

His hair was close cropped, and on his cheeks was a three days' growth of beard.

He held out a grimy hand.

"*Senor*," he murmured. "*Por Dios*—"

"Git."

The man looked at him appealingly.

"*Diez centimes, Senor,*" he whined.

Baggin raised his hand, but checked its descent. He had seen something behind the ragged jacket closely buttoned at the throat.

"Wait for me on the road to Jerez," he commanded, and tossed the man a silver piece. The beggar caught it with the skill of an expert.

The American cut short the torrent of thanks, blessings, and protestations.

"Meet me in half an hour; you understand?"

"What the devil are you going to do?" demanded Meyers.

"You shall see."

Half an hour later they emerged from the Cafe, Baggin to his horse, and the fat man to a capacious victoria, that he had summoned from the hotel stables.

A mile along the road they came up with the beggar.

"Get down, Meyers, and send the victoria on; you can signal it when you want it."

He waited until the empty victoria had driven away; then he turned to the waiting ragamuffin.

"What is your name?"

"Carlos Cabindez," said the man hesitatingly.

"Where do you live?"

"At Ronda."

"Where do you come from?"

"Tarifa."

"What is your trade?"

The man grinned and shuffled his feet.

"A fisherman," he said at last.

Baggin's hand suddenly shot out; and, grasping his collar, tore open the frayed jacket.

The man wrenched himself free with an imprecation.

"Take your hand from that knife," commanded Baggin. "I will do you no harm. Where did you get that shirt?"

The beggar scowled and drew the threadbare coat across his chest.

"I bought it," he said.

"That's a lie," said Baggin. "It's a prisoner's shirt; you are an escaped convict.

The man made no answer.

"From Ceutra?"

Again no reply.

"What was your sentence? Answer."

"Life," said the other sullenly.

"Your crime?"

"*Asesinatos.*"

"How many?"

"*Tres.*"

Baggin's eyes narrowed.

"Three murders, eh?" he said. "Then you would like to earn a thousand *pesetas?*" he asked.

The man's eyes lit up.

"You can go on, Meyers," he said. "I shall see you tonight. In the meantime, I wish to have a little talk with our friend here."

CHAPTER 23

The House on the Hill

Beyond the town of Jerez and on the road that runs westward to San Lucar, there is a hill. Once upon a time, a grey old watchtower stood upon its steepest place, but one day there came an eccentric American who purchased the land on which it stood, demolished the tower, and erected a castellated mansion. Rumour had it that he was mad, but no American would be confined on a Spaniard's appreciation of sanity.

The American consul at Jerez, of his charity and kindliness of heart, journeyed out to call upon him, but the proprietor was in bed with gout, and neither then or at any time desired visitors, which so enraged the well-meaning consul that he never called again. The American's visits were of a fleeting character. He was in residence less than a month in the year. Then one day he came and remained. His name was registered as Senor Walter G. Brown, of New York. The English police sought him as George T. Baggin, an absconding promoter, broker, bucket-shopkeeper, and all-round thief. After a time he began to receive visitors, who stayed on also.

Then came a period when Mr. Walter G. Brown became aggressively patriotic.

He caused to be erected on the topmost tower of his mansion an enormous flagstaff, from which flew on rare occasions a ridiculously small Stars and Stripes.

At night, the place of the flag was taken by a number of thick copper strands, and simple-minded villagers in the country about reported strange noises, for all the world like the rattling of dried peas in a tin canister.

On the evening of a wintry day, many people journeyed up the steep pathway that led to the mansion on the hill. They came singly and in pairs, mostly riding, although one exceedingly stout man drove up in a little victoria drawn by two panting mules.

The last to come was Mr. Baggin, an unpleasant smile on his square face.

By the side of his horse trotted a breathless man in a tattered coat, his cropped head bare.

"I will show you where to stand," Baggin said. "There is a curtain that covers a door. The man will pass by that curtain, and I shall be with him. I will hold his arm—so. Then I will say 'Senor Silinski I do not trust you,' and then—"

The ragged man swept the sweat from his forehead with the back of his hand, for the path was steep.

"And then," he grunted, "I will strike."

"Surely," warned the other.

The man grinned.

"I shall not fail," he said significantly.

They disappeared into the great house—it is worthy of note that Baggin opened the door with a key of his own—and darkness fell upon the hill and upon the valley.

Far away, lights twinkling through the trees showed where Jerez lay.

CHAPTER 24

The Nine Bears

The room in which the Nine Men sat was large even as rooms go in Spain. It had the appearance of a small lecture hall. Heavy curtains of dark blue velvet hid the tall windows, and electric lights, set at intervals in the ceiling, provided light.

The little desks at which the men sat were placed so as to form a horseshoe.

Of the nine, it is possible that one knew the other, and that some guessed the identity of all. It was difficult to disguise Meyers with his unwieldy bulk, yet with all the trickery of the black cloaks they wore and the crepe masks that hid their faces, it was hard enough to single even him from his fellows.

The last man had reached his seat when one who was sat at the extreme end of the horseshoe on the president's right, rose and asked: "What of Silinski, brother?"

"He has not yet arrived," was the muffled reply.

"Perhaps, then, it is well that I should say what I have to say before his return," said the first speaker.

He rose to his feet, and eight pairs of eyes turned towards him.

"Gentlemen," he began, "the time has come when our operations must cease."

A murmur interrupted him, and he stopped.

"What is it?" he asked sharply.

"Let us have more light," said a mask at the end of the horseshoe, and pointed to the ceiling where only half of the lights glowed.

Baggins nodded, and the man rose and made his way to the curtained recess where the switches were.

"No, no, no!" said Baggin quickly—for he suddenly realised that there was something hidden by the curtain, a sinister figure of a man in convict shirt, fingering the edge of a brand new knife. So Baggin pictured him.

The masked man halted in surprise.

"No, no," repeated Baggin, and beckoned him back. "For what I have to say I need no light; you interrupt me, brother."

With a muttered apology the man resumed his seat.

"I have said," continued Baggin, "that the time has come when we must seriously consider the advisability of dispersing."

A murmur of assent met these words.

"This organisation of ours has grown and grown until it has become unwieldy," he went on. "We are all business men, so there is no need for me to enlarge upon the danger that attends the house that undertakes responsibilities which it cannot personally attend to.

"We have completed a most wonderful organisation. We have employed all the ingenuities of modern science to further our plans. We have agents in every part of Europe, in Indian Egypt, and America. So long as these agents have been ignorant of the identity and location of their employers, we were safe. To ensure this, we have worked through M. Gregory Silinski, a gentleman who came to us four years ago— under peculiar conditions.

"We have employed, too, and gratefully employed, Catherine Silinski, a charming lady, as to whose future, you need have no fear. Some time ago, as you will all know, we established wireless stations in the great capitals, as being the safest method by which our instructions might be transmitted without revealing to our agents the origin of these commands. A code was drawn up, certain arrangements of letters and words, and this code was deciphered and our secret revealed through the ingenuity of one man. We were prepared to meet him on a business basis. We communicated with him by wireless, and agreed to pay a sum not only to himself, but to two others, if he kept our secret and agreed to make no written record of their discovery. They promised, but their promise was broken, and it was necessary to employ other methods.

"I am fully prepared to accept responsibility for my share of the result, just as I am prepared to share responsibility for any other act, which circumstances may have rendered necessary.

"And now, gentlemen, I come to the important part in my speech. By sharing the result of our operations we may each go our way, in whatever guise we think most suitable, to the enjoyment of our labours.

"In a short time for many of us the Statute of Limitations will have worked effectively; and for others there are States in South America that would welcome us and offer us every luxury that money can buy or heart desire.

"Yet I would not advise the scattering of our forces. Rather, I have a scheme which will, I think, enable us to extract the maximum of enjoyment from life, at a minimum of risk. With that end in view, I have expended from our common fund a sum equal to half a million English pounds. I have completed elaborate arrangements, which I shall ask you to approve of; I have fashioned our future." He threw out his hands with a gesture of pride. "It is for you to decide whether we shall go our several ways, each in fear of the weakness of the other, our days filled with dread, our nights sleepless with doubt, or whether in new circumstances we shall live together in freedom, in happiness, and in unity."

Again the murmured applause.

"But there is an element of danger which must be removed," Baggin went on, "between freedom and us there lies a shadow."

He stopped and looked from mask to mask.

"That shadow," he said slowly, "is Gregory Silinski, the man who knows our secret, who has done our work, the one man in the world who holds our lives in the hollow of his hand."

Before he had finished he saw their eyes leave his face and seek the door, and he turned to meet the calm scrutiny of the subject of his discourse. He entered the room whilst Baggin was speaking and stood listening.

Silinski had an air of his own; a deferential, yet menacing air, which impressed you. He had been described by T. B. Smith as a combination of head-waiter and hangman—not an unhappy description.

Now he stood with his eyes fixed on Baggin.

"Monsieur Baggin does me an honour that I do not deserve," he said suavely, in his high lisping voice.

Baggin shot a swift glance at a curtained recess behind which stooped a crop-haired man in a convict shirt, fingering a brand-new knife.

Monsieur Baggin," Silinski went on, "is wrong when he says I am the only man who stands between The Nine Bears of Cadiz and freedom—there is another, and his name is T. B. Smith."

"T. B. Smith is dead, or dying," said Baggin angrily, "We have your word for it."

Silinski favoured him with the slightest bow.

"Even Silinski may fall into error," he said magnanimously. "T. B. is neither dead nor hurt."

"But he fell?"

Silinski smiled.

"It was clever, and even I was deceived," he confessed; "the ambulance that took him away was an artistic conception—he is alive and—"

He walked forward until he was opposite the curtain where the assassin waited.

"He is in Jerez, *messieurs*."

"It's a lie," shouted Baggin. "Strike, Carlos."

He wrenched the curtain aside, revealing the sinister figure behind.

Silinski fell back with an ashen face, but the convict made no move.

Baggin sprang at him in a fury, and struck madly, blindly, but Silinski's arm caught his, and wrenched him backward.

In Silinski's other hand was a revolver, and the muzzle covered the convict.

"Gentlemen," said Silinski, and his eyes blazed with triumph, "I have told you that T. B. Smith was alive—behold him!"

And T. B. Smith, in his convict shirt, standing with one hand against the wall of the recess, and the other on his hip, smiled ruefully.

"That is very true," he said.

Under his hand were the three switches that controlled the light in the room.

"It is also true," said Silinski, who dearly loved a speech, "that you are virtually dead."

T. B. nodded; he knew his man by now.

"Wasn't it a Polish philosopher," he began with all the hesitation of one who is beginning a long discourse, who said—"

Then he switched out the light and dropped flat on the floor. The revolvers cracked together, and Silinski uttered an oath.

There was a wild scramble in the dark. A knot of men swayed over a prostrate form; then a trembling hand found the switch, and the room was flooded with light.

Silinski lay flat on his back with a bullet through his leg, but the man they sought, the man in the striped shirt and with three days' growth of beard, was gone.

CHAPTER 25

T. B. Smith Reports

In red, blue, and green; in type varying in size according to the temperament of the newspapers; in words wild or sedate, as the character of the journal demanded, the newspaper contents bills gave London its first intimation of the breaking up of the Nine Bears.

"Never in the history of our time," began the leading article of the *Telegram*.

"A story which reads like the imaginative conception of the romantic writer," began the leader of *the London Times and Courier*.

That the Nine Bears were dispersed was hailed as a triumph for the English police. Unfortunately, the popular view is not always the correct view, and T. B. Smith came back to London a very angry man.

It had been no fault of his that the majority of the band had escaped.

The Civil Guard was twenty minutes late in taking up its position, (wrote T. B. in his private report.)

No blame attached to the Guard, which is one of the finest police forces in the world, but of the local authorities, who at the eleventh hour detected some obscurity in their instructions from Madrid, and must needs telegraph for elucidation. So that the ring about the House on the Hill was not completed until long after the whole lot had escaped. We caught Francois Zillier, who has been handed over to the French police, but the remainder of the gang got clean away. Apparently they have taken Silinski with them; he may or may not be dangerously wounded, but such indications as we have point to his having been badly hurt. How the remainder managed to carry him off passes my comprehension; the 'why' of it is apparent. He knows too much. We have secured a few documents. There is one mysterious scrap of paper discovered in Baggin's private room which is incoherent to a point of wildness, and apparently the rough note of some future scheme; it will bear re-examination.

CHAPTER 26

The Lady Who Lost £200

There was, in the Record Office at Scotland Yard, and is probably still, a stout package containing a number of telegrams written in French, English, Spanish, German, Portuguese and Italian. Each one of these wires is to the same effect as the others.

"Exhaustive enquiries throughout the country have failed to discover any trace of the Nine Bears of Cadiz."

The story of these men, inscribed in the records of Scotland Yard, is not perhaps as complete as that in the possession of the French police, for M. Escoltier, sometime confidential wireless operator of the Eiffel Tower, had placed the police of Paris in possession of a great deal of useful information that he had denied the Metropolitan authorities.

From the rough notes of the telegrams he had received and transmitted to the unfortunate Hyatt, the French police, with the aid of codes obligingly supplied by Scotland Yard, had been able to grasp the magnitude of the operations conducted by the Nine. The extent of these operations revealed the extraordinary thoroughness of their organisation. In various names, and under cover very often of innocent-looking commercial concerns, they had conducted their nefarious business with impunity. There is now no doubt whatever that the Deutsch Ost-Amerika Handel, with its gorgeous offices at The Hague, was part of the chain of operating centres. Equally certain it is that the Compagnie de Maritime de Solent was another. The Credit Sud-Espagna—despite threats of libel actions—was a third. One could multiply the list, covering bogus concerns in Vienna, Petersburg, Moscow, Milan, Rome, Budapest, Bukarest, and Brussels.

So far as we have been able to trace, there was no office in Copenhagen or in either of the Scandinavian capitals. By means of M. Escoltier's telegrams the French police made an approximate estimate of the extent of the profits secured by the band.

Slump in *Kaffirs* (anticipating the announcements that the Portuguese Government refused recruiting facilities for native labour)   £1,750,000
Slump in New York steel (anticipating the "suicide" of the President of the National Bank of Baltimore) £2,850,000
Slump in copper   £1,340,000
(Coincident with the arrest of Mr. Hilas B. Cuttering on a charge of misappropriation. The documents on which the arrest was effected were afterwards discovered to be forgeries) £1,000,000
Slump in British Industrials (expert opinions held that this was one of the failures of the Nine)   £100,000
Slump in Spanish Fours   £2,000,000
(see page 49 of the Appendix of M. Gaultier's Report.)

It well may be that the French police have overestimated the hauls, just as they have entirely failed to connect the disastrous fall of Argentine securities with the revolution of '07—a revolution which owed its origin to the machinations of the Nine Men of Cadiz.

The discovery of the band and the revelations of its *modus operandi* must stand as the greatest sensation in the history of crime. It was followed by the world-famous "International Convention of 1910," and the adoption of its recommendation prohibiting the working of private wireless instruments without a licence from the Government, making any breach of the ordinance a penal offence.

Thanks to the industry and perseverance of the English police, (said the *London Morning Journal*, commenting upon this law,) the Nine Men of Cadiz are dispersed, their power destroyed, their brilliant villainies a memory. It is only a matter of time before they will fall into the hands of the police, and the full measure of Society's punishment be awarded them. Scattered as they are—

T. B. Smith put down his paper when he came to this part, and smiled grimly.

"Scattered, are they!" he said. "I doubt it."

For all the praise that was lavished upon him and upon his department, he was not satisfied with himself. He knew that he had failed. To break up the gang had always been possible. To arrest them and seize the huge fortune they had amassed would have been an achievement justifying the encomia that was being lavished upon him.

"The only satisfaction I have," he said to the Chief Commissioner, "is that we are so often cursed for inefficiency when we do the right thing, that we can afford to take a little credit when we've made a hash of things."

"I wouldn't say that," demurred the Chief. "you did all that was humanly possible."

T. B. sniffed.

"Eight men and Silinski slipped through my fingers," he answered briefly; "that's a bad best."

He rose from the chair and paced the room, his head sunk on his breast.

"If Silinski had delayed his entrance another ten minutes," he said, stopping suddenly. "Baggin would have told me all that I wanted to know. This wonderful scheme of his was to secure them all ease and security for the rest of their lives."

"He may have been boasting," suggested the other, but T. B. shook his head.

"It was no boast," he said, with assurance, "and if it were, he has made it good, for where are the Nine? One of them is on Devil's Island, because he had the misfortune to fall into our hands. But where are the others? Vanished! Dissolved into the elements—and their money with them. I tell you, sir, there is not even the suspicion of a trace of these men. How did they get away from Cadiz? Not by rail, for all the northward trains were stopped at Bobadilla and searched. Not by sea, for the only Brazilian man-o'-war, *Maria Braganza*."

"Airship," suggested his Chief flippantly, as he moved towards the door.

"It is unlikely, sir," replied T. B. coldly.

The Chief Commissioner stood with his hand on the edge of the open door.

"At any rate, they are finished," he said, "their power for further mischief is destroyed."

"I appreciate your optimism, sir," said T. B. impertinently, "which I regret to say I do not share."

Three months had passed since the disappearance of the "bears"; from that day no news had come which might even remotely associate them with a hiding place.

"One thing is evident, and must be remembered," T. B. went on, as his Chief still lingered. "Outside of the Nine Men there must be in Europe hundreds of agents, who without being aware of their principals, have been acting blindly for years in their interest. What of the men who went to the length of murder at Silinski's orders? What of the assassins in Europe and America who 'arranged' the suicide of the Bank President and the wreck of the Sud Express? Not one of these men have we been able to track down. I tell you, sir, that outside of the inner council of this gang, Silinski organised as great a band of villains as the world has ever seen. They remain; this is an indisputable fact; somewhere in the world, scattered materially, but bound together by bonds of Silinski's weaving, are a number of men who formed the working parts of the Nine Men's great machine. For the moment the steam is absent—Yes?"

A constable was at the door.

"There is a lady to see you, sir," he said.

"Lady?" said T. B. wonderingly, for the ladies were rare amongst his regular callers. "What does she want?"

"I don't know, sir, except that she wants to see you about some money," said the man.

T. B. looked up at his Chief in blank astonishment, and the elder man shook his head sadly.

"I should never have suspected you, T. B.," he said sorrowfully, with very cryptic utterance he left T. B. alone to his interview.

The lady was stout and voluble, respectable, middle class. Her ample bosom was a chaos of brooches, ranging in size from a half-crown to a coffee saucer. She was red of face and scant of breath, and with a gracious inclination of her head she took the seat to which T. B. motioned her.

"Mr. Smith?"

T. B. nodded, and the lady fumbled in a little black satin bag that hung from her wrist. It contained many things that rattled; it also contained a little notebook, which the lady extracted and opened.

"On the 4th *ultimo*," she said.

"May I ask, madam." Interrupted T. B. Smith, with some little evidence of irritation, "exactly what your business is ?"

The lady shot him a look in which reproof and indignation were blended.

"I have some experience of the police," she said bitingly, "having given evidence against Gustav Heilberg, a house-boy charged at the West London Sessions with having stolen a ring valued at four guin-

297

eas, the property of—"

"But—"

"The legal mind," she said, with a magnanimous sweep of her hand, "is not beyond my comprehension, 'These police officials are busy people; they want all the facts set forth clearly, concisely'—er, another word begins with an 's' which has for the moment escaped me—yes, 'succinctly,' that is it."

"To all this I agree," said T. B.; he walked to his desk and pressed a bell. "If it is another case of Gustav Heilberg, I will see that you are escorted to the proper department. I do not deal with these matters myself—"

"Stop!" The lady raised a gleaming hand.

"This is a matter of greater importance—it concerns you—and a lady."

If his visitor intended shocking him she succeeded admirably.

T. B.'s eyebrows rose, his lean jaw dropped.

"A matter of two hundred and fifty-five," said madam, holding her head till the ornament of her bonnet shivered again, "advanced to a friend of yours last week—I say advanced, because I want no unpleasantness. I think that it is right to explain that we were fellow-passengers—the money never left me day or night, being always wrapped up in my nightdress bag, placed under the pillow—"

"I see!" A light was beginning to dawn on T. B. "You have been robbed and somebody has told you to come and see me—"

"Wait," said the lady imposingly; "wait; by day I carried it in my bodice—such a nice gal she was, used to sit for hours talking about my late husband, and her brother was such a gentlemanly man with a little peaky beard and eyeglasses, like a young man I used to know at the Hydro at Malvern. Well, she talked and talked, she helped me with my packing; I went down to help her with hers, though she never asked me, and," said the lady wagging an impressive finger; "the first thing I saw in her cabin was you."

Eh?"

T. B. stared at the lady blankly.

"You," repeated the visitor, with evidence of the satisfaction that her startling news had produced. "You as large as life; in a silver frame, propped up on the bunk."

"'Who's that?' says I

"'A friend of mine,' says she, snatching up the photo. That was all. But I have a memory for faces; the other day I saw your portrait in the *Police News*—"

T. B. made a little grimace.

"I saw your portrait in the *Police News*," she repeated, "and I says to myself, 'Ah, ha, my lady! I'm going to call on this friend of yours.'"

She paused and looked triumphantly at the detective.

"Two hundred and fifty-five pounds in Bank of England notes," she said slowly, emphasizing each word with a jab of her right finger in the palm of her left hand. "Gone!"

"When did you find this out?"

T. B. was interested now, although filling in the spaces of her disjointed narrative, he perceived little more than a fairly common story of an ordinary theft.

"When I got to Euston the money was in my jewel-case; my card-case was packed in it, and I wanted to give my card to a very charming girl I met in the train—niece of Lord Somebody or other—I opened the case—gone!"

Again she stopped.

"Well?" said the detective. "What do you expect me to do?"

"Find my money," said the lady complacently. "If she knows you, you must know her."

"What was her name?"

"Mad'moosle de Verdum."

The detective shook his head.

"I don't know the name," he said, "and if I did, I don't suppose I could find her; you may be sure that if she is a professional thief she has left England—"

"She is here; I saw her today. I was on the top of a 'bus and she was in a carriage," said the lady bitterly, "paid for out of my money; you don't know her name de Verdum?"

"I do not," said T. B., and rose to signify that the interview was finished.

"Suppose she had another name; suppose the name I saw on a card in her cabin was her name?"

"In that case," said T. B. wearily, "you had better give me that also."

For a moment the lady groped in the recess of her satin bag, and after what looked like developing into an interminable search, she produced a card.

"here it is," she said, and read:

"'Catherine Silinski.'"

In the Record Office

T. B. spun round as though the lash of a whip had caught him.

"Silinski—Catherine Silinski—here?" he breathed.

"Here!" said the triumphant lady. "Now, will you tell me that you can't get my money back?"

"It's incredible, unthinkable!"

Silinski in London.

As he stood, his mind busily engaged in speculation, his visitor grew impatient.

"Two hundred and fifty-five pounds," she murmured absently'

He looked up. "Your money, madam," he said briskly, "is the least important aspect of the question,"

The lady was not unnaturally annoyed.

★★★★★★

The little telegraph instrument near the chief inspector's desk began to click. In every police station throughout the Metropolis it snapped back and forth its message. In Highgate, in Camberwell, in sleepy Greenwich, in Ladywell, as in Stoke Newington. "*Clickerty, clickerty, click*," it went, hastily, breathlessly. It ran:

> To all Stations:—Arrest and detain man and woman (here the descriptions followed) on a charge of having stolen banknotes to the amount of £255 from Louisa Breddell, of Sloe Grove, Bayswater. All reserves out in plain clothes.

All reserves out!

That was a remarkable order. What was the importance of this theft of £255 that the whole of the London police force should be mobilised to find the thief?

London did not know of the happening; the homeward-bound

suburbanite may have noticed a couple of keen-faced men standing idly near the entrance of the railway station, may have seen a loiterer on the platform—a loiterer who apparently had no train to catch. Curious men, too, came to the hotels, lounging away the whole evening in the entrance hall, mildly interested in people who came or went. Even the tram termini were not neglected, nor the theatre queues, nor the boarding-houses of Bloomsbury. Throughout London, from East to West, North to South, the work that Scotland yard had set emissaries to perform, was swiftly and expeditiously carried out.

T. B. sat all that evening in his office waiting. One by one little pink slips were carried in to him and laid upon the desk before him.

As the evening advanced they increased in number and length.

At eight o'clock came a wire:

"Not leaving by Hook of Holland route."

Soon after nine:

"Continental mail clear."

Then in rapid succession the great *caravanserai* reported themselves. Theatres, bars, restaurants, every place in London where men and women gather together, sent, through the plain-clothes watchers, their messages.

T. B.'s hope lay in the woman. Without her, Silinski might hide himself in some obscure slum in the Metropolis. At eleven o'clock he was reading a telegram from Harwich when the telephone at his elbow buzzed.

He took up the receiver.

"Hullo," he said curtly.

For a second there was no reply, and then, very clear and distinct, came a voice.

"T. B. Smith, I presume."

It was the voice of Silinski.

If there had been anybody in the room, but T. B. they might have imagined it was a very ordinary call he was receiving. Save for the fact that his face twitched, as was characteristic of his when labouring under any great excitement, he gave no sign if the varied emotions Silinski's voice had aroused.

"Yes, I am T. B. Smith; you are of course, Silinski?"

"I am, of course, Silinski," said the voice suavely, "and it is on the tip of your tongue to ask me where I am."

"I am hardly as foolish as that," said T. B. drily; "but wherever you are—and I gather from the clearness of your voice that you are in

London—I shall have you."

There was a little laugh at the other end of the wire.

T. B.'s hand stole out and pressed a little bell-push that rested on the table.

"Yes," said Silinski's voice mockingly. "I am in London. I am desirous of knowing where my friends have hidden."

"Your friends?" T. B. was genuinely astonished.

"My friends," said the voice gravely, "who so ungenerously left me to die on the salt plains near Jerez whilst they were making their escape."

A constable entered the room whilst Silinski was talking, and T. B. raised his hand warningly.

"Tell me," he said carelessly, "why you have not joined them."

Then like a flash, he brought his hand down over the transmitter and turned to the waiting constable.

"Run across to Mr. Elk's room," he said rapidly; "call the Treasury Exchange and ask what part of London—what office—this man is speaking to me from."

Silinski was talking before T. B. had finished giving his instructions.

"Why have I not joined them," said Silinski, and there was a little bitterness in his voice, "because they do not wish to have me. Silinski has served his purpose. Where are they now? That is what I wish to know. More important still, I greatly desire a piece of information which you alone, *senor*, can afford me."

The sublime audacity of the man brought a grin to T. B.'s face.

"And that is?" he asked.

"There was," said Silinski, "amongst the documents you found at our headquarters in Jerez a scrap of paper written somewhat unintelligibly, and apparently—I should imagine, for I have not seen it— without much meaning?"

"There was," said T. B. cheerfully.

"So much I gathered from Baggin's agitation on our retreat," said Silinski. "Where, may I ask, is this interesting piece of literature deposited?"

The cool, matter-of-fact demand almost took T. B.'s breath away.

"It is at present at Scotland Yard," he said.

"With my—er—*dossier?*" asked the voice, and a little laugh followed.

"Rather with the dossier of your friend, Baggin," said T. B.

"In case I should ever want to burgle Scotland Yard," said the drawling voice again, "could you give me explicit instructions where to find it?"

T. B.'s anxiety was to keep Silinski engaged in conversation until the officer he had dispatched to the telephone returned.

"Yes," he said, "at present it is in the cabinet marked 'Unclassified Data,' but I cannot promise you that it will remain there. You see, Silinski, I have too high an opinion of your enterprise and daring."

He waited for a reply, but no reply came, and at that moment the door opened and the constable he had sent on the errand appeared.

T. B. covered the transmitter again.

"The Treasury say that you are not connected with anybody, sir," he said.

"What?"

T. B. stared at him.

He moved his hand from the transmitter and called softly, "Silinski."

There was no reply, and he called again.

He looked up with the receiver still at his ear.

"He's rung off."

Then a new voice spoke.

"Finished, sir?"

"No, who are you?" demanded T. B. quickly.

"Exchange, sir—Private Exchange, Scotland Yard."

"Who was talking to me then? Where was he talking from?"

"Why, from the Record Office."

T. B., his face white, leaped to his feet.

"Follow me," he said, and went racing down the long corridor. He went down the broad stairs three at a time.

A constable on duty in the hall turned in astonishment.

"Has anybody left here recently?" asked T. B. breathlessly.

"A gentleman has just gone out, sir," said the man; "went away in a motorcar—lady driving."

"Is Mr. Elk in the building?"

"In the Record Office, sir," said the man.

Up the stairs again flew the detective. The Record Office was at the far end of the building.

The door was ajar and the room in darkness, but T. B. was in the room and had switched on the light.

In the centre of the room was stretched the unfortunate Elk, in a pool of blood. A life-preserver lay near him. T. B. leant over him; he was alive, but terribly injured; then he shot a swift glance round the room. He saw the telephone with the receiver off; he saw an open cabinet marked "Unclassified Data," and it was empty.

CHAPTER 28

The Lost Warship

Translation of an Extract from a little memorandum book found in Gregory Silinski's house in St. John Street and now in possession of the Police Authorities.

It may be said that life is fairly crude, from the standpoint of the professional writer, and 'True Stories' have a singular knack of being remarkably dull.

Thus in actuality it very often happens that *dénouements* have a knack of postponing themselves for a dozen years or so—a dozen years that enables the hero to grow fat and the heroine to lose a little of the bloom of youth and develop characteristics which are not in harmony with one's original conception of her character.

Very few indeed of the stories, tragic, or comic, of real life, make good 'book tales,' because life is made up of anti-climaxes, and because the villains of life more often than not live to be respected, and virtue so frequently goes to the wall before an unappreciative world can realise its immense and gratifying worth.

One need not be an admirer of Silinski's to agree with the truth of much that he had said.

Silinski was a philosopher, without being a gentleman.

It may be that on the slender basis of his philosophy he depended too implicitly. He would argue that since his case was one of actuality he was safe in putting back the *dénouement* for a dozen years or so. More he may have entertained visions of a respectable old age—of a Silinski white-haired, benevolent, and venerated, musing in his dotage of virtuous competitors buried and forgotten.

Unfortunately the story of the "Nine Bears" is a "book" story—one of a very few, and the *dénouement* came with disconcerting swiftness. To such comfort as he might extract from his philosophy he was welcome.

T. B. Smith was a philosopher, but of another type; his attitude in the face of blame was one of stoical equanimity; before a too lavish award of praise he was cynically tolerant.

There might have been blame in plenty, if the news of the outrage at Scotland Yard leaked out, but, fortunately, Elk was not killed and the world was unaware of the happening.

Silinski had escaped; there was pother enough; eight of the Nine Bears had melted into nothingness; no official feather came to T. B.'s cap for that, whatever praise the mistaken public might award. Worst of all, the Record Office at Scotland Yard had been burgled and important documents had been stolen.

Their contents were not lost to the police, for Scotland Yard does not put all its eggs into one basket, even when the basket is as secure a one as the Record Office. There were photographs innumerable of the scrap of paper, and one of these was on T. B. Smith's desk the morning after the robbery.

The memorandum, for such it was, was contained in less than a hundred words. Literally, and with all its erasures written out, it ran:

Idea (crossed out). Ideas (written again). Suppose we separated; where to meet; allowing for accidental partings; must be some spot; yet that would be dangerous; otherwise, must be figures easily remembered; especially as none of these people have knowledge (crossed out and rewritten); especially as difficult for non-technical (word undecipherable) to fix in mind, and one cipher makes all difference. Lolo be good, accessible, unfrequented. Suggest on first Ju every year we rendezvous at Lolo. (Mem.—Lolo would indeed be nowhere!)
So far have only explained to Zillier.

That was all, and T. B. read and reread the memorandum. Zillier was the only man who knew. By the oddest of chances, Baggin had confided his plans to the one man who might have found them useful if Providence had given him one chance of escape. But the French Government had him safe enough on Devil's Island.

For the rest, the "note" needed much more explanation than he could give it.

He took a pen and began to group the sentences he could not understand.

"Must be some spot, yet that would be dangerous? He was perplexed, and showed it. What was meant by "spot"?

He grinned faintly, remembering a famous legal quibble as to what was a "place" within the meaning of an Act. Any given point on the earth's surface was a "spot," so what could the "otherwise" mean? Somewhere that was not on earth? He smiled again. In the air? What were the figures—and technical figures at that?

"On the 1st Ju we rendezvous at Lolo—nowhere!"

"This is absolute nonsense!" The detective threw down his pen and jumped up. "I'll go over to the hospital and see old man Elk."

He called at the Chief Commissioner's office and was received cordially.

"Any news, T. B.? what do make of your puzzle?"

T. B. made a little grimace.

"Nothing," he said, "and if the original had not been stolen I should not have troubled to study it again."

He gained the Strand by a shortcut.

A contents bill attracted his attention, and he stopped to buy an evening paper.

"Loss of a Warship"

He turned the paper before he discovered the small paragraph that justified so large a bill.

The Brazilian Government has sent another cruiser to search for the Brazilian man-of-war, *Maria Braganza*, which is a month overdue. It is feared that the warship foundered in the recent cyclone in the South Atlantic.

"*Maria Braganza?*" thought T. B.—and remembered where he had seen the vessel.

The ship and her fate passed out of his mind soon afterward, for he had a great deal of routine work requiring his attention; but the name cropped up again in the course of the again in the course of the day and in a curious manner.

★★★★★★

A drunken sailor, obviously of foreign extraction, was ejected, fighting from a small public-house in the Edgware Road. He rose from the ground slowly, and stood apparently debating in his mind whether he should go away quietly or whether he should return to the attack. It is not too much to say that he had decided upon the pacific course, the mystery of the whereabouts of the Nine Bears might never have been elucidated. In that two seconds of deliberation hung the fates of Baggin and his confederates, of Silinski and his sister, indeed of the reputation of Scotland Yard.

The foreign sailor made up his mind. Back to the swing doors of the tavern he staggered, pushed them open and entered.

A few seconds later a police whistle blew, a commonplace constable strolled leisurely to the scene of the disturbance and took into custody the pugnacious foreigner on a charge of "drunk and disorderly."

This was the beginning of the final fight with the "bears," a fight which cost Europe a million of money and many lives, but which closed for ever the account of the Nine Bears of Cadiz.

CHAPTER 29

Silinski Understands

What "double chambers" are to the dramatist, parallel columns are to the journalist; in the former you see two actions going on at the same time, in the latter you may observe two minds working differently to the same end.

Thus Gregory Silinski of Paris and T. B. Smith in London.

You may picture Silinski on a day in April, when Paris was awakening to spring-time, and the branches of the trees in the Bois de Boulogne vivid green. A day very barmy, with a hint of early summer, with no bite in the breeze that came in soft gusts along the Boulevard des Capucines.

Every day to the *Coq d'Or* came a thoughtful student, clean-shaven, dressed in shabby black, with a cravat sufficiently extravagant to suggest art, and spectacles business-like enough to hint at medicine. This Monsieur Flamarrion lived in the Montmartre, and described himself as a mechanical engineer. He was—so said his papers—from Bayonne.

He came naturally enough, under the observation of the police, and was reported to be a bachelor of "studious and virtuous" habits; he had, said the report, "*ne pas ami intime*." Your Parisian detective, by nature suspicious, differs materially from his brother at Scotland yard. In the first place, he concentrates his attention too fiercely and is too readily swayed by first impressions. Under his terrific scrutiny and examinations the newly observed takes on a permanent character. Thus M. Flamarrion, a newcomer to Paris, endured the embarrassing attention of the French police for exactly two days, and was passed as "harmless."

And all this time, T. B. Smith was imploring the French authorities to keep a strict watch on Silinski. Every day came M. Flamarrion to soak his *brioch* in his coffee and read patiently and thoroughly the *Journal des Débats*.

Every day, too, to this admirable tavern came a young lady, heavily veiled and wearing the evidence of recent widowhood.

They did not sit at the same table, but generally they were near enough to exchange furtive glances and conventional politeness.

"May I offer you *Le Matin, madame?*"

"I am obliged to you, *monsieur.*"

Thus would Silinski communicate with his sister, for always, with the newspaper he so politely tendered, would be a letter giving her his news, his plans, and for such money as she required.

This April morning, Catherine read her note with some trepidation. There was a little flush on Silinski's cheek when he greeted her, his eyes were a thought too bright, and his nod lacked the pretence of deference which usually marked it.

More than this, he threw away all pretence of strangership and called her to his table.

"Catherine," he said quickly, "we must leave Paris."

She nodded.

"Our friend Zillier!" he said, dropping his voice. "Consider it, little one! Whilst we are at liberty he languishes on in chains! A prisoner, a dog!"

She looked at him curiously.

His eyes were dancing, that little patch of red was in his face; she knew they stood on the threshold of a great enterprise.

"I cannot sleep at nights," he went on. "I start up and see Zillier in his cage—"

"Gregory," she said steadily, "why do you talk thus to me?"

He was not abashed.

"Little one," he said exultingly, "I talk thus because I feel thus. Zillier means a return to the grip of things. Baggin has gone, and with him my good fortune; you cannot any more secure employment; we have had to descend to petty robberies to sustain life. The Nine Men I made!" he said, and, since the *café* was empty, he indulged in his favourite gesture. "I created them, their machinery, their organisation, their very code. And now—! I have on my hands a hundred and one bold gentlemen who, their fortunes being bound in mine, find their means of living gone. On the one hand, I am sought by the police, who want my life, on the other by my agents, who want my money— of the two I fear the police least."

He paused to sip his coffee.

"From police and friends I have one refuge—the Nine Men of Cadiz; now the eight men of nowhere and the one of Devil's Island. How to join forces—how to reach Mr. Baggin, that is the question."

He took a scrap of paper from his pocket-book

"This was valueless to me until today," he said, tapping the paper. "It gave me no clue as to the means by which my friends escaped, vanished into the void; but today has come a great light. We go to join our friends!"

So much for Silinski, who, as we now know, left Paris that night.

CHAPTER 30

What the Sailor Said

The solution of the "note" did not come so quickly to T. B., because his mind could not jump as Silinski's did.

"Here is a case that will amuse you, T. B.," said the Chief, strolling into his bureau; "a man, giving the name of Silva, who has been taken to the police-station on the prosaic charge of 'D. and D.', is found to be a walking cash deposit. Twelve hundred pounds in Bank of England notes and 26,000 *francs* in French money was found in his possession. He speaks little or no English, has the appearance of being a sailor—will you go down and see what you can make of him?"

In a quarter of an hour the Assistant-Commissioner was at the police-station.

"Yes, sir," said the station sergeant, "he's quiet now. I don't think he's so very drunk, only pugilistically so."

"What do you make of him?"

"He's a sailor; a deserter from some foreign navy, I should say. He has underclothes of a uniform type, and there's a sort of device on his singlet—three stars and a number."

"Brazilian Navy," said T. B. with promptness. "Talkative?"

The sergeant smiled.

"In his own language, very," he said drily. "When I searched him, he said a great number of things which were probably very rude."

T. B. nodded.

"I'll see him," he said.

A gaoler led him down a long corridor.

On either side were long stone-painted doors, each with a little steel wicket.

Stopping before one door, he inserted his bright key in the lock, snapped back a polished bolt, and the door swung open.

A man who was sitting on a wooden bench with his head in his hands, jumped to his feet as the Assistant-Commissioner entered, and poured forth a volume of language.

"Softly, softly," said T. B. "You speak Spanish, my friend."

"*Si, senor*," said the man. "I am Spanish."

"That is good, for I cannot speak Portuguese," said T. B.

"I know nothing of Portuguese," said the man quickly.

"Yet you are deserter from a Brazilian warship?" said T. B.

The man stared at him defiantly.

"Is that not so, friend?"

The prisoned shrugged his shoulders.

"I should like to smoke," was all that he said.

T. B. took his gold case from an inside pocket and opened it.

"Many thanks," said the sailor, and took the lighted match the gaoler had struck.

If he had known the ways of the English police, he would have grown very suspicious. Elsewhere, a man might be bullied, brow-beaten, frightened into a confession. In France, *Juge d'Instruction* and detective would combine to wring from his reluctant lips a damaging admission. In America, the Third Degree, most despicable of police methods, would have been similarly employed.

But the English police do most things by kindness, and do them very well.

The sailor puffed at his cigarette, from time to time looking up from the bench on which he sat at the detective's smiling face.

T. B. asked no questions; he had none to ask; he did not demand to how the man came by his wealth; he would not be guilty of such a crudity. He waited for the sailor to talk. At last he spoke.

"*Senor*," he said, "you wish to know where I got my money?"

T. B. said nothing.

"Honestly," said the sailor, loudly, and with emphatic gesture, "honestly, *senor*," and he went on earnestly, "By my way of reckoning a man has a price."

"Undoubtedly," agreed T. B.

"A price for body and soul." The sailor blew a ring of smoke and watched it rise to the vaulted roof of the cell.

"Some men," continued the man, "in their calm moments set their value at twenty million dollars—only to sell themselves in the heat of the moment for—" he snapped his fingers.

"I have never," thought T. B., "come into contact with so many philosophical criminals in my life."

"Yet I would beg you to believe," said the sailor—and I would ask the reader to realise he was speaking in Spanish, which gives even to the educated speech a certain literary pedantry—"it is a question of opportunity and need. There are moments when I would not risk my liberty for a million *pesetas*—there have been days when I would have sold my soul for ten *mil-reis*."

He paused again, for he had all the Latin's appreciation of an audience; all the Latin's desire for dramatic effect.

"Sixty thousand *pesetas* is a large sum, *senor*, it amounts to more than £2,000 in your money—that was my price."

"For what?"

"I will set you a riddle: on the *Maria Braganza* we had one hundred officers and men—"

T. B. saw light.

"You are deserter from the *Maria Braganza*," he said—but the man shook his head smilingly.

"On the contrary I have my discharge from the navy, properly attested and signed by my good Captain. You will find it at my lodgings, in a tin trunk under a picture of the blessed Saint Teressa of Avila, or as some say, Sergovia. No, *senor* officer, I am discharged honourably. Listen."

His cigarette was nearly finished and T. B. opened his case again, and the man, with a grateful inclination of his head, helped himself. Slowly he began his story, a story which before all the others, I think, helps the mind to grasp the magnitude of a combination which made the events he described possible.

I was a sub-officer on the *Maria Braganza*," he began, and went on to narrate the history of the voyage of that remarkable battleship from the day it left Rio, until it steamed into the roadstead off Cadiz.

We stayed at Cadiz much longer than we expected, and the men were grumbling—because our next port was to have been Rio. But for some reason our Captain did not wish to sail. Then one day he came on board—he spent most of his time ashore—looking extremely happy. Previous to this he had lived and walked in gloom, as though some matter were preying on his mind. But this was all changed now. Whatever troubles he had were evaporated. He walked about the deck, smiling and cracking jokes, and we naturally concluded that he had received his orders to sail back to Brazil at once.

That same day we were ordered to take on board stores which the government had purchased. Whatever stores these were, they were extremely heavy. They were packed in little square boxes, strongly made and clamped with steel. Of these boxes we took two hundred and fifty, and the business of transporting them occupied the greater part of the day.

"What was the weight of them?" asked T. B.

"About fifty kilos," said the man, "and," he added with an assumption of carelessness, "they each contained gold."

T. B. did a little sum in his head.

"In fact a million and a half of English pounds," he said half to himself.

As to that I do not know, (said the other), but it was enormous; I discovered the gold by accident, for I and another officer had been chosen to store the boxes in one of the ammunition flats, and owing to the breaking of a box I saw—what I saw."

However, to get back to the Captain. In the evening he came aboard, having first given orders for steam to be ready and every preparation made for slipping.

Then it was I told him I had seen the contents of one of the boxes, and he was distressed.

'Who else has seen this?' he asked, and I informed him of the sub-officer who had been with me.

'Do not speak of this matter, as you value your soul,' he said, 'for this is a high Government secret—send sub-officer Alverez to me'—that was the name of my companion. I obeyed and sent Alverez aft. He, too, received similar injunctions, and was dismissed."

At ten o'clock that night, the quartermasters went to their stations, and all stood ready for dropping our mooring.

As the hours wore on, the Captain began to show signs of impatience. I was on the bridge with the officer of the watch, and the Captain was pacing up and down, now looking at his watch and swearing, now training his binocular on a portion of the land to the north of the town.

I had forgotten to say that at 8.30 the ship's *pinnace* had been sent away, and that it had not returned.

315

It was for the coming of the *pinnace*, and whoever was coming with it, that our Captain displayed so much anxiety.

It was eleven o'clock before the boat came alongside. We heard it racing across the water—for the night was very still. Then it drew alongside, and a number of gentlemen came on board. They were talking excitedly, and seemed as though they had walked a long distance, for, by the light of the branch lamp that lit the gangway I saw that their boots and trousers were white with dust, such as I believe lies on the road outside Cadiz. One was in a state of great fear; he was very stout. Another, and he was the leader, spoke to our Captain, and soon after I heard the order given—'Quartermaster, stand by for going out of harbour,' and the Captain gave the navigating officer his course. We went at full speed, steering a course due west.

It was a perfectly calm night, with stars, but no moon. When (as near as I can guess) we were twenty miles from the coast, the captain sent for me and Alverez to his cabin.

'My friends,' he said, 'I have a proposition to make to you, but first let me ask you if you are good patriots?'

We said that we were.

'What,' said the captain, addressing himself to me, 'do you value your patriotism at?'

I was silent.

("*Senor*," said the prisoner earnestly, "I assure you I was not considering the insult offered to me, because we had not got to a point outside of abstract morality. In my mind was a dilemma—if I ask too little I should assuredly lose money. Such was also the consideration in Alverez's mind.)

'Senor Captain,' I said, 'as an honest man—'

'We will leave that out of the question,' said the Captain. 'Name a price.'

And so, at random, I suggested a sum equal to £3,000, and Alverez, not a man of any originality, repeated '£3,000'.

The Captain nodded; 'This sum I will pay you,' he said. 'Moreover, I will give you your discharge from the navy of Brazil, and you may leave the ship tonight.'

I did not ask him why. I realised he had some high scheme which it was not proper I should know, besides which I had not been ashore for a month—and there was the £3,000.

'Before you go,' said the Captain, 'I will explain to you that my honour and my reputation may not suffer. In a few days' time, when we are at sea, the comrades you leave behind will be offered a new service, a service under a new and wealthier Government, a Government that will offer large and generous rewards for faithful service and obedience.'

The prisoner chuckled softly, as at some thought which amused him.

We went ashore in the steam *pinnace*; the Captain himself superintending our landing. It was a remarkable journey, *senor*.

You may imagine us in the open sea, with nothing but the '*chica-clucka, clucka!*' of the engine of our little boat; Alverez and myself sitting at the bow with our hands on the butts of our revolvers—we knew our Captain—and he himself steering us for the lights that soon came up over the horizon. We landed at Cadiz, and were provided with papers to the Brazilian Consul, should our return be noticed. But none saw us, or if they did, thought nothing of the spectacle of two Brazilian seamen walking through the streets at that hour of the night; remember that none but the port authorities were aware that the *Maria Braganza* had sailed. The next morning we procured some civilian clothing, and left by the afternoon train for Seville. By easy stages we came first to Madrid, then to Paris. Here we stayed some time.

He chuckled again.

"Alverez," he resumed, "is a man of spirit, but, as I have said, of no great originality. In Paris a man of spirit may go far, a man of money farther, always providing that behind the spirit and the wealth there is intelligence. My poor Alverez went his own way in Paris. He made friends."

Again he smiled thoughtfully.

"Alverez I left," he explained; "his ways are not my ways. I came to England. I do not like this country," he said frankly. "Your lower classes are gross people, and very quarrelsome."

A few more questions were asked, and answered, and ten minutes later T. B. was flying back to Scotland Yard with the story of the stolen battleship.

CHAPTER 31

The Maria Braganza

Once more were the Nine Men in the bill of every newspaper in London. Once more the cables hummed from world's end to world's end, and slowly, item by item, came fragmentary scraps of news which Scotland Yard pieced together.

Of all extraordinary developments, (said the *London Journal*), in any great criminal case, nothing has ever equalled in its improbability, the present phase of this remarkable case. Our readers will remember . . . . . . (here the *Journal* went on to give the story of the inception and progress of the Nine Men in their schemes—a story with which the reader is already familiar).

And now we have reached the stage which we confidently hope will be a final one. It is clear that these men, having command of enormous riches, gained at the sacrifice of life, and by the ruin of thousands of innocent people, secured to their service the Captain of the Brazilian warship, *Maria Braganza*.

Captain Lombroza holds an unenviable reputation in the Brazilian Navy. A court of Inquiry had discovered that, for years, he had been systematically robbing the Brazilian Treasury, and the discovery of his speculation coincided with his disappearance; but not only with his disappearance but with the vanishing of the Brazilian Government's battleship.

It is not difficult to understand what arguments the Nine Men used to win over the crew of this unfortunate battleship. They had enormous wealth at their command; they could offer to pay salaries which, to the untutored men of the Brazilian Navy, must have seemed beyond the dreams of avarice.

But what is the explanation of the discharge of Alverez and his companion?

To our minds it would seem tolerably easy. These two men of all the crew knew the extent of the riches brought on board the *Maria Braganza*. They of all the crew had a comprehension of the wealth of the Nine Men. They were dangerous men to have on board; their presence might mean mutiny, strikes, all the extraordinary consequences of a position which would be Gilbertian were it not for the note of tragedy that underlies the whole remarkable story.

From the day the *Maria Braganza* left Cadiz it has, apparently, been lost to sight. We say 'apparently' because a closer inspection of shipping records leads us to the belief that this ship has not only been sighted, but has coaled at a British port. On the 16th of January, Lloyds published, amongst other arrivals, that of the *Spinoza* at Port Elizabeth. At first, this was reported to be a warship flying the flag of Venezuela. This was later corrected to Colombia, a mistake very easy to make if one were to judge the nationality of a ship by its ensign; for, save for a small emblem in the centre of the flags, both these countries display a similar ensign.

A reference to the battleships of the world, shows us that no such warship exists, and later advices from the Cape go to prove that the vessel that came in, coaled and took stores so hurriedly, was none other than the *Maria Braganza*. So that somewhere in the wide seas of the world is a stolen battleship, having on board a congregation of the world's worst rascals, Napoleonic in the largeness of their crimes. But money which can do much, cannot do all, and it is necessary that these men, no less than the ship's company, should obtain stores and food, and the necessities of life; more important still, that they should secure the coal that is so necessary a part of the ship's equipment. In this respect we have made one or two important discoveries.

An examination of the shipping list shows that two months ago three colliers were chartered out of Cardiff. There is nothing remarkable in this fact, and their apparent destination excited no comment at the time. They were ordered to very usual ports in South America, but it is an extraordinary fact that the consignor in each case gave the captain sealed orders which were only to be opened at sea. So far, we have had no news from these ships, and it is the merest conjecture on our parts when we suppose the colliers were intended for the *Maria Braganza* and, that at some rendezvous, and at some appointed time, they were met by the warship in mid-ocean, and there transferred their cargo.

But more mysterious is the chartering of the *Hedleigh Head*, a tramp steamer of 2,000 tons, which took on board, on the 16th of last month, one of the strangest cargoes that ship has ever taken. We now know that a month prior to this, one of the largest furnishing firms of the West End received an order to the extent of £10,000, for the delivery of elaborate ship's fittings, intended, as it was said, for a South American yacht owner. The firm in question makes a speciality of such luxurious appointments, and such an order was not regarded as unusual, and so chairs, panels, upholstery of all kinds, paints, mouldings, and twelve magnificent cabin suites were placed on board the *Hedleigh Head*, and were ostentatiously consigned to Valparaiso, the cargo was met on the high seas and taken over.

Many and fantastic are the suggestions that have been put forward as to the whereabouts of the Nine Men of Cadiz. One of our contemporaries draws a fanciful picture of life on some gorgeous Southern Pacific Isle, out of the track of steamers, and pictures the Nine Men living in a condition of Oriental splendour, an existence of *dolce far niente*. Such supposition is, of course, on the face of it, absurd. Such an island exists only in the fancy of the romantic writer. The uninhabited portions of the globe are few, and are in the main, of the character of the Sahara desert. Wherever life can be sustained, wherever comfort and freedom from disease waits the newcomer, be sure the newcomer has already arrived.

I quote this much from the *Journal* because it is near enough to truth and actuality to merit quotation.

That Baggin had based all his plans on the supposition that such an island existed, and could be discovered, we now know. He was the possessor of an imagination, but his geographical knowledge was faulty. The "idea," that scrap of paper which Silinski had risked his neck to obtain, was simple enough now—up to a point.

The "Idea"	The Solution
Suppose we separated, where to meet? Must be some spot yet that would be dangerous.	"Some spot," meant some place on land.

Otherwise, must be easily remembered. Especially as it is difficult for non-technical (?) to fix in mind, and one cipher makes all the difference.
Suggest we rendezvous at Lolo.

The latitude and longitude of the sea rendezvous must be easy to remember.

This last was the only part of the little clue that offered any difficulty to T. B. The *Gazetteer* supplied no explanation.

Nor could the Admiralty help. The naval authorities did their best to unravel the mystery of "Lolo."

T. B., who saw no reason to suppress such news as he had, and following the precedent he had established when he revealed the story of the deserter to the Press, called the engine to his aid, and all the newspaperdom racked its brains to discover in "Lolo," a cryptic reference to some lonely Pacific island.

Many and ingenious were the suggestions offered, but none found favour.

A conference of the Ambassadors met in London, and as it was jointly agreed that the nations should act in concert to bring the *Maria Braganza* and her crew to justice as speedily as possible. The Brazilian Government agreed to indemnify the Powers in their action, and in the event of the destruction of the ship being necessitated by resistance on the part of its rebel captain, to accept an agreed sum as compensation.

There are surprising periods of inaction in the record of all great accomplishments, which those who read the stories of achievements, realise.

There were weeks of fretting, and days of blank despair in one room at Scotland Yard. For the examination of all clues led to the one end. Somewhere in the world were the Nine Men of Cadiz— but where none could say. Every port in every civilised land was alert. Captains of mail steamers, of grimy little tramps, of war vessels of every nation, watched for the battleship. Three British cruisers, detached unostentatiously from the Home Fleet, cruised unlikely seas, but with no good result.

Then began the new terror.

T. B. had always had one uncomfortable feeling, a feeling that the dissipation of the Nine had not dispelled, and that was the knowledge that somewhere in Europe the machinery set up with devilish ingenuity by Silinski, still existed. Who were the desperate and broken men who acted as agents to the Nine? Whoever they were, they had been well chosen.

Silinski possessed an extraordinary acquaintance with the criminal world. There was scarcely a land in which he had not been a *sojourner*, a citizen of the shades, more often than not, a fugitive of justice.

That he then had a splendid opportunity of meeting with the very type which was ultimately to prove of such value to him, there can be no doubt.

Investigations had not brought any of these men to the light of day; they lurked in the background—ominous, menacing, a constant danger.

That danger was all the greater if Silinski had rejoined his accomplices, or if by chance he had come into touch with them, as he boasted he had.

This knowledge of danger was irritating, more irritating since it ran with the impatience engendered by inaction. For three weeks—three whole eternities—no word came of the *Maria Braganza*; then a Cape steamer picked up a ship's boat with a dead man and a rough wooden chest filled with English gold coins. There were no papers, no name was painted on the little boat, but for the mystery of the tragic find T. B. had a solution which received official support. One of the crew of the *Maria Braganza* had looted the treasure and attempted to steal away by night. He had succeeded only too well.

"This suggests," said T. B., "that at the time of the desertion the warship was within sailing distance from some coast, probably the Isle of Sao Thome or Principe. The man, having no compass, took a wrong course; from the description he must have died of thirst."

Two gunboats from the Cape station were sent to search these latitudes, but drew blank. The commander of the *Dwarf*, a small British gunboat, however, was partially successful, for it fell in with a Monrovian fishing-boat, which had sighted a "big steamer" three weeks before, heading south.

The British Government had taken every precaution to prevent supplies reaching the Nine. It was forbidden by a special Order in Council (colloquially known as "The 'Port to Port' Ordinance,") for ship's masters to sail with "sealed orders," or to discharge their cargoes elsewhere than at the ports specified on the ship's papers. Other nations had followed the lead, and the German Government instituted a vigilant surveillance of charters, a sort of charter parties' censorship which is in vogue to this day.

The weeks passed without further news of the ship, and T. B. was beginning to worry, for good reasons. He had an elaborate chart supplied to him by the Admiralty, which showed him from day to day, the amount of provisions and coal such a ship as the *Maria Braganza* would require, and he knew that she must be running short.

Then came news from Paris that trace of Silinski had been found; and, although the scent was old, T. B. crossed the Channel the day the message came.

★★★★★★

The night of the 1st of March saw T. B. Smith in Paris. He stayed at the Hotel D'Antin in the Rue D'antin, one of those cosy little hostels in which Paris abounds. His visit was partially successful. He had been able to find traces of Silinski and his sister; he found their lodgings without much difficulty. He found, with the aid of a French detective, the *café* affected by the precious pair, and in one way or another was able to collect quite a considerable amount of useful information regarding the Silinskis. He was idling away an evening, sitting before the Café de la Paix, watching the ceaseless procession of people passing to and fro. This was favourite amusement of his; indeed, is it not of every Englishman who finds himself in Paris with time on his hands?

As he sat there sipping his coffee, a man left the pavement; and pulling a chair towards the next table, seated himself. He was a thickset man with a straggling beard, and there was little to distinguish him from the ordinary citizen. T. B. gave him a glance and resumed his survey of the passing crowd. By and by, his attention was again attracted to the neighbouring table by the arrival of another man equally undistinguished. The two men apparently knew one another, for after a curt meeting, they plunged into a conversation, which was carried on in such low tones that no word reached the detective.

Now, if T. B. had not been a born policeman, he would have been a born journalist, for his ruling passion was an intense curiosity. For aught that he knew, these two might have been engaged in the discussion of some private business matter; the subject of their conversation might indeed have had reference to some intimate family secret. But no sooner had these two very ordinary citizens given evidence of their wish for privacy, than T. B. was overpowered with a desire to act the eavesdropper.

But his unpardonable curiosity was unrewarded save that, by one expression which reached him, he gathered that the conversation was either in Low German or Flemish.

"Mumble, mumble, mumble, mumble," said one rapidly.

"*Soh!*" said the other nodding.

"Mumble, mumble, mumble, mumble."

"*Ja,*" said the other, and added something in a lower tone.

T. B. was annoyed, not with himself that he should be acting the spy on apparently innocent people; he had no conscience in the matter—but because of the extraordinary and unnecessary care these people were taking to keep their affairs to themselves.

He had a good working knowledge of Flemish—which is Cape Dutch with variations—and he was in a position to understand anything they might say, if they would only have the grace to say it aloud.

At last he gave up his attempt at hearing, in disgust, and opened the *Journal du Soir*, began to read a particular lurid story of an Apache murder in the Montmartre.

""Mumble, mumble, mumble, mumble," went on the voices; and T. B., in his unjustifiable annoyance, thought twice about the inadvisability of changing his seat.

He read the case through, turned over a leaf to a brilliant, if wholly illogical article on one of France's inevitable "situations," and was half way through it; then suddenly he stopped reading, and, though his eyes did not leave the printed page, every nerve in his body awoke to life.

""Mumble, mumble, mumble, Silinski, mumble, ship, mumble." He waited. The voices kept up their monotonous burden.

"Silinski—ship!"

That was all; he heard no other word that gave him further clue to the subject of the conversation, but "Silinski—ship" was enough. By and by, he saw a French detective stroll past, saw the swift and apparently careless scrutiny of the officer, and caught his eye. The sign T. B. gave was imperceptible to any save one acquainted with the universal sign-language of the great police world, but the French detective, seeing T. B. rubbing his right eye as if to keep himself awake, knew that he was required and walking along to the Place de l'Opera, waited. T. B. was with him in less than a minute, and rapidly explained. The detective listened. He had noticed the men.

"If *Monsieur le Commissaire* will return to the *café* and invent some excuse for detaining them, I will do all that is necessary."

T. B. nodded and returned to the *café*. The men were settling with the waiter when T. B. returned to his seat, with two or three newspapers he had hurriedly purchased at the corner *kiosque* as an excuse for his absence.

As they rose, T. B. looked the man with the beard in the face, and, smiling, nodded.

He saw the gathering frown of suspicion, and said. "Mr. Herhault, *n'est ce que pas?*"

"You are mistaken, *monsieur*," said the man coldly.

"*Pardon*," T. B. made haste to say with profound humility, "but I am in error. I thought—"

"Goodnight, *m'sieur*," said the other curtly, and turned to go.

"One moment." T. B. laid his hand on the man's arm. "I cannot allow you to go under a misapprehension; will you be seated whilst I explain how I came to make the mistake?"

"Your explanation is unnecessary," said the man shortly. "I beg you not to detain me."

T. B. with one eye for the promenading crowd saw the French detective pass.

"I will not detain you, *m'sieur*," he said, with a slight bow.

The two men turned out of the *café*. He watched them as they crossed the Place, going in the direction of the Rue de la Paix.

At a distance he followed, and saw them turn into a side street. He quickened his steps; and, as he rounded the corner, he came upon a little group in the deserted street. The two men were surrounded by half a dozen plain clothes officers. They were expostulating vigorously, and their captors stood impassively by.

As T. B. came up to the group two of the French officers took an arm each of the arrested men, whilst one whistled a cab.

T. B. did not follow to the *Commissaire's* office. He had told the detective all he had heard, and he was content to leave the matter at that.

He returned to his hotel, and waited. It was near midnight before the French officer came.

"We have searched their lodgings, and can find nothing but a little drawing of the cardinal points of the compass," he said.

"Do they deny knowledge of Silinski?"

The Frenchman shrugged his shoulders.

"They deny nothing; they affirm nothing," he said. "It is unusual for my countrymen in the exultation of arrest to make confessions. But I am placing a spy in the same cell, and tomorrow we may learn something. All that we know at the present is that they are Frenchmen, although they are visitors from Brussels, that they have been in this city for a month, and are engaged in no known business."

The next morning brought T. B. no further information. The men had remained dumb in the presence of the spy.

"I am afraid that unless we get further evidence, we must release them," said the officer who brought the information. "I am with you in believing that these two men are, or have been, agents of Silinski; but we need a stronger case."

That stronger case did not materialise, and that same night T. B. was informed that the men had been released.

They were carefully watched, but that same night they left by the mail train for Liège.

So much the detective officer related to T. B. over coffee and a cigarette at the Café de la Paix.

"It is very curious," said the French detective thoughtfully; it was La Croix of Lefeu's staff; "that you should have heard them, or one of them, speak of Silinski and a ship. You are sure you were not mistaken?"

T. B. shook his head.

"I do not think you were," said La Croix. "I questioned them and they denied that they knew any such person, or that they had ever mentioned his name. That in itself is suspicious."

"You found nothing in their lodgings?"

"Nothing—except the compass points."

He felt in his breast pocket, took out a notebook. Opened it, and extracted a folded sheet of paper. This he smoothed on the marble-topped table at which they sat. There was no word of writing on it, only a simple diagram. It was a cross with tiny circles at the end of each arm, and a large circle in the centre.

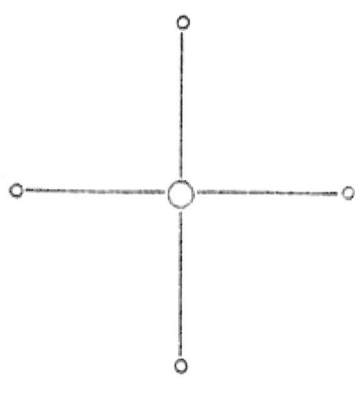

T. B.'s frown spoke eloquently his disappointment.

"This," bantered La Croix, "gives you no clue to this mysterious 'Lolo' of yours, I suppose?"

T. B. shook his head.

"Does it you?" he asked, and the Frenchman laughed.

"No," he said, "to me it is only a curious little cross with no significance."

T. B. smoothed the paper again, and pursed his lips in thought.

"Can I have this?" he demanded after a little while.

"You may have a photograph of it," said the cautious La Croix. "These documents, even the least of them, have some value, and are part of the *dossier*, until we know enough to be able to distinguish between those that count and those that have no bearing whatever on the case, we cannot destroy any of them, or part with them. As it happens, I have anticipated your wishes, for a photograph has already been taken and will be in your possession today."

It was the 9th of March when T. B., with the meagre evidence he had been able to secure, together with the unpromising photograph of the meaningless cross, drove down the Gare du Nord on his way back to town. The train was on the point of drawing out when a man came racing along the platform. T. B.'s carriage had been reserved, so that the man had no difficulty in discovering it. He jumped up on the footboard, and thrust a bulky blue package into T. B.'s hand.

"I am from the Chief of the Police," he said breathlessly; "this telegram is for you, and has just arrived."

T. B. thanked him, and the train began to move.

Leaning back amidst the cushions, he unfolded the blue sheets and read.

The telegram was from Scotland Yard, and began:—

Officer commanding Gibraltar reports that his wireless station has been intercepting messages in code which bear some resemblance to those of N. H. C. Full messages have been forwarded here for decoding. Some of them are unintelligible, but one portion of a message we have been able to make read: '. . Accept your assurance and explanation; we have will splendid field for enterprise; I will join you at Lolo with shipload of provisions and collier on June 1st. In meantime, if you do as I suggest we can make terms with Governments and, moreover, find employment agents who are at present discontented. . . .'

Message beyond this undecipherable with exception of words 'destruction,' 'easily obtainable,' and 'insure.' This message obviously between Silinski and *Maria Braganza*"—Stop. 'Commander Fleet, Gibraltar, has sent H. M. S. *Duncan, Essex, Kent,* with six destroyers into Atlantic pick up *Maria Braganza*. Return immediately.—Commissioner.

T. B. read the message again, folded it carefully, and placed it in his breast pocket. There was one word in Silinski's message that revealed in a flash the nature of the new terror with which the Nine Men of Cadiz threatened the world.

CHAPTER 32

A Matter of Insurance

You pass up a broad stone staircase at one end of the Royal Exchange, and come to a landing where, confronting you, are two big swing doors that are constantly opening and closing as bareheaded clerks and top-hatted brokers go swiftly in and out.

On the other side of the doors is a small counter where a man in uniform checks, with keen glance, each passerby. Beyond the counter are two rooms, one leading to the other, shaped like the letter "L," and in the longer of the two sit innumerable pews, quiet men with fat notebooks. From desk to desk flutter the brokers bargaining their risks, and there is a quiet but eager buzz of voices through which at intervals booms the stentorian tones of the porter calling by name the members whose presence is required outside.

A stout man made a slow progress down one of the aisles, calling at the little pews *en route*, making notes in a silver-mounted book he held in his hand.

He stopped before the pew of one of the biggest underwriters. "*Taglan Castle?*" he said laconically, and the underwriter looked up over his spectacles, then down at the slip of paper the man put before him.

"One *per cent.?*" he asked, in some surprise, and the other nodded.

"How much?" he asked.

The underwriter tapped the slip of paper before him.

"Ten thousand ponds at 5s. *per centum*," he said. "I can do that." He initialled the slip and the man passed on.

He went the round of the room, stopped to exchange a joke with an acquaintance, then descended the stone stairs.

Back to his scruffy little office went the broker with little thought that he had been engaged in any unusual variety of business. In his private room he found his client; a thickset man with a straggling beard, who rose politely as the broker entered, and removed the cigar he had been smoking.

"You have finish," he said with a slightly foreign accent, and the broker smiled.

"Oh, yes!"—a little pompously, after the manner of all Lloyd's brokers—"no difficulty about the *Taglan*, you know. Mail ship, new steamer, no risks practically on the Cape route; rather a bad business for you; you'll lose your premium."

He shook his head with a show of melancholy and took a pinch of snuff.

"I have a dream," said the foreigner hastily, "ver' bad dream. I have belief in dreams."

"I daresay," said the broker indulgently. "A sister of mine used to have 'em, or she said she had; dreamt a tiger bit her, and sure enough next day she lost her brooch."

He sat at his desk, signed a receipt, counted some notes, and locked them in his drawer.

"You won't get your policies for a day or so," he said; "you're stay-ing—"

"At the Hotel Belgique," said the client, and, pocketing his re-ceipts, he rose.

"Good-day," said the broker, and opened the door.

With a slight bow his client departed, and reached the street.

There was a taxicab drawn up before the door, and two or three gentlemen standing on the pavement before the office.

"Cab, sir?" said the driver, but the foreigner shook his head.

"I think you had better," said a voice in French, and a strong hand grasped his arm.

Before he realised what had happened, the Frenchman was hustled into the cab, two men jumped in with him, the door banged, and the car whirled westward.

It was a car which had extraordinary privileges, for at a nod from the man who sat by the side of the driver, the City police held up the traffic to allow it to pass. It flew down Queen Victoria Street at a much greater speed than is permissible within the city boundaries, and the gloved hands of the policemen on duty at the end of Black-friars Bridge made a clear way for it.

It turned into Scotland Yard, remained a few minutes, then re-turned along the Embankment, up Northumberland Avenue, and through a side thoroughfare, to Bow street.

Thereafter, the Frenchman's experience was bewildering. He was searched, hurried through a passage to a small court where a benevolent-looking gentleman sat behind a small table, on a raised dais.

The prisoner was placed in a steel pen, and a quietly-dressed man rose from the solicitors' table, and made a brief statement.

"We shall charge this man with being a suspected person, your worship," he said, "and ask for a remand."

Then another man went into the witness box.

"My name is Detective-Sergeant Kiegnell, of 'A' Division," he said; "and from information received, I went to 976, Throgmorton Street, where I saw the prisoner. I told him I was a police officer, and should take him into custody."

That was all.

The magistrate scribbled something on a paper before him, and said briefly, "Remanded."

Before the prisoner could say a word, or utter anything more than a "*Sacré!*" he was beckoned from the dock and disappeared from court.

So unimportant was this case that none of the reporters in court troubled to record more than the fact that a "well-dressed man of foreign appearance was charged with loitering with intent."

Certainly nobody associated his arrest with the announcement that the *Taglan Castle* had left Cape Town, homeward bound.

It was an interesting voyage for the passengers of the *Taglan Castle*, which by the way, carried specie to the amount of £600,000. She left Cape Town soon after dusk. The next morning, to the surprise of her Captain, he fell in with a little British fleet—the *Doris*, the *Philomel*, and the *St. George*, flying a Commodore's flag.

Greatest surprise of all came to Captain of the *Taglan Castle* when he received the following signal:

"Slow down to thirteen knots, and do not part company."

To the Captain's "I am carrying the mails," came the laconic message, "I know."

For ten days the four ships kept together, then came the sensation of the voyage. At dawn of the tenth day, a big steamer came into view over the horizon. She was in the direct path of the flotilla and to all appearance she was stationary. Those who were on deck at that early hour, heard shrill bugle sounds from the escorting warships, then suddenly the engine of the *Taglan* stopped, and a crowd of curious passengers came running up from below. The *Taglan Castle* had obeyed a peremptory order given by the *St. George*, and was hove-to.

The *St. George* and *Doris* went on; then from the funnels of the stationary steamer came clouds of smoke, and through their telescope the passengers saw her turn slowly and move.

Slowly, slowly, she got under way, then—

"*Bang!*"

The forward 9.2 guns of the *St.* George emitted a thin straight streak of flame, and there was a strange whining noise in the air.

"*Bang! Bang!*"

The *Doris* came into action at the same time as the *St. George* fired her second gun. Both shots fell short, and the spray of the ricochets leapt up into the air.

The fugitive steamer was now moving at full speed; there was a great fan-shaped patch of white water at her stern.

"*Bang!*"

All this time the two British warships were going ahead firing as they went. Then from the stern of the strange steamer floated a whiff of white smoke, and, in a second, the eerie whine of a shell came to the passengers who crowded the deck of the *Taglan Castle*. The shell missed the firing warships; indeed, it did not seem aimed in their direction, but it fell uncomfortably close to the mail boat. Another shell fell wide of the steamer but in line with her. The manoeuvre of the flying vessel was now apparent. She carried heavier metal than the second-class cruisers of the British fleet, but her object was to disable the mail boat.

The Captain of the *Taglan* did not wait for orders; he rung his engines full speed ahead, and swung his helm hard aport. He was going to steam back out of range.

But no other shot came from the *Maria Braganza*.

Smaller and smaller she grew until a pall of smoke on the horizon showed where she lay.

Obeying a signal from the distant warship, the *Taglan* came round again, and in half an hour had come abreast of the two warships, the faithful *Philomel* in attendance.

There was a swift exchange of signals between the warships, and their semaphore arms whirled furiously.

Then the Commodore's ship signalled.

"Hope you are not alarmed; you will not be troubled again; go ahead."

On the twelfth day there was another shock for the excited passengers of the *Taglan Castle*, for, nearing Cape Verde Islands, they came upon not one warship but six—six big black hulls lying at regular intervals along the horizon. But there was no cause for alarm. They were the six Dreadnought cruisers that had been sent down from Gibraltar to take up the burden of the Cape Fleet.

It was all a mystery to the bewildered passengers, whatever it might be to the officers of the *Taglan*, who had receive a long "lamp" message in the middle of the night.

There was a two hours' delay whilst the Captain of the *St. George* went on board the *Indefatigable* to report.

This was the end of the adventures that awaited the *Taglan*. She was escorted to the Needles by six warships, and came into Southampton, her passengers a-flutter with that excitement peculiar to men who have come through a great danger, and are exhilarated to find themselves alive.

The arrival of the *Taglan* was opportune; it gave confirmation to the rumours which had been in circulation, and synchronised with the issue of the manifesto of the Nine Men—a manifesto unique in history.

CHAPTER 33

The Mad Warship

The manifesto had arrived simultaneously at every newspaper office in London, Paris, and Berlin.

It was printed, (says the official record of the incident, with its cold precision and its passion for detail), on paper of a texture and quality which is generally in use in small Continental newspaper offices. From certain peculiarities of the printed characters, it was seen that the type from which it was printed must have been cast in Spain. Wherever the letter W occurred it was replaced by VV. . . . The manifesto was neatly folded and enclosed in an envelope of *octavo* size, and the actual sheet-size was what is known in the printing trade as double-crown. The postage stamps were Spanish, the place of posting, as revealed by the office postmarks, were in some cases Malaga, and in some, Algeciras. The fact that, whether posted at one place or the other the date of the posting was identical, supports the view that at least two persons had been concerned in the dispatch.

The manifesto itself ran:—

To the Civilised Nation (*sic*).
Whereas, we, the company known as the Nine Men of Cadiz, have been placed by universal decree outside the law, and whereas it is against our desires that such decrees of outlawry should exist against us, both from the point of view of our own personal comfort and safety, and from the point of view of the free exchange of commercial (*sic*) relationships.
Now, therefore, we decree—
That unless an immediate free pardon be granted to each and

every man on board the *Maria Braganza* and liberty to be given him to go his way peaceably without arrest or fear of molestations (*sic*), the owners and crew of the *Maria Braganza* will declare war upon the commerce of the world. It will loot and destroy such shipping as may with advantage be so looted and destroyed, and in the end will fight to the last against its aggressor.

(Signed) By order of the Nine,

Silinski.

It is no exaggeration to say that the publication of this manifesto caused a panic, not only in shipping circles, but throughout the civilised world. The sea held a hidden danger, neither life nor property were secure. There came to stay-at-home people a realisation of the dependence of these islands upon its oversea trade. That insurance rated should rise was only a natural and immaterial result of the publication of the threat. But a more serious aspect was the instant effect the manifesto had upon the grain market. Bread rose in two days from *4d* .to *6d.*, and in some parts of the country *7d.*, a loaf.

That the fears of the community were justified was proved by the story of the *Taglan* Castle, and was proved beyond doubt two days after the publishing of the Nine Men's proclamation by what happened to the *Zeider Prince*, a welsh collier bound from Cardiff to Valparaiso. The port authorities at St. Vincent (Teneriffe) reported that heavy cannonading had been heard by the coastguards on the western shore of the island. The firing lasted three minutes and then ceased. Fortunately, there was in the harbour of St. Vincent at the time, the British destroyer *Alert*, which, on receipt of the news, went out at full speed to investigate. The *Alert* came up to the scene of the crime after the *Zeider Prince* had been sunk (a lifebuoy and a waterlogged boat were taken on board the destroyer to establish the identity of the doomed ship).

When the *Alert* came up, the *Maria Braganza* was hull down, and steaming due west, and the Captain of the destroyer very pluckily have chase. With the *Alert's* enormous speed she overhauled the battleship hand over hand, but long before she could get within striking distance, the *Maria Braganza* opened fire on her, and it was only by a miracle that the *Alert* escaped destruction. The destroyer had neither coal nor the stores necessary for a long chase, and returned to Teneriffe.

The theory in regard to the *Zeider Prince* is that she was first brought alongside the battleship, her cargo taken aboard, and then the little tramp was sunk. No member of her crew was found, dead or alive, and the assumption at the time was that the crew were prisoners on board the warship—an assumption which afterwards proved to be accurate.

Less fortunate were the men who manned the German steamer *Aosan Werthan*, bound from Hamburg to the ivory coast with a general cargo. The dead body of a sailor washed up near Cape Blanca was the first intimation of the tragedy. It was the only intimation, for from that day to this no word has ever reached the world of its fate.

There was consternation enough at these events, but within a fortnight came the story of the North Atlantic outrage.

The *Caratana*, the fastest mail-ship afloat, as well as being nearly the largest, was sixty hours out of New York with 350 passengers on board, when she came up with a strange warship flying a red flag. The warship hoisted an unintelligible signal, which the Captain of the *Caratana* did not understand. It was followed by one of which there could be no mistaking the meaning.

"Stop, or I will sink you."

The Captain of the Atlantic liner knew all that was known about the *Maria Braganza*, and at once realised his danger. If he did not realise it, there came a shell from the warship, which passed astern. Fortunately, there was a mist on the water which grew in density every minute—a real "bank" fog, not usually met with so far east.

The Captain of the *Caratana* decided upon the course of action he would take. Very quickly he signalled "I surrender," and rang his engines to "stop." The men on the warship seemed satisfied with his action, and no further demonstration was made against the liner. Such was the "way" on the big ship, that although her propellers had ceased to revolve, she continued her course, nearer and nearer she grew to a thick patch of fog that lay ahead of her. The *Maria Braganza* may have suspected the manoeuvre, for she signalled, "Go astern."

For answer, the Captain of the *Caratana* put port and starboard engine full ahead, and, whilst men were running to their stations on the warship, the *Caratana* slipped into the fog belt.

In an instant the *Maria Braganza* was blotted from view.

The liner Captain put his helm over to starboard, and it was well that he did so, for with a reverberating crash, the warship opened fire in the direction he had disappeared. Shell after shell came flying through the thick mist, and the thud of their impact as they struck the water came to the ears of the affrighted passengers.

The sound of spasmodic firing grew fainter and fainter every minute as the great steamer went threshing through the swirling fog, until it ceased altogether.

Although no harm had befallen the liner, the news of the attack produced a profound sensation. Its effect was to paralyse the business of ocean travel. "The Mad Warship" terrorised the seas.

Immediately intelligence of the outrage was flashed by wireless telegraphy to America, the American Fleet, which had been cruising up the Atlantic coast, steamed out to intercept the *Maria Braganza*; and, simultaneously, the Home Fleet, which was lying in Queenstown Harbour, sailed to meet them. The American Fleet consisted of the battleships *New Jersey*, *Connecticut*, *Idaho*, and *Michigan*; the armoured cruisers *St. Louis* and *Maryland*; and the protected cruisers *Salem*, *Chattanooga*, *Olympia*, and *Tacoma*. The cruisers went on, and two and a half days later came up with the *Warrior*, *Achilles*, *Invincible* and *Indomitable*, of the British Fleet.

But no sign had they seen of the *Maria Braganza*, which must have headed due south.

It was on the day the report of their non-success reached England that T. B. Smith located Silinski.

★★★★★★

There languished in a prosaic prison cell at Brixton gaol a Monsieur Torquet, who was admittedly a victim of police persecution. That much I think T. B. himself was prepared to admit. He had come before a police magistrate; had been remanded and again remanded; he had communicated first with the Belgian Ambassador, who found it convenient to disown him as a Belgian; he had applied to the French Consul, and that gentleman had replied to the communication with a promptitude and a finality which suggest that the whole of the circumstances of the case had been in possession of the Consulate, and the application anticipated.

This was indeed the fact.

M. Torquet was suspected not of a crime against any particular section of society, but indeed of being accessory to a crime against humanity; and T. B. was prepared to run a tilt at the very *Habeas Corpus* Act rather than release his grip upon the stranger with the straggling beard, whom he had recognised as being the mumbling gentleman of the Café de la Paix, who knew of Silinski and of "ships"; and knowing so much about the latter, had heavily insured the *Taglan Castle* before she started out on her adventurous voyage.

337

So, through the days of the terror, M. Torquet was a prisoner in Brixton, watched day and night, taking his exercise aloof and at separate hours from the other prisoners; and, moreover, denied the satisfaction of knowing that public interest was excited in his fate.

For nobody knew of M. Torquet. The most astute reporters who had seen the thickset figure stumble up the steps of the dock in the Extradition Court had failed to connect him with the subject that was filling every mind, and, incidentally, every available column in the newspapers. It is a fact that all through the period of incarceration no man had attempted by threat, entreaty, or promise, to extract from him the secret he undoubtedly held.

The police had waited for a voluntary statement; they applied to him the supreme torture of indifference.

Day by day men had brought him food, warders who were apparently dumb had led him forth to the paved exercise yard, and had led him back again. He had been kept supplied with books and writing materials, the food that came to him was well cooked, every consideration was shown to him; but nobody displayed any desire to share his confidence, or to be interested in any way in him, save as a rare animal to be fed and exercised.

He had been remanded and remanded. Finally, he had been committed for trial.

It does not seem possible that evidence could be produced in open court—evidence sufficient to constitute a *primâ facie* case for trial—without the event being reported, yet this was what happened.

Into the Extradition Court at Bow Street, generally supposed to be closed for the day, the man was hurried. A magistrate took his seat on the bench, evidence was given—there were two police witnesses—the committal was signed, and before the faintest rumour reached the general court that the other court was open, before a reporter could gather up his block and pad and hurry out, the sitting was completed, and no man was wiser.

This M. Torquet, brooding in the loneliness of his cell at Brixton, had very nearly reached the limits of his patience; the silence and the indifference had crushed what little there was in him.

For two months he had lain without trial, in a cell which had a table on which were pen, paper, and ink. He had not in all that time touched the one or the other, but on the day that the Atlantic liner came across the *Maria Braganza* he sat at the table and wrote a brief note to the governor of the prison. Within an hour T. B. Smith was ushered into the cell and remained with the man for some time. Then he came out and sent for a shorthand clerk, and together they returned.

For four hours the three men worked, one questioning and translating, one answering, at first sullenly and with periodic outbursts of temper, and later eagerly, volubly—and all this time the clerk wrote and wrote, until one notebook was exhausted and he sent out for another.

It was late in the evening when he said:

"And that, *monsieur*, is all."

"All?" T. B.'s eyebrows rose. "All? But you have not explained the whereabouts of Lolo?"

The prisoner was frankly puzzled.

"Lolo?" he repeated. "*M'sieur,* I do not understand."

It was T. B.'s turn to be astonished.

"But the rendezvous—there was to be some rendezvous where the ship would come to pick up any member of the Nine who might become detached."

The man shook his head, and at that moment an idea occurred to T. B. He drew from his pocket a copy of the little "cross with the nobs," as it had been named at Scotland Yard.

"Do you know this?" he asked.

The man looked at it, and smiled.

"Yes—Silinski drew that for me on the last occasion I met him in Paris."

"What does it mean?"

Again the prisoner shook his head.

"I do not know," he said simply. "Silinski was telling me something of his plans. He drew the cross and was beginning to explain its meaning and then for some reason he stopped, crumpled up the paper, and threw it into the fireplace. At the time I attached some importance to it, and after he had gone I rescued it, but—"

"You don't understand it?"

"I don't," said the man, and T. B. knew that he spoke the truth.

CHAPTER 34

In Tangier

Many little houses are on the Marshan, the *plateau* that commands Tangier. They are villas in which Moorish, Spanish, and English styles of architecture, struggle for supremacy, have compromised in a conglomerate type. In one of these house lived Gregory Silinski and his sister. There is every excuse for a rich Madrid merchant taking up his residence in this pleasant land, most especially when the rich Madrid merchant is an invalid. This was Silinski's *rôle* for the moment.

Like most people of the Polish race, he had an aptitude for languages, and his Arabic was well-nigh faultless.

The man had a passion for organisation, and in an incredibly short space of time he had created a secret service of his own.

In Tangier, the very centre of international intrigue, where the Embassies beamed at one another over the dinner-table, and plotted their host's ruin in the dark of night, Silinski might be sure that if his presence in tangier excited any comment, it would be of a harmless character to himself. Each Embassy would write him down as the agent of the other.

Silinski found the African city a convenient hiding place for many reasons, and was content to remain in his pleasant villa overlooking the Straits, until the *Maria Braganza* forced from a reluctant Europe pardon on her own terms.

It is well to mention that Catherine Silinski shared neither the patience nor the optimism of her brother.

Catherine Silinski must pay the penalty of being her brother's sister. It had been suggested that she is worthy of a whole biography to herself, but such particulars as I have been able to secure of her life do not support this view. Had Catherine lived up to her excommunication—for she once fell under the ban of Holy Church—she might

340

have been great; had she rivalled her brother in villainy, she would have merited the respectful notice of criminologists. As it was, she excites the curiosity only of that section of the morbid and unlettered public which finds more gloomy pleasure in surveying the instrument with which a crime is committed, than in the psychology which enables the thoughtful student to appreciate the criminal's state of mind before the deed.

I believe she had no morals sense; that she was one of those strange creatures without love or fear. I cannot think that even for her brother she entertained the slightest spark of affection. An accident of nature that made them interdependent; circumstances had thrown them together more than either of them could have desired.

Catherine was by nature luxurious. Adventure separable from comfort she had no heart in. As agent, and well-paid agent, of the Nine Men, she had come to London, and gladly accepted the music-hall engagement for which her talent fitted her.

She was prepared to work adventure within adventure, to let private enterprise run with larger scheming.

Then, of a sudden, the ground had been cut from underneath her feet, first by an urbane detective who had shipped her whither she had no desire to go, secondly by the disappearance of the golden source of her comfort.

Nor was Silinski himself in much better case. He had sufficient money at hand to take him to the West Indies once he was clear of Spain.

He went to Jamaica because, frugal soul that he was, he discovered that it was almost as cheap to go in person, as it would be to cable—and much safer. Then he thought, Catherine would have money with her, or the means of getting it.

When they had paid their fares back to England—Silinski affected a little beard in those troublous days—they exhausted their stock of ready money.

It must have been whilst Silinski was in Paris that the ruling spirit of the Maria Braganza discovered that Silinski was indispensible, and that strange reconciliation occurred. Through what agency Baggin and he came into touch is not known. It is generally supposed that the warship ventured close to the French or Spanish coast and sent a message of goodwill flickering through space, and that some receiving station, undiscovered and undemolished—there must have been a score of such stations—received it, and transmitted it to Silinski. At any rate, it would appear that Silinski became suddenly affluent, and that he was—in Tangier—reputedly wealthy.

For this accession to comfort, I find an explanation, more simple than that offered by the majority of biographers of the "Nine Men of Cadiz." There can be little doubt, that by one of those extraordinary coincidences which no writer of fiction could dare fabricate, Silinski had met the second Brazilian sailor—that Alverez who was "not of great mentality and preferred Paris," and had succeeded in securing no small amount of the ex-quartermaster's money.

But to return to Catherine Silinski.

I reconstruct the scene when Catherine delivered her ultimatum—Catherine grown weary of waiting, grown tired with forced seclusion; Catherine divorced of an admiring audience, and being moreover a recipient of daily doles, for as I have explained Silinski was a careful man where money was concerned.

They sat on either side of a table in the spacious living-room of their villa. The night was unusually warm, and the French windows were open, but the *jalousies* were closed.

The room in which they sat was well furnished for Silinski was a man of some taste.

He himself was engaged in making notes in a large exercise book, and Catherine was pretending to read. From time to time she glanced across the table at him, but he did not look. Once, her glance rested that look up. Once, her glance rested longer than usual, and he might have seen that look of calm dispassionate speculation which was the peculiar possession of the Silinski family—a cold appraisement.

When she spoke it was patiently and quietly.

"Gregory," she said suddenly, "how does this end?"

"This?" He looked up enquiringly.

"This," she repeated. "This hiding and seeking; these mysteries—and poverty?"

He smiled gently, and shook his head as one reluctant to reprove, but compelled by circumstances to administer a chiding.

"Poverty, as the great Cervantes once he said—" he began.

"I would rather not discuss Cervantes," she interrupted coolly. "I do not know who Cervantes was, though there was a little man in Madrid who showed me a great deal of attention, who had that name. Gregory, what is the end of this, for me, and you?"

He stroked his moustache with caressing white fingers.

"Wealth," he said, after a while, "enormous wealth; our share of the profits we secured for our friends of Cadiz. It will not be difficult to reach the *Maria Braganza*. It will be less difficult to leave her when our share has been apportioned. More than our share," he added, thoughtfully, "for there is a man on the ship with whom I have some score to settle?"

She made no answer, but absently fingered the paper of her book.

"You are once more in touch with them?" she asked, and Silinski nodded.

"How?"

He smiled. He loved a mystery, yet there was no mystery in the matter. In the days before the Nine men had been scattered, Silinski had foreseen the necessity for establishing wireless stations that would be, because of their very openness, free from suspicion. He had no difficulty in persuading the young *sultan*, Abdul Asziz, to grant a concession empowering the erection of experimental wireless stations, for Abdul Asziz dearly loved a toy, greatly desired, too, amongst Europeans the reputation of being a progressive monarch. So that the high masts of the Anglo-Sevilla Wireless Company stood by the lighthouse, at Cape Spartel, and had so stood for two years. When the hasty inspection of existing stations had been made by the powers, the Cape Spartel installation had not been suspected, and Silinski's agents had been permitted to continue their experiments. It was a simple explanation; it explained in fact Silinski's presence in Tangier, but he did not feel disposed to offer it.

So his cryptic smile was all the answer that Catherine received.

"Is there not a reward for the arrest of the Nine Men?" she asked.

"There is, my child." He replied.

"And a pardon?"

"And a pardon."

She was silent and sat with her eyes fixed on the table.

"A reward of ten thousand pounds?" she repeated. "How much is that?"

"A little more than a quarter of a million *francs*. Why do you ask?"

He looked at her keenly as he spoke, searching her every feature as though he would surprise a secret.

"Why do you not take the reward?" she said calmly, and he stifled a little sigh of relief.

"Because, my dear Catherine, I am what these English call a party to the crime—and in the amiable proclamation which the English Government issued a short time since, I was specifically named."

She was silent for such a long time, that he had resumed his work. Then—

"What will they do to you, if they capture you?" she asked, and he laid down his pen again, with an exaggerated air of impatience.

"They will hang me by the neck until I am dead," he said, and Catherine did not shudder as a thousand other women would have done, but nodded.

"And me?"

"You, my dear Catherine?" Silinski looked at her again, with swift suspicion. "You? I think because of your youth and beauty, but more because you are not as deeply involved as the rest of us, you might escape with a few years' imprisonment—let us say seven."

"I see."

She took up her book again, and idly turned the leaves. "Seven years is a long time," she commented reflectively.

"Eternity is longer," said Silinski.

Catherine did not answer. She was apparently interested in her book, and Silinski, after waiting for her to speak, took up his pen again.

He worked steadily for two hours, during which time Catherine made no further attempts to speak.

He finished his work, read it over carefully, blotted the book, and rose.

He pushed open the *jalousies* and stepped into the little garden. From the villa, a hill sloped downward to the town. It was a calm moonlight night, and the crude white of Tangier was softened in the silver beams. There were many twinkling lights in the town, and the bay was laced with light.

He walked through the garden, and moved toward the sea.

From where he stood he could not distinguish the little ship that lay under steam round the shoulder of the cliff. A tiny Spanish steamer that wandered from port to port, from Casa Blanca to Ceutra, from Tangier to Mogador, carrying passengers in the tourist season and cargo all the year round. Silinski had a "friend" in command of the *Doro*. The fact that he was a friend of Silinski's is sufficient to indicate that he was none of Nature's noblemen, and I say this in no uncharity. It was rumoured in Gibraltar that the *Doro* had been engaged in not a few gun-running adventures on the Moorish coast, and on one occasion there had been a Court of Inquiry following upon a seizure, but nothing had come of that.

Silinski walked back to the villa, and stood for a time on the white road that led past the house, his head on one side, absorbing the beauty of the scene—for there was poetry in the man.

Then he walked slowly to the house.

Catherine was sitting as he had left her, the book—it was one of Guadilva's romances, and bore a gaudy picture on its cover—before her. She too had been thinking, for Silinski noted that the page was open at the identical illustration he had seen when he went out.

He took up his work where he left off, opened his little book, unscrewed his stylographic pen, and began to work.

Suddenly he stopped and, looking up, caught his sister's eyes fixed on him.

"My friend," he said, picking up the conversation where they had dropped it, "you worry too much about things that do not concern you."

She shrugged her shoulders.

"I think seven years' imprisonment concerns me very much," she said. "I should be an old woman at the end of that time."

"It will never come to that," said Silinski sharply—for him. "You seem to think that we shall fail. Do you not realise that we are on the verge of our greatest success?"

She smiled, a little scornfully.

"Men are always on the verge of success who end their lives in failure," she said. "There is no verge to real success; it opens under you and you fall into it."

"You are too clever," said Silinski. "You have read that somewhere. After all," he went on, "you have less to fear than most of us; and you forget that you are only a very small piece in the game."

Then he made a mistake, a bad mistake for a man of his *finesse*.

"We will find you a husband, Catherine," he said, with humour. "It shall be Baggin or Meyers—somebody immensely rich, and you shall live on a beautiful island, and have thousands of slaves."

All the time she was looking at him thoughtfully.

She nodded slightly when he had finished, and went on reading.

Silinski retired that night just before there came floating up from the town below the voice of the *muezzin* calling the faithful to prayer. He slept on the ground floor, and he was dozing when there was a tapping on his window pane.

He got up and opened the window, for he recognised an agent from the wireless station.

"*Senor*," whispered the man, "have you heard the news?"

"No; what is it?"

"Monsieur Zillier has escaped from the Devil's Island—the news came across from Gibraltar tonight."

"Are you sure?" whispered Silinski, eagerly.

For answer the man produced a slip of paper.

Silinski took it, closed the shutters, and turned up the electric light.

The paper, crumpled and soiled, was a copy of the garrison orders of Gibraltar, and under the routine duties appeared the "News of the Day."

Yes, there it was.

"The man Zillier, convicted in connection with the Nine Men of Cadiz conspiracy, has escaped from Devil's Island."

That was all.

Silinski read it again, then he extinguished the lights, and reopened the window.

"Take this," he said, handing the paper to the man. "All night call the Nine, and if you get an answer convey the news to them. They must know, for Zillier will endeavour to reach the rendezvous on June the first."

After the man had gone, he returned to bed, and lay staring into the darkness. If Zillier joined the *Maria Braganza*, he must join it also; that much he decided. And Catherine—? He frowned. Catherine was getting a little difficult to manage. Before he fell asleep he decided to cut himself adrift from her. Curiously enough some such resolution had already been made by Catherine.

★★★★★★

Three days later Silinski returned from a walk in the best of humours. He had been out to the station near Cape Spartel. After two days the operators had got into communication with the *Maria Braganza*, and the news was satisfactory.

He burst in upon Catherine as she was settling herself down for a *siesta*.

"Catherine, my child," he said, with a gesture that was peculiarly his, "soon you are to lose your unsympathetic brother, my little one; yet be assured that his thoughts will ever be with you, his eyes tearful—"

"And what does all this mean?" she added, very wakeful indeed now.

346

He waved his hands airily.

"A little separation," he said. "I must go to meet the Nine Men; after a while I shall, of course, return—"

"But what of me?" she said. "Do I stay in this town of dogs and smells? Do I bury myself in Tangier and grow old?"

"I will leave you money," he said. "I have made certain arrangements; you will have ten thousand *pesetas*."

She laughed.

"Ten thousand *pesetas!*" she scoffed; to last me for eternity!"

"*Madame*," he said gravely—Silinski was unusually impressive when he was grave—"I shall return."

She made a little grimace, was about to speak, then shut her mouth tightly as though to check something that were better not said.

"When do you purpose leaving?" she asked.

"Tomorrow—the next day—who knows?" he answered vaguely. "There are many things to do. The English Government have become interested in the wireless station. They have been putting on foot inquiries, which are not likely to allay any suspicion we have aroused. It would be better if some of our instruments were dismantled and taken away; they will be difficult to replace."

He rattled on, giving her, amongst other things, such purely domestic instructions as to the disposal of such of his linen as was still with their Moorish laundry.

To all this she listened patiently, even interposed a few suggestions of her own.

Silinski, prepared for something of a scene at his barefaced desertion, was relieved, and showed it. He was in an exultant mood throughout that day, hummed such airs as occurred to him, whistled, made little jokes, and went on with his packing for all the world like some everyday clerk released from the bondage of office work to his annual holiday.

Less boisterous was Catherine, She, too, was busy in a quiet way. In the confusion of his packing, Silinski did not notice at first that Catherine was packing also. When he did he dropped the work he was at the moment engaged in, and came to her.

"Beloved," he said seriously, "what are you doing?"

"I am packing," she replied calmly.

"But," he urged gently; "you do not understand. I will return—"

"I shall not be here," she said, without raising her voice, "You did not expect me to stay in this place, did you?"

"At least, you will wait until I have gone?" he asked, ignoring her question. He had only the vaguest interest in her fate thereafter. Indeed, he thought it likely that Catherine might remain at liberty less than a week following his disappearance. You may be sure that Silinski had studied the situation well in all its aspects. He had thought at first of taking her with him on board the *Maria Braganza*, but he foresaw complication. Her presence might strengthen his position with the Nine; at the same time it might easily bring about his own undoing.

"Have no fear," she answered his question. "I shall wait for your departure."

"That might well be," thought Silinski, for he had timed his departure for that very night. The *Doro* waited for him, and the dark of the night would bring a boat to shore to take him and his belongings aboard.

"Where do you meet your friends?" she asked suddenly.

"At the rendezvous," Silinski answered instantly, "Although it is a great secret, little one, I will tell you; it is a spot on the map nine hundred miles south of Bermuda, in the midst of a desolation of water; here will Gregory Silinski. An outlaw, join his fellow outcasts."

He grew pensive at the melancholy picture he drew, and sighed.

"Nine hundred miles south of the Bermuda," she repeated absently.

"To be exact," said Silinski carefully, "eight hundred and ninety-four miles."

She nodded.

"I wonder where the rendezvous really is!" she said with a smile.

"I have told you—"

"You have told me a lie," she interrupted him, still smiling, and Silinski smiled in sympathy.

He made many visits to the wireless station that day. It was a hot and dusky walk, but he regarded neither heat nor discomfort. Late in the afternoon, just as darkness fell, returning to the villa, he found it deserted, save for the two Moorish servants of the house. Their mistress had gone out, so they said, into the town. They had scarcely finished answering the questions that Silinski put to them when Catherine walked in.

"Where have you been?" he asked. He made no pretence at being polite, for he was perturbed in mind.

"To the city," she said coolly.

"Why?"

"To book my passage by the *Petalygo!*"

"Why?"

She made no answer.

"Why?" he asked again.

She shrugged her shoulders.

"Have I not answered? As soon as you have left Tangier, I also leave."

"Why did you go into Tangier?" he was insistent, and she saw she had need for caution.

"I have told you—to book my passage to Cadiz."

He laughed harshly.

"Book your passage to Hades, my friend!" he said. "You went to Tangier for a purpose."

For answer she turned upon him with a contemptuous gesture, and walked quickly to her room. She heard him follow with quick steps, and shut the door in his face; before he could grasp the handle of the door, he heard the key turn in the lock. He was in a mind to kick in the door, for he had an instinct for danger, and knew that he was in deadly peril.

Instead he knocked at the door gently.

"Catherine," he said softly, "Catherine, little one; I am sorry I offended you."

There was no answer.

"I was annoyed because you went into Tangier without telling me. It was indiscreet, my dear. Open the door and I will explain."

He heard her footsteps on the floor of the room, and slipped from his hip-pocket the thin-bladed knife he had found so useful many times before.

But she did not come to the door. He heard a drawer open, the soft "*click*" of a Browning pistol being charged, and replaced his knife with a little grin which meant many things.

He went back to the sitting-room. It was quite dark now, but he did not attempt to turn on the lights.

He sat down to think. His baggage he had sent away during the afternoon. The men would now be waiting for him with the boat, though it was early. He could have wished to settle matters with Catherine. How much did she know? He did not rate the intelligence of women very highly, but Catherine was a Silinski. Yet, remarkably enough, he had never before seriously considered the extent of Catherine's knowledge.

A suspicious man sitting in the dark, rapidly reviewing such a position as this, is not likely to think evenly or justly, and perhaps Silinski overestimated Catherine's astuteness. Be that as it may, he came to a decision.

He stepped softly into the garden, and came to a spot beneath her window.

"Catherine," he called, and he saw her dimly, for there was no light in her room.

She stood a little way back from the open casement, but he judged the distance between himself and her with tolerable precision.

Like a flash, his arm rose, and the thin-bladed knife went whistling through the air.

He heard a sharp cry; then silence.

He waited a little while, and walked through the garden. There was a man standing in the middle of the white road. His hands in his overcoat pocket, the red glow of his cigar a point of light in the gloom. Farther away, he saw the figures of three horsemen.

"Silinski, I suppose," drawled a voice—the voice of T. B. Smith. "Put up your hands or you're a dead man."

CHAPTER 35

Silinski Leaves Hurriedly

In an instant the road was filled with men; they must have been crouching in the shadow of the grassy *plateau*, but in that same instant Silinski had leapt back to the cover of the garden. A revolver banged behind him; and, as he ran, he snatched his own revolver from his pocket, and sent two quick shots into the thick of the surrounding circle. There was another gate at the farther end of the garden; there would be men there, but he must risk it. He was slight and had some speed as a runner; he must depend upon these gifts.

He opened the gate swiftly and sprang out. There were three or four men standing in his path. He shot at one point blank, dodged the others, and ran. He judged that his pursuers would not know the road as well as he. Shot after shot rang out behind him. He was an easy mark on the white road, and he turned aside and took to the grass. He was clear of the houses now, and there was no danger ahead, but the men who followed him were untiring.

Presently, he struck the footpath across the sloping plain that led to the shore, and the going was easier.

It was Silinski's luck that his pursuers should have missed the path. His every arrangement worked smoothly, for the boat was waiting, the men at their oars, and he sprang breathlessly into the stern.

It was a circumstance, which might have struck him as strange, had he been in a condition for calm thought, that the horsemen who were of the party that surrounded him had not joined the pursuit.

But there was another mystery that the night revealed. He had been on board the *Doro* for an hour, and the crew of the little ship was pushing her southward before he went to the cabin that had been made for him.

His first act was to take his revolver from his pocket, preparatory to reloading it from the cartridges stored in one of his trunks.

Two chambers of the pistol were undischarged, and, as he jerked back the extractor, these two shells fell on the bed. He looked at them stupidly.

Both cartridges were blank.

★★★★★★

Had he heard T. B. Smith speaking as he went flying down the road, Silinski might have understood.

"Where's the dead man?" said T. B. cheerfully.

"Here, sir," said a voice.

"Good." Then in Spanish he addressed a figure that stood in the doorway.

"Were you hurt, *senora?*"

Catherine's little laugh of contempt came out to him.

"I know Gregory," she said quietly; "there is not a trick of his that I have not seen. I was expecting the knife before he raised his arm; has he got safely away?"

"I hope so," said T. B. Then, "You have learnt nothing more?"

"Nothing," she said. "He told me a story of the rendezvous, but it was, of course, a lie; but I have earned my reward."

"I think you need have no fear as to that," said the detective. "Although I knew that your brother was somewhere on this coast, I should, in all probability, have arrived days too late but for your telegram; you will remain in Tangier under the protection of the British Consul."

He was going away, but she called him.

"I cannot understand why you allowed my brother to escape—" she began. "That you should desire blank cartridges to be placed in his revolver is not so difficult, but I do not see—"

"I suppose not," said T. B. politely, and left her abruptly.

He sprang on to a horse that was waiting, and went clattering down the hill, through the Sök, down the narrow main street that passes the mosque; dismounting by the Custom House, he placed his horse in charge of a waiting soldier, and walked swiftly along a narrow wooden pier.

At the same time as Silinski was boarding the *Doro*, T. B. was being rowed in a cockleshell of a *pinnace* to the long destroyer which lay, without lights, in the bay,.

He swung himself up a tiny ladder on to the steel deck that rang hollow under his feet.

"All right?" said a voice in the darkness.

"All right," said T. B.; a bell tinkled somewhere, the destroyer moved slowly ahead, and swung out to sea.

"Will you have any difficulty in picking her up?" He was standing in the cramped space of the little bridge, wedged between a quick-firing gun and the navigation desk.

"No—I think not," said the officer; "our difficulty will be to keep out of sight of her. It will be an easy matter to keep her in view because she stands high out of the water, and she is pretty sure to burn her regulation lights. By day I shall let her get her hull down and take her masts for guide."

It was the strangest procession that followed the southern bend of the African Coast. First went the *Doro*, its passengers serenely unconscious of the fact that six miles away, below the rim of the horizon, followed a slim ugly destroyer, and three miles distant, came six destroyers steaming abreast. Behind them, four miles away, six swift cruisers.

That same night there steamed from Funchal in the Island of Madeira, the *Victor Hugo*, *Condé*, *Gloire*, and the *Edgard Quinet* of the French fleet; the *Roon*, *Yorck*, *Prinz Adalbert*, and the battleship *Pommern*, of the German navy, with sixteen destroyers, and followed a parallel ocean path.

After three days' steaming, the Doro turned sharply to starboard, and the unseen fleets that dogged her turned too. In that circle of death, for a whole week, the little Spanish steamer twisted and turned, and, obedient to the message that went from destroyer to cruiser, the fleets followed her every movement. For the *Doro* was unconsciously leading the nations to the mad battleship. She had been slipped with that object. So far every part of the plan had worked well. To make doubly sure, the news of Zillier's escape from Devil's Island had been circulated in every country. It was essential that if they missed the *Maria Braganza* this time, they should catch her on the first of June at "Lolo."

"And where that is," said T. B. in despair, "heaven only knows."

Wearing a heavy overcoat, he was standing on the narrow deck of the destroyer as she pounded through the seas. They had found the South-East trade winds at a surprisingly northerly latitude, and the sea was choppy and cold.

Young Marchcourt, the youthful skipper of the *Martine*, grinned.

"'Lolo' is 'nowhere,' isn't it?" he said. "You'll find it charted on all

Admiralty maps; it's the place where the supply transport is always waiting on manoeuvres—I wish to heaven these squalls would drop," he added irritably, as a sudden gust of wind and rain struck the tiny ship.

"Feel seasick?" suggested T. B. maliciously.

"Not much—but I'm horribly afraid of losing sight of this hooker ahead."

He lifted the flexible end of a speaking tube, and pressed a button.

"Give her more revolutions, Cole," he said. He hung up the tube. "We look like carrying this weather with us for a few days," he said, "and as I don't feel competent to depend entirely upon my own eyesight, I shall bring up the *Magneto* and the *Solus* to help me with this beggar."

Obedient to his signal, two destroyers were detached from the following flotilla, and came abreast at dusk.

The weather grew rapidly worse, the squalls of greater frequence. The sea rose, so that life upon the destroyer was anything but pleasant. At midnight, T. B. Smith was awakened from a restless sleep by a figure in gleaming oilskins.

"I say," said a gloomy voice, "we've lost sight of that dashed *Doro*."

"Eh?"

T. B. jumped from his bunk, to be immediately precipitated against the other side of the cabin.

"Lost her light—it has either gone out or been put out. We're going ahead now full speed in the hope of overhauling her—"

Another oil-skinned figure came to the door.

"Light ahead, sir."

"Thank heaven!" said the other fervently, and bolted to the deck.

T. B. struggled into his clothing, and with some difficulty made his way to the bridge. As he climbed the little steel ladder, he heard the engine bell ring, and instantly the rattle and jar of the engines ceased.

"She's stationary," explained the officer, "so we've stopped. She has probably upset herself in this sea."

"How do you know she is stationary?" asked T. B., for the two faint stars ahead told him nothing.

"Got her riding lights," said the other laconically.

Those two riding lights stopped the destroyer; it stopped six other cruisers, far out of sight, six obedient cruisers came to a halt, and a hundred miles or so away, the combined French and German fleets became stationary.

All through the night the watchers lay, heaving, rolling, and pitching, like so many logs on the troubled seas. Dawn broke mistily, but the lights still gleamed. Day came in dull greyness, and the young officer, with his eyes fastened to his binoculars, looked long and earnestly ahead.

"I can see a mast," he said doubtfully, "but there's something very curious about it."

Then he put down his glasses suddenly, put out his hand, and rang his engines full ahead.

He turned to the quartermaster at his side.

"Get the Commodore by wireless," he said rapidly, "the *Doro* has gone."

Gone, indeed, was the *Doro*—gone six hours since.

They found the lights. They were still burning when the destroyer came up with them.

A roughly built raft with a pole lashed upright, and from this was suspended two lanterns.

Whilst the fleet had watched this raft, the Doro had gone on. Nailed to the pole was a letter. It was sodden with spray, but T. B. had no difficulty in reading it.

Cher ami, (it ran), much as I value the honour of a naval escort, its presence is embarrassing at the moment. I saw your destroyer this morning through my glasses, and guessed the rest. You are ingenious. Now I understand why you allowed me to escape. My love and duty to Catherine, if she still lives; for yourself, my respectful salutations, most admirable of policemen.

It was signed "Silinski."

******

I am happy to think that the court-martial held on Lieutenant-Commander George Septimus Marchcourt, on a charge of "neglect of duty, in that he failed to carry out the instructions of his superior officer," resulted in an honourable acquittal for that young officer. It was an acquittal, which had a far-reaching effect, though at the time it did not promise well.

T. B. was a witness at the trial, which was a purely formal one, in spite of the attention it excited.

T. B. remained at Gibraltar, pending further developments. For the affair of the Nine Men had got beyond Scotland Yard—they were an international problem.

Thanks to the information supplied by Torquet in Brixton prison, supplemented by such particulars as Catherine Silinski was able to supply, the European agents had been arrested. Their trials—if one may anticipate a little—were of the most sensational character, but in no case, whether the investigation was before the gentle tribunals peculiar to English law, or whether they were instituted by the more vigorous courts of France, Germany, or Russia, was the mystery of "Lolo" solved.

But of "Lolo" she had no information to give.

Catherine's evidence, however, was particularly valuable to T. B., not so much because she was able to assist him in his search for the Nine, but from the inside history she was able to give of the working of this colossal organisation of crime. We know the cause of many market "breaks" which were, at the time, inexplicable. We catch a glimpse, in her fascinating story of the method adopted by the Nine, their directors' meetings, to which apparently, she was admitted.[1] Catherine appears to have shared the confidence of Meyers, who from time to time confided his fears to her; she knew, intimately, Baggin, and it was through her that Silinski and he met.

T. B. was walking over from La Linea, across the strip of neutral ground which separated Gibraltar from Spain, with young Marchcourt, when he confessed that he despaired of ever bringing the Nine to justice.

"The nations cannot stand the racket much longer," he said, "these Nine Men are costing civilisation a million a week! Think of it! A million pounds a week! We must either capture them soon or effect a compromise. I am afraid they will make peace on their own terms."

"But they must be caught soon," urged the other.

"Why?" demanded T. B. irritably. "Why 'must'. Man, we couldn't catch De Wet in the restricted area of the Orange River Colony; how can we hope to capture one of the fastest war vessels afloat when the men who control her have all the seas to run in?"

"The crew will get tired. After all, they have nothing to gain," persisted the officer; "that is the weakness of their position.

"And their strength," said T. B. "If these men have been persuaded to take the first step in piracy, the rest is easy; if by promise of huge rewards, they have been induced to put their necks in the noose, the

1. The evidence of Catherine Maria Silinski in relation to the operations of "The Cadiz Conspirators"—Blue Book, 747-11 (Home Office).

realisation of their danger will only make them the more determined to go through with their enterprise."

They had reached the waterport, and T. B. stopped before his hotel.

"Come in," he said suddenly. The two men passed through the paved vestibule and mounted the stair, to T. B.'s room. I'm going to show you our clue," he said grimly, and extracted from his portfolio the drawing of the little cross with the circular ends.

T. B. himself does not know to this day why he was moved to produce this disappointing little diagram at that moment. It may have been that, as a forlorn hope, he relied upon the application of a fresh young mind to the problem which was so stale in his.

The officer looked and frowned.

"Is that all?" asked Marchcourt, without disguising his disappointment.

"That is all," responded T. B.

They sat looking at the diagram in silence, and T. B., as was his peculiarity, scribbled mechanically on the blotting pad before him.

He drew flowers, and men's heads, and impossible structures of all kinds; he made inaccurate tracings of maps, of columns, pediments, squares, and triangles. Then, in the same absent way, he made a rough copy of the diagram.

Then his pencil stopped and he sat bolt upright.

"Gee!" he whispered.

The young naval officer looked up in astonishment.

"Whew!" whistled T. B.

He jumped up, walked to his trunk, and drew out an atlas.

He turned the leaves, looked long and earnestly at something he saw, closed the book, and turned a little white; but his eyes were blazing.

"I have found 'Lolo'," he said simply.

He took up his pencil and quickly sketched the diagram.

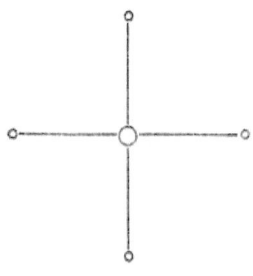

"What this means perhaps our nautical friend will tell us," he said triumphantly, and with a return to his old mannerism.

But young Marchcourt only shook his head.

"Look," said T. B., and added a few letters.

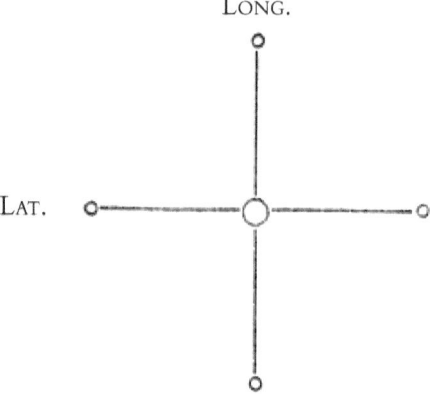

"Longitude nought; latitude nought—L0, L0!" whispered the officer. "By Jove! Why, this is off the African coast."

T. B. nodded.

"It is where the Greenwich meridian crosses the Equator," he said. "It's 'nowhere'! The only 'nowhere' in the world!"

CHAPTER 36

At "Lolo"

Under an awning on the quarterdeck of the *Maria Braganza,* George T. Baggin was stretched out in the easiest of easy-chairs in an attitude of luxurious comfort.

"Admiral" Lombrosa, passing on his way to his cabin, smacked him familiarly upon the shoulder—an attitude which epitomised the changed relationships of the pair.

The *Maria Braganza* was steaming slowly eastward, and since it was the hour of *siesta,* the deck was strewn with the recumbent forms of men.

Baggin looked with a scowl.

"Where is Silinski?" he asked, and the other laughed.

"He sleeps, *Senor President,*" said the "Admiral."—there had been some curious promotions on board the *Maria Braganza*—"he is amusing, your Silinski."

Baggin wriggled uncomfortably in his chair, but made no answer, and the other man eyed him keenly.

Baggin must have felt rather than observed the scrutiny, for suddenly he looked up and caught the sailor's eye.

"Eh?" he asked, as though to some unspoken question. Then, "Where is Meyers?"

Again the smile on the swart face of the Brazilian.

"He is here," he said, as a stout figure in white ducks shuffled awkwardly along the canting deck.

He came opposite to Baggin; and drawing a chair towards him, with a grunt, he dropped into it with a crash.

"You get fatter and fatter, my friend," said Baggin, regarding the monstrous figure with the interest he would have given to some strange beast.

"Fatter!" gasped the other—ever short of breath was Lucas Meyers—"Course 'm fatter! No exercise—this cursed ship! Oh, what a fool, what a fool I've been!"

He wriggled his big head, and the rolling fat of his neck creased and bulged.

"Forget it," said Baggin. He took a long gold case from his inside pocket, opened it, and selected with care a black *cheroot*. "Forget it."

"Wish I could! Oh, heaven, I wish I could!" wheezed Meyers. "I'd give half a million to be safe in the hands of the Official Receiver! I'd give half a million to be servin' five years in Portland! Baggin," he said, with comic earnestness, "we've got to compromise! It's got to be done. Where do we stand, eh?"

Baggin puffed leisurely at his cigar, but made no attempt to elucidate the position.

The other man did not wait for any answer. He wheezed on, whining, complaining, cursing.

Baggin was used to all this; he had had years of it, but now, with his nerves on edge, this cowardice of Meyers' grated.

"I've got an idea, see?" Meyers was saying, with unwonted eagerness. "I'm a nuisance to you ain't I? I know I am. Now, suppose you ventured into some little port, eh? Put me on shore in a boat. I'd turn King's evidence—them London murders, Hyatt an' Moss—it wouldn't do you any harm, but it'd save me, see? You'd still be at sea; still be free, eh? I'll make over my share to you—just enough to get ashore an' live comfortably, if they let me—"

"Splendid, splendid!" said the silky voice of Silinski.

Meyers jerked himself erect, with a start.

"Hey!" he breathed. "Hey, Silinski! You go sneakin' about in your bare feet. Don't do it! I hate it, Silinski; it unnerves me. I hate people who come creepin' on a man unawares! That's what you do, Silinski! It's—it's not gentlemanly."

"It is not gentlemanly to talk of deserting your comrades; deserting this ocean republic we have founded," said Silinski gently; "that is treason, high treason."

"Rot!" exploded Meyers. "Rot! Never approved of it; never saw any sense in it! Presidents! Admirals! Citizens! Oaths! Bah!"

The Admiral had walked away to the after-rail.

"Where are the Nine Men of Cadiz?" demanded Meyers, the sweat rolling down his cheeks, a tragic-comic figure. "Where is Bortuski? Where is Morson? Where is Couthwright? Zillier, we know where he is, or was, but where are the others? You an' me an' this feller Silinski, an' the rest—phutt!" He made a little noise with his mouth. "I know!" he said. He raised a trembling finger accusingly. They were all here when Silinski came aboard—less'n a week ago."

"My dear man," said Baggin lazily, though his face was white and his lips firm-pressed. "There was the storm—"

"That's a lie!" screamed the fat man, beating the air with his hands; "that's a lie! The storm didn't take Kohr from his bunk an' leave blood on his pillow! It didn't make Morson's cabin smell of chloroform! I know, I know!"

"There is such a thing as knowing too much," said George T. Baggin, rising unsteadily. "Meyers," he said, "I've been a good friend of yours because I sort of like you in spite of your foolishness. Our friends perished in the storm; it wasn't a bad thing for us, taking matters all round. If this manifesto of ours doesn't secure us a pardon, we can risk making a run for safety. There are fewer of us to blab. See here"—he sat down on the side of the other's chair and dropped his voice— "suppose we can't shock this old world into giving us a free pardon, and the sun gets too warm for us, as it will sooner or later—"

"Suppose it!" Meyers burst in. "D'ye think there's an hour of the day or night when I don't suppose it? Lord! I—"

"Listen, can't you?" said Baggin savagely. "When that happens, what are we to do? We've buried gold on the African coast; we've buried it on the South American coast—"

"All the crew know," grunted the fat man, "we're at the mercy—"

"Wait! Wait!" said the other wearily. "Suppose there comes a time when we must make a dash for safety—with the steam *pinnace*. Slipping away in the night when the men of the watch are doped. You and me, Silinski and the Admiral!"—he bent his head lower—"leaving a time-fuse in the magazine"—he whispered—"there's a way out for us, my friend!"

Meyers said nothing. The cold-blooded villainy of the proposal did not shock him; for a moment a gleam of hope lit the dark places of his miserable soul.

"But Zillier," he whispered huskily; "We're going to pick up Zillier; why not leave him?"

"He knows more than any other of our plans," said Baggin; "he will be safer with us—for a time."

"We're going to make one last effort," he went on, "between here and 'Lolo' we fall in with the outward bound intermediate Cape mail.

It shall be our last attack upon civilisation—"

"Don't do it!" begged Meyers; "for the love of heaven, don't do it! I can't stand it!"

He stood on the deck, his feet wide apart, his big body quivering with fear. Terror gave him a certain dignity; he was grotesque rather than ridiculous.

"Drop Zillier! Drop everything! Let us clear out—"

Baggin left him babbling and walked to where Silinski strolled with the Captain.

"I've done my best," he said shortly; "he's just mad with fright; there's no backbone in him."

Silinski nodded.

They ate a silent meal in the magnificently upholstered wardroom, which had been converted into a saloon for the officers of the Republic.[1] After dinner, Silinski and Baggin promenaded the quarter deck together.

"Meyers has gone below," reported the latter in answer to a question; "he got no sleep last night."

"He's a greater danger than any of the others," said Silinski quietly.

They stood for a while watching phosphorescence on the water till Lombrosa's voice recalled them.

"Are you there?" he called quickly. They detected the agitation in his tone and turned together.

"It's Meyers," said the Captain rapidly. "I found him in the wireless cabin, trying to send a message. He's half mad."

"Where is he?" demanded Silinski, but, before his tongue had formed the words, the voice of the fat man came to him. He came along, the centre of a swaying body of sailors, who held him.

"For God's sake, silence him!" said the Brazilian hoarsely. "Don't you hear—"

"Dead! Ye'll all be dead!" yelled Meyers. He was screaming at the top of his voice in English. "Eh" a time-fuse in your dam' magazine! Whilst they get away with the money! Hold 'em! Catch 'em, ye fools!"

At any moment he might remember that the Brazilians who held him could not understand a word he said.

---

1. The exact constitution of this extraordinary Republic is not very clear. We have to depend upon the evidence of the warship's crew for such information as we possess, and it would appear that their knowledge was of the slightest.—E. W.

Silinski gave an order, and the struggling man was flung to the deck.

"Murder!" he screamed. "Hyatt, an' the other feller! An' poor Morson, an' Kohr. I see the blood on his pillow! An' a time-fuse in the magazine—"

Silinski thrust a handkerchief in his mouth.

"Chloroform," he said in Spanish. "Our friend has been drinking."

In a few seconds Baggin was back with a bottle of colourless liquid, and a saturated handkerchief was pressed over the struggling man's mouth.

He was silent at last, and, at a word from their captain, the men who held him released their hold, and went forward to their quarters.

The three men stood in silence, gazing down at the huddled figure. Then, "He must go," said Silinski, and Baggin nodded.

Nobody heard the splash of him as he fell into the water, or heard the one scream of horror that came from his lips as the cold of the water revived him, or saw his large white face staring blanly into the darkness ere he went down to his death.

CHAPTER 37

The Last of the Nine

To a calm sea, to a dawn all pearl and rose, the crew of the *Maria Braganza* woke. In the night the speed of the warship had been accelerated until she was moving at her top speed, and two columns of black smoke belched from her great funnels. The two men who came on deck at the same moment did not speak one to the other. Baggin was pale; there were dark circles about his eyes; he looked like a man who had not slept. But Silinski was unperturbed to the last.

Dapper, shaven, not unusually pallid, he woke as from a pleasant dream, and appeared on deck trim from point of shoe to fingernail—a singular man.

All the morning preparations were going on. Ammunition came up from the magazine, dilatory quartermasters swung out guns; on the masthead was an under-officer armed with a telescope.

He was the principle object of interest to the man on the quarter deck. Every few minutes their eyes would go sweeping aloft.

Beyond the curtest "*bueno dias*" neither the Captain, Baggin, nor the calm Silinski spoke. In Baggin's heart grew a new terror, and he avoided Silinski.

The sun beat down on the stretch of awning that protected the privileged three, but for some reason Baggin did not feel the heat.

He had a something on his mind; a question to ask; and at last he summoned his resolution to put it. He walked over to where Silinski sat reading.

"Gregory," he said—he had never so addressed him before—"is the end near?"

Silinski had raised his eyes when the other had come toward him; he smiled.

"Which variety of end?" he asked.

"There is only one variety," said Baggin steadily. "There is only one thing in the world that counts, and that is life."

"Not money?" sneered the Pole.

"Not money," repeated Baggin; "least of all money."

"You have been reading," said Silinski promptly—it was a point with him that all disturbing thought came as a result of book-reading; "we are at the very beginning of a new life, my friend—look, look!"

From where they stood the man on the mainmast was visible; he was shouting to somebody on the bridge and pointing northward.

"You see?" said Silinski triumphantly, "at the moment of your despair comes the spur to action; throw your philosophies overboard, my friend; they killed Meyers because they developed into fear. We will make our final appeal to the world."

It came reluctantly into view, a big grey-painted steamer with red and black funnels, a great lumbering ocean beast.

Through their glasses the three men watched her, a puzzled frown upon the Captain's face.

"I do not recognise her," he said. "She is larger than the *Ross Castle*; she looks like a gigantic cargo steamer."

"Her decks are crowded with passengers," said Baggin. "I can see women's hats and men in white; what is that structure forward?" He indicated a long superstructure before the steamer's bridge.

"There goes her flag."

A little ball crept up to the mainmast.

"We will show her ours," said the Captain pleasantly, and pushed a button.

Instantly, with a crash that shook the ship, the forward gun of the *Maria Braganza* sent a shell whizzing through the air.

It fell short and wide of the steamer.

The Captain turned to Silinski as for instructions.

"Sink her," said Silinski.

But the steamer was never sunk.

The little ball that hung at the main suddenly broke, and out to the breeze there floated not the red ensign of the merchant service, but the stars and stripes of America—more, on the little flagstaff at the bow of the ship fluttered a tiny blue flag spangled with stars.

Livid of face, Captain Lombrosa sprang to the wheel.

"It's a Yankee man-o'-war!" he cried, and his voice was cracked. "We've—"

As he spoke the superstructure on the "intermediate," which had excited Baggin's curiosity, fell apart like a house of canvas—as it was—and the long slim barrel of a nine-inch gun swung round.

"*Pang!*"

The shell carried away a boat and a part of the wireless cabin.

"Every gun!" yelled Lombrosa, frantically pressing the buttons on the bridge before him. "We must run for it!"

Instantly, with an ear-splitting succession of crashes, the guns of the *Maria Braganza* came into action.

To the last, fortune was with the Nine, for the second or third shot sent the American over with a list to starboard.

Round swung the *Maria Braganza* like a frightened hare; the water foamed under her bows as, running under every ounce of steam, she made her retreat.

"We must drop all idea of picking up Zillier," said Baggin, white to the lips; "this damned warship is probably in wireless communication with a fleet; can you tap her messages?"

Silinski shook his head.

"The first shell smashed our apparatus," he said. "What is that ahead?"

Lombrosa, with his telescope glued to his eye, was scanning the horizon.

"It looks like a sea fog."

But the Captain made no reply.

Over the edge of the ocean hung a thin red haze. He put the glass down, and turned a troubled face to the two men.

"In other latitudes I should say that it was a gathering typhoon," he said. He took another long look, put down the telescope, closed it mechanically, and hung it in the rack.

"Smoke," he said briefly. "We are running into a fleet."

He brought the *Maria Braganza's* bows northward but the smoke haze was there, too.

East, north, south, west, a great circle of smoke and the *Maria Braganza* trapped in the very centre.

Out of the smoke haze grey shadowy shapes, dirty grey hulls, white hulls, hulls black as pitch loomed into view.

The Captain rang his engines to "stop."

"We are caught," he said.

He opened a locker on the bridge leisurely, and took out a revolver.

"I have no regrets," he said—it was a challenge to fate.

Then he shot himself and fell dead at the feet of the two. Baggin sprang forward, but too late.

"You coward! You coward!" he screamed. He shook his fist in the dead man's face, then he turned like a wild beast on Silinski. "This is the end of it! This is the end of your scheme! Curse you! Curse you!"

He leaped at the Pole's throat.

For a moment they swayed and struggled, then suddenly Baggin released his hold, dropped his head like a tired man, and slid to the deck.

Silinski wiped his knife on the white duck coat of his fallen fellow, and lit a cigar with a hand that did not tremble.

★★★★★★

One last expiring effort the *Maria Braganza* made; you could almost follow Silinski as he sped from one side of the ship to the other, by the spasmodic shots that came from the doomed ship.

Then four men-of-war—the *Roon*, the *Connecticut*, the *Black Prince*, and the *Gloire*—detached themselves from the encircling fleets and steamed in toward the Brazilian. Shell after shell beat upon the steel hull of the "Mad Battleship," a great hole gaped in her side, her funnels were shot away, her foremast hung limply.

A white flag waved feebly from her bridge and a British destroyer came with a swift run across the smoky seas.

Up the companion-ladder came a rush of marines; and, after them, a revolver in his hand, T. B. Smith, a prosaic Assistant-Commissioner from Scotland Yard.

And the end of this extraordinary story of crime was as commonplace as it could well be.

T. B. came upon Silinski standing with his back to a bulkhead, grimy—blood-stained, but with the butt of a cigar still glowing in the corner of his mouth.

"You are Gregory Silinski," said T. B., and snapped a pair of handcuffs on his wrists. "I shall take you into custody on a charge of wilful murder, and I caution you that anything you now say may be used in evidence against you at your trial."

Silinski said nothing.

LEONAUR

ALSO FROM LEONAUR

AVAILABLE IN SOFTCOVER OR HARDCOVER WITH DUST JACKET

THE LONG PATROL *by George Berrie*—A Novel of Light Horsemen from Gallipoli to the Palestine campaign of the First World War.

NAPOLEONIC WAR STORIES *by Arthur Quiller-Couch*—Tales of soldiers, spies, battles & sieges from the Peninsular & Waterloo campaingns.

THE FIRST DETECTIVE *by Edgar Allan Poe*—The Complete Auguste Dupin Stories—The Murders in the Rue Morgue, The Mystery of Marie Rogêt & The Purloined Letter.

THE COMPLETE DR NIKOLA—MAN OF MYSTERY: 1 *by Guy Boothby*—*A Bid for Fortune & Dr Nikola Returns*—Guy Boothby's Dr.Nikola adventures continue to fascinate readers and enthusiasts of crime and mystery fiction because—in the manner of Raffles, the gentleman cracksman—here is character far removed from the uncompromising goodness of Holmes and Watson or the uncompromising evil of Professor Moriarty.

THE COMPLETE DR NIKOLA—MAN OF MYSTERY: 2 *by Guy Boothby*— *The Lust of Hate, Dr Nikola's Experiment & Farewell, Nikola*—Guy Boothby's Dr.Nikola adventures continue to fascinate readers and enthusiasts of crime and mystery fiction because—in the manner of Raffles, the gentleman cracksman—here is character far removed from the uncompromising goodness of Holmes and Watson or the uncompromising evil of Professor Moriarty.

THE CASEBOOKS OF MR J. G. REEDER: BOOK 1 *by Edgar Wallace*— *Room 13, The Mind of Mr J. G. Reeder* and *Terror Keep*—Edgar Wallace's sleuth—whose territory is the London of the 1920s—is an unlikely figure, more bank clerk than detective in appearance, ever wearing his square topped bowler, frock coat, cravat and muffler, Mr Reeder is usually inseparable from his umbrella.

THE CASEBOOKS OF MR J. G. REEDER: BOOK 2 *by Edgar Wallace*— *Red Aces, Mr J. G. Reeder Returns, The Guv'nor* and *The Man Who Passed*—Edgar Wallace's sleuth—whose territory is the London of the 1920s—is an unlikely figure, more bank clerk than detective in appearance, ever wearing his square topped bowler, frock coat, cravat and muffler, Mr Reeder is usually inseparable from his umbrella.

THE COMPLETE FOUR JUST MEN: VOLUME 1 *by Edgar Wallace*—*The Four Just Men, The Council of Justice & The Just Men of Cordova*—disillusioned with a world where the wicked and the abusers of power perpetually go unpunished, the Just Men set about to rectify matters according to their own standards, and retribution is dispensed on swift and deadly wings.

AVAILABLE ONLINE AT **www.leonaur.com**
AND FROM ALL GOOD BOOK STORES
07/09

LEONAUR

ALSO FROM LEONAUR

AVAILABLE IN SOFTCOVER OR HARDCOVER WITH DUST JACKET

THE COMPLETE FOUR JUST MEN: VOLUME 2 *by Edgar Wallace*—*The Law of the Four Just Men & The Three Just Men*—disillusioned with a world where the wicked and the abusers of power perpetually go unpunished, the Just Men set about to rectify matters according to their own standards, and retribution is dispensed on swift and deadly wings.

THE COMPLETE RAFFLES: 1 *by E. W. Hornung*—*The Amateur Cracksman & The Black Mask*—By turns urbane gentleman about town and accomplished cricketer, life is just too ordinary for Raffles and that sets him on a series of adventures that have long been treasured as a real antidote to the 'white knights' who are the usual heroes of the crime fiction of this period.

THE COMPLETE RAFFLES: 2 *by E. W. Hornung*—*A Thief in the Night & Mr Justice Raffles*—By turns urbane gentleman about town and accomplished cricketer, life is just too ordinary for Raffles and that sets him on a series of adventures that have long been treasured as a real antidote to the 'white knights' who are the usual heroes of the crime fiction of this period.

THE COLLECTED SUPERNATURAL AND WEIRD FICTION OF WILKIE COLLINS: VOLUME 1 *by Wilkie Collins*—Contains one novel 'The Haunted Hotel', one novella 'Mad Monkton', three novelettes 'Mr Percy and the Prophet', 'The Biter Bit' and 'The Dead Alive' and eight short stories to chill the blood.

THE COLLECTED SUPERNATURAL AND WEIRD FICTION OF WILKIE COLLINS: VOLUME 2 *by Wilkie Collins*—Contains one novel 'The Two Destinies', three novellas 'The Frozen deep', 'Sister Rose' and 'The Yellow Mask' and two short stories to chill the blood.

THE COLLECTED SUPERNATURAL AND WEIRD FICTION OF WILKIE COLLINS: VOLUME 3 *by Wilkie Collins*—Contains one novel 'Dead Secret,' two novelettes 'Mrs Zant and the Ghost' and 'The Nun's Story of Gabriel's Marriage' and five short stories to chill the blood.

FUNNY BONES *selected by Dorothy Scarborough*—An Anthology of Humorous Ghost Stories.

MONTEZUMA'S CASTLE AND OTHER WEIRD TALES *by Charles B. Cory*—Cory has written a superb collection of eighteen ghostly and weird stories to chill and thrill the avid enthusiast of supernatural fiction.

SUPERNATURAL BUCHAN *by John Buchan*—Stories of Ancient Spirits, Uncanny Places & Strange Creatures.

AVAILABLE ONLINE AT **www.leonaur.com**
AND FROM ALL GOOD BOOK STORES
07/09

LEONAUR

ALSO FROM LEONAUR

AVAILABLE IN SOFTCOVER OR HARDCOVER WITH DUST JACKET

THE COLLECTED SUPERNATURAL AND WEIRD FICTION OF J. SHERIDAN LE FANU: VOLUME 1 *by J. Sheridan le Fanu*—Contains Two Novels 'The Haunted Baronet' and 'The Evil Guest', One Novella 'Carmilla',One Novelette and Ten Short Stories of the Ghostly and Gothic.

THE COLLECTED SUPERNATURAL AND WEIRD FICTION OF J. SHERIDAN LE FANU: VOLUME 2 *by J. Sheridan le Fanu*—Contains One Novel 'Uncle Silas', One Novelette 'Green Tea' and Five Short Stories of the Ghostly and Gothic.

THE COLLECTED SUPERNATURAL AND WEIRD FICTION OF J. SHERIDAN LE FANU: VOLUME 3 *by J. Sheridan le Fanu*—Contains One Novel 'The House by the Churchyard', and One Short Story 'Dickon the Devil' of the Ghostly and Gothic.

THE COLLECTED SUPERNATURAL AND WEIRD FICTION OF J. SHERIDAN LE FANU: VOLUME 4 *by J. Sheridan le Fanu*—Contains One Novel 'The Wyvern Mystery', One Novelette 'Mr. Justice Harbottle,' and Nine Short Stories of the Ghostly and Gothic.

THE COLLECTED SUPERNATURAL AND WEIRD FICTION OF J. SHERIDAN LE FANU: VOLUME 5 *by J. Sheridan le Fanu*—Contains One Novel 'The Rose and the Key', One Novelette 'Spalatro, From the Notes of Fra Giacomo', and Two Short Stories of the Ghostly and Gothic

THE COLLECTED SUPERNATURAL AND WEIRD FICTION OF J. SHERIDAN LE FANU: VOLUME 6 *by J. Sheridan le Fanu*—Contains One Novel 'Checkmate', and Six Short Stories of the Ghostly and Gothic

THE COLLECTED SUPERNATURAL AND WEIRD FICTION OF J. SHERIDAN LE FANU: VOLUME 7 *by J. Sheridan le Fanu*—Contains Two Novels 'All in the Dark' and 'The Room in the Dragon Volant', Two Novelettes 'The Mysterious Lodger' and 'The Watcher' and Four Short Stories of the Ghostly and Gothic

THE COLLECTED SUPERNATURAL AND WEIRD FICTION OF J. SHERIDAN LE FANU: VOLUME 8 *by J. Sheridan le Fanu*—Contains One Novel 'A Lost Name', One Novelette 'The Last Heir of Castle Connor', and Six Short Stoies of the Ghostly and Gothic

AVAILABLE ONLINE AT **www.leonaur.com**
AND FROM ALL GOOD BOOK STORES
07/09

www.ingramcontent.com/pod-product-compliance
Lightning Source LLC
Chambersburg PA
CBHW022144010726
47493CB00002B/334